To Alicja

GUARDIAN'S G

BOOK ONE OF THE RUANE SAGA

Scott J Kenna

Scott J Kenna

Michael Terence Publishing

First published in paperback by
Michael Terence Publishing in 2020
www.mtp.agency

ISBN 9781800940369

This book is dedicated to my father, Sean Kenna.
A true Warrior, who taught me right from wrong.

Also, sorry for stealing your condoms out of your top drawer when I was younger. Yes, that was me. I really wanted a brother.

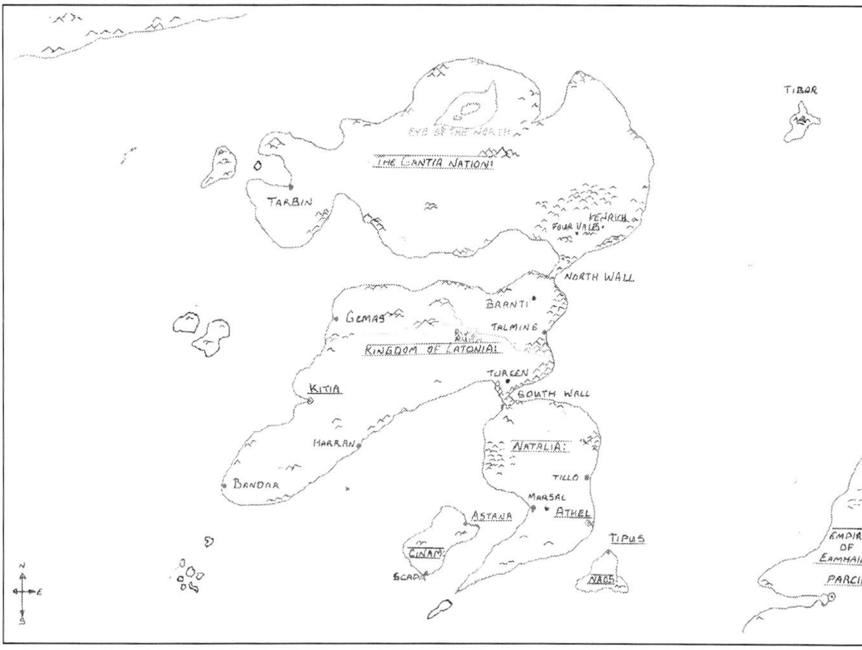
TIBAR
EYE OF THE NORTH
THE LANTIA NATION
TARBIN
FENRICK
FOUR VALES
NORTH WALL
BRANTI
GEMAS
TALMINE
KINGDOM OF LATONIA
TUREEN
SOUTH WALL
KITIA
HARRAN
NATALIA
TILLO
BANDAR
MARSAL
ATHEL
ASTANA
TIPUS
CINAM
NAOS
PARCIF
N
E
S

Prologue

The sun was setting low in the sky and the frozen ground seemed to grow even colder. It cast long shadows across the white, snow-covered ground as it subsided down below the distant mountains. Karra stood alone on the mountaintop at the centre of the old ruins. Even though the darkening sky was free from clouds, he sensed that there was more snow on its way. It was nearing the end of winter and all around the hilltop the trees and vegetation were covered with a blanket of snow, except for the two giant black pillars set in the centre of the ruins. The pillars themselves seemed strangely out of place. Karra heard a shriek in the sky and looked up to see a great eagle soaring high above. It was late in the evening for this predator to be hunting he thought, but then again to survive out here you had to adapt. All around him was quiet and he felt at ease with his solitude. He reached deep into his pocket and pulled out a small, crescent shaped, black amulet, attached to a silver chain. It had a faint glow at its centre and felt slightly warm to touch.

'Nearly time!' he whispered to himself.

He walked a small way down the mountainside to a small cabin. Here he had logs stacked against the cabin wall that he had chopped earlier. He brought a bundle up to the centre of the ruins in front of the pillars and started to light a large fire some ways back from the black stones. Several times he added large logs to the fire, building it bigger and bigger to a fiery mound. It was heating up the surroundings now. The snow around it was melting away and thick smoke floated into the air. He looked at the amulet once more and the light from it had intensified, shining bright now in his hand. Sliding it securely back into his pocket, he walked towards the two huge pillars and stood several steps back from them. Karra stood waiting, feeling the warmth of the fire at his back and the warmth of the amulet in his pocket. Then, Golden symbols appeared and started to illuminate within the blackness of the stones. Slowly the two black pillars started to glow and a mist between the pillars formed and started to glow brightly with an intense light. Lighting started to flash from pillar to pillar, but there was no sound. Then he could see a shadow starting to move within the mist. The shadows started to come into focus, and four huge figures walked from the mist and out onto the snow-covered ground. They looked down at Karra silhouetted in the fire's blaze. Everything was still, except the swirling mist between the pillars. The huge creatures stared at Karra. They towered over him, and Karra noticed them tightening their grips and adjusting their weapons in their hands. Karra remained calm and stood very still. Then he spoke with a stern voice breaking the silence.

'I will give you but one word of advice, you hideous dogs. Go back through the gate from where you came, or I will end all your lives right here and now. You do not belong here. This is my world.'

The creature nearest him began to laugh with a booming sound, and then spoke with a deep growl in words Karra could not understand. Karra's eyes narrowed on him and his hands shot behind his head and pulled two swords from their scabbards behind his back. The four creatures held their ground. Karra smiled at them. 'Then come and face your end you ugly puppies.' The closest Creature took a step towards him and Karra shot forward with blistering speed. He leapt high into the air and his left sword flashed out and sank deep into the throat of the lead creature. Karra landed smoothly and stood back. The creature dropped his huge axe to the snow. He swayed, and then fell forward on to his knees, grabbing at his neck trying to stem the flow of bubbling purple blood that gushed out onto the white ground. The creature then fell face-first down into the snow. Dead. Karra looked up at the remaining three. 'Who is next?' The three remaining creatures pushed forward swinging their enormous axe-like weapons. But Karra was too fast for them and darted between them hacking and stabbing as he moved among them. The fight did not last long. Karra had brought down three of the intruders and the last remaining creature stood breathing heavily and bleeding badly. Karra stood drenched with the creatures' blood. 'You have not got long left to live you foul mutt. You are mortally wounded.' The creature clumsily staggered forward in an attempt at one last attack, but his legs would not carry him any further and he fell, face down. Karra sheathed one sword behind his back as he walked close to the struggling giant. He reversed the remaining sword and grasping it with two hands he plunged it deep into the back of the creature's neck ending his misery. 'I told you, this is my world.' As the night sky grew darker Karra sat beside the fire, wiping the blood from his arms and cleaning his swords with a cloth. The mist between the pillars had gone and the amulet was once more, black and cold. The four huge bodies lay still on the frozen ground. Satisfied that the blades were clean, Karra sheathed them behind his back. He let out a small groan as he raised his left hand. His tunic was stained, and blood oozed from a large cut in his left shoulder. 'I must be getting old.' He sighed. He stood and walked back toward the dead bodies and with great effort he started to roll them towards the entrance of the ruins. Karra walked on down to a small stable beside the hut and untied his horse. He then returned to the bodies and one at a time tied them to the horse and dragged them clear of the ruins and out onto a cliff where he rolled them off the side into a huge crevice down in the rock face. He then returned to the stable, secured his horse and entered the hut. Once inside, Karra took out the amulet, it was black as night and the glow had vanished. He placed it on a table. Happy now, he undid the straps that held his swords on his back and placed them beside the amulet. He then removed his wrist guards and then his fur boots and sat down in an oversized armchair and stretched out. There was a small table next to the chair with a cup and a half bottle of red wine. He poured himself a cup and sipped it slowly. He looked sideways at his shoulder and cursed at the sight of the wound. He was tired now and the weariness of the night's events swarmed over him. He drained the cup and replaced it on the table and, slumping back into his chair, he was soon asleep.

1

The woods were all quiet except for some birds singing in the distance. There was a cold breeze slowly moving through the trees bringing leafless branches and vegetation to life. The winter was at its end and the snow was almost gone. The sun was high in the sky and the forest bathed in the weak warmth of its rays. Kalin was breathing heavily and he could feel the sweat trickling down his lower back under his tunic as he ran along a deer trail. He suddenly turned off the trail and stopped at a large tree. He pressed his back against the trunk of the old oak hiding from the trail. His tunic was wet now and stuck to his back. His hand clenched tightly around the hilt of his sword as it hung in his belt. He could feel his heart pounding hard in his chest and struggled to take control of his breathing. Steam rose up from the heat of his body in the cool air and he took several deep breaths and let them out very slowly, regaining control of his breathing. Gradually, his heartbeat began to slow now. He peered around the tree looking back along the trail. There was no sign of any one there, but he knew his enemy was close, he knew his enemy was on his way. He closed his eyes, focusing on sounds that might appear further up along the trail, but could hear nothing. The breeze was cooling on his skin and he started to relax. It was a good hiding place for an ambush, he thought, and a surprise attack might give me an advantage. He peered out once more and this time he could see a figure moving along some distance down the trail. He could feel his heart pounding once again. Perspiration started to bead on Kalin's forehead, and he wiped his brow slowly. I'll take him by surprise, he thought. He drew his sword silently from his belt and gripped it with two hands, preparing himself for the attack. He turned so his shoulder was leaning against the tree and waited at the ready. His enemy was taking his time and Kalin was ready to spring but no one passed on the trail. Just then a sudden snap of a twig sounded behind him and as he spun around his pursuer was upon him, striking down with his sword. Kalin barely blocked the blow with his own sword and fell back out onto the forest trail with the ferocity of the attack. His attacker was looking down at him smiling now.

'Think you could get away from me, you rat?'

Kalin struggled to get back to his feet and backed away to gain a better foot hold. Steadying himself for another attack, Kalin looked his attacker in the eyes and spoke with a mocking tone in his voice.

'I hope that wasn't your best shot, you couldn't hit water if you fell out of a boat.'

With that his attacker lunged forward surprisingly, jabbing his sword for Kalin's face. Kalin was ready this time and side stepped and blocked it with a back thrust, knocking his opponent off balance as he surged forward. The two separated and slowly circled one other with outstretched swords. The pursuer spoke,

'I see you have been practicing.' He laughed, 'But it will take more than just practice to beat me. Come on and show me everything you know; it should only take but a few heart beats.'

Kalin smiled at the statement.

'I'm afraid that won't happen, the dead do not learn much!'

'You made a big mistake hiding behind that tree, your big head gave you away. You should have run for your life while you still had it.'

Kalin's hands felt slippery now with the sweat and he stepped back slowly, trying to create distance between them both. Kalin retorted, 'If you really want to know about mistakes you should ask your parents, dung breath.' With that the attacker sprang forward with a frenzied attack, hacking and cutting with his sword from left to right. Kalin could barely protect himself from the force of his enemy's attack. His opponent pushed forward with remarkable speed, hacking and slicing with his sword. Then with a hacking downward cross Kalin's hand lost its grip on his sword hilt and the sword slipped free of his hand and hit the ground. Knowing he had lost the fight Kalin fell forward onto his knees, submitting to the outcome. His enemy stepped in front of him and smiled a broad victory smile and brought his sword high into the sunny sky and as he brought it down Kalin closed his eyes for the impact. The sword came down with speed and stopped within inches of Kalin's face. Kalin opened one eye and smiled.

'Am I dead yet?'

Chal looked down and Kalin had his arm extended with a knife an inch away from his groin. He laughed out loud and sheathed his wooden sword.

'Dead? I think not, we will live forever you and me. You had me with that knife. How is it I spend hours each week training with the sword with one of the best teachers in Latonia and still you always find a way to better me?'

'I do get lucky sometimes, but I am finding it harder and harder to come up with new ways to try and get the better of you. Your sword skills are always far better than mine,' smiled Kalin.

'I love our mock fights Kalin. But next time you can hunt me. I am out of breath trying to catch you.'

Chal reached out his hand and helped his friend Kalin to his feet.

'I love all the name calling and vulgarities; but I think it is getting more farfetched.'

Chal laughed again and picked up Kalin's wooden sword and handed it to him, hilt first. Kalin put his sword down through his belt and dusted his knees off.

'It is getting out of hand alright we will have to improve on our profanities.'

Kalin looked at the sun in the sky through a gap in the trees.

'We should really be getting back Chal.'

Chal looked up to see the sun also.

'You are right Kalin, it is getting late. I will be having my lessons shortly; it is almost midday. I wish you could join me today Kalin, in the sword training at least, it would really help you with your fencing.'

'I think I have had enough torture for one day Chal. Besides, you have my measure with the sword.'

'It's only because my father pays for a good teacher for me. Mother said he will be home in a few weeks, and I will ask him again can you join me in my training and studies.'

'No please don't Chal, as much as I would love to join in, remember the trouble you got into the last time you took me training with you. Your father is a well-respected General in the King's army. He doesn't want people thinking his son has his studies with a… a savage boy.'

'It's not like that Kalin, you know that. My father knows you are my best friend. We have spoken about this before, just because you come from Gantia doesn't make you a savage or any less than people living in Latonia.'

'Tell that to the rest of the city Chal. They all despise me and my Aunt because I come from a different land. It is that way and I feel it will always be that way. And besides, you know the law. Outsiders are not allowed to put a hand on any weapon in Latonia Lands, even if it is merely a wooden sword. If I were to be seen holding this wooden sword I would be punished severely or worse.'

'They have small minds, Kalin that's all, small minds, and some day things will be different.'

'Any way Chal, let's get back to the city before you miss your training, you shouldn't leave Master Ultan waiting again. He will make you pay for it, tenfold next time.' The two boys made their way back down the hill through the forest towards the city of Kitia. Just before they cleared the tree line, they stopped by an old oak tree. Its roots were exposed from the earth and the boys hid their wooden swords in a hollow beneath them. They had several hiding places along the roads and in the woods where they would hide the wooden swords, they used for their sword playing. Then they made their way down towards the main road to the city. The great walls that protected Kitia looked immense in the distance with their huge defensive turrets soaring high into the sky. It was almost midday and smoke plumed up and out over the city, hanging in the air above; giving the impression the city was alive and breathing out the waste of the inhabitants. The two friends chatted and laughed together as they strolled on down reaching the main road that led to the Eastern Gate of the city. As they neared the gate Kalin heard hooves behind them and turned to look. Three riders approached at a fast speed. Chal turned to look also.

'They look like Royal Messenger Riders to me.'

He said as he squinted to see.

'And by the look of the blue flag the middle rider is carrying, he is one of my Father's troops. My Father told me that once the Royal Messengers are dispatched, they don't stop for anything until they have delivered their message.'

As the Riders approached, the two boys stepped from the road to let them pass. Without as much as a glance the riders galloped by. They could feel the rush of air as each rider shot past on to the city. They watched as they disappeared through the open gates just ahead. Chal and Kalin strode back on to the road and walked in silence for a short while until Chal broke the silence.

'It won't be long you know.'

'What won't be long Chal?'

'It won't be long now until I will be signing up to the Royal Army and start my training as a soldier, I'm sixteen in two months. Father says the training is very hard.'

'I'm sure you will make a fine soldier Chal. They'll probably make you an Officer or a Captain within a year. Your Father will be very proud of you. I wish I had been born here in the Kingdom of Latonia; I would love to be a Royal Latonian soldier. Maybe when you become General Chal, like your father you will change the rules for me.'

'That will be the first thing I will change Kalin. I promise you one day you will be able to hold a sword in public on this land and no one will bat an eyelid.' The two boys looked at one another; Kalin knew he was serious and decided not to jest.

'I believe you my friend and look forward to that day,' said Kalin as he nodded.

The two boys walked on through the main gates and in under the huge walls of the city without being stopped by the gate guards and on through to the city. The busy life inside the Capital was everywhere as people went on with their daily life. The city markets stalls started just a short walk inside the gates, lining both sides of the main road, Kings Avenue, right up and around the City Square.

'I think I will have to take the shortcut home through the alleys if I am going to make it in time for my lesson Kalin, so here I will leave you.'

'Until tomorrow my friend, enjoy your lessons.' replied Kalin and patted his friend on the back. Chal smiled.

'See you tomorrow.'

Kalin watched as Chal took off at a run and was soon swallowed up by the city's inhabitants. Kalin then turned and walked on through the marketplace taking his time to look at what was on offer on some of the stalls. As he reached the City Square, he noticed Brin and two of his friends were heading straight towards him. Kalin cursed softly and turned his back, pretending to be interested in buying an item of clothing on one of the stalls, in an effort to hide himself from his foe.

Suddenly he was pushed from behind and fell against the stall table, knocking over some fabric piles. He spun around and came face to face with Brin. Kalin noticed Brin had a fresh burn on his forearm that he must have got working with his father, the Armory Blacksmith. Brin was a big lad for his age of 15, the same age as Kalin and Chal. He was slightly taller than Kalin. He took pride in degrading and bullying other boys.

'Buying something nice for your boyfriend are we Kalin?' Brin said, with malice in his voice. His two friends started to laugh at the jest. Kalin could feel his anger growing now and was about to retort when the stall owner called out.

'You boys be gone with you before I come over there and move you myself.' Kalin looked at him and then back to the other boys. No one moved and the tension started to rise.

'GO! Get away from my stall now. That is my last warning,' the owner shouted.

Kalin turned and walked on swiftly trying to lose himself in the crowded market square. He could feel the presence of the three boys following him and his mind struggled to think of a way to outsmart them and shake them off. He noticed a narrow alley up ahead and as he approached the entrance, he turned down it swiftly and ran. After turning down several more alleyways he came out onto a larger road. Kalin felt his breath quicken now and stopped to look behind him to see if he was being followed. There was no one pursuing him. He noticed that he recognized the street. It was one of the poorer roads. While running he was so busy trying to get away that he hadn't noticed where he was running to. The city was a vast place and there were hundreds of streets, but Kalin knew most of them from delivering to homes and establishments for his uncle's bakery. He could not remember the name of this street and there were no people around except for some young children at the far end of the road. As he walked on, he heard running coming up behind him. He turned to see Brin and his two friends running towards him, he cursed under his breath.

'Think you could get away from us that easy, did you?'

Brin walked up close to Kalin and pushed his head down hard against Kalin's. Kalin stood back to give himself room from Brin's invading breath.

'Brin, your breath smells like pig shit!'

With that, Brin lashed out a punch and hit Kalin on the left side of his face. Kalin turned with the force of the blow but did not go down. He faced into Brin and felt his anger taking hold of him. He then lurched forward and let fire his own punches, knocking Brin to the ground. As Brin fell down, his two friends ran forward and started to hammer punches into Kalin. Kalin raised his hands up trying to block most of the punches and moved back and to the side to make it harder for them to hit him. Waiting for a break in the attack Kalin then fought back, pushing forward on the two. Blocking and punching. The two attackers seemed to give as Kalin fought back. Both were overcome by the aggressiveness of Kalin's counterattack they fell back, wanting no more of the conflict. They turned and ran. As Brin got back to his feet Kalin could see he had a badly bruised eye.

'Come on then Brin.' Kalin said with a smug grin.

Brin cursed out loud and was about to attack again, but with his friends gone for backup Brin hesitated. He felt a bit dizzy and could still feel the blow that Kalin dealt out. His hand moved up and, rubbing at the bruise that was starting to swell on his face, Brin thought better of it.

'You just wait, Savage. You'll get yours; you'll get what's coming to you, and I'll get you for this.'

Then, he turned and ran after his two friends. Kalin rubbed his own bruised face and walked on, trying to figure out what street would take him back home the quickest. He glanced back once more to see if Brin was gone and noticed a figure partially hidden in the shadow of a doorway. He was very tall, and his face was shaded with a hood. As the figure noticed Kalin had spotted him he just stepped back into the dark doorway and was gone. Kalin turned and hurried on home. After some time, he reached home and went inside. The house was owned by his Aunt, Reesa. Reesa was also from the Northlands of Gantia. She was a large rounded lady, sister to Kalins father. She had met and fallen in love with a Latonian man called Mara on a trading trip to the North Wall some years back. Mara had a trading stall there and was interested in some of the foods that the Gantian people had for sale. The people in the city called him Fat Mara, he was a baker and very well known in Kitia for his sweet cakes and honey delicacies. Like Kalin, Reesa was a victim of prejudice in the land of Latonia. She tried her best to keep her head held high and shelter Kalin from it. Kalin knew she was unhappy living in the city, but Mara was happy here with his business. She loved her husband Mara and endured it for him. Mara knew about the troubles that they both had to endure but he always tried to see the light side of things. It was just in his nature to be jolly. Kalin called out to his Aunt as he walked in through the door.

'Reesa are you home?'

Reesa came to the hallway with her finger on her lips shushing Kalin as he came in the door.

'Shush! Mara is asleep trying to get some rest, how did you get on with your deliveries this morning?'

'It went grand, we have an extra six customers to cater for, so it took a bit longer today to get the cakes and pies to them.'

'Were you out with Chal today?'

'Yes, we had a walk in the woods.'

'Well you must be hungry so, there's some bread and cheese and milk on the kitchen table. Go help yourself.'

As Kalin passed her Reesa grabbed his arm.

'Is that a bruise on the side of your face?'

'It's nothing Auntie, I just walked into a branch while in the woods today with Chal, that's all.'

'I just don't want to see you getting into any more trouble here in Kitia. It is hard enough for us both being from the North.'

'It's fine Auntie, really.'

'Well then, go and have yourself some food. I need to pop out to the market for a while and bring some supplies to the bakery for Mara.'

Reesa wrapped a shawl around her shoulders and left the house, closing the door behind her. Kalin went into the kitchen and sat and ate. After a while he heard Mara stirring in his room and moments later, he joined Kalin at the kitchen table. Mara noticed the red mark on Kalins face but said nothing. Reesa returned to the house after a few hours. Kalin talked and laughed with his Auntie and Uncle through the evening time, but by the time the sun started to set Kalin felt himself getting very sleepy. He said good night and he went to bed early for he had an early start again the next day delivering food for Mara. Sleep came swiftly once he was under his warm blanket.

Kalin felt wet grass under his shoeless feet; it felt pleasant as he moved his toes upon it. He looked down and his feet and legs were covered in dirt and he was standing on a grass meadow. He was surprised to find he was standing there naked. Just then he heard his name spoken, 'Kalin!' as if someone whispered it close to his ear. He spun around, surprised to find himself alone. It was nighttime and there was not a sound. He could see a slow mist gently moving across a nearby meadow and his mind struggled to think how he had got here. He heard his name called again, this time it came from directly in front of him, it sounded like it was in the distance. He started to walk in the direction of the sound. The mist was getting thicker now and as he ran, he could just make out there was no ground in front of him, he stopped abruptly. He looked out across the cliff and in the distance, there was another cliff.

'I do not know this place, where am I, he thought to himself.'

He heard his name called again, this time it sounded closer. The mist was coming in towards him but then it started to clear. He could just make out a figure standing on the far cliff through the breaks in the mist as it swept by. It then cleared completely and Kalin could see that there was a huge stoned wall along the edge of the cliff.

'Where am I? How did I get here?'

He spoke out loud. His mind raced. There was a snapping sound of branches coming from behind him, Kalin turned to find an entanglement of thorns and bushes directly behind him that were not there moments before. He felt panic starting to set in. He could hear something moving in the bushes but could not make out what it was. The thorns were thick and matted. Again, he heard his name being called, He went to look out over the cliff once more. The cliff was no longer there. He was now standing outside the wall that he had just been looking at from across the other cliff. Nothing was making any sense. There was a large, dark, wooden door in the recess of the wall. Kalin approached it and called out.

'Hello, who is there?'

There was no answer. Kalin decided to try to open the door but there was no handle, so he knocked twice on the hardwood. It sounded loud and echoed from behind the door. The door gave a loud groan and opened outwards. Kalin could not see inside as it was very dark inside. As he moved closer and peered inside, he heard a voice call out.

'Help me! Help me please!'

It came from the bushes from behind him. Kalin spun around and could see a small child, of around three years of age, caught in the thorns. She was wearing a loose, white dress. The thorns and bushes started moving around her and curling around her limbs. She cried out as the thorns pierced her skin and blood started to flow on to her white dress, staining it. Kalin tried to run to her aid and realised he could not move his legs. He looked down and could see large black hands holding his legs in a tight grip. Then, more black hands came shooting out of the darkness from behind the door and grabbed him, pulling him into the darkness. Kalin was panicking now and tried to free himself from the black hands, but they were too strong, and pulled him even closer into the blackness of the door. The little girl screamed out in pain and Kalin felt a sense of helplessness as he watched her being engulfed by the branches. The thorns then twisted around her small neck and stabbed into her flesh. They twisted sharply and broke her neck. Kalin cried out.

'Nooo!'

Kalin bolted up right in his bed with sweat dripping from his face, breathing heavily. He swung his legs out over the bed, feeling numb from the dream. There was a knock and his bedroom door opened. Mara peered in to Kalin's room with a candle in his hands,

'Is everything OK Kalin? I heard you cry out.'

'it's OK uncle, I just had another bad dream again, that's all.'

'OK then, once you are OK. Try and get some sleep. We are up for work in a few hours.'

Mara closed the door quietly and was gone. Kalin lay back down on his bed, trying to push the bad dreams from his thoughts. He eventually drifted off into a dreamless sleep. He woke just before dawn still feeling tired. The bad dreams seemed to be happening more frequently now, and he always felt drained after them. He swung from his bed and stretched, and then dressed and went to the kitchen and broke off a chunk of bread and poured himself a cup of milk. He woke around the same time every morning to start his days' work. Mara would be at the bakery now getting everything ready for the day ahead. Kalin grabbed his cloak and left the house. The bakery was getting very busy, a lot of people relied on Mara's food and the orders were coming in more and more every day. Last year Kalin helped out in the kitchen but now all his focus was on delivering the baked goods around Kitia. He even had to hire extra help to keep up with the demand but Kalin didn't mind. He liked the job he had with his uncle. It gave him a chance to meet new people and see all the city. Sometimes he had to deliver to the

Palace. The pay was a small amount, but he was grateful for it, and the fact that he had a roof over his head. He owed his auntie a lot and Mara too. He would not let them down. As he made his way to the Bakery he repeated over and over in his head. I will not get into trouble today. Today will be a good day.

2

King Roban sat on his throne, listening to his assembly of four Royal Councilors argue around a small table that was placed on the podium. The party present consisted of five men, the King Roban and the four men that held the most power under the King: Arthen The Royal Primary General, Sabat the Kings Mystic Lord, Ulauth The High Priest of The House of Light and Giram the Financial Custodian of The Kingdom. For over an hour the meeting had continued, and the King was growing tired of the bickering. The heated debate kept coming back again and again to the same thing, the over expenditure of the city's gold. The King liked to let the advisers get everything off their chests before he had the final say. It was true though; the City of Kitia had run into financial difficulty in the last few years and the King was finding it harder to find revenue in other avenues. The Royal Capital was rapidly depleting. There was less and less money coming in from his Kingdom, Latonia. The mines in the east, just south of Talmine in the Black Mountains, were starting to run dry.

Giram took a deep breath and spoke, 'we might be left with no choice but to up the taxes again, and this would alleviate the pressure within the capital.'

Ulauth shook his head vigorously at this. 'No, no, morale would be affected by this and then trade would suffer across the land, I would not recommend another tax hike our people are at breaking point with paying taxes. We must look at a different avenue.'

Sabat then spoke in a low deep tone, 'If I may make a suggestion, our Kingdom has been at peace now for many years and we can see no threat from other nations. We are building friendships with neighbouring lands and the offshore trading is good, maybe it is time to start looking at other areas? Maybe we should start looking at downsizing our armies? The annual expenditure on training and weapons and soldiers pay is colossal, and for what? There is no enemy to fight, there are no lands we must conquer. We have a huge army just eating our food stock and draining the Kingdom of its gold and for what? These are times of peace, not war and yet we spend like we are preparing for a campaign. Does the assembly not agree with this?'

Arthen thundered his fist down on the table, 'I will not allow the Kingdom to be weakened by reducing our army; this would be a very bad decision to make, just to save on expenditure.'

Sabat leaned forward, 'I'm not saying that we don't have an army, all I am saying is we should reduce the size. We have 3000 troops in Cinam, peace keeping. A place where they do not belong. Another 2000 on the South Wall in Natalan, at least 2500 on the North Wall to Gantia guarding the pass from the north savages, at least 1000 in Naos and another 10000 within these walls here in Kitia and another 1000 royal guards within this palace and who knows how many we have scattered across the Latonia lands. I am not going to mention our naval forces, and now we are making new improved armour for troops that have no need of it. Where does it end?'

The General Arthen sniggered, 'I see you have done your homework on The King's army Sabat.'

'It is a case of having to. Do you honestly think we need all these men protecting us from nothing? The cost of maintaining such an army is enormous.'

Arthen sat back in his chair and folded his arms and took in a deep breath trying to calm himself.

'I am not in favour of this Sabat, and like I said, I will not allow The Kingdom of Latonia to be weakened in any way.'

'So, what would you suggest General?'

'I think we should look at opening a new campaign. A new expedition into new lands and, maybe an invasion to the north? There are still plenty of riches to obtain in the north, the natural resources are endless. Their mountains are full of wealth.'

Giram had remained quiet for most of the talks. Now it was time for him to speak up. He sighed at the thoughts of a new campaign and the heavy weight that a war would bring.

'I am sorry, Arthen, but killing and plundering is never the answer.'

Arthen grinned at Giram. 'Sometimes it must be done. A man's feelings have no place in war. In any case, the Kingdom has a fine balance and we control that balance with our forces.'

Sabat laughed out loud. 'You know little about balance, General, what you are talking about is fear. The people of Latonia are kept in line due to fear, fear of the Kingdom's Iron Hand.'

King Roban could see Arthen was getting angry at Sabat's statement, and decided it was time to step in before it got out of hand. He took a large drink of his red wine and cleared his throat.

'Well my friends.'

The assembly stopped talking and looked to their King.

'I have listened carefully to everything you have had to say, and I will have to take some time to consider where best to take things from here. You all have argued logical points and I thank you for this.'

The King looked around at the men at the table nodding. The room fell silent for a couple of heart beats as The King took another drink from his goblet and then wiped his mouth.

'But I think we should all have a drink now and get our minds off these subjects. Is there other business on our agenda for today?'

Ulauth nodded, 'Yes your highness, we have the Summer Celebrations and your Birthday to organise, and the 10th anniversary of your rule.'

'Ah that's more like it, I like hearing the word Celebration.' The King said with a proud smile.

After another hour of talks the meeting was adjourned for another week. The King called a halt to the meeting and the four Councillors bowed and then went about their business, leaving the room without saying a word. Sabat left the room and one of his Partisans was waiting for him. They both headed out of the palace past the Royal Guards and out into the streets.

'Have you made the preparations?' Sabat asked as they walked.

'Yes, all is ready, Rector.'

'Good, we have plenty of work to do now that things are underway. I will inform you of all the plans when we reach the apostolic. We have some work to do.'

The two moved on through the streets and up a hill leading to Sabat's place of worship. It had large walls around it and a huge iron gate. As the men approached the gates, they opened. It seemed very dark inside and they both walked through. The gates were shut behind them. The

King sat alone drinking his wine. He was starting to feel hungry now and ordered for some food to be brought to him. One of his Coordinator's entered the room and bowed before him.

'You have a Royal Messenger waiting to see you, your Highness; will I tell him to come on through?'

'Yes of course let him in.'

The messenger was led forward, and he bowed to the King. 'I have letters from Turren and a full report from General Titus Cassian at the South Wall.'

'Excellent, I have been waiting for some news. It gets rather boring around here. How are things on the wall there? And how are things in Natalia? I believe the problem with the rebel horde is now under control.'

'Yes, your Honour, things are running well. Following your last orders, General Titus has sent a peace keeping force into Natalia and they have disbanded the rebels.'

'When do you head back?'

'I leave at first light tomorrow morning your Highness.'

'Good. I will have a letter drawn up to be taken to the General, make sure you take this with you tomorrow. I have already sent a letter down, requesting his return but I will send another just in case.'

'Yes, your Highness.'

The King turned to one of his staff.

'Make sure this man is well fed and gets plenty of rest. That is all'

The King gestured to his Coordinator that the meeting had ended, and the messenger handed the letters to the Coordinator, thanked the King, bowed and left the room.

'I need you to write a letter to General Titus Cassian, tell him he needs to start making preparations to come home. He must return to Kitia in time for the summer celebrations. I'm sure he could do with a break for the wall. He must be missing his family. It would be good to have him back in the city, he is a man to drink and laugh with. Now bring me some more wine.'

It was late into the night. Sabat changed from his white gown to a black gown and entered the side door from his chambers to the food hall. Two of his followers brought in a young orphan boy around 6 years of age and sat him down, presenting him with a plate of food. The child devoured it within seconds. A priest then came out of the kitchen with a small bowl. He tilted the child's head back and opened his mouth. He then put his finger into the boy's mouth and smeared a green paste on to his gums and walked away. The young boy made a face at the taste of the paste in his mouth.

'I don't like that.'

He said as the priest went back into the kitchen without saying a word. The boy seemed to look sleepy and started rocking from side to side trying to keep awake. He then slumped forward onto the table as if he were sleeping only his eyes were wide open. Two priests dressed in black came in and lifted the boy from the table and brought him through a door and down steps to the lower section on the church. They lifted him onto a large stone table and then locked the door they had entered by. They then tied the boy's wrists and ankles to the four corners of the table. The boy moaned as they stretched his limbs out to their full spread. The two priests then left through a different door and closed it behind them. They waited outside silently. The room was large with a high ceiling and the only light came from a few candles, scattered around the outskirts of the floor, flickering the light onto the dark walls. The sound of a muffled voice echoed from the walls, coming from the young boy as he tried to speak but could not. The drug had taken full effect now, rendering him helpless and void from movement. Moments later the door opened again. Sabat walked in and the priests outside closed the door once more behind him. Sabat strode over to the altar. He looked down at the helpless boy, who looked back up at him with terrified eyes. From a shelf to the side of the altar, he produced a short-curved knife. With this he cut open the boy's tunic to expose his pale, small, skinny frame. He raised his hands high into the air and started chanting unrecognisable words. The two priests outside the room stood fast guarding the door. They heard noises coming from the room that they had never heard before. Flashing lights could be seen from the crack at the bottom of the door. The only way to comprehend what was happening in the room was that there was a thunder and lightning storm taking place within. It lasted for a short while and then suddenly there was silence. Then a scream came from the room that made the hairs on the backs of their necks stand up. A powerful voice boomed out in a language unknown to them, causing the doors to shake on their hinges. They looked at one another with fear and a sense of uneasiness, but they waited dutifully, guarding the doors. Some time had passed, and the noises had died down within the room, all was quiet now. They heard footsteps coming towards them from the other side of the door and then it opened. Sabat walked past them without saying a word. He was drenched in blood and looked very frail and weak, like he had not slept in days. Sabat then stopped and turned to the priests.

'I have contacted the Dark Lord. We have a lot of work to do, but first I need to rest. Clean up that mess in the room and we will meet and talk later.'

He then turned and made his way to his chambers. The two priests turned and walked into the room. They were stopped in their tracks with shock to see what was left inside. One of the priests turned and threw up, spilling his vomit onto the stone floor. The other one looked at him.

'It is not a time to be fragile, my fellow brother. You have just added to the mess we have to clean up. Be strong if you want to survive this. For the Dark Lord is watching us.'

The two reluctantly went inside and started cleaning up the room, trying not to be sick. Sabat woke from a deep sleep. He felt better now but still not back to normal after contacting The Dark Lord. It always took its toll on him. He stood from his bed and made his way from his room to the hall. There were several men waiting for him to arrive. They all bowed as he walked into the hall.

'Please be seated.' They all sat in silence.

'The next few weeks will be vital to our plan. As you all are aware, I contacted The Dark Lord last night and he has instructed me in what he wants from us all. I am about to tell you of the bigger plan we have to act on. Firstly, there will be an invasion from the Emahair Emperor. This will take place very soon. Before the Dark Lord is able to come to our world, we must have certain things completed here first. Our goal is to create chaos and bring this world to its knees. This will allow us to take control of the Gate between worlds. So be ready and act swiftly when I order it. Our time here is near its end and then we will all bathe in the glory of The Dark Lords rule. Now I must try and contact my brother Oranius.'

Oranius stood over the Emperor as he lay on his back on the bed. His healing hands floated just above the Emperor's naked body. No one was permitted to touch the God Emperor. Only his daughter. He could feel the energy flow through his body and down to his hands and then into the Emperor's body. This energy also brought pleasure and blissfulness with it as it flowed. This was evident by the Emperor's visible erection as he lay there on the bed. As the healing took place, he also forced his own thoughts and will onto the Emperor. He was able to mask these thoughts with the healing energy. He transferred the thoughts of war, thoughts of conquering other lands and invading countries across the seas. As the emperor felt these thoughts, he associated them with the feeling of pleasure and longed for them. Through this, Oranius had control over him and the Empire. The treatment was almost complete when he had a feeling, a feeling of someone reaching out to him. Someone wanted to connect with him.

'The treatment is complete now, your Highness.'

The Emperor opened his eyes with the sound of the words. He still had a smile on his face.

'That did not seem as long as the last treatments. Can you keep the process going for longer?'

'I must stop now your Highness, as you are fully healed. I do not want to overdo it, as it might make you sick.'

'Very well then hand me my robe.' The Emperor said in a disappointed voice.

He dressed and walked from the room. Oranius bowed as he left. Oranius then made his way to his house of prayer. Arriving at his chambers, he lit a fire in the fire pit and sat on the floor beside it. He then closed his eyes and concentrated. The flames from the fire grew larger and turned blue. He opened his eyes and gazed into the blue flames. He could see the face of his brother Sabat.

'Hello, my brother, how are you?'

Came the voice in his head matching the motions from the face in the fire.

'I am well. How is your work going?'

'I am on track. I have the Emperor ready and he is preparing for war.'

'That is good news indeed. I have contacted The Dark Lord and he is pleased with our progress.'

'I will keep working on our goal here and hope to see you in the lands of Latonia soon.'

'There is one thing we did not plan for. There is a prophecy that The Dark Lord told me. It is of the utmost of importance. It is to do with a boy.'

'Where is this boy? Do you need me to find him? Or kill him?'

'No, I will deal with him. I do not know who he is as yet. This boy will be our only weakness and is a great threat to us and our plans, but I will find him and kill him for he must die.'

3

General Titus Cassian was a strict and stern man. He did everything by the book and his men knew this. If anyone stepped out of line, or failed to follow a command, they would be punished. His orders would be carried out to the letter, no matter what. The Country of Natalia had been in trouble. There had been disagreements within their governing body, and an internal struggle had transpired. This had brought about protests, rioting, and finally a rebellion. The Natalian Guard had fought hard to contain it, but the groups were growing in size and the Guard had found it increasingly difficult to maintain order. The Chancellors fears of a revolution had led him to reach out for help, and King Roban had naturally offered support. The King had allocated troops to help disband these rebels and brought peace back to the land, but in doing so he had broken a treaty that had been set in place many years ago by all the nations; that no foreign military force would be allowed to enter any of those nations. General Titus had completed his task, and now his job was one of maintaining the wall, and the traffic of people and trade that passed through its gates. It was a fresh morning as he walked the ramparts of the wall, sipping on his cup of lemon tisane. His morning routine was to check the walls and make sure that troops were all at their posts. The wall guards all stood to attention as he passed. All was quiet and in order and he was satisfied. He stopped at the entrance of the keep, and then wandered over to the edge. As he looked out over the lands of Latonia, his thoughts strayed to his family. He was starting to miss his home now. He missed his wife and his son Chal and the life at his villa. He was away from home nearly a year now, although it often seemed shorter. He tipped the remains of his tisane out over the wall and was about to head back into the keep when he spotted riders coming towards the wall. He waited as they came into sight. When their flags came into view, he could see that they were the Royal riders returning. He hoped there was mail from his wife. He left the wall and made his way down through the keep to meet the messengers. He received three letters, one from his wife, one from a merchant he had business with, and one from the King. This last was sealed with the Royal wax seal. The King had ordered him to return to Kitia before the Summer Festival so he could join in the celebrations.

He was happy to return, but he would not share that sentiment with his men. The General called for a meeting with his commanders to share the details of his news and to organise an assembly to notify the troops, and hand over the command to the Captain of the wall. The next morning, the entire force of 2000 Royal Soldiers of the south wall assembled in the courtyard below the ramparts. General Titus addressed them all. His voice boomed out over his men.

'I have received a letter from the King. He has ordered me to return to Kitia to carry out orders that are more pressing than those here at the wall. I will be leaving today. The King has said that the level of work being done here is immense, and that the disbanding of the rebel forces and the aid given to the Natalian people has been hugely appreciated by both the King and the Chancellor of Natalia. Well done to you all for achieving this. To express his gratitude, the King has sent 6 wagons loaded with alcohol for your enjoyment and a celebration will be held in the next day or two. It is well deserved by all.'

A buzz of excitement spread through the ranks as the troops started to discuss the benefits of having some free time.

'Before I leave today, I want to thank you all for your hard work and service to the Kingdom. It was a pleasure working with you all and I am very proud to be your General. Now, it is time for me to hand over my command to Captain Brota. He may be a little more lenient than I have been, but he is a great Captain. You will be in good hands.'

The captain smiled and walked forward, and the General handed over the Royal shield with the Lions head engraved on the front. General Titus smiled back at Captain Brota and then saluted to the troops, who in turn saluted back, and a cheer went up. The general marched from the wall and headed straight for Kitia with 500 of his troops, leaving 1500 to man the south wall. It took almost a month for the army to arrive back in Kitia. They arrived just in time for the Summer Celebrations. The General wanted to make his way to his villa, which was located a few miles outside the city of Kitia, but his duty dictated where he had to go first. He would have to report to the King immediately on his arrival, and no doubt the King would want to hear all about his time at the wall. This in turn would then lead to the King wanting to get drunk and the General would have to join him. It might be another 2 days before he would get to see his family, but they would have to wait. The King's needs always came first. Chal was outside moving hay from the shed to the stables to feed the horses. His friend

Kalin was with him, helping him finish his chores. The two boys were in competition with each other to see who could carry the most hay, and who could complete the job fastest. There was great excitement. Chal's mother Mordeena was washing and peeling vegetables in the kitchen as she gazed at the boys through a window. She was laughing to herself at the boy's antics. She looked out through the gate in the 10-foot walls that surrounded the villa and spotted a lone horseman coming up along the path. She was not expecting a visitor. As the man came closer and dismounted, she caught a glimpse of sun on armour and knew he was a soldier. She walked outside to greet the man. Realising at the last moment that it was her husband, she raised her hands to her mouth to stop from crying out. Chal noticed his mother's reaction and turned around to see what she was staring at. It was his father, General Titus Cassian coming through the gate.

'FATHER!' He shouted out and ran to meet him.

Chal hugged his father and Mordeena ran out from the house and joined them in an embrace. Kalin stood watching the emotional event unfold. They walked back towards the house and General Titus stopped before Kalin.

'You are looking well Kalin, and much bigger since the last time I saw you. We are about to prepare some food and catch up around the dinner table, would you like to join us?'

'I think you all need some time alone. Thank you for the offer but I must be getting back home, it's getting late.'

'Well it is good to see you Kalin. Please come around again soon and we can have that meal together.'

'Thank you. I will, and it is good to see you too General. I will see you tomorrow Chal.'

With that Kalin left and made his way back to the city, and the General and his family went inside. As Kalin walked back he found himself in a good mood after witnessing Chal's happiness at his father arriving home. It made him think about what it would have been like if he had known his own father and mother. He knew he loved his auntie and uncle, and he knew they loved him, but would that love have been even greater towards his father and mother? He had not seen his friend react like that before. Chal's face had lit up with joy at seeing his father. He must have missed him immensely. Even though the General had invited him to stay, Kalin knew that this was a special moment for Chal and his family and did not want to intrude on their reunion. It was for them, and them alone. Kalin entered through the gates and made his way towards his home. It was getting late and the sun was starting to set. There were less people on the streets and the evening was drawing to an end as the stall owners were closing their trading posts. Kalin entered an empty street. He looked up as he walked along and could see a lone person standing in the middle of the road looking back at him. As Kalin got closer he realised that it was Brin waiting for him. As he got closer, several more boys came out of alleyways to join Brin. There were six boys in total, including Brin. Kalin stopped walking towards them. He was tempted to run straight into the gang and start beating on all of them, but even six was a push for Kalin to take on. Brin spat on the ground in front of Kalin.

'Well well well, look who we have come across lads. It's the savage. I think he must be lost, because he's thousands of miles away from his home.'

The rest of the boys laughed. Kalin forced himself to remain calm.

'You know Brin, I was having a good day until I saw your ugly face. What do you want?'

'You know what I want Kalin, I want you to go back to where you came from. Back to your savage land.'

Kalin laughed at Brin's statement 'And you think that the six of you will be strong enough to achieve that?'

Brin grew angry and started to walk forward, leaving his five comrades behind him.

'I told you I'd get you, savage, now you will know not to mess with me.'

Brin pulled a long hunting knife from his sleeve and pointed it towards Kalin.

'I forged this knife myself. I call it the Savage Killer.'

Kalin could feel panic starting to set in, and his survival instinct kicked in and his mind told him to run, but his heart said fight. Brin came closer and Kalin stood his ground ready for the first attack. Brin pulled his arm back, preparing for a forward thrust to Kalin's mid-section, when a shout halted him just before he slashed forward with the knife.

'STOP!' Came a loud, deep voice.

Everyone turned in the direction of the shout. A very tall dark-skinned man walked from the shadows. His movements were steady and smooth as he approached the boys.

'Drop that knife or I will shove it so far up your ass you'll have to sharpen it through your mouth,' he said.

His cold voice startled all the boys. Brin instantly dropped the knife and spun on his foot. He was surprised to see that the other boys were already running down the street. Brin then took off in the direction of the five other boys and disappeared around a corner out of sight. Kalin sighed with relief and turned to meet the man. He had very dark skin and a bald head. He noticed a scar over his left eye that came down onto his left cheek. Kalin felt he knew the man's face, but could not think from where.

'Thank you for your help,' said Kalin.

'You are welcome. You are a very brave young man to take on another with a knife, backed up by five of his friends, when you yourself are unarmed, but courage can get you killed sometimes.'

Kalin thought about what the man had said as he bent down to pick up Brin's knife. He was about to ask the man for his name when he turned and walked back into the darkness of the alley and was gone.

4

Princess Thianni ran through the corridors of the Royal Palace, holding up her long dress so it wouldn't catch on her feet as she ran. She could feel a butterfly feeling fluttering in the pit of her stomach, and she felt giddy. Her auntie, Queen Lesta had released her from her royal duties for the day and mentioned that the King was in a meeting and most of the staff were having lunch in the servant's food hall. This was the perfect opportunity to steal away for a while. She had been assigned new duties a few months back and they were taking up a lot of her day. Thianni now had to look after the food stock and supplies, and the running of the kitchens. She remembered the Queen's words. 'It will be good for you to take on a more important role and it will broaden your knowledge of how the Palace operates. I am also assigning you two ladies-in-waiting.' The Queen then introduced the two young female personal assistants. One, called Sabby, was a very pleasant girl a little younger than Thianni, and Tiffin, a slightly older girl that did not smile. 'These ladies will help you in your new duties and will deal with all the business outside of the palace. So, you can concentrate on your duties.' The Princess ran to her chambers and undressed; she then let her long blonde hair down and went to a hidden closet in her wardrobe, donning a simple dress and a caped hood. She slipped a well-worn, grubby pair of shoes on. There was a knock on her door.

Thianni called out. 'Who is it?'

'It is Tiffin and Sabby my lady.'

'Come in.'

The two girls entered the room and saw Thianni dressed in old scruffy clothing.

'Do you require any help my Lady?'

'No, I am fine; I am on my way out to get some bread for the kitchen.'

'Oh, we can do that for you.'

'No, it is OK I would like to do it myself. I need a break from this palace.'

Thianni walked past the two girls and then stopped. 'But I would prefer if you didn't mention this to anyone. Especially the Queen.'

'Then we shall go with you,' said the older girl.

'No, I would rather go by myself.'

The two bowed to the princess. Thianni then left the room and, pulling the hood over her head, she quickly walked towards the servant's section of the palace, through the kitchen area and out a side door into the sunlight. Still walking quickly, she headed for the secondary palace gate. As she approached the gate, a guard stepped out to confront her. She looked up and smiled, 'it's OK, it's only me!' the guard smiled back, and she placed a copper coin into his hand. Without a word, he moved aside to let the Princess pass out onto the streets. Thianni walked on through the alleyways and streets towards the market unnoticed. She felt butterflies in her stomach again, as she thought about her freedom for the day. She had a good life at the palace, but she often needed to get away from her duties and the pressures of being a member of the royal family. By masquerading as one of the common folk, she was free to move among the people of Kitia without being noticed. Every few weeks she would sneak out to walk, talk and haggle with the people at the market. This she lived for. There were so many wonderful characters, she had even made friends and got to know some of them by name. Thianni was now sixteen years old, and as the Queen said, 'You are becoming a woman.' With these new bigger tasks, she often felt completely overwhelmed but it gave her this opportunity to get out of the Palace. Although her auntie and uncle, the King and the Queen, were strict on her, she knew they loved her, and she was extremely appreciative of that. It was over ten years now since her father and mother had been ambushed, robbed and killed while they were traveling to the city of Harren, in the southeast. Her father had been the King then and it had been a great blow to the Kingdom. His younger brother Roban had taken up the role as the new King. Often, when she tried to remember her father's face it wouldn't come to her, no matter how hard she tried. This upset her greatly, but she was reminded of her beautiful mother Caitria every day as she had a large painting of her in her room beside her bed. She was only six when her parents were taken from her, but she missed them every day. She was supposed to have been traveling with them that day, but she had fallen from her horse and banged her head the day before and they felt she would not be able to accompany them. In some way, that horse had saved her life. The Royal Court suspected it had been an assassination by the Eamhair Empire but could find no proof. Arthen, the Primary Chief General had declared that he would not rest until the murderers were captured, and justice was served. They had eventually caught the offenders, there were 21 of them. A band of outcasts and thieves. They were all tried, proven guilty and hanged. After a short walk through the streets, Thianni arrived at the marketplace. The various perfumes and scents, and the aroma of food cooking, always hit her before she arrived at the first market stall. Thianni could feel a smile widening across her face as she moved on through the hustle and bustle of the crowds. She stopped at a familiar stall; it was a jewellery stall. There were some exquisite pieces of jewellery here. Each time she was here she admired a certain piece. It was a necklace made of silver. The chain was thin but strong and there was a small carved silver dove with its wings spread. The craftsmanship was excellent; the dove looked like it was alive and in mid-flight. Just then, the owner of the stall spoke to her,

'Good day madam, every time you're here you just stare at that damn necklace, are you ever going to buy it?'

'I will someday,' she replied.

Thianni knew she could not buy just anything and had to be careful to remain unrecognised. But every time she saw this necklace, she longed to own it. 'Some day,' she whispered to herself. She moved on through the stalls unnoticed, taking in everything. There were some stalls that she liked to spend time at, one was the jewellery stall the other was a fabric stall. She loved to touch the different fabrics, and the textures, designs, and patterns always held her attention. After some time, she could feel her stomach growling and decided to sample some food, so she made her way to the baker's stall owned by a man called Mara. He had one of the largest tents in the market and sometimes hosted cooking demonstrations. He was famous for his cakes in Kitia, his food was always delicious, and she often had them sent to the palace. There were all sorts of sweet cakes on display and she could feel her mouth starting to water with the thought. Mara came to the counter drying his large hands.

'Now what can I get you madam?'

'Could I have one of your honey cakes please?'

'Most certainly!' he spoke with a friendly voice.

Thianni liked him. As Mara was reaching out to get the cake for Thianni, she heard a commotion, a noise coming from behind Mara at the back of the stall. She looked around him and saw a boy struggling to catch a large cake that had slipped off a tray he was holding. The boy, in his effort to try and keep hold of the cake, lost his balance and slipped backwards. He then crashed into a stack of shelves and brought down trays of fresh cakes and baking ingredients on top of himself, including a bag of baking flour that crashed down on his head and launched a cloud of smoke out across the stall. The boy cursed out loud as Mara turned around. As the cloud cleared Thianni let out a loud giggle as she saw the boy sitting there covered in flour apart from his wide eyes.

Mara turned to her and said, 'I sometimes think that boy has fingers made of butter.' Mara turned to the boy, 'That will be coming out of your wages, again!'

Thianni giggled again, but she wanted to help the boy.

'Are you OK?' she called out.

The boy stood up and in embarrassed silence, he angrily brushed the flour from himself. As he cleaned himself off, she noticed he was not from Latonia. He hadn't the same look as most here. She could see that his hair was black, and his eyes were a pale blue with a hint of grey and a distinct black rim around his iris, giving him an unusual look. Almost like a storm could be seen raging within his eyes. Most of the people from Latonia had fair hair with brown eyes so he looked out of place. She turned to Mara and asked if it would be ok to help him.

'He looks to be in a spot of bother. Would you mind if I went in there to help him?'

'Be my guest.'

Mara lifted the hatch on the counter and let her into the tented area at the back of the stall which Mara used as a stock room. The boy was picking up small cakes from the floor and putting the spoiled ones in a small pile. Thianni started to help him and the boy looked surprised. They cleaned up in silence until all the cakes were accounted for, then they swept as much of the flour as they could.

Then Thianni spoke, 'I am sorry for laughing.'

'It's ok,' the boy said in a low tone.

'Oh, you speak Latonian!'

'Of course, I do, I live here. Do you think I can't speak? Do you think I'm stupid?' Kalin said angrily. Still vexed at himself for causing such an incident in front of a girl.

'No, not at all, forgive me. I did not mean to be rude. Please allow me to start again, I'm…!'

She paused for a second; her mind struggled to come up with a name other than her own, in fear of giving away her identity. The first thing that came to her was her mother's name, Caitria.

'I'm Caitria.'

'Nice to meet you Caitria, I'm Kalin.'

As the two talked, Kalin's embarrassment and anger seeped away. He found himself chatting away to this girl he just met with ease. Usually he felt shy and awkward and got tongue tied while he talked to girls, but with this girl, Caitria, it was different. He felt comfortable with her. As the two chatted away they talked about the weather, cakes, the festival and the King's Birthday Feast. The conversation just flowed. After a while,

Mara butted in, 'Sorry Kalin, I will need you to deliver the rest of the fresh bread now.'

He looked at Caitria with disappointment knowing their meeting would come to an end. She could see this in his face and gave him a weary smile.

'And I must be getting off, I still have several stalls to visit.'

Kalin walked her out to the front of the stall.

'Thank you for helping me clean up the mess I made.'

'That's no problem; I'm always there to save a stranger in their time of trouble.'

Mara came out to the front of the stall and handed the girl the honey cake she originally came to buy.

'Oh! I almost forgot. How much do I owe you for this honey cake?'

'Nothing at all, it's on the house, for helping Kalin clean up.'

Thianni wanted to insist on paying but knew somehow that the baker would not accept the payment.

'Thank you' she replied.

Mara walked back, leaving the two alone. There was silence for a few seconds as they looked at each other.

'I really must go.'

'I know, me too.' said Kalin. 'I liked chatting to you; maybe we could talk again sometime?'

'Yes, I would really like that Kalin. Goodbye, for now.' Thianni walked away and then stopped and looked back at Kalin. He was looking straight at her.

'I hope you drop a cake again soon.'

'Why?' Kalin spoke back.

'So, I can come and save you again.'

'It'll be my turn to save you next time Caitria.' Kalin called back.

Caitria gave him a smile, then she turned and walked away. Kalin watched her until she disappeared into the crowd. He could feel a want within him that he had not felt before, and he could feel he was missing this girl already. For the rest of the day Kalin worked, delivering cakes and breads with a smile on his face thinking about Caitria, the girl he met that day. He could not seem to get the image of her beautiful face out of his mind. He could not wait to tell Chal all about it. He would laugh at him and tease him about it, but he would not mind. It was his friend's job to mock him. He remembered he would not see Chal for a few days. He went about his work with Caitria's face in his mind. The next couple of days passed and Kalin worked with his uncle. He was still thinking about the girl he met. Every time a customer came to the stall, he would look out from the back of the tent in hopes she had returned, but she had not. As he delivered around the city, he was looking out to see if he could see her. Each day, he would come back disappointed. The following week, Kalin was finished his work for the day and headed off to meet up with Chal. He headed out through the city gates and made his way towards Chal's family villa a couple of miles outside the city. It was a nice day out, and he could feel a spring breeze on his skin as he walked. A short while later, Kalin arrived at the Villa. High, whitewashed walls surrounded the villa, shining in the midday sun. As he walked through the open gates, he could see Chal was training in the front courtyard with his teacher, Master Ultan. He decided not to walk in on them, but instead waited at the gate. Master Ultan noticed his presence. Chal was in the middle of a routine, he was dancing and spinning with his sword. Slashing and stabbing into the air as if he were fighting imaginary opponents.

'Freeze!' Ultan sharply shouted.

Chal stopped still, right in the middle of a forward thrust. Master Ultan walked over to Chal, and with a swift movement, pushed Chal's shoulder and Chal fell to the side.

'See? You must obtain complete balance, even in motion. This is the key to speed. You are still overextending with your offence.'

Chal got up from the ground and dusted himself off.

'Now try it again, but this time let it flow, trust your body. Do not force the movements. Let your body take over and your actions will flow like the river. Let it feel natural.' Chal started again, as he spun around, he noticed Kalin was watching from the gate.

'Concentrate!' Master Ultan called out. 'Do not let outside forces distract you from your goal.'

Chal continued with his training. The sweat was dripping from him now and he looked tired. After several more times repeating the exercise, Master Ultan was happy with his performance and called an end to the training session.

'That's enough for today Chal you have done extremely well. You have a friend waiting for you and it would be impolite to keep someone waiting. You will need to practice this form again and again until it flows from you without thought. Practice this several times daily. So, until next time, I bid you good day Master Chal.' He placed his hands behind his back and smoothly walked out from the Villa, bowing his head to Kalin as he walked by. Kalin reciprocated the action and then rushed in to meet Chal.

'That looked really good. You are coming on very well.'

Chal wiped the sweat from his forehead. 'I was doing OK until I saw you watching me. He is a tough teacher Kalin, he doesn't let me away with anything.'

'Master Ultan is one of the best, you are very lucky to have him as your teacher Chal. No wonder I can never beat you in our sword bouts.'

Chal laughed, 'So how are things with you?'

'All good,' said Kalin. 'I met a girl.'

'What! Do tell?' Asked Chal surprised.

Kalin told Chal the story of how they met and how he hasn't stopped thinking about her since. He was surprised that Chal did not try to mock him over it.

'I don't think I know any girls named Caitria, what does she look like?'

'Oh, Chal she is very beautiful, she has a lovely face with big brown eyes.'

'And big round boobs too?' Chal added. They both laughed.

'Let me get this right. You meet this girl once and now you can't stop thinking about her. Well I'm very much looking forward to meeting her now. She must have really large breasts.'

They both laughed again.

Chal changed the subject. 'Would you be up for a run?'

'I would Chal, but I think you might be too tired after all your training with Ultan.'

'I'll be OK. I could go for a small run. I think we need to start training so we will be fit enough to enter the summer games at this year's festival. After all, it's not too far away now. I know you are not allowed to enter in the sword fighting events Kalin, but you will be allowed to enter into the running.'

'You are right Chal, you are always right, let's get running so. You can tell me about this girl with the large breasts on the way.'

The two boys set off on a slow run around the wooded hills around Chal's parent's villa. As the weeks passed, their training increased as the games drew closer. Chal would take a lesson from Ultan twice a week and when the lesson had ended, he would show Kalin what he had learned, and they would work on the new techniques together with the wooden swords. They would also go running together three times a week over the hills and through the surrounding woods. Slowly increasing their pace and distance. Pushing themselves further each time. Kalin had not seen Caitria since they first met, but he thought about her often and was starting to wonder if he would ever see her again. It was getting late in the day when the Princess was finally able to escape to the market for a few hours without Tiffin and Sabby knowing. She had not been able to get away from the palace for a while and was getting excited at the thoughts of the break away, even if it was only for a few hours. She slipped out and made her way straight to Mara's stall. Mara was serving some customers and the Princess queued in her raggy clothes and waited for her turn. She was feeling very excited, more so than usual. She could not help herself from trying to look in the back of the stall, hoping to see Kalin there. She was next to being served and Mara gave her a big smile.

'Well hello there, good to see you again young lady. Are you looking for my fresh honey cakes or is it my nephew you are looking for?' He gave her a wink.

Thianni felt herself getting embarrassed and could feel her face getting warm, she knew she was blushing.

'Well I was hoping I could have both.' She was surprised she said that and gave a giggle.

'Well I can give you a honey cake, but Kalin is not here today. He is off out with his friend.'

The smile fell from her face with disappointment.

'Well I will have to settle for just the honey cake then.' The Princess paid Mara and thanked him. 'Can you tell him I was asking for him?'

'Of course, he is mostly here in the morning when I need deliveries done, if you want to come back another day to see him.'

She thanked him again and headed back toward the palace. She was making her way through the market when she turned around and saw Kalin walking towards her amongst the crowds. He noticed her at the very same time and gave her a big smile, and she smiled back. She could feel her heart flutter in that instant. He looked just as handsome as the first time they had met. He came running over and called her by her mother's name.

'Caitria, how are you?'

The Princess smiled. 'I am good, and you?'

'I am good too.' Kalin looked down at her hand and saw that she was holding a honey cake and felt good that she had been at the stall.

'I was just talking to Mara. What have you been up to?'

'I was out running with my friend Chal. We are training for the festival games.'

'That is very exciting. Do you think you have a chance at winning?'

'I'm not sure, I never actually thought about that. I think I do. I am just happy that I will be allowed to take part in the race. I would really love to take part in the sword fighting, but unfortunately, I am not allowed.'

'Why would you not be allowed?'

'You know, because of me being who I am.' He paused. 'Me being a savage.'

She laughed. 'Oh, Kalin you are far from a savage. And that is a silly rule any way.'

Kalin went red in the face and turned away. She noticed he was uncomfortable and decided to change the subject.

'I will have to get back to the…' She paused in the middle of the sentence, conscious that she had almost given her secret away.

'I must get back home soon, but I have a little while if you would care to take a walk with me?'

Kalin looked straight at her. 'I would like that.'

They walked together along the city's streets, talking about whatever came to mind. Kalin found he was talking about his auntie and uncle, but it was getting late and Thianni reluctantly said she would have to get back home. They stopped walking and faced each other.

'When can I see you again?'

Thianni gave a wide smile. 'You want to see me again?'

'Yes of course. I… I like you.' Kalin said bashfully. 'And there is a lot about you I would like to know.'

'I like you too, Kalin.' Thianni's smile faded. 'I'm not sure though; I find it hard to get the time to visit the markets. I am very busy with my new job lately.'

'What job do you work at?'

Thianni thought hard on how to answer the question without giving away her identity. 'I work in a kitchen.'

'That's a good job, you will never go hungry. When can I see you again? Or do you want to see me?'

'Of course, I do, I like you too you know.'

Kalin's smile stretched out wide and he longed to just kiss her but was afraid that it might be too soon to try to steal a kiss.

'I don't know when I can get some free time, but when I was talking to your uncle, he said that you work most mornings with him so I know where to find you when I need to.'

They looked into each other's eyes. Thianni reached down and took Kalin's hand in hers.

'I really must go now. Thank you for today I really enjoy being with you.'

'And me too. I will be thinking about you until our next meeting, whenever that might be.'

'I will be thinking about you too Kalin.'

Thianni leaned in close and for a second Kalin thought she was about to kiss him but at the last second, she let go of his hand and pulled away.

'See you soon Kalin.' She said as she slowly walked away.

Kalin watched as she walked. She did not look back and disappeared down by a stall. Kalin felt that she looked worried as they departed and decided to walk after her. She came into sight again. She had stopped by a jewellery stall and was looking at a small silver necklace. She was talking to the stall owner. He could see that they were exchanging words and they were both laughing. She then put the necklace back and was on her way. He decided that he would not follow her. If she saw him following her, she might not like it. He did not want to have any bad feelings between them. He was curious to know what she was looking at. He made his way over to the stall to get a better look. He picked up a delicate piece; it was a silver chain with a small bird attached to it.

'Are you wanting to buy that?' said the stall owner.

'No, I am just looking at it.'

'I don't know what it is about that necklace. No one ever wants to buy it. There is a girl that was just here moments ago before you. She comes here every few weeks and just looks at it. But never wants to buy it. I don't think anyone will ever buy it.'

'How much is it?' Asked Kalin with a grin.

'I will sell it to you right now for a silver coin. Just so I can be rid of it'

'Can you put it to one side, and I can be back here in a few minutes with a silver coin?'

'I can do that for you, but if you are not back in a short while I will put it back out on the stall so people can look at it without buying it. You had better be fast I am closing up the stall in a very short time.'

Kalin handed back the necklace and rushed off to see if he could get a silver coin from his savings from Mara. He arrived back just in time, as Mara was starting to close his stall too.

'Mara could I have some of my savings please?'

'Of course, Kalin, after all it is your money. How much do you require?'

'One silver coin.' Kalin said proudly.

5

All of the highest rankings of the Eamhair Empire gathered in the Great Realm Hall. The rustling of armour echoed throughout the high rafters of the hall as the Generals, Admirals Captains and Masters all piled in and lined up facing the Emperor's Throne. The hall was packed when the doors boomed shut behind the assembly. There was an eerie silence, not a whisper, and then the Imperial Speaker walked out and took the floor, announced the entry of Emperor Casimir, and bowed. Trumpet horns sounded and the entire hall saluted in sync, fists thumping on their black chest plates as the Emperor entered the hall from two large side doors followed by his six advisors, his daughter Leta and his mystic priest Oranius. His long white gown with gold trim flowed behind him as he made his way along. He looked like he was gliding as he walked elegantly up the steps to the podium and seated himself on the large golden throne made up of two carved dragon heads breathing fire. The emperor was a tall lean man with a stern face. He had ruled now for almost 16 years, succeeding his father before him. His daughter Leta sat alongside him on a chair to the Emperor's right and the six advisors sat behind him with Oranius. The Speaker then addressed the assembly,

'Thank you all for coming. I would like to call forth Imperial General Jargo to speak to this assembly.'

He turned to face the Emperor and bow once more, and then scurried off to the side, walking backwards while holding his bow. General Jargo walked from the gathering, bowed his wide shoulders to the throne and took the floor.

'The highest rankings are gathered here today to set a mark on the history of this great empire of ours. We are about to take to the seas and claim back the lands of Cinam and Naos. There have been long debates about this, and both the Imperial council and Emperor Eamhair have stated that this is the best direction to take. The Kingdom of Latonia has set troops in Cinam and in doing so has broken our peace treaty. The Empire must take action on this. Latonia also has armies in Natalan and the island of Naos, this has hampered trade with these small nations, and has affected the Empire greatly. On the next full moon, we will set sail, landing in Cinam, Naos and Natalan. We will take these lands back under the flag of our Empire by force. We will also take the South Wall and if the Kingdom of Latonia retaliates, we will be in a position to push on through into Latonia and claim the capital Kitia and take The Kingdom. We have four weeks to prepare for this, and although we have been planning this undertaking for some time, we still have plenty of preparations to make. This will be a controlled attack, and I expect the Emperor to have full support from all regiments.'

Whispers started throughout the gathering. They were hushed as the Emperor Casimir stood and took the floor. Jargo turned and bowed with a thump on his breastplate to the Emperor and backed away. The room became silent once more. The Emperor peered out over his assembly.

'I know this comes as a shock to most of you, especially as we have been at peace with The Kingdom of Latonia for so long now, but over the last few weeks we have discussed all options, and all of our debating led to but one path. To take back what belongs to us. Latonia has broken the treaty by sending troops into Natalia and Naos and Cinam. We cannot stand by and let them get away unpunished. The empire will not stand for this. We are an empire of strength, with rules and beliefs, and we do not stand by while our inferiors try to take advantage, and break those rules, and disrespect what we have built and what we stand for. So, it is time for our great nation to show its power once again.'

Casimir's voice started to grow louder, 'It is time for the great dragon to breathe its fire and punish those that oppose it. I ask you,' Casimir paused and looked out over the assembly and shouted.

'Are you with me?'

The assembly responded, shouting, 'The power and glory to the empire!'

The Emperor smiled and whispered, 'well, let us begin, and let them feel the heat of our fire.'

Casimir turned and left the room, followed by his party of advisors, his daughter, and the priest Oranius, to a chamber at the back of the hall. They all sat down around a table.

Leta spoke first, 'That went well, but I would say there will be some talk in Parcia tonight.'

The Emperor held out his hand and a servant rushed over and handed him a cup while another servant filled it with wine.

'Let them talk,' said the Emperor. 'It will do them good to air their thoughts to one another.'

He then turned to Oranius. 'Have you made the preparations that we have discussed?'

'Yes, your Majesty, all is under way. My ships will set sail next week.'

'Excellent! I like when my orders are met.'

Just then there was a knock at the entrance to the room and the guards opened the large doors.

General Jargo strolled in with his black helmet under his arm.

'Please take a seat General,' the Emperor gestured to an empty seat at the table.

The General bowed and sat, laying his helmet on the table.

'There is some talk out there right now, but mostly positive words, well, in my presence anyway.'

The Emperor gestured for wine to be brought to the table.

'Let us talk, I want you to go through the campaign in detail, so we are all clear on what has to happen?'

The Emperor sat back and listened contentedly. The General was passed a large map, which was unrolled on the table. It showed all the lands to the West. Leta sighed as she was handed a cup of wine, she knew it would be a long night listening to the plan that she had heard at least 10 times now. The Emperor ignored her as she slumped in her chair and slowly sipped at her cup. The General outlined everything that was to happen with the campaign from start to finish. It would take the troops over a week at full sail to reach Naos, and a couple more days to hit Athel, the Capital of Natalia. This would have to be a surprise attack. The first wave of ships would carry 25000 troops. 5000 would land at Naos and take the city. Then 15000 would land in Natalia and sack the city Athel. Once this has been accomplished, these 15000 troops will march north and lay claim to Latonia's south border wall. The remaining 5000 troops will sail on to Cinam and land less than a week later. We estimate that there are around 3000 Latonian troops there, peacekeeping. The cities in Cinam and Naos have no defence walls, so this should help greatly. Athel does have a surrounding wall, but the port will be open; this will be our access to the city, providing we have the element of surprise. There are only 1000 city guards shielding the capital of Natalia. Once these countries are taken and controlled, a second wave of 25000 troops will be deployed from the Eamhair Empire. This army will then march up through the Latonian Kingdom and lay siege to the city of Kitia. We will cut off all supplies from land and sea. This will be the biggest test of this campaign, the taking of Kitia, as the city walls are legendary. They have never been breached in the history of the city. The talks went on late into the night, and as Leta sipped her wine, she watched the General. He was a powerfully built man, with quite a full head of hair for his age. He was married, but that had not stopped her in the past. His movement was smooth for an older man and he held the floor and everyone's attention with his authority. She was admiring how his voice projected across the room. Maybe if he is lucky, I might consider sleeping with him tonight, Leta thought. She then looked over at the priest Oranius. A shiver went through her and he looked back at her and gave a creepy smile. She averted her gaze. She disliked the priest immensely. The more the General talked about the plan, the more excited he became, sitting there with a devious smile on his face. She did not like him in any way. There was something about him that her every instinct told recoiled from. In her 22 years, she had learned to listen to this inner voice. There was not much known about the man, he had come into the Emperor's council four years ago after helping deal with trading with the lands to the East and had been asked to stay due to his diplomatic skills. He never talked about his past, or where he was from. His influence on her father was much too strong for her liking. She started to feel light-headed and the room began to spin. The Emperor looked over at his daughter and could see the wine was going to her head. He ignored this. He focused his attention on the General. The meeting did not go on as long as everyone had predicted, and Leta was glad it was over. They all left the room and Leta was about to try and catch up with General Jargo when her father called her back.

'Please join me for a while my daughter.' She sat back down facing him.

'Do you know your role in this strategy?'

'Of course!' She replied sharply, annoyed at the thought that her father would question her, and that she might have missed her chance to seduce Jargo.

'I know this will be your first campaign, but the experience you will gain from this will be great. It will help you to become a better leader and will give you a greater love for our Empire.'

She nodded as he spoke.

'I will make sure that you have the backing of a large army and the best of guards, you will need them if you are to rule Natalia. Do you know why this invasion must happen?

No!' She replied honestly.

The Emperor looked at her for a second. 'Sometimes the young do not understand, but that is OK for now. Once you follow my orders correctly everything will be fine.'

'I will not let you down Father.'

'I know, my daughter, for I will not allow you to. Now, there has been enough talk of this campaign. Let us talk about something else, for tomorrow we have other celebrations. Your cousin will be home from the wars in the east land and there will be a parade in his honour.'

It was a hot day and the streets of Parcia were packed with people, each side of the main road leading to the Palace of the Sun was lined with people cheering, and everyone came out for the spectacle. Trumpets were sounded and the parade started to make its way towards the Palace with a gold chariot at its head. Skarin stood in the chariot, waving to the crowds as he passed. His black and gold armor shone in the sunlight, and he looked almost Godlike as he rolled slowly forward, followed by his two captains leading 2 carts full of gold and riches, and his battle-hardened Dragon army marching behind him. The Emperor sat on his throne with his daughter beside him and his General and advisers around him. They were all seated at the top step to the palace, watching the procession come towards them. Casimir sat waiting patiently for his nephew to reach the steps. Skarin was taking his time, milking the crowd and basking in all the glory. Casimir despised the young man for he had it all, good looks, intelligence, youth and fame, but most of all he despised him for his ruthlessness. Skarin would stop at nothing to get what he wanted, but he was loyal to the Empire and everyone loved him. The Emperor needed him, so

Casimir tolerated him. The chariot finally arrived at the base of the steps with the procession stopping behind it. Skarin stepped down and raised his hand high into the air, basking in all the glory. The crowd went wild, shouting and cheering for their hero. He reached into the chariot and took out a leather sack and, swinging it over his shoulders, he made his way up the steps to the awaiting assembly. The Emperor stood, followed by the rest of them. Skarin stopped just before Casimir and laid the sack onto the ground. He then bowed and reached into the sack, pulling out a severed human head by its hair, and held it up to the masses lining the street. The head was disfigured and rotten. The crowd cheered. He removed a gold crown from the crest of the severed head and then threw the head down the stone steps towards the parade. It bounced down the steps, coming to a halt near the two horses that pulled his chariot. He then placed the crown at the feet of the Emperor, drew his sword, and knelt.

'Your Imperial Majesty, this is the crown of your enemy from the lands far to the East and this is my sword of a thousand deaths.'

He held his sword out and laid it on the stone ground at the Emperor's feet, beside the gold crown.

'I offer you these, and my pledge to serve you and the lands you rule, now and always.'

The cheers echoed down the street from the onlookers.

The Emperor held out his hand. 'Rise my general.'

Skarin stood and the Emperor took hold of his arm, raising it into the air to the delight of the cheering crowd.

'You have done well my nephew, not only have you managed to squash the armies to the East and expand the Empire. You have also brought the head of one of my enemies.'

The gathering moved from the steps and into the palace. The Emperor walked with his arm around Skarins shoulder.

'Come let us celebrate.' The Emperor said with a joyous smile.

Skarin looked over at Leta as they all walked together and gave her a grin.

'Welcome home cousin.' She said to him with a smile back.

Carts and stalls with food and wine were brought into the street and the celebrations were under way. The palace hall was filled with the best of foods and delicacies. Cups of wine were handed to everyone in the hall.

The Emperor spoke and everyone raised their cups. 'Welcome back nephew. We have been waiting for your return and looking forward to hearing about your victories in the east.'

'It has been a long time, too long to be away from home.'

They all gathered around while Skarin told the stories of his exploits in the east to the Emperor and the gathered party. The ladies that were present laughed loudly and giggled as he talked.

'How fake their laughs were?' Leta thought. She watched him as he gestured and spoke. She had missed him and the secret meetings they'd had together. He was a couple of years older than her and she had watched him over the years grow into a man, but he looked different now. His black hair was long and tied back. His face seemed more defined and sterner and his shoulders seemed to have grown even wider. He looked taller and leaner. All the women were captivated in his presence and she was no different. He was keeping his attention on his audience, but his eyes would scan the hall every now and then to see where Leta was. She wanted him. She could feel a warmth building deep within her and wanted to bed him right now. She could not contain herself any longer. Leta interrupted the conversations.

'Sorry for interrupting, I'd like to speak with my cousin if you don't mind?'

Leta took his hand and led him away from the group.

'So, when were you thinking of paying me some attention?'

'I am home for good now, so you will have all the attention you require from me.'

'Come with me now, to my chamber.'

'Leta I can't leave just yet. Your father, The Emperor has put this celebration on for me and I can't just steal away. It would not seem right.'

Leta looked disappointed. 'So, you would rather choose all these boring people over me?'

'No, it is not like that. I have a duty to carry out. I must stay for a while at least.'

'Well then, you have chosen. Do not try to come to me later when the wine is all gone and there is no one left in the hall to listen and laugh at your stories.' In a temper, Leta turned and stormed off.

Skarin tried to catch her hand but she was too fast. He looked over at the Emperor and noticed he was watching. He was sitting alone on his throne watching the party. Skarin took an open bottle of wine from a table and made his way over to him.

'More wine uncle?' He held out his cup and Skarin filled it for him.

'That's Emperor to you General.' Skarin smiled at the sarcasm.

'I take it you have heard by now that we are heading into a new campaign?'

'I had heard that before I had reached Parcia my Emperor. What is my role in this?'

'You have served the Empire well Skarin, I think you should rest a while and enjoy life for a bit before you head back into the chaos of war.'

'Do you not require me to lead my army across the water and join your soldiers?'

'Not right away. I am planning to travel to Latonia next year, to see the Kingdom fall. I might need you with me then.'

'Whatever you call for, it will be done, my Emperor.'

6

Karra woke from a deep sleep with a startle. He thought he had heard his name being called. He looked around the room, the fire had gone out. It was no longer night-time and there was daylight beaming through the small window near the door.

'Karra!' he heard his name called out once more, 'are you in there?'

Karra stood up and felt his shoulder sting as his fresh wound stretched. Grabbing his two swords from the table, he walked over to the door and opened it. His eyes squinted, adjusting to the sudden light outside as he focused on the two figures standing at the tree line a little way from his cabin. It was his old friend Tucus and his son Blan.

Tucus shouted over as he walked towards the cabin. 'How are you keeping, my old friend? We were fixing some traps last night and saw the smoke from the fire at the old ruins. Is everything alright?'

Karra gave a rare smile, 'Just taking care of some pests. It is good to see you Tucus, please come in!'

Karra left the door open and walked back inside. He tried to poke the fire alive as Tucus came into his cabin. Greeting Karra with the Warriors Handshake, he shook the cold off and then sat on a chair by the table, while Blan remained outside to skin and gut some rabbits that he had snared that morning. Tucus noticed the blood stain on Karra's shoulder. 'I see you have survived another winter, you old goat.'

'I could say the same about you. How is life with you Tucus?'

'I am good, and my family is doing well, so I can't complain.'

'How are things in four Vales lately?'

'They are all well, nothing much changes there.'

'Ah that's what I like about it. I was stuck up here guarding the gate the whole winter, and to make it worse, that heavy snowfall had me snowed in for these last few weeks. I'm surprised you could make it up through the pass with the snow still bad.'

'It was tough going at stages, but we needed to get food and we wanted to see how you were doing. Then last night, we just finished fixing the last of the traps and were about to set camp and bed down for the night when we saw the smoke from your fire and decided to pay you a visit. How many beasts did you slay last night?' Tucus gestured with a pretend sword slice into the air.

'There were only four that came through the gate, easy pickings!'

'I see one of them got lucky.' Tucus pointed to the blood stain on Karra's shirt. 'Should that not have healed by now?'

'Yes, it should have, maybe I am starting to get old!'

'I hope you're not getting slow?'

'Getting old maybe, but never getting slow.'

'I still stand by my words that I spoke to you last year, you need help here guarding the gate.'

Karra relit the fire as the two friends caught up on things. Blan came into the cabin with the rabbits ready to cook, and Karra greeted him with a pat on the back.

'How are you keeping lad? Come in and get warm.'

Karra took the rabbits from him and, setting up a spit over the fire, started to roast the first of the meat. When the meat was ready, Karra dished it out onto some wooden plates and the three men ate in silence. The cabin was nice and warm again.

'Are you planning on staying the night here tonight?'

'Yes, that would be good; we were hoping you'd ask.' Tucus said. 'The hard-cold ground is starting to have an effect with my back.'

Blan opened a leather pouch and pulled out a needle and some thread. He then stood and said, 'Let me seal that cut on your arm Karra before it gets infected.' Karra stood and took his shirt off. Blan had seen Karra stripped to the waist before, but it was still hard not to stare at the scars the man had on his huge muscular frame, from battles and from fights and from guarding the gate. There were a lot criss-crossed on his forearms and shoulders and chest, but very little on his back. Karra sat in the chair while Blan slowly cleaned and stitched the four-inch gash in Karra's huge shoulder. It looked clean and looked like it was a week old.

'When did you receive this cut?' asked Blan.

'Last night, one of those pox ridden dogs managed to catch me.'

Blan scratch his head. 'Well it is nearly healed already Karra. Did you put any ointment on it?'

'Nope! I usually just leave the cuts to themselves.'

'Well, it is almost healed. That will make my job easier, and I'll only have to put a couple of stitches in just to make sure it closes.' Said Blan.

Karra continued talking to Tucus, seemingly oblivious to the needle point piercing his skin and the tightening of the thread.

'You seem tired Karra.' Tucus said. 'Would you not start looking for help with the gate? You are not getting any younger. You must be at least 50 now?'

'Ha-ha!' laughed Karra with a jerk which made Blan pull away from the cut with his needle.

'I'm 48 this summer Tucus, and yes, I am feeling tired. It has been a long winter this year. I think it is time I found my nephew and brought him here to train him in the ways of The Guardian.'

'Do you know if he is still living with your sister in Kitia?'

'Aye, I believe so. I have not heard from her in a few years. According to the symbols on the stone slab, there should not be an opening of the gate for at least three months. This might be enough time to pay my nephew a visit.'

'It sounds like a good plan Karra.'

After Blan had finished stitching Karras shoulder, Karra opened a bottle of wine and the three men talked and drank for most of the day, telling old stories to Blan about Tucus and Karra's adventures. As it got dark, the men roasted another rabbit and shared it between them for their supper and Karra then showed his visitors into their bedrooms. The two small rooms off the kitchen were very small, but Tucus and Blan were grateful for the soft bedding. Karra slept in his chair by the fire. He found it hard to fall asleep, as his plans to organise a trip down to the Kingdom to see his nephew kept going through his mind. This made him feel uncomfortable. The next morning, Karra arranged with Tucus and Blan to look after things with his cabin and, in the event that he was late getting back, that Tucus would arrange to man the Guarding of The Gate. A couple of days had passed and Karra was waiting for the snow to subside a bit more before he journeyed down south. On the third morning the sun was shining and Karra figured that this would be a good day to set out. He loaded up his two horses with the provisions he needed, and then strapped two large axes to the horse and set out. It would take him at least a week to reach the North gate that divided Gantia and The Kingdom of Latonia, so this meant sleeping on the cold ground. Karra was not looking forward to that part of the journey. He paused and looked out over the vast mountains from the hillside.

'Another damned adventure,' he whispered and disappeared into the trees below.

7

The quote went through his head as he listened carefully from the shadows of the night for any sounds of movement. A light breeze whispered through the darkness. He blocked this sound out and concentrated on any other noise. There was none. The moon came out from behind the clouds and illuminated his surroundings momentarily. Jann watched the man's house closely. He could see that there was a dimly lit room within the house but could see no movement. He watched for some time, from a rooftop some way away. Making sure that the man was not awake. This was a perfect observation position. He could look down on the man's property. There was no one around this late. This was his fifth job, and he knew that above all else he had to be patient. This was one of the first rules of The Assassins Code, which he had been taught on the Island of Tibar. He had finished his training and left the island nearly a year ago now, but the training was still fresh in his mind. The previous four people he had killed were executed easily enough, except for the young woman, Teel. She had screamed at the last second, and Jann was nearly caught. It had been an error on his part as she had been naked, and just before he came face to face with the woman, he was distracted by a large scar she had on her body. It travelled the full length on her upper torso from the shoulder right down to her thigh. He wondered for a split second how she had obtained such a wound and how she had survived it. In that split second of distraction the woman had screamed, giving away his position. Nonetheless, he had completed his mission and was gone without detection. This new target was different; there was something about him that set all Jann's senses off. He had done his homework on the man. His name was Porcia. He was a well-respected noble man and the people of Talmine thought him to be a very fair man, but after watching him for a few weeks now Jann had noticed some very strange behaviour. Porcia liked small children. Jann noticed he would spend a lot of time around the schools and play areas where the children would be, and Jann saw, on several occasions, the man touching them. This would make the kill easier for Jann. The price for this job was a good one but killing someone that had evil in them was always easier for an assassin. Jann had studied his patterns, and now he knew when the best time would be to strike. He would kill the man tonight. Porcia would make his way to the bathhouse, where he would bathe and get a massage as was his routine. After this, he would make his way home and fall into a deep sleep. This would be the best time to enter his home and take his life, Jann thought. Jann quickly climbed down from the rooftop and slipped into the shadow of the gate pillar below. The night was starting to get cold, and snow clouds were starting to move across the sky again, making it even darker. He glanced out to see if the door of Porcia's house was guarded, but there was none there. He quickly checked the gate, it was locked. Jann then scaled the high wall that surrounded the premises with ease. He jumped down to the garden within and quickly moved to a tree, disappearing into its shadow. He could feel his heart beating and the blood coursing through his veins. He only felt alive when he was doing his job, the job of an assassin. The target lived alone. This would make things a lot easier. He knew the front door would be locked so he made his way around the side of the house and checked for an opening. All the windows were shut tight, so he moved around to the back of the house. The back entrance was locked too. The door was in the shade of a porch and this made the back entrance even darker. Jann slipped his hand into his pocket and pulled out a device that looked like a long key with wires coming out of it. He adjusted this device and pushed it carefully into the lock. He made several, minute adjustments and turned the key. There was a click, and the door was finally unlocked. Jann slipped inside, closing the door silently behind him. He made his way up the dark corridor to Porcia's sleeping quarters. Even before he entered the room, he could hear the loud snores coming from the man. Jann took a small canister and oiled the hinges on the door. He had learned from experience that some doors would make loud creaking noises when opened, giving away his objectives. He opened the door without a sound and moved inside. Porcia was a large man; he nearly took up the whole bed. He was asleep on his back snoring loudly. The room was dimly lit from a candle that was burning by the bedside. Jann moved around to the left-hand side of the bed and drew his knife slowly. He then blew out the candle. The room was instantly in darkness. He waited for a few moments so his eyes could get accustomed to the darkness. He spun the knife in his hand, so the point was facing downwards, and placed the tip an inch away from the far side of the man's throat. In one movement, he placed his left hand over the man's mouth and plunged the knife deep into his neck with his right, dragging the blade across his target's throat towards himself.

The man tried to scream and sit up, but Jann held him down with his left hand over his mouth. The man grasped at his neck as blood spread out over the white bed covers from the wound. Muffled shouts sounded out, but they were quashed by the blood flooding out of the dying man's nose and mouth and around Jann's forceful hand. Choking noises faded as the man slowly died. The mission was complete. Jann wiped his knife clean on the bed covers and then cleaned his blood drenched hands. He could just make out that there was a basin of water on the other side of the bed. He made his way around to it and washed his hands clean of the blood, drying them with a towel that was placed by the basin. He had considered making this death look like an accident, but after discovering that the man had been touching the children, he did not mind killing him outright. Jann left the room, making his way out of the building the same way he had come in, and climbed back out over the wall. He then made his way to the tavern on the other side of the city. He had arranged to meet up with a man there and would receive the second half of his payment. After a long walk, he entered the tavern and ordered a mug of ale, sitting at a table alone sipping his drink. He was surprised how busy it was, as it was very late at night. Before long, a man approached his table. He wore a long, hooded robe, and sat down across from Jann. He removed his hood, and Jann recognised his face. He watched the hooded man as he moved his chair closer to the table. He looked like a priest. He had a shaved head and wore a necklace with a silver goat's skull on it, indicating he was a follower of The Dark Sect.

'I take it everything went well?'

Jann nodded, 'the job has been completed.'

The priest reached down into his pocket and produced a leather pouch, sliding it across the table to Jann. 'That is the rest of the payment.'

Jann quickly took it and placed it in an inner pocket in his tunic and continued sipping his ale. The man sat across from him watching as he drank. It made Jann feel uncomfortable.

'Is there anything else I can help you with?'

'Yes, as a matter of fact, we have another job for you. It is a rather large task.'

'I think I could manage that,' Jann replied, making eye contact. 'How much will the payment be?'

'1000 gold coins.'

Jann spat out a mouth full of ale. 'Did I hear you right? 1000 gold coins?'

The man nodded. 'That is correct.'

'And who is the target?'

The man leaned in close across the table and spoke in almost a whisper. 'King Roban.'

8

Captain Vimeo sat at his desk looking through maps and designs. He had been awake for most of the night, working on plans and problems. He had dozed off a couple of times, but his mind had not rested and kept him awake. The sun had come up and there was a long shaft of light beaming in through a small window by the door. He was staring into the light in a daze, when a knock came at the door.

'Come in!' he announced hesitantly.

Carson walked through the door with a stern look on his face.

'Please take a seat.' Vimeo gestured.

Vimeo felt very nervous now, he knew that Carson's visit was to see how his investment was coming along.

'Well Captain Vimeo, it seems that you have been trying to avoid me these past few weeks, how is the ship coming along?'

'I am a very busy man, Carson. It is almost finished, we are just putting the finishing touches to it, and just to ease your mind, this project was my sole focus.'

'Well that is good to hear; I have put a lot of money into this project and would like to see your results. I have to say, if the new design is as good as I am hearing it is, I have a lot of interested people that would like to invest in a ship like this. Can I see it?'

Vimeo looked very worried now. 'Yes, of course, we shall go right away.'

Vimeo put his coat on and tied a red scarf around his neck and they both left the office and walked down to the dock area. His office was near the harbour as he liked to be close to the sea, it helped him think. The two men walked out onto a long boardwalk as the harbour came into sight. There were all types of ships in the docks and there was plenty of activity going on with men working. They were loading cargo on and taking cargo off vessels. Vimeo talked most of the time about new inventions he had planned. As they got closer to the building yards and the docks, Carson's eyes widened. There, in the bay of Athel, was a huge ship. It stood out among the other ships because of its huge size.

'It looks magnificent, can we board her?'

'Yes of course, but I have to warn you, there is still work being done on her, so please be patient.'

Vimeo's worries were starting to dissolve, he always got anxious when he had to reveal his new ideas or inventions, but seeing Carson get excited was a big lift for the Captain. As they got closer, Carson could make out the name carved onto the upper front of the ship.

'The Sea Wolf!' Carson was taken back by the immense size of the vessel. 'The size of the ship is enormous; I was not expecting that, will this make her slow on the sea?'

'No not in the slightest. I have had the wood for her shipped in from the far south. The wood comes from a tree called a Trike tree, it is much lighter than any other wood I know of and just as strong as any wood we have here in Natalia, but the wood has better buoyancy to it, thus, it floats better. With the wider deck we can have bigger sails attached to the masts. The keel does sit deeper in the water but with my new design, with the timber planks overlapping on each other, it can cut through the water much faster than any other ship, and because it is much lighter, I have reinforced the hull. So, it's much stronger that a normal ship.'

'That truly is amazing Vimeo, have you taken her out yet?'

'No not yet, we are just finishing the last of the work on her. The sails are being attached today. I have used a new type of fabric on the sails and have yet to test their strength.'

'I have to admit Vimeo, you had me worried for a while. I have invested a lot of money in this and at first though the idea of a bigger ship was ludicrous, but now seeing it in the flesh I am overwhelmed with what you have created. It will make us a lot of money and may even change the way ships are built in the future. Will she be ready for a test sail tomorrow?'

'I'm not sure, there is still plenty to be done.'

'Well she looks like it could fly, I want to see her out on the sea first thing tomorrow. No excuses!'

Vimeo called for the ramp to be lowered to the dock and the two men boarded The Sea Wolf. Vimeo was excited, showing his investor all that had been done since they had last talked. As the new sails were starting to be hoisted in place to the mast, Vimeo pointed out the brace rings that he invented. They were to add extra durability to the sails, so the fabric wouldn't tear in high winds. This in turn would allow the vessel to sail in stormy weather. In combination with the new wide design of the bow and keel, this would help steady her on high seas. Carson was amazed with everything, but unlike Vimeo all he was thinking about was, how much money he would make.

'I have to admit Vimeo, this is such a wonder! I really like what you have created here!'

'Thank you, Carson.' Vimeo replied with relief. 'It has been a hectic few months but I am pleased with the outcome. All my workers have worked so hard to build and develop this ship and will be looking to get their final pay.'

'I understand, I will have the final payment sent to you later tomorrow, but I want to see her out on the sea at first light tomorrow morning, no excuses! The Sea Wolf looks ready to sail.'

He leaned in close to the Captain, 'And I am very happy with the work you have put into this.'

Vimeo agreed to the request reluctantly. The two men shook hands, and Vimeo escorted Carson from the docks and saw him on his way. He then walked back to the ship to seek out Barus. Barus was tying off a rope at the bow of the ship. The battle rope was thick in width and looked very heavy. There was sweat rolling off Barus's bald head as he heaved the rope down along the deck. Barus was much older than Vimeo and had been in Vimeo's employment for a long time now, he was Vimeo's Number One. Barus was a big powerful man. A sea veteran, born and raised on the sea. He knew almost everything there was to know about sailing. He was strict with the crew and they respected him, but most of all Vimeo could trust him.

'Barus!' Vimeo called out as he approached him.

'Well Captain, what has you down on the ship this early?'

'I have good news and bad news for you today.'

Barus smiled a toothless smile, 'Well that can't be true; you always only bring me bad news.'

Vimeo explained to Barus about Carson's visit and that he wanted the Ship out on the open water first thing in the morning to test her.

'Well I had better get cracking the whip. There is a lot of work to be done before tomorrow. What about crew members? We have only 12 on board at the moment. This won't even be enough to work the oars on one side of the ship.'

'I haven't even thought about that, what would you suggest?'

'I can pop into the Harbour Ale House tonight. There are always men looking for work. I will see if I can muster up a few seaworthy men, that will do us for testing the ship.'

Happy with this, Vimeo left Barus to do his checks and left to make his way back to his office.

9

Pittana sat alone on the beach crying, with his face in his hands. He was only a boy of 12 years old. In his short life he had lost family member after family member, and now the last of his family, his Grandfather, had died that morning. The grief was immense. He never knew his Father; his mother had told him he had died at sea just before Pittana was born, and then two years ago his mother had passed away from a fever. He had nothing now. No money, no food, and no family. To make matters worse, the landlord had said that, now his Grandfather was dead, he wouldn't be able to pay the rent, so he should take his things and go. Nothing, he thought, I have nothing. No family, no money, no home, nothing. Pittana sat there, thinking of what he could do. Where could he spend the night that would be safe. It was still early in the day, he still had lots of time. Then the hunger pains started again in his stomach. Pittana looked up from his hands and looked out at the sea. Then a thought hit him like a hammer. I should just run down to the sea and drown myself, at least then I can join my family in the afterlife. I have nothing! No one will miss me! Pittana stood on shaky legs and made his way down to the shoreline. He remembered he had experienced loss and pain in the past, but this pain of complete loneliness was immense, more than he could cope with. He looked out over the sea and started to walk into the crashing waves, with one thought in his head. I have nothing! The sea was very cold but somehow, he did not feel its icy embrace. He was chest deep now and the waves were pushing him back into shore, but he was determined to keep going. Pittana sighed and took one last look at the land behind him as if to say goodbye, when he saw a man walking towards him along the beach.

'Hello! You there! Hey! You! Boy! Come here!'

Pittana turned around and found himself coming back into shore, drenched with sea water. The stranger was well dressed, a red scarf around his neck, and as he approached, he put out his hand as they met. Pittana shook his hand, feeling silly that his hands were wet.

'Hello, my name is Captain Vimeo. I am a businessman and an inventor. I have a new ship that is docked in the bay,' There was a pause, 'Well? Have you a name boy? The proper retort when someone introduces themselves is for you to introduce yourself in return.'

'Oh, my name is Pittana, sorry!'

'That's sorry Sir!'

'Sorry Sir,' said Pittana shaking his head as if to try and wake from a bad dream.

'Now, the reason I called you over is, I am taking my ship to sea tomorrow morning and I am looking for some good crew members to help sail her. You look to me as a strong young man. I know it is short notice, but you will be paid well and if things work out, I may have other work for you. Are you interested?'

Pittana heard himself say 'Yes' 'Yes Sir!'

The man smiled 'Very good. Now have you any experience in sailing?'

'My Grandfather is a sailor, was a sailor.'

'Ah so it's in your blood then. Be on the docks at sunrise tomorrow. The ship's name is the Sea Wolf. You can't miss it; it's the largest vessel in the harbour.'

With that, Captain Vimeo tossed Pittana a large silver coin and Pittana caught it. 'Make sure you get plenty of rest tonight and show up with a full belly, it might be hard work tomorrow. Meet me at the gates to the docks, and definitely no more swimming in the sea today.' The Captain winked, then continued walking along the shoreline. Pittana looked down at his hand admiring the large silver coin he was given. He placed it in his pocket and walked back towards the docks. As Vimeo walked along the beach, many thoughts ran through his head. The pressure was on him again. This vessel weighed heavily on his mind. It had been constantly in his thoughts for a long time now, but all his projects seemed to work out quite well in the end. His thoughts flickered back to the child on the beach. He knew by the pain on his face what he had been about to do. This young boy would be an extra burden on top of everything else, but The Captain could not bear to watch him kill himself. He had known his Grandfather in the past; he was a good man and an excellent sailor. One of the best. The news of his death had spread fast among the sailing community and it was news that had saddened him. Everyone deserves a second chance, especially in life, and especially a young boy.

'I will make sure he is looked after.' He whispered in the sea breeze and continued on with his walk.

10

It was just past sunrise and the harbour was quiet, apart from the odd cry from some early seagulls. The Sea Wolf sat still in the waters around the dock as the crew shuffled around on board, making preparations. The Captain approached along the pier with a young boy and they were the last to board. The Captain introduced the young boy, Pittana, to Barus. Barus shook his hand and brought him down along the ship to meet the helmsman, Old Talip, and then to meet Tipin, the ship's drummer and the rest of the makeshift crew. Barus had managed to muster up 42 veteran sailors from the bars around the docks. Some were still drunk from the night before. He assigned 38 of these men to work the oars below deck, and the other four were to work the upper deck and sails. The Sea Wolf had the capability to run on 120 oars with a second deck below, but the 38 would be sufficient to test the ship, 19 oars on each side. The ship was then untied from its moorings and was pushed quietly, with the aid of large poles, away from its resting place. Once they were fully clear, the Ship's Master, Barus, gave orders for all oarsmen below deck to take their positions. Captain Vimeo gave the signal to Barus, Barus nodded back and walked slowly along the top deck. He stopped at the main hatch and shouted down to the 38 waiting oarsmen below deck. The oars were extended out through their oar holes and hoisted at a steep angle high into the air. Moments later, a second shout went out and all oars splashed down into the water and were held in ready position. The Drum-Man Tipin hit his drum, the beat boomed out across the harbour and in perfect sync, the oarsmen began to row. The ship pulled through the water with ease as it moved slowly away from the pier, traveling through the still harbour water. There was a light fog sitting on the sea giving the impression the ship was gliding through the clouds. Its sheer size dwarfed all the other boats and ships in the harbour as it moved on by. Captain Vimeo walked along the deck until he reached the Bow of the ship where Barus stood. They quickly went through the plans for the day ahead. As the ship approached the Harbour Gatehouse he could see the Harbour Sentries in the watchtowers taking note of the vessel's departure. As they passed between the two huge harbour towers, he gave them a wave. The Captain walked back along the deck, checking the tied knots holding the sails firmly in their ready position. The ship moved out onto open water, oars moving to the slow beat of the drum, drifting through the morning fog. Barus called out another command, it echoed out over the sea and the drum beat quickened, as Tipin's large arms banged out the beat. The ship launched forward with the quickening of the oars as they cut through the water with great speed, out into the vastness. Pittana stood at the front of the ship, feeling exhilarated as the morning breeze passed by him with the ship's swiftness. After some time, the water became a bit rougher. The fog had cleared and the harbour of Athel was but a thin line on the horizon. The Captain gave a nod to Barus, Barus shouted out the order to halt and have the oars stopped and retrieved and the anchor then lowered.

'Take some rest men!' He shouted.

Barus walked over to his Captain with a smile. 'She is a smooth ship indeed. You were right about the reinforced hull, there is not much creaking in the wood, and she feels steady on the water and very well balanced.'

Vimeo gave a rare smile back, 'she does feel good, doesn't she?'

'The sea is calm today and there is very little wind to get her up to high speeds. But she will have greater tests ahead of her before I am satisfied, today is just a small step in her journey.'

'Call all hands-on deck Barus, I wish to address the entire crew.'

Every man made their way to the ship's Master on deck. The Captain stood on the upper back deck, looking down on his crew.

'Today is the start of a new venture, and you are all part of it. There is no ship like this one on these seas, she is one of a kind. We have spent a lot of time and money in building this ship and when word gets out, and it will, every nobleman and merchant that is heavy with coin will want a ship like this. This is the start of a new future in ship building. Today will be a day to remember. We will put this ship through some tough maneuvers today and see what she can do. I know we are short on crew, so I am asking you all to endure this for now, let us enjoy some breakfast and the drinks that flow tonight at the Harbour Tavern where we will celebrate properly, for those drinks tonight will be on me.'

With this, a huge roar let out from the crew. One man vomited over the side of the ship at the thoughts of drinking more beer. Pittana scrambled over the boxes and sacks of supplies on the lower deck in the hold and pulled out a bag of loaves and 3 large blocks of cheese. He quickly took these to the crew on the main deck and passed them out among the men as they sat chatting amongst themselves. He then handed out cups of fresh water. The mood was good, and the food was welcome, as some of the men were still nursing a sore head from the night before. Vimeo and Barus stood together a small way from the main body of the crew. They both stood in silence as they chewed on the cheese and bread.

'Is there any beer down in the hold?' Barus said, trying to swallow down large lumps of food.

'I'm not sure, you packed the cargo yesterday yourself.'

Suddenly Barus noticed a strange dark line that had appeared on the horizon.

'That's peculiar!' he said to his Captain as he focused and pointed out to the East.

The Captain squinted at the sight of it.

'I think it may be a storm?' replied The Captain.

They watched it for a while, trying to figure out what this low dark cloud was. Barus gave out a sigh of disbelief.

'I've never seen anything like that before, but it's getting bigger and it seems to be heading in our direction. There is very little wind today, maybe it is a storm?'

'I think we should have a look. Barus, give the men the order to get back to their posts and we will sail towards it and have a closer look at what this is.'

The Sea Wolf moved towards the cloud, the oars holding a steady rhythm. The cloud was spread out across the sea now as far as the eye could see, and it approached towards the ship with speed, getting closer and closer.

Barus looked over at Vimeo, 'It seems to be some sort of rolling fog, but I've never seen a fog as dark or as dense as that before. We should turn around before we are engulfed in it.'

Just then, the fog started to lighten in colour and slowed its advancement. The Captain gave the order for the Sea Wolf to halt. Every man on the ship glared at the fog as it slowly came to a stop. Everything was quiet, only the sound of the gentle waves could be heard. Slowly, scores of lights appeared and seemed to be getting brighter within the fog as it started to dissipate. Then, to the astonishment of everyone, scores of huge heads with glowing eyes appeared through the fog, black war ships burst out of the fog heading straight towards The Sea Wolf. There were too many ships to count. Every man aboard the Sea Wolf knew what this was; they were Dragon Ships belonging to the Empire. It was an invasion, an invasion on a huge scale and instant panic set in.

Barus shouted 'Captain, they look to be Imperial Dragon War ships!'

Vimeo shouted out. 'Turn this ship at once and row, row as hard as you can, all our lives depend on it!'

The Imperial Dragon fleet drifted through the fog at a steady speed. The fog was extremely dense, darkening the sky and the surroundings, giving the impression that it was nighttime. The sun could just be seen but the black clouds were blocking out the light from it. It had been like this now for days and the troops were beginning to feel anxious with the lack of sunshine. There was little talk amongst the men, mostly they worked in silence. For days, the only sound was the oars hitting the water and the waves hitting against the hulls.

General Zukata slowly walked along the upper deck, watching his men. He looked out over the bow, checking the distance between the ships was adequately spaced. Sailing in this lack of light could be dangerous. Each ship had two large lanterns at its bow, lighting the way. These lights were placed on each side of the huge, carved Dragon heads, giving the impression that the Dragon's eyes were on fire. The sea was covered with ships, as far as he could see were dotted lights through the fog, all traveling in formation. Satisfied, Zukata walked to the stern of the vessel, and joined the Captain.

The Captain turned as he approached. 'Good morning General. I hope you have slept well.'

'I always sleep well. How could you not? It has been night-time for a week and a half now.'

'I know what you mean; I have never sailed in such thick fog for so long before. It does not feel right. We must be nearly there; this can't last for much longer.'

'I hope not, my men are beginning to get restless.'

Just then, a shout went out from a neighbouring ship. 'The fog is clearing; the fog is clearing!'

They could see that the fog had come to an end. Gaps of light beamed through as the Dragon Ships emerged from thick, dark fog to dazzling sunshine.

'Ship sighted!' went out another shout and all eyes squinted to see the biggest ship they had ever seen. Zukata turned to the Captain. 'Unless I am mistaken, that is a huge vessel.'

The Captain nodded in disbelief and then spoke. 'It is huge! It doesn't look like a War Ship, maybe a cargo vessel?'

'Nevertheless, I can't have our surprise spoiled. I want this ship taken right away.'

The General called out to Captain Tulk on a neighbouring ship off his Starboard.

'I want this ship captured. Take two other fast ships with you and take this ship' He paused… 'Captain, do whatever it takes to seize it, do you understand?'

The Captain saluted, turned, and started to bark orders at his crew. A number of flags were waved in the air and his ship and two others surged forward, pulling away from the fleet in pursuit of the large vessel. Zukata watched as the huge ship turned with ease and took off, skimming over the sea at an angle. The Dragon fleet steadily moved on course for the Capital of Natalia, leaving the fading fog behind. Captain Tulk called out for the ships; archers to stand ready as they shortened their distance on their target. Such a large ship will be easily caught, he thought to himself.

'We will be upon her in minutes.' he shouted out. 'Dragon soldiers! Make yourselves ready for boarding!'

Scores of Dragon soldiers rushed to the main deck. They were all clad in black armour and moved into ranks with great efficiency. The Sea Wolf had just completed a full turn and was starting to gain speed with all its 38 oars in the water. But it was not fast enough. The Dragon ships were gaining on them.

Barus shouted out to the oarsmen, 'Keep her steady men, and listen to the beat of the drum. Stay in rhythm.'

He looked up at Vimeo with panic in his eyes. The Sea Wolf, with less than half its oars manned due to a skeleton crew, was no match for these Dragon Ships. They were coming in fast. Vimeo heard a distant shout, and moments later a wave of arrows hit their ship. A few screams went out from the ship's crew. One crew member was hit in the back of the neck and fell sideways onto the deck, dead. Others were luckier, only getting an arrow in the shoulder or slicing through their arms. One arrow managed to get beneath the deck and glanced off a rower's head leaving him with a large gash. Blood flooded down his neck and back, but he kept rowing. He knew, like all the crew knew, to stop rowing was to die. Barus felt the ship drift to the side and looked back at Old Talip at the helm. He was leaning to the side and pulling the ship starboard. Barus ran to him and saw that he had been hit by an arrow in the back of his shoulder and was struggling to keep the ship on a straight line. Barus lifted him aside and placed him on the deck, under cover of the rigging, and took control of the steering. With a strong heave, he pulled on the wheel and the ship straightened. Sweat was beading now on his bald head and he looked around for Vimeo. Captain Vimeo shouted to the boy to get below deck and see to the oarsmen. Panic swept through the crew as a fresh wave of arrows thundered into the ship. Another oarsman was hit in the leg, the arrow standing upright from his thigh. He roared in pain as it thudded into his leg. He looked down at the arrow and hobbled off below deck to get cover. Vimeo scanned the deck to see if there was anyone else hurt. He then looked back at the Dragon ship. It was nearly upon them. He could see that the approaching ships were all full of Dragon soldiers in full battle armour and the Dragon ships were flying their war flag. He paused for a moment. Think! What can we do? Think! Just then, the Captain felt a breeze on his face. He spun around and shouted to the three remaining men on the main deck. 'We have wind! Release the sails; release the sails.' the men scrambled with the bark of the order and untied the holding ropes. The first main sail dropped, and it immediately opened fully with the wind. The Ship jumped forward with speed. Another wave of arrows hit the back end of the ship. Thankfully this time none of them hit their targets. The Sea Wolf was pulling away now from the three ships giving chase. Vimeo looked back and could see the pursuers also had dropped their sails to catch the same winds in an effort to gain some distance on them. For a time, they did not seem to be gaining any distance. Another wave of arrows was launched but these all fell short of the Sea Wolf, plunging into the sea behind them. The archers were just out of range now. The Captain walked to the bow of the ship and tugged on a rope. Another large sail dropped and billowed out as the wind caught it. The ship seemed to pull forward again as it cut through the water and the Sea Wolf started to pull away from the Dragon ships that were hunting them. A yell of relief went up from one of the deckhands. Vimeo walked back to the stern of the ship and watched with relief as the three ships fell behind. He then went to check on his crew.

'Are you OK Barus?'

'Yes, I'm fine, but you might want to see to Old Talip.'

He pointed down to where Talip was sitting, Still holding onto the ship's wheel, holding her course steady. Captain Vimeo called for one of the crew to come over and gave him orders to climb to the top of the mast to keep watch on their pursuers. He then saw to Talip's wound. There was an arrow jutting out of the back of his right shoulder. It had passed right through the shoulder and he was able to remove it without doing further damage. He then called for Pittana to bring water and see to the men. He then gave orders to reduce the drum speed, as the men were very fatigued. The wind had picked up, and the sails were at full flight. The injured men were seen to, and the dead crew member was brought below deck and placed in the hold, where he was covered with a cloth. The Captain approached Barus at the helm.

'What the hell was that?'

'It can only be one thing, it's an invasion. There was a huge fleet of Dragon ships heading towards Athel.'

Vimeo nodded in agreement. 'By all the Gods this is a bad day. They are heading straight for our home city and there is nothing we can do about it. If we go back now, we will surely have the same fate as everyone in the city.'

Barus wiped the sweat from his bald head and shouted up to the lookout.

'How far are they?'

'They have fallen back, nearly a half mile by the looks of it.' Barus seemed to relax slightly.

'So, Captain, what do we do now?'

'That is a good question.' He thought for a bit and then answered. 'By the looks of it, it is an invasion. They are flying their battle flag. This means that all the cities will be taken under control. Naos has probably already been taken and they will also have to take Cinam.' He paused for thought again.

'How many ships did you see?'

'I reckon there had to be anywhere from 150 to 200 ships. That must nearly be their whole fleet. I've never seen so many ships on the sea at the one time.'

'I saw the same. A fleet of that size could easily support 20,000 troops. With that many, they would be able to take all of Natalia and then push on up through the South Wall and invade The Kingdom of Latonia.'

'What do we do?' Barus asked worriedly. 'We have really no choice, we will have to sail for Kitia and notify the King of the news. Even if word reaches the South Wall in a month, it will take at least another few weeks before word reaches King Roban. If we sail straight to Kitia now, we could be there in less than a month's time, providing the wind is good to us.'

'We would arrive just in time for their Summer Celebrations.' Barus put in with a smile. Vimeo fixed his scarf around his neck. 'How much food and water did you bring on board?'

'We have maybe enough for 4 days. I thought we would have a full crew, so I stocked up to accommodate that. If we can stay ahead of the Dragon ships, we might gain some time to pull into some of the fishing ports along the southern coast of Natalia and restock the ship and warn them.'

'Hopefully the wind will stay strong and they will disappear from view.'

'As soon as we lose sight of them, I think we should change course and try and lose them.'

Vimeo looked back behind them to see if he could spot any ships and shook his head.

'How is this happening? Maybe we should move inland then, and travel along the coast in case they catch us. At least we could try and beach the Sea Wolf and then we could run in land. These are troublesome times.'

Captain Tulk was in disbelief. How could such a large vessel move so fast? He was sure they would catch the huge ship with ease, but when its sails dropped, they could not keep up. It was also the first time he had seen a ship with more than one sail. This was fascinating to him. What were the ship's dimensions? How many crewmen would be required to run the ship? What wood was used in making it? It would have to be very light in weight for it to move through the water with such ease. All these questions were going through his mind. He needed these questions answered. He needed to catch and take this ship. His orders were clear.

'Do whatever it takes to seize it.' were the words General Zukata spoke.

The ship they were hunting had disappeared out of sight now. They could not keep up with its speed. Even with their sail in full flight and the oarsmen rowing at full speed. It was not enough. He shouted out orders to the two ships accompanying him in their pursuit.

'Spread out as wide as you can to cover more sea area. Do not lose sight of this ship, stay in view.'

They had been sailing for hours now, but still there was no sign of the ship and it was getting dark. It was time to rest, for the oarsmen were near exhaustion. He called for the signal to be sent to the other two ships to start making their way towards them and they would anchor for the night. The hunt would resume at first light. Captain Tulk gave orders for food and water to be served first to his men, and then to the slave oarsmen below deck. He then ordered his second to follow him below deck to his room. The two men sat in silence as Captain Tulk poured two glasses of fire wine. They each took a small sip.

'Tell me Dakra, how did that monstrous ship escape capture?'

'It is a simple answer,' Dakra replied, it was faster than any of our ships.'

'But it was huge. A vessel of such enormous size should not have been able to achieve such speeds. How is this possible?'

'It baffles me also Captain, but it did.'

'We need to formulate a plan. Maybe we might catch them if they stop for the night. Tomorrow we will set out early, before the sun rises. I have a feeling they will head for land.'

It was almost dark when the Sea Wolf anchored for the night. Her crew were all weary from the day's events. Vimeo looked out into the blackness of the night. There were no other ships in sight. He felt slightly relieved. Barus had called everyone on deck and had the ship's boy Pittana hand out food and water to the men.

'I will take the first watch tonight. Everyone should try and get some rest as we do not know what tomorrow will bring.'

There was little talk amongst the crew and, after they had eaten, they were all asleep quickly. Captain Vimeo climbed up the mast to the Crow's Nest and kept look-out across the vastness of the sea. It was a clear night and there was a sickle shaped moon shining brightly in the night sky. The stars appeared, endlessly scattered across the heavens. He watched intently and after a few hours he climbed back down and woke Barus to take his turn at watch. After an hour, Barus felt like he could not keep his eyes open and also climbed down, waking the nearest crew member for his turn. Barus lay down, pulled an old blanket over himself, and was instantly asleep. Barus slowly became aware of the rocking of the ship as he opened his eyes to the light of the day. He sat up and rubbed his eyes to awaken himself. He still felt tired, so he tried to sleep some more, but his throat felt dry and he was thirsty. He rose from his makeshift bed and made his way over to a barrel of water, scooping out a cup full and drinking deeply. He looked around; everyone was still asleep. The sea felt choppy now and he looked out over the edge of the ship. His heart almost stopped as he could see three Dragon ships coming at them at full speed. He let out a shout. 'SHIPS IN SIGHT!'

Captain Vimeo jumped up and also let out a yell. 'Rowers at your position! Raise the anchor!'

Barus unhitched the anchor rope, cranked the pulley and started to retrieve the anchor. The crew scrambled with fear and a fast drumbeat sounded out. The ship started to turn direction away from the attackers. The Dragon ships were closing in fast. Vimeo turned to Barus as soon as he secured the anchor on board. 'There is a good wind behind us, drop the sails.' Barus did not even try to untie the ropes that held the sails. He took out his curved sword and hammered down on the ropes, cutting through them instantly. The sails dropped down into place and opened up with a gust of wind and the Sea Wolf was propelled forward. Almost immediately, the Sea Wolf matched the speed of the Dragon ships and as Barus dropped the second sail into place, the Sea Wolf started to pull away, increasing the distance between them. The early morning waves were much bigger, and as the ship cut through them, a spray of salty sea water came spraying over the front of the ship. Vimeo wiped his forehead with his scarf and fixed it back in place around his neck. He looked at Barus who was fixing a knot in place.

'That was lucky, who was supposed to be keeping watch?'

'I'm not sure Captain, but we can find out if you want?'

'Damn.' He cursed. 'No, we don't need to know that right away, we have more pressing issues at the minute.' As he looked back at the three ships in pursuit, he could see that they were losing them.

'From tonight onwards, we will keep the ship moving. We cannot afford to be caught off guard like that again. All our lives were jeopardized by someone not doing their job.'

Barus cursed out loud and clenched his fists.

'When I find out who was meant to be on watch, I will wring their necks.'

'I am willing to let this go, Barus, and so should you. We need all the help we can get to man this ship. I will talk to the crew later when we are at a safe distance from these ships, but for now we must concentrate on getting as much distance as possible between us and those Dragon ships.'

The wind kept up and after a while, the three ships disappeared beyond the horizon. Barus formed 3 groups to take shifts on the oars, to keep the ship at a steady speed. Each group would row for two hours and then rest for four hours. Everyone had to take a turn rowing, including young Pittana. Old Talip stayed at the helm, even with his shoulder wounded from the arrow. He was looking tired. Tipin, the Drum-Man, could hardly hold up his huge arms to keep a steady beat. Barus relieved him so he could rest, and Vimeo took over from Talip to keep the ship on course. This continued throughout the night. A few days passed, and the food was starting to run out. They could see the southern coastline of Natalia. They had not seen any Dragon ships since the night they had nearly been caught sleeping and decided to harbour at a small fishing town to restock with food and water. Vimeo had some coins that he had been keeping to pay the men for their work after testing the ship, but decided to use this to buy food, water and supplies to last them weeks at sea. They called out to every fishing ship they could, to inform them of what had happened. Vimeo spoke with the harbour Master, and panic spread through the village. They restocked as fast as they could. Two crew members left the ship in hopes of returning to their families back in Athel. Barus managed to recruit five new crew members, and they returned to sea with no sign of their pursuers. The winds were still good, and after another day of sailing, they passed the Southern Tip of Natalia. Here, they changed course to a more North Westerly heading and continued towards Cinam, to bring them the bad news. As the first signs of the coast of Cinam came into sight, they could see smoke rising from the city of Scada in the distance. They knew straight away that the city had been taken by the Empire. Vimeo called the crew together to discuss their options.

'I want to make this quick before we are seen by any Dragon ships. As you can see, Scada has been sacked, so this leaves us with but two options. We can run and hide, and hope to escape the Dragon ships for good, or we can keep going on course and sail to Kitia. If we run, the pirate islands are our only destination in that direction. This will bring its own set of problems.'

The men voted and it was almost a unanimous decision. They would sail to Kitia and seek refuge there. As they pulled away from the coast of Cinam, they could see that they had been spotted by the distant Dragon ships, who were now coming after them, but they were no match for the speed of The Sea Wolf. Before long they were out to deep sea, with no land or ship in sight, and on course for The Kingdom of Latonia.

11

Fray, the barmaid, had worked in the Ale House for around a year now. She enjoyed the work and got to know most of the customers. The Tavern was well established in the city of Gemas, in the north west of the Kingdom. Most of the customers were nice and pleasant except for the odd few. Today seemed to be busier than normal. The long winter was over, and Spring was in full motion with buds and flowers starting to come to life. Everyone seemed happier when the sun started to shine. These busier days were hard going, and she knew she might have to miss her breaks and be on her feet until closing time. When she got home after the chaos of work, she would only be fit for her bed. She had started cleaning down an empty table when she noticed a tall man that had just entered the Ale House. Her eyes were instantly drawn to him. He walked to the back of the room and sat alone at a vacant table. There was something about this man. She had not seen him before, but she felt unease. She hesitantly walked over to him.

'How can I help you sir?'

He looked up at her from under his peaked hat and stared at her for a moment. She felt a chill go down her spine.

'I would like a large Wiskin please.'

She was about to walk off, but the man spoke again.

'Is Tarrin here today? I would like to speak to him if he is free?'

She turned back to the man. 'Yes, but he is busy with his books at the moment. He does not like to be disturbed when he is working in his office. I will let him know there is some one that wants to speak with him as soon as he is finished. Can I give him your name?'

'That will be fine. I can wait. Just tell him an old friend would like a word with him please.'

'Very well, Sir.'

She walked off and brought him back a glass and poured a measure into it from a bottle. He paid and thanked her. He was pleasant in his manner but, working as a barmaid, she had learned to trust her instincts. As she walked back to the bar, she could feel his eyes upon her, and she wanted to be far away from him. Tarrin was busy trying to balance his account books when a knock on the door came.

'WHAT?'

He shouted with frustration. Fray opened the door and peeped her head around. Tarrin smiled as he saw it was Fray. His mood instantly changed.

'Sorry for disturbing you sir, but there is a man asking to speak with you.'

'Who is he?'

'I'm not sure Sir but he says he is an old friend.'

'Alright I'll be out in a bit. I just need to finish this first.'

'Yes Sir, I will let him know.'

As she left, she gently closed the door. He felt frustrated with himself for shouting, as he liked Fray. As a matter of fact, he liked her a lot. Ever since she had started working for him, he liked her, but he had never built up the courage to make his feelings known. He poured himself a goblet of water and continued with his work. After some time, he caught a movement in the corner of his eye. He looked over at the other end of the room and was startled to see Renik sitting in a chair watching him.

'Is work that bad that you cannot hear an old friend sneak into your office?'

'I am glad to see you have not lost your touch on stalking people.'

'I know. It's a huge burden on me, possessing these skills, but I am learning to live with it.' Renik said with a sarcastic smirk.

'I haven't seen you in a while, you must be keeping busy?'

'Business is good these days. A lot of people want a lot of other people dead for some reason. So, have you any work for me, to add to my ever-increasing workload?'

'As a matter of fact, I do. I have a client that needs some business taking care of.'

Tarrin stood and poured a cup of wine and offered a cup to Renik.

'No thank you, I have Wiskin waiting for me on a table outside.' Tarrin walked over to Renik with his water in hand and sat down in a deep armchair next to the Assassin. 'How are you keeping Tarrin?'

'I am good, and as I said, business is good too.'

'I have always thought to myself that you would have sold this old building and moved on. The pressures of running such a noisy place should only be for the youngest and most ambitious of men.'

'That is true Renik, but I have invested a lot of money into this old place. Speaking of money, let me talk about these jobs I have for you. One of them could be quite profitable, but I have a small matter that I need you to take care of for me first.'

Tarrin paused and seemed a bit distracted. 'It is a delicate matter, one that is close to home for me.' Renik looked intrigued as he observed Tarrin's emotions coming into play. He had never seen him react like this before. Usually the man played a stone face. 'I need a man taking care of. I will pay above the usual price for this. The bar girl that served you started working for me around a year ago. I am very fond of her.'

Renik noticed he was struggling telling him.

'Well she got involved with a rather unworthy man. Everything was grand until a short while ago. He started to beat her. I noticed bruises on her, so I confronted her about it, and she told me what had been going on. He is a very jealous and violent man. She told him it was over, so he raped her.' Tarrin paused in mid-sentence and cleared his throat. 'Now he keeps harassing her and has continued to rape her when he can. The woman is living in fear. I have been trying to help her as best I can, but this man is relentless and will not let her go. She often comes into work badly beaten. He has also threatened me for my interference. So, I want to put an end to this. I want this evil man taken care of. Will you do this job for me?'

The Assassin smiled at Tarrin's discomfort. 'Of course, sure is it not what I do?'

'It is what you do, and I am asking you to do this because you are the best at what you do.'

'What is this man's name? Tell me everything you know about him and don't abbreviate on the detail.'

'His name is Gualtha.'

Tarrin began to tell Renik everything he knew. Renik sat back and listened while Tarrin went into detail about this man.

'He sounds like a nice piece of work alright. I will take great pleasure in eradicating a rodent like him. Give me one week and what you ask will be done.'

Tarrin felt a little more at ease now knowing that this problem would be taken care of.

'We have been friends for a long time now Tarrin, and I like the business that we have together. So, as a friend I have no wish to charge you for this job.'

Tarrin felt even better now hearing that it would not cost him money. 'That is nice to hear.' Tarrin said as he finished the water.

'Tell me, Tarrin, what is this other job that you mentioned?'

'I have to say I was a bit concerned by the way it was brought to me. A priest from The Dark Sect has asked to meet with you tonight to discuss a job he would like to hire you for. This religious group are not to be trusted, but I said I would say it to you in case you might be interested.'

'I feel you do not want me to take this job?' Tarrin did not reply.

'The fact that you are uncomfortable with this Priest has intrigued me a little. I will meet with him to see what he has to say.'

'Well if you must, he will be in the Tavern tonight.'

'What is his name?'

'He did not give his name, and to be honest, I didn't want to know it. I said I would introduce you both.'

'I will come in later tonight and see what job entails.'

As promised, Renik came back into Tarrin's Ale House later that night. The place was very crowded now, with music playing and people having a good time. Renik especially noticed the noise level was high. This bothered him greatly, as he was used to more quiet evenings. Renik could see why Tarrin kept the place. The business here was good. It seemed it was a very popular place indeed. Renik moved through the people. As he walked, he could feel their emotions. Some were happy, some were sad and some, he could feel, were angry. Tarrin saw Renik coming through and came out from behind the bar to guide him into his study, closing the door behind them.

'I had a feeling you would not come tonight.'

'I had thought about turning back with all that noise out there.'

'It does get noisy, but you get used to it. Now, you can wait in here and I will send the priest in to you when he gets here. Can I get you anything to drink?'

'Yes, I will have a Wiskin. When I left this room earlier today my Wiskin was gone from the table I was sitting at.'

'That tends to happen around here. I must get back to the bar. I will have Fray bring you in another Wiskin.'

Tarrin left the room and closed the door behind him, shutting out the noise. Renik moved a chair from the table and placed it in the darkened corner. He sat and waited for his drink to be brought to him. Moments later, the barmaid brought in his drink, and left without saying a word. Renik sat and waited, sipping on his drink in the shadows. Some time had passed, and the noise out in the bar seemed to get even louder. A sharp knock on the door almost startled him. The door was then opened by Tarrin, and a small man in a dark cloak walked in. Tarrin closed the door and left the two alone. The priest moved towards Renik and held out his hand.

'Pleased to meet you.'

Renik did not move to shake the priest's hand. 'Do you have a name?' Renik asked.

'We do not have names in our Sect. We only go by numbers. I am 19.'

The priest withdrew his hand.

'Well 19, what is it that you require of me?'

The priest turned and pulled a chair up closer, much to the annoyance of Renik.

'I have heard a great deal about you, The Whisper. I have heard that you are the best at what you do and for this job I will need the best. I would like to pay for your services.'

'That will depend on what it is?'

'What if I offer you a large amount to complete this task? Let's say 1000 gold.'

Renik sipped his drink as if the price had no bearing.

'In my experience, when there is a large amount offered, there is always a large risk to take.'

'The risk is high; I won't lie to you.'

There was silence between the two.

Then Renik spoke. 'Who is the target?'

The priest cleared his throat, 'You must make your way to Kitia and kill the man who is sitting on the Throne.'

Renik laughed, 'Now that is a large risk alright.'

'What about 2000 gold?' The priest offered.

Renik's laughter stopped and he sipped his drink again. 'Make it 3000 gold and you have a deal.'

The priest smiled, 'Every man has his price. 3000 gold it is.'

Renik then reached out his hand to the priest and the priest shook it.

'I will pay you half now and half when the job is finished.'

'Leave the money with the bar man, Tarrin.'

The priest then looked at Renik.

'Make sure this job is successful, as you don't want to fail the Dark Sect.'

'I will. Your orders are very clear. Kill the man that sits on the Throne.'

12

Karra moved slowly through the forest; it was a calm day. The forest came to life as the day unfolded. As he rode through, he had already seen a Red Deer and a score of rabbits and squirrels. There were scores of tracks left on the snow-covered ground. Contentedly, he rode, watching the sun glint through the trees. He hadn't had any breakfast that morning as he had eaten his remaining rations the evening before. The edge of the woods came into view and he could make out the vast plain of snow-covered land yonder that led up to the expanse of the North Wall. He breached the last of the woods and, in the distance, he could see the huge wall of the North Pass where it stretched out between two mountain ranges. This wall was one of two that isolated the North Lands from the South Lands. There was a half mile separation between the two walls, giving plenty of room for outposts and village life for the Kingdom between the two walls. With the mountain range on both sides, it made for a natural fortress. No North clan had ever taken these walls by force. Bar the sea; this was the only access to the Latonian Kingdom from the North. The walls looked impenetrable but seemed out of place here against the winter trees and plant life. Every year, the Latonian soldiers had to come out and cut back the vegetation away from the wall as it encroached. It was as if the land was attacking the wall and did not want it there. Karra could feel his horse was jittery beneath him and decided to dismount and walk the last mile to the gates. He held on to both horses' reins as he went. Karra felt his hunger build and his mouth salivate at the thoughts of the meat pies in the food houses and taverns that awaited him beyond the wall. He walked on with thoughts of food on his mind. As he got closer, he could make out the figures of the guards upon the high wall. They were silhouetted against the blue-sky background. Karra approached the closed gates, his feeling of contentment rapidly dissolving away as he felt eyes upon him and the wall looming above him. He had not been this far South in a long time and the last time he was here he had left on bad terms.

A guard called down to him, 'There is no trading today, you have missed it by two days, come back early next week.'

Karra shouted back up to the Guard. 'I am not here for trade.'

'What is your business here stranger?'

'I am Karra from the clan Ruane. I am here to seek passage into the lands of Latonia.'

'I am sorry, you cannot pass. I have orders to keep these gates closed until trading day.'

'Tell Captain Groth I wish to speak to him.'

The guard on the wall fell silent and then moved away. Karra waited patiently at the entrance for what seemed eternity. Then he heard a loud banging noise and a huge creak echoed out from the wall. The massive wooden doors started to open inwards. As they parted, Karra could see maybe twelve guards through the opening. They appeared uneasy as they looked back at him, with their hands on the hilts of their swords, at the ready. Then he spotted Captain Groth walking through the pack of guards, fixing his leather tunic in place as he strode. Karra walked on through the opening gates, leading his two horses behind him. The approaching North Wall Captain stopped a few yards from Karra and spoke.

'You know the rules in Latonian Lands Karra, no weapons are permitted to be held by outsiders beyond this gate.'

Karra turned and took two swords and two large axes from the scabbards on each side of his saddle. Groth gestured to one of the guards to retrieve the weapons, which he did with great caution backing away from the North man without taking his eyes from him.

'And I want that hunting knife you have on your belt too,' said the Captain as he pointed to the knife.

Without a word, Karra drew the knife, walking forward and handing it to Groth hilt first. The two men stood looking at one another for a few heartbeats. Then Captain Groth offered an outstretched hand with a smile on his face. The two men clasped forearms in the warrior's handshake.

'How are you keeping Karra?'

'I am well, and I hope you are in a fit state?'

The guards that stood around looked more at ease now and started to relax. Groth was a big heavy man with a large protruding stomach and chest.

'I see you have lost weight.' Karra spoke in a mocking manner.

The Captain laughed out loud. 'I have missed you too my old friend. I take it you will need accommodation for the night?'

'Yes. if that is OK?'

'Of course, I'll arrange for you to stay in the same tavern you had the last time you visited. Although I can remember the last time you did visit you left it in a shamble.'

'Good. I remember they do a nice meat pie, and it was not my fault that I had to teach those men a lesson in manners.'

The Captain pointed to one of the guards to take Karra 's horses. Karra took his bags from his two horses and handed the reins to the guard. 'Make sure you treat these well.' The guard nodded and led them to the stables. The Gate close and the two old friends walked past the waiting guards and on to the tavern. Karra sat at a table with Captain Groth, enjoying some ale with a full belly from a most enjoyable meat pie. The Tavern was full, and the noise was loud with talking and laughter, but Karra didn't mind. He was comfortable and warm, and he knew he would get a good night's sleep. He had found it tough sleeping the last few nights on the frozen ground. He chatted to Groth about old times. Groth took a drink from his cup and wiped his mouth.

'So, tell me Karra how come you are traveling south? Is it getting too cold for you in the North these days?'

'I am on my way to Kitia to visit my nephew.'

'Kitia is a long way away, it will take you nearly 2 months to reach there and it will be busy at that time with the Summer celebrations and the King's birthday. You'll be away from your duties guarding the gateway for quite a while.'

'I know this. I have friends guarding the gate for me while I am away. It is in good hands. Everyone needs a holiday now and again. What is the news with you?'

'Nothing of note has happened. I probably need a visit back to my home in Talmine. I have been stuck up here on the wall for the last 7 years.' The two men talked and drank long into the night. The bartender was trying to encourage his customers to leave as it was very late, and he wanted to close for the night. A fight broke out between 2 large men at the far end of the tavern and was making its way towards Karra and Groth's table. A man came flying through the air and landed on their table unconscious. Both Karra and Groth managed to lift their drinks free before he landed. He slid off the table and onto the floor. The man that had hit him was standing with a bloody nose and his fists clenched, smiling. He wiped the blood from his nose and announced.

'I'm still unbeaten!'

Karra sniggered, and the young man saw this. 'What about you, old man… do you think you can take me?'

Karra was about to stand and confront the man when Groth intervened. Groth stood quickly, 'that's enough of the entertainment, time to go home now lads.'

The young man stood there with his eyes on Karra, ignoring the Captain's request.

Groth talked louder, 'Time to go home.'

The young man still did not listen.

'That's an order Torgo, you don't want to end up in a cell again tonight, do you?'

Torgo turned slowly, all the while staring at Karra, and left the tavern. The tavern emptied fast after that.

Groth sat back down. 'I apologise on Torgos behalf. He is a young man with strength to burn but he is as dumb as an ox.'

'Youth is wasted on the young.' added Karra, as he drank down the last of his ale. 'He will find his match some day and that will tame him.'

'I will leave you to your rest Karra. What time will you start your journey tomorrow?'

'I think as soon as I get some food in the morning I will leave.'

'I will see you off then, so. Please stay out of trouble.'

The two men parted and Karra made his way to his soft bed. He slept better than he had done in a few nights and when he woke, he felt rested. Groth joined him for breakfast. Karra purchased some provisions for the trek south, while Groth saw to an issue with one of his soldiers. Karra threw two sacks of provisions over each shoulder and then made his way to the stables to collect his horses. A group of men were walking towards him. Karra could see at the head of the group was the young man, Torgo, from the night before. He walked right up to Karra's face.

'Well old man, let me see you sniggering now.'

Karra could smell the stale ale from the young man's breath and was in no mood for a fight. He was still holding onto the sacks, so he raised his right knee and hit home into Torgo's groin. The group of men jumped back as Torgo doubled over in pain, grabbing his crotch area. Karra then raised his knee again and caught Torgo with a huge thud to the side of the young man's jaw. He fell backwards to the ground unconscious. As Karra continued to walk on, a cheer went up from the group of men at the felling of this bully. When he got to the stables, he gave the soldier a silver coin for looking after his horses and began to load his supplies.

Groth came trundling in, laughing. 'I have left you for five minutes. Somehow, I knew you'd get in a fight during your short visit here.'

'I wouldn't call that a fight.'

Groth's laugh boomed out. 'Well he had it coming to him. He had bested most of the other soldiers that had challenged him, and I think he was getting a big head about it.'

Groth walked Karra to the gate in the smaller wall that led to the south. He then called up to the guards on the wall and the gate opened.

'Here you might be in need of this.' Groth handed Karra back his hunting knife. 'I will make sure your swords and axes are safe and give them back to you on your return.'

'I will need my axes for firewood.'

The Captain looked at his friend. 'What size trees will you be cutting down with them?'

'I have to keep warm on my travels, Groth.'

'Very well then, you can have your axes.' Groth sent a guard to fetch them and handed them back to Karra. Karra thanked Groth and the two men shook hands and Karra mounted and rode off into the Kingdom of Latonia on his long journey. It only took 4 days to reach the city of Branti. Karra's food had just lasted the duration and he was glad to secure a bed for the night. He only stayed one night, setting off again at dawn, traveling further and further south. The deeper he went into Latonian land, the better the weather was, and the temperature felt much warmer. There was less snow covering the ground now. He looked for beds where he could in villages and farms. He had enjoyed meeting fellow travellers. The roads were good, as he entered the central plains, where the population was much less. He noticed the plants and trees were different here. Within seven weeks his weary mounts crested a hill and he could just make out the huge walls of Kitia. The lands here were rich and the colour was vibrant across meadows, farms and woods. The farms here were rich with crops and livestock. His legs were now tired, and both his horses were very weary. He stopped on the hill for a moment's rest, and to take in the views of the countryside. His long journey was almost done. He then moved on down the road to the gates of the great city Kitia.

13

Imperial General Zukata stood at the bow of the Dragon Ship, as it closed in on the mouth of the harbour of Athel, Natalia's Capital. The rest of the fleet was a few miles back. Zukata wanted to secure the entrance of the harbour first. This would allow the rest of the ships to enter without resistance and then move in and take the city. The key to this attack would be the element of surprise. Zukata could see the guards had spotted them and were moving out from the watchtower.

'Pull in the sail' the Imperial General commanded. 'And prepare the oars.'

The sail was pulled down and ropes held it in its resting place. The ship started to slow.

'Deploy the oars,' he commanded, as the ship drew closer to the mouth.

The oars splashed down and started to move at a slow pace. There were several guards waiting on the dock, trying to identify the approaching ship.

'How many guards can you see?' Zukata asked Raim, his second.

'I can count maybe 12.'

'Get the archers ready. Tell them and the rest of the soldiers to keep down until I give the word.'

The ship glided ever closer. The Harbour Master, who had been standing among the 11 guards, walked to the edge of the pier. As it came closer, the Harbour Master's heart sank as he recognised the black ship as an Imperial Dragon war ship. She had very little crew on board apart from the oarsmen and a few of the crew on the main deck. He held out his hand as the ship came to a halt just a few feet off the pier.

'What business do you have here?' he shouted.

Zukata ignored the question. He called out an order for the oars to be retracted and then turned to the waiting Harbour Master and replied to his question.

'My business is simple; I am in the business of killing.' He then shouted, 'NOW!' With that command, 20 Imperial archers jumped up and launched a volley of arrows at the 12 harbour guards. The Harbour Master took an arrow through his outstretched hand. He was about to shout out, but another arrow hit him through his right eye socket. He was dead before he hit the ground. There was instant panic as arrows sliced into the other guards at speed. Grappling hooks were thrown to the pier as the rest of the soldiers stood and the ship was pulled close enough for them to jump across. Two guards fell into the water below with arrows jutting from their chests, six others were downed with arrows. The Imperial Soldiers swarmed the pier, executing any survivors they found. Three guards had run, and two of them had been shot and killed by the archers. The remaining guard was trying to run away with an arrow sticking out of his upper leg. Arrows whizzed past him as he struggled to run away. General Zukata quickly ran to the nearest archer and grabbed the bow from him. Extracting an arrow from the man's quiver, he took aim at the fleeing guard, who was nearing the end of the pier in an effort to sound the alarm that they were being attacked. Zukata would not allow this to happen. He let fly his arrow and a heartbeat later the guard fell face down with an arrow embedded in the back of his neck. Zukata shoved the bow back at the archer. 'You need more practice,' he said with disdain.

The Dragon ship was pulled around to the inside of the pier to make space for the incoming fleet. Zukata turned to Raim, 'Make sure you look after the ship, and that the oarsmen are well fed and ready to sail if needed.' Raim acknowledged the order, and Zukata drew his long-curved sword and jumped down to the pier, shouting out another command.

'Make sure there are no survivors.'

100 Dragon Soldiers stormed the harbour killing everyone they came across, jumping onto all the docked fishing ships and slashing and stabbing everyone. Zukata looked back out to sea. On the horizon, he could see the fleet appearing. He then looked into the sky. It was midday, and the sun was high. Satisfied now, he moved on with his men to secure the rest of the harbour. 150 Dragon Ships crowded the Athel harbour, most of the ships could not get in, so each ship would pull up to the pier, unload soldiers and move back out to sea to allow the next ship to come in and do the same. 15000 Imperial Dragon soldiers pushed on through the city, killing and slaughtering every man

and young child they came across. They were given strict orders to enslave all healthy women and children that could walk, everyone else would die. The city was taken even faster than they expected, the city guards being no match for the Imperial Soldiers. Zukata sat, slumped, on some steps that led to a large building. He felt tired now. He looked down at his hands and noticed that he was covered in blood from all the killing. He felt a wave of sorrow come over him. There were dead bodies everywhere, and the streets were covered in blood. There was no honor in slaughter, but it was an order and had to be obeyed. The sun was now beginning to set, and the evening air was filled with the cries of the city's survivors, still in shock at what they had witnessed. They were all tied up or chained, not knowing their fate. Most of the houses had been searched and scores of them had been set alight. The smoke billowed up into the evening sky. All the guards had been killed and the city now belonged to the Empire of Eamhair. There were a few hundred Latonian soldiers within the city that fought well but had simply been overwhelmed by the sheer size of the Dragon force. Reports said that around 20 of the Latonian soldiers escaped on horses and headed off to the north. No doubt they would make their way to the North Wall and report the invasion. This was expected. There were groups of soldiers sitting around, eating and talking, all exhausted from a day of killing. Zukata did not feel hungry, just tired. He heard a loud scream coming from down along the road to his right. As he looked down, he could see three Imperial Soldiers taunting a young girl. They were jabbing at her with their spears. She only looked to be around 12 years of age; she had a small knife in her hand and seemed to be trying to defend a small body that lay at her feet. Zukata slowly pushed himself to his feet and walked towards the scene.

'What is going on here?'

As he spoke the frightened girl turned in his direction, slashing the air with her knife. One of the soldiers took advantage of the girl's distraction, thrusting his spear forward into her shoulder. She screamed with pain. Her free hand grabbed the shaft of the implanted spear and slashed at her attacker. He pulled the spear free as he moved back out of reach of the knife. Angry now, Zukata shouted.

'Put those spears away at once.'

The men backed away at his command. The young girl fell to her knees, holding her shoulder with one hand, and her knife high in the air with the other, in defense. Blood started to flow, rapidly soaking her tunic. The three soldiers stood to attention as soon as they saw General Zukata approach.

'We were just having some fun sir,' one of the soldiers said.

Zukata walked forward and grabbed the knife from the girl, tossing it aside. The girl looked up at the General, 'Don't harm my brother.' She spat in a foreign language. Zukata could speak the Natalian tongue and understood her. He looked down at the dead boy beneath the girl and realised she was trying to protect him, and with her frightened state she had not realised he was dead.

'What is your name?' he asked.

'Sabia, she replied, as she started to cry.

'You can come away from your brother, he is dead.'

The tears stopped and she looked down at the body. In a sudden rage, she leapt at the General and lashed out with her fist. Zukata stepped back to avoid the strike and, with a swift movement, backhanded the girl across her jaw, rendering her unconscious. He caught her before she hit the ground.

'You there!' He pointed to the soldier that had wielded the spear. 'Take this girl to my ship at the end of the North Pier and tell Raim to look after her.'

The General gave the soldier a stern look.

'Know this, if this girl gets hurt again, you will know my fury.'

The soldier carefully lifted her from the General and carried her away towards the harbour. The sun had just gone down below the city of Athel. The night was clear with stars shining brightly, but there was a cold breeze blowing in from the sea. The screams and shouts coming from within the city had ceased. Raim was walking along the deck, enjoying the quiet, when he saw a soldier coming down the pier towards him. He was carrying a young girl.

'I am looking for Raim.' he shouted up.

'I am Raim.' Raim bellowed back down at him.

'I was ordered to take this girl to you by General Zukata. He said to tell you to make sure you look after her.'

Raim lowered the loading ramp and the soldier carried her on board. Raim noticed how gently the soldier lowered the girl to the deck and as soon as he did, he was gone. Raim noticed the blood stain on the girl's tunic and pulled it down from her shoulder to expose a large wound. He fetched some clean water and cleaned it as best he could and then he took out a needle and some thread and started to stitch the cut. The girl woke suddenly as he inserted the first stitch. She cried out. Raim spoke to her in the Natalian tongue. His voice was low and gentle.

'You have a bad wound in your shoulder, if I do not seal it, it will most likely get infected and believe me you don't want that.'

The girl nodded and turned her head away and endured the pain of the stitching. Raim continued to talk to her in a low calm voice. The girl began to shake uncontrollably.

'You have been through a traumatic time and you are most likely in shock, but I promise you there will come no more harm to you.'

Once this was done, Raim covered the girl with a wool blanket and let her rest. She was asleep in moments. Raim settled down for the night across from her. Sabia woke with the memory of the day before. It hit her like a hammer's blow. Sadness swept over her again as she remembered that her little brother was dead. It was bright out and she could see the man that had treated her organizing food on the deck of the boat. He turned and looked in her direction. Sabia closed her eyes and pretended to be still asleep. She heard his footsteps come towards her and then they walked away again. She opened her eyes slightly and noticed he had left her some food and a cup of water. She noticed he was coming back so she closed her eyes again. When she opened them again he was sitting opposite her.

'You should really try eating something; it will make you feel better.'

Sabia started to sit up, but as she did, she felt a sharp pain shoot down her right shoulder and she cried out.

'You might want to take things slow for a while.' The man said. 'Those stitches are very tight you might tear them.'

The girl turned to her left side and sat up. She lifted the bowl with her left hand and started to eat.

'What is your name?'

The girl did not answer him at first, but after she drank deeply from the cup, she wiped her mouth and looked at Riam.

'Where is my brother?'

'I am sorry to say, your brother is dead.'

The girl turned away and glared out to sea for a while and then went back to eating.

'My name is Sabia and my brother is all I had. Now I have nothing.'

'General Zukata told me what happened and ordered one of the soldiers to bring you here.'

'Is he the man that struck me?'

'Yes, that is him. He only struck you because he was afraid you would hurt yourself; you were out of control.'

'I don't like him. I was only looking after my younger brother.'

'The General knows that. He was impressed by how brave you were, defending your brother against three Dragon Soldiers. He is asleep below in his quarters and would like to see you later when he rises.'

'Well I don't want to see him; I don't like him.'

'General Zukata is an honourable man and very well respected'

'I don't like people that hit me.'

'You will learn to like him.'

'What will happen to me now, will I be put in chains like all the other people and made a slave?'

'Oh no my dear, General Zukata has looked favourably on you. You will not be a slave and there will be no chains attached to any of your limbs. You will be well looked after. You will be given an education befitting of a lady. Things will change for you now. You will start a new life, a better one than you have had here. Today is the first day of your new destiny.'

Zukata arose from his bed and stretched. His body was sore and the ribs on his right side were badly bruised from charging a Natalian guard in the heat of battle. He drank a couple of cups of water, put on his black armour and headed up to the main deck. As he passed the slave oarsmen, he could smell the stench of stale sweat. The slaves were talking quietly amongst themselves, but when the General drew close there was silence. He walked past them and up the wooden steps onto the deck and felt the warmth of sunshine on his face. Raim was busy preparing food. He moved to him.

'Good day General, did you sleep well?'

'I did, thank you. How is our guest?'

'She is better than she was.'

The girl was sitting at the back of the ship, looking out to sea. She noticed the General was on deck and looking over at her. She turned away and continued looking out to sea.

'I see she is beginning to like you already,' said Raim with a smile.

'She doesn't know How lucky she is. Make sure you take really good care of her. When do you leave for home?'

'We will set sail tomorrow morning. The slaves will be brought on board the ships tonight. We should be back at home within 2 weeks. The reinforcements and supplies should arrive in the next couple of days. You will have your horse then.'

'I will need her to make the journey to the Latonian Wall. It will be around 1000 miles from here. It will be over a month's march.'

'I noticed that the oarsmen are well overdue a wash. Make sure that they all get a good swim in the sea before you set sail again.'

'I will, General.'

Zukata walked over to Sabia. She turned to face him. He was a small man, much smaller than Raim, but his presence demanded authority. 'How are you feeling?'

Sabia shrugged. 'I'm OK.'

'I am sorry for hitting you, I felt it was the only thing I could do at the time. I know you feel like you have lost everything, but I am offering you a new start, a new life. There is nothing left for you in this land. I promise you will be looked after. Will you accept?'

There was a long pause, Sabia did not know what to do. She looked behind Zukata and Raim was standing there watching he nodded his head to try prompting her. She followed suit and nodded to Zukata and said. 'Yes!'

Raim set sail for Parci. The ship was full now with gold and valuables and slaves taken from the city of Athel. Sabia watched from the stern of the ship as the city disappeared beyond the horizon. She wondered if she would ever see her home again. A day later, the reinforcements and provision ships docked in the harbour. It took a long time to unload the contents. Hundreds of horses were walked out on shaky legs from the carrier ships and to solid ground. Wagons of food and livestock were unloaded and organised for the campaign. There was a new city guard put in place, and the Imperial Eamhair war machine of 15000 Dragon Soldiers marched out from the City of Athel and headed north towards the city of Tillo. The line of the march would trail on for miles, followed by hundreds of supply carts. They would sack any small towns, villages and farms along the way and bleed them for resources as they marched, feeding the campaign, and leaving the lands behind them waste. While they were marching, ships would also land in Cinam, taking their main cities of Scapa and Astana. The city Tipus had already fallen, and the Land of Naos was now under the rule of The Empire. It was all going to plan. 54 Latonian riders rode in through the gates of the South wall. They all looked exhausted. The original 23 riders that had escaped from Athel had gathered as many Latonian soldiers as they could. They travelled at speed to warn the South Wall of the coming invasion. It took them almost 2 weeks to get there, riding nonstop. The order went out, and the gates were all closed, and the wall was now on high alert. The lookout scouts were doubled, and preparations were made. The Royal messenger riders were dispatched to the Capital Kitia to notify the King and ask for reinforcements in case The Empire had further plans to invade Latonia. Scores of Latonian soldiers now poured in, returning from their peace keeping in the lands of Natalia. A month had passed, and the first signs of the Dragon army could be seen moving towards the wall. Within a day, 15000 troops were camped a mile from the south wall. Captain Brota stood on the wall, looking out to the land of Natalia, staring out at the huge army. It seemed like the whole Empire of Eamhair was camped on the doorstep of the Kingdom. He had sent word back to the King, in Kitia, when he had first received reports that the Eamhair army had sacked the Natatian capital, Athel. It was hard to believe that it had happened, but realisation had hit him like an arrow when he had seen the first of the Dragon soldiers arriving. Now, the invading army spanned out the full length of the wall, and more were arriving each day. 500 Royal troops had come to their aid, to help defend the wall from the surrounding areas and from Tureen. It would be another few weeks before there would be reinforcements arriving from Kitia. He was nervous. This force was much too large for him to hold with only 2000 men. Everyone was on high alert. Most of the guards were sleeping on the ramparts now, at the ready. All spears and swords were kept sharpened, and hundreds of extra arrows were being made each day in preparation for pending attack. The tension was high. Every day, he looked out over the projection of the wall, watching and waiting. What are they waiting for? The thought kept niggling at him. Why do they not attack? He heard a faint horn sound and he could see a lot of commotion and then, as he looked out, he realised, and fear swamped him.

14

Twenty ships sailed into the already packed harbour of Athel with a force of 2000 soldiers, led by the Emperor's daughter, Leta. She was met by a Dragon Captain called Velez. Velez was temporarily in charge until her arrival. He was waiting with guards and a chariot that would bring her up through the broken city. She greeted him quickly and they set off towards the most luxurious of buildings in Athel, the dead Chancellor's palace. Captain Velez joined her in her chariot and briefed her as they moved through the streets. Leta noticed that there were very few inhabitants left in the city. The Captain explained that most of the Natalians within the city had been killed and the rest had fled to the countryside, but they had managed to capture many slaves. Most of these had been shipped back to Parcia, to serve The Empire, but there were a few hundred left behind to serve the troops and help maintain the city. This gave an eerie feeling to a once vibrant city. A city that had once been the leader in many subjects, Science, Mathematics, Art and Culture and many more. Now it looked like a waste land. Only the imperial Dragon Troops were free to walk the deserted streets. This made Leta feel saddened. For when she was young, she was told amazing stories about the city of Athel in her studies. She had fantasized about visiting this city when she was younger and now, she was here, and it lay in shambles. She looked out towards the perimeter at the outer wall. She could see that they were well manned with guards. The Captain explained that troops were sent out daily to raid the countryside for food and that they now had a large stock available to them. Ships from Parcia, the Empire's capital, also arrived daily with supplies and food to feed the Campaign. Most of these supplies were sent to the wall in preparation to move into the land of Latonia. All was working to plan. Her father, The Emperor, would arrive the following summer and she did not want to disappoint him. Her job was to maintain the city and the progress of the campaign until his arrival. His orders were also to start rebuilding the city. She would gather all riches and gold and send these back home to her father. There was an enormous amount of old texts and historical artefacts also in the city that would be claimed by her father. Athel was once the leading city in the known world for medicine, this would be a great asset to the empire in years to come. Most of the world's greatest minds would have come from Athel. Now, most of these men were dead or on the run, and their work and studies in ruins. Leta knew she had a colossal job ahead of her, she knew this from the start, and she had some plans of her own. She arrived at the palace and Velez led her into the huge building. She was pleasantly surprised to see that the inside was undamaged from the battles. She liked it straight away, and thought The Chancellor had good taste. It was beautifully fashioned with fine fabrics and pleasant colours. The architecture of the building itself was a marvel. The halls and rooms were very large, and the ceilings were high, giving the feeling of open space.

'Yes, this will suit me.' she said aloud.

Within 2 weeks Leta had turned the city around. She had everyone working. She even joined in and helped with the lighter work. The streets were now cleaned up and the buildings were being repaired and rebuilt. The city's walls and defences were being improved on, and the harbour had been altered and had security in place, so that no other army could do what the Empire had done by just sailing in and invading. The mood had changed in Athel. There were rules and laws set in place by Leta and she enforced them with all her power. She had started a senate with intelligent men handpicked by herself from her troops. These men held a forum once a week in order to prioritise which areas needed looking at next. Leta was fair to the slaves and made sure they were treated right. She also made sure she was always surrounded by 20 of her most trusted guards and Velez. All was going to plan until the third week, when three imperial ships arrived, and word was sent back to the palace that on board was the mystic priest Oranius. Leta took her place on her throne within the palace and sent orders for Oranius to join her there. She waited for hours, but he did not show. Leta was getting very angry now at Oranius's lack of respect. She called for her captain, Velez. She then sent an order for him to join her straight away. A short time had passed when the doors to the palace hall opened and Oranius was announced by her Scribe. He walked up the long aisle with two of his followers by his sides. The walls of the hall were lined with Leta's guards. He did not look happy. He reached the steps to the throne but did not bow.

'You have summoned me, my lady?'

Leta gave him a stern look. 'I requested your presence hours ago, what has taken you so long?'

'We have just arrived and have preparations to make and orders from your father, The Emperor, to carry out. I am busy preparing the temple for the Order.' He hissed back at her.'

'My father has given me orders too, and one of them is to rule Natalia until he reaches here. All here are my subjects, including you Oranius. My orders must and will be obeyed. Do you understand?'

Oranius paused for a second and gave her a slimy sneer. He was not used to being talked to in that manner. 'Yes, your Highness.'

One of Oranius's followers placed his hand on a short sword on his belt and looked like he was about to draw it. Leta's guards jumped forward, hands on their swords, when Captain Velez walked from behind a pillar with his hands raised to halt the guard's advancement. Velez walked down the hall and placed his own hand on the hilt of his sword and looked at the Follower.

'If that sword is drawn in the presence of Her Highness, you will die where you stand.'

Leta could not help smirk at the drama that was unfolding and the satisfaction it brought. Oranius looked at Velez for a split second, then at his follower and gave him a nod. The follower slowly took his hand away and folded his arms. The guards moved back to their places along the walls. Velez walked slowly up to Leta's side by the Throne and stood on guard. Oranius looked on with a sneer on his face.

'As you wish your Highness. How can I be of service to you?'

'I also have work for you to do Oranius.'

Oranius interrupted her as she spoke, 'I have plenty to be getting on with. My tasks are many.'

Leta glared at him intensely. 'If you interrupt me again when I am speaking, you will have to go about your work with only one hand. As I will have Velez cut the other one from your arm. Now, as you can see there is plenty to be done in this city. I myself have had to help with tasks. I myself have had to get dirty and sweaty. So, you can see there are more important issues here than religious work. This is what I need from you Oranius.'

Oranius listened closely now without any interruptions. Leta laid down her plans and orders for what she wanted from the priest. She purposely held him longer than necessary, in retaliation for his tardiness, keeping him and his followers standing for the duration. After some time, she dismissed him. The priest left, with his two followers close behind him, looking very unhappy. This pleased Leta immensely. She then rose, and her scribe opened the doors for her. As she left the room, she gave orders. 'I will be in my chambers and I do not want to be disturbed.' Velez stopped at the door.

'You may come with me Velez; I wish to speak to you.'

Velez followed close by. Leta entered the room and gestured Velez in and then closed the door to the two guards standing outside. She turned to Velez and looked at him.

'You are a loyal soldier and I value your commitment to the Imperial house, and on top of that you are a very handsome man. I had not realised that until a short while ago.'

She moved around him running her finger over his shoulders.

'Yes, very handsome indeed. I know you have a wife and child back in Parcia. That is a long way away and we have been here some weeks now. You must be feeling very lonely?'

Velez could feel himself getting aroused now as Leta circled around him and tried to hide it from her. She stopped in front of him. Now, take off all your armour and clothing. We don't have long.'

Velez looked confused and was about to speak.

'Well hurry up then. It is a direct order, Velez.'

She moved in and kissed him forcefully. Velez did not protest and kissed her back. He slowly undressed from his armour as the Emperor's daughter watched. After all, it was a direct order.

15

The Conri, Chieftain of Four Vales, walked through the wooded area and up to the old door of the wooden cabin. He was just about to knock on the door when he heard a low voice call out from within.

'Enter!'

The Chieftain turned the handle and walked into a dimly lit room. It smelled musty inside with dampness. He could see the old man sitting in a low chair by a small fire. Only the glow from the fire was illuminating the room. The old man's wispy white hair seemed to look yellow now in the fire light.

'There was a time when people came to my home frequently to see me, to talk and spend time with me. Now, it seems, people only come to visit when they are looking for something from me. How time changes things. What do you seek Chieftain?'

'I thought you knew all, old man?'

'The positive thinker sees the invisible, feels the intangible and, on rare occasions, achieves the impossible. But I never claimed to know all, for that is very much impossible. Now I am tired, and in no mood for games. So just tell me what it is you want?'

The Chieftain moved closer to the old man. The wrinkled skin of his face was more pronounced in the soft glow and made him look even older. His voice matched his age, weak and crackly. No one in the Vale knew how old Sallin was. The people would say that he had been there forever, and maybe they were right. The man had the gift of the third sight and his visions were never wrong. He had been a gift to the people of Four Vales, and they trusted his guidance. The Chieftain quickly gathered his thoughts.

'A little girl from the Vale has gone missing and I was looking for your help in finding her.'

The old man closed his eyes. 'Give me a name that I can concentrate on?'

'The girl's name is Eanna.'

'Ah yes I see her, little Eanna, full of spirit. She is in danger. Her life hangs in the balance. I can see teeth and claws coming for her from out of the woods. Time is dwindling for this young girl.'

'Do you know where she is?'

'I do not know the whereabouts, but I do know she will be found.'

'By whom?'

'Who does not matter, what matters is that she is found. You need to offer something to entice the people to look. You need to offer some gold. Gold always gets people motivated, but you must be swift. The little girl's time is running out.'

'Thank you, old man! I will see to it straight away and I will make sure food and drink are sent to you today as my appreciation for your help.'

The old man nodded, and the Chieftain turned to leave. The old man then raised his arm. 'Wait!' and called him back.

'Conri, before you go. There is something that you must know.'

The Chieftain stopped and came back to the side of the old man. 'What is it, old man?'

'I have just seen something that might be of concern to you, a concern to all of us.' The Conri listened carefully.

Cahira stood with the rest of the villagers of The Four Vales, listening intently. The Conri, Chieftain of the Four Vales, stood on the back of a wagon, addressing a large crowd of a few hundred.

'Listen up, we have a task at hand. Little Eanna has gone missing. She has not been seen since this morning and her Mother and Father have been frantically searching for her to no avail. Some of the other children that were playing with her said that she wandered off into the woods to the North. I am asking for your help today to look for her. Gather yourselves into small groups and spread out and let's start looking for her. We will start looking around the village first and then spread out in these groups and cover as much ground as we can outside the village until we find her. The first one to find her will be awarded this gold coin.'

There was a wow sound within the crowd as they started to chatter amongst themselves. The Conri then raised the coin up high into the air so all could see. Cahira got a rush of excitement as it glinted in the sunlight. She had only seen a gold coin once before, and the thought of having a chance to own one was captivating. The Conri asked for silence.

'Tucus, the Tracker and his son Blan are away on a hunt, so this should give you a chance to find the girl. Go now and bring this little Eanna home safe.'

The crowd started to break down into searching groups. Cahira fixed her bow and quiver of arrows on her back and headed off to the North by herself. She wanted to get ahead of the crowd so she could read the tracks, before they were spoiled by hundreds of footsteps. On her way through the village, she stopped to ask the other children where they had last seen Eanna. They pointed off to an opening in the woods and she headed in that direction. She reached the woods quickly and there were lots of trails going in different directions. Cahira knew these woods well from hunting here, and straight away she could see small footprints trailing into the North. She moved into the woods without haste. Her tall, lean body enabled her to move through the thickets with ease. Cahira was used to tracking on the move and she pushed on fast through the vegetation. She followed the little girl's trail for a while. The woods were getting dense now. She stopped at a darker part of the woods, where the sunlight had very little penetration because of the thick covering of trees above. She noticed that the girl's footsteps had looped around and crossed over her earlier footsteps and headed out to the West. Cahira knew then that the girl had lost her direction and was heading back home in the wrong direction. She could hear groups of people getting closer now, but she was determined to get to the girl first and earn the gold coin. It was getting late, but Cahira was still tracking the girl's trail to the West. She stopped to read some footprints and just then she could hear a child crying up ahead on the trail. She followed in the direction of the sounds and came to an opening in the woods and there, on a large fallen tree, sat the little girl Eanna, crying and rubbing her eyes with her hands.

'Well hello there little one.' Cahira said in a soft voice, trying not to scare the girl.

Eanna instantly stopped crying and looked up from her hands to stare at Cahira.

'We've all been looking for you. Your family are all worried.'

Cahira then noticed that the girl had blood on her tunic. Her right arm was drenched in blood and she could see scratches on her hands and three lines of scratches across her left cheek. The little girl stood and went statue still. She then slowly pointed in a direction off to her left to a wide tree. A young mountain cat gradually came into view, baring its long fangs and hissing at them both. Cahira gently moved towards the girl to try and get between them. It hissed at Cahira as it moved towards them. Cahira held out her hand to the little girl and she took it, and Cahira pulled the girl in close behind her, ever so slowly so as not to provoke the cat.

'It's OK now Eanna, I have you now.'

The frightened little girl clung to Cahira's leg with fear. It looked like Eanna had been attacked by this lion and, judging by the leaves and under growth under the falling tree, the girl must have hidden there. By reading the sign, Cahira guessed that the girl had received her wounds when she had hidden under the fallen tree and the lion had tried to pull her out. The cat must have withdrawn from its attack when it heard Cahira coming. The Mountain Lion started to circle them both. Cahira moved her right hand and unclipped the safety strap from the hunting knife on her belt. She then took her bow from her shoulder, drew an arrow from behind her head, notched it to her bow and took aim. The Lion started to move closer and hissed louder. Cahira stood her ground, for to run now would be a mistake. The lion was not happy that Cahira was here, it hissed and spat at her. Then suddenly the lion lurched forward, it leaped high into the air at Cahira. Cahira fired her arrow and it hit home into the lion's chest. The Lion landed with a scream to Cahira's right. The cat swiped at her, catching her high on her right hip. She felt instant pain as the cat's claws sliced through her leather trousers and tore into her skin. The cat turned for another attack with an arrow sticking out of its chest. Cahira dropped her bow and spun to her left pulling the girl behind her. She drew her hunting knife with speed, but the Lion leaped and attacked again, opening its large jaws and exposing its dagger-like teeth as it came close to snapping down on Cahira's neck. In a flash, Cahira thrust upwards with her knife, driving it hard into the lion's throat and sliced up towards its head. It slammed into Cahira, knocking her and the girl to the ground. Cahira managed to push the girl away and the lion's lifeless body landed hard on top of her. She pushed the cat aside. It felt like a dead weight. Little Eanna sat up and started to cry again. Cahira stood and walked over to her, picking her up from the ground, and held her in a tight embrace.

'It's OK now little one, let's get you home.'

Just then a group of about 20 villagers rushed into the clearing and crowded around Cahira and the girl and the dead mountain lion. The girl's mother and father also rushed in and Cahira handed over the child to the mother where she hugged and kissed her irrepressibly.

'Thank you Cahira.' Said the father of the girl as he put his hand on her shoulder.

'You are most welcome.' she said in return.

The father noticed that she was hurt and pointed to her torn and blood-stained trousers.

'You have been hurt!'

'It is OK, I think the little girl has more injuries than I do.'

A horn was sounded to indicate a halt to the search, and they all made their way back to Four Vales, bringing the dead mountain lion with them. When they arrived, the whole village was there to greet them. The Conri, Chieftain called Cahira forth, thanked her for her efforts and awarded her the gold coin. Cahira was smiling from ear to ear. She noticed a young warrior called Akala watching her, as she put the gold coin into an inner pocket on the inside of her tunic. The villagers let out a big cheer as she made her way back to her home on the outskirts of Four Vales. Even with the pain of her injury, she could not stop smiling as she went. As she passed by Akala, he walked over to her.

'Well done on finding the girl.'

She nodded to him and kept walking. She could feel he was following her and turned to meet him.

'What do you want Akala?'

'I was just wondering if you needed any help in dressing that wound you received on your hip.'

He looked down along her body slowly. 'You do know I have very gentle hands and would be more than willing to help?'

Cahira smiled at him 'I'm thinking it's an undressing you want rather than a dressing.'

'Well I wouldn't complain about undressing you. If you are offering?' He retorted with a snicker.

'Or is it my shiny gold coin you want?'

'Come now Cahira, who do you take me for? I am only looking to be of some help.'

Akala looked her up and down again. Cahira stepped in close to him and grabbed him between the legs and squeezed a little. Akala let out a shout of pain and went to push her hand aside and she squeezed even harder. He put his hands out to the side.

'OK, OK. I am sorry please let go. I am only playing with you. Please let go.'

Cahira moved her face very close to Akala's. Their noses were almost touching.

'If you had anything to offer me, I would come and take it. Now stop following me or I will inflict some real pain.'

She let go, turned and walked away. Akala instantly fell to one knee in pain holding his groin. He looked up, shouting at her as she walked away. 'You look even better from this angle.'

Cahira ignored him and kept walking. She reached her house and locked the door behind her, in case Akala decided to follow. Firstly, she hid the gold coin under a wooden panel in under the floor where she kept some silver coins. She then stripped off her clothes and saw to her wound. She was lucky it was not too deep, but it was starting to sting. She filled a large bowl of water and bathed the wound until it looked clean. Any scratches or bites from wild animals would usually get infected if not treated. The wound did not look like it needed stitching. She took out a Mortar and pestle and ground down some garlic cloves and a piece of ginger root. She then added a small white flower and some honey. This all made a paste and she then smeared it onto the wound. Happy now, she lay down on her bed, recalling the day's events. She liked to be part of the village, but most of the time she was left out. Especially by the other girls. When she was younger, they used to tease her. She found herself playing with the boys more than the girls. Then, when she got older, the boys only wanted one thing from her, so she limited her time with them also. Now she spent most of her time alone. She was 18 now, and had no friends, no husband and no children she could call her own. Her own parents had moved north last year, and she did not want to go and make a new start in a new village. So, she was alone now. She thought about them often and wondered how they were getting on. Maybe one day I will travel to them and see how life is treating them. Akala came into her thoughts, then she slept.

General Zukata walked from the war tent with the other nine Generals. They all mounted their war horses and took their places in front of their Dragon troops sections. General Zukata gave the nod and a loud trumpet sounded out, and flags were raised and waved high into the air. Thousands of troops moved with efficiency into their positions. There came a low rumble and scores of siege towers were being pulled and pushed forward into place in front of the lines of troops. Another flag waved and a slow drumbeat sounded out, and the Eamhair war machine began to move forward with a slow pace. Back at the wall, a look-out yelled to Captain Brota. Captain Brota let out a shout.

'Take your places, they're coming.'

The Royal guards rushed into their defensive positions and within minutes everyone was in their places, just as they had practiced hundreds of times before. All wearing armour and garbed with the official white cloak of the Kingdom, but they were not equipped with the newly designed battle armour, for it had been years since there had been any fighting in Latonia. The walls were packed with lines of men. The back lines all had spears and swords and the front lines were armed with bows and scores of arrows in quivers at their feet, waiting for the chaos to start. If the attackers breached the wall, the archers would fall back and allow the spear men forward to deal with the invaders. Captain Brota walked along the wall.

'Wait until I give the word to shoot. When the towers come into range, make sure your arrows are lit with fire.'

Closer and closer, the black armoured Dragon men made their way to the walls. They were nearly in range when another trumpet sounded, and hundreds of Dragon men ran forward with long ladders and shields held high into the air to provide protection from above. Captain Brota let out a shout. 'Fire!'

Hundreds of arrows were released into the air and came down on the attacking troops, felling large numbers. Most arrows missed or were deflected from the black armour. They reloaded and took aim again and the Captain shouted again 'Fire.' Even more Dragon soldiers went down with horrible wounds, but they still came. The men running with the ladders reached the base of the walls and heaved the ladders up against them, rushing upwards to the ramparts. Men fell as they climbed, with arrows jutting out of their bodies. As they reached the tops of the ladders, they were met with long spears thrusting out at them.

'Kill any man that breaches this wall,' the Captain shouted.

The noise level increased as more and more soldiers reached the top of the wall, but none were able to gain ground on the ramparts. The siege towers were moving in close, and a rain of fiery arrows were launched against them. The arrows stuck in, but were unable to catch the towers alight, as they had been drenched with water to keep them fire resistant. The huge siege towers were moved into place just short of the wall, with all the fighting going on around them. Then the bridges were dropped with a thud into place from the top of the towers, allowing the Dragon soldiers to pour out along the bridges and onto the battlements of the wall. The fighting was furious. The sound was almost unbearable now with shouting and yelling, as men died with horrible wounds and fear in their eyes. At first, the Dragon soldiers looked like they were unstoppable, as they pushed the defence back on the wall. Captain Brota gave orders to the bowmen to shoot at the men coming along the bridges from the towers. The defenders on the wall focused their arrows on the attackers coming across the bridge. They were getting cut down as they tried to cross over. This slowed the ferocity of the attack, and the Royal soldiers started to push them back, regaining control of the wall. Waves upon waves of Dragon soldiers ran to the walls and amongst them, an enormous battering ram was pushed into place at the gates to the wall. A loud boom sounded out as a rhythm started, with a swinging arm being smashed into the gate with its iron ramming tip. Hearing this, Brota pushed his way to the back of the defenders and down the stone steps to the ground, where 300 ground defence forces were standing at the ready.

'Have your arrows notched and ready and hold steady men.'

The banging on the gates increased as the battle continued up on the wall. Then, a loud cracking noise sounded out over all the chaos and the ram came through the wooden gate with a burst of splintered wood. The ram was moved a few feet to the side, and then continued striking. Then, one of the gates shifted on its hinges and on the next bang, it broke open and the Dragon soldiers pushed through. Arrows flew into them, cutting and piercing the attacking force. Captain Brota fell back to his awaiting 150 Royal horsemen, who were carrying long lances. He mounted his horse, and they prepared for their attack on the black masses bursting through the gates. The 300 defending the gate were overcome and killed in a matter of minutes. The Mounted Royal lancers then charged and smashed into the oncoming hordes, killing a multitude of men, but still they came. They thrusted with their lances, spearing and stabbing as they moved forward into the crowd. The Captain stabbed out at a Dragon Soldier. The lance sliced through the gap between the top of his breast plate and his face guard and buried itself in his neck. The dying soldier clung to the shaft as he fell to the ground, pulling the lance from the Captain's grip. The Captain then drew his sword, hacking left and right. The horsemen were soon overcome. A short sword sliced down from his blocking thrust and buried itself into his leg. Pain shot through him. He could no longer hold off the attackers. He felt his horse weaken as they stabbed at its flank, and the horse stumbled. He was nearly surrounded now as he fought. He heard a rush from behind him as two mounted Royal horsemen pushed in to help him. As the Captain's horse fell beneath him, he felt his white cloak being tugged backwards. One of his men pulled him back and the Captain turned and climbed onto the horse behind his rescuer. The man kicked his mount and the horse broke through onto open ground and galloped away. He could hear thudding noises as arrows hit the ground behind them as they moved away further from the fighting. At a safe distance, Captain Brota looked back as they sped off. The wall was overcome, and he could see the last of his men being swamped by the black hordes of the Empire. The last thing he saw was the Royal white flag with the Red Lion's head, being cut down. The wall was taken, and now the Empire was free to move their forces into the lands of The Latonian Kingdom. They needed to get back to Kitia as fast as they could, so they could inform the King of what had just happened here. As they rode on, Captain Brota could feel the pain in his leg where he had been injured. He realised then that his whole leg was covered in blood. There was nothing he could do but to keep holding onto the rider, and hope that they would not be pursued by the Dragon soldiers.

16

Thianni rushed to her room and changed into her old clothes. She could not wait to see Kalin. As she opened her door, she jumped back with a fright to see her Auntie, Queen Lesta, standing on the other side.

'Thianni, we need to talk.'

Thianni sighed as she knew she had been caught and her heart sank for she knew this could be the end of her relationship with her new friend Kalin and her trips to the market. The Queen entered and sat at a table at the other side of the room. Thianni closed the door and joined her. The Queen spoke first.

'Now I need you to listen to me. I know you have been sneaking to the market. This I don't mind, as we all need time away from our duties, but it can be very dangerous for a princess to go beyond the palace walls unaccompanied. If you must go out, you will need an escort, but I will draw the line at you fraternizing with foreigners. I have been informed that you have been meeting with a savage boy.'

The Queen paused and corrected herself. 'A northern boy, outside of the palace, in secret.' Thianni went to defend herself, but the Queen cut her off. 'Please do not try to deny this.' Thianni looked like she was about to cry, and the Queen noticed and did not want to upset her further. 'Thianni you must understand, the King and I have vowed to take care of you as best we can, and if that means leading you in a different direction, well, that is what we will do. This is one of the reasons that we keep you and Little Rain out of the public eye.'

The Queen took in a deep breath and reached out and held Thianni's hand.

'You are becoming a woman, and the last thing you want is to have your thoughts being led astray. You have a very important role here as a Princess. You are needed here at the palace.'

Thianni remained quiet for a while and then spoke.

'how did you know?'

'Little goes on within this city that I do not know. I have my little birds watching everywhere.'

Thianni looked uncomfortable.

'I really like this boy. He is my friend.'

'I know. Just give it some time and see how you feel then. We love you very much and we just want to see the best for you.'

The Queen then rose and kissed her cheek and left the room. As soon as she was gone, tears started to form in Thianni's eyes. She then threw herself on her bed and cried.

Kalin and Chal spent all of their spare time either running through the woods and hills, or practicing sword fighting in secret. They would go over all the techniques and drills that Master Ultan had taught Chal in his training sessions. Kalin had noticed that Chal's sword fighting had improved greatly. As the weeks sped by, the snow slowly melted away and the promise of summer was closing in as the days got warmer. Both Kalin and Chal's fitness improved, and the hill runs were becoming easier and faster. Kalin met with Caitria when he could. Her visits to Mara's stall were infrequent but Kalin enjoyed her company immensely and even though she was very secretive of her home life Kalin had got to know her well. He found himself thinking about her often and this made him feel happy.

More and more people were arriving in Kitia for the summer celebrations and for the King's Birthday. The marketplace was crowded every day now and all inns and guest houses were full. There were tents set up outside the city walls to accommodate further travelers that needed places to stay. There were also areas cordoned off with rope for the various venues and events that were to take place, such as the wrestling, archery and sword fighting, and the start and finish of the hill running. Kalin was only entering into the hill running event, while Chal was entering into both. Kalin would not be allowed to enter the sword fighting because he was a foreigner, and not permitted to hold a weapon, and he did not want to enter into the wrestling event because of his size. He knew he would be unfairly put in against men. It was the evening before the start of the feast, and Kalin was making his way back to the city. He was coming back from Chal's parents' villa, where they had gone over the plan and tactics for the next day. He had reached the tented area set up outside the city walls when he saw a few girls handing out food to some of the poorer people that had arrived for the festival. He stopped still in disbelief when he noticed Caitria was among them. She looked magnificent. Her hair was tied up in a design that only the nobles wore, and she was wearing a long white gown with fine detailed patterns on it. There were two Royal Guards following the group of girls closely. He could feel a powerful attraction towards her and had to go to her. As he got close, she looked up and, seeing him approach, her smile left her face and her cheeks started to go red. She looked around to see if any of the other girls that she was with were watching.

'Hi Caitria!' Kalin said in a friendly voice.

'Oh! Hi.' she replied, hesitantly.

Kalin went to hold her hand and kiss it, but as soon as he touched her hand, she pulled away from him. There was a pause as he thought she was playing.

'Can I offer you some food?'

Kalin was confused by her reaction towards him. Had he done something wrong?

'You look beautiful.'

She turned away and handed out some bread to a few young children sitting on the grass playing and glanced towards the other girls again. This time they were watching her.

'I am very sorry; I can't speak to you right now I am very busy at the moment.'

She turned and walked away. Her abruptness tore through him; he felt his heart sink as he watched her walk away from him. He had never seen her like this before; did he do or say something wrong? He felt like he had always felt, an outsider in these lands, he felt alone. The final preparations for the summer feast and the King's Birthday were made and the day had finally come. Kalin did not sleep too well that night as he could not stop thinking about Caitria and her reaction towards him. What had gone wrong? He did not want to lose her. He was up early to help prepare the food with Mara, but Mara was letting Kalin off early that day as he knew he was entered into the hill run. Kalin set off to the bakery. Normally there would be very few people around on the streets this early, but already there were crowds of people getting ready for the day's events. Kalin had not seen so many people in one place before. The morning went in fast and, after he was done helping Mara, he made his way outside the city to meet up with Chal. Chal was standing talking to a few boys around his own age when Kalin reached him.

'Good morning Chal, how are you today?'

As soon as he spoke the other boys turned and walked away.

'Good morning Kalin, are you ready for a nice run today?'

'I am, and I am hoping to beat some of these boys, especially the ones that can't even stand to be around me.'

Kalin gestured to the boys that Chal had just been talking to.

'Pay no attention to them Kalin.' Chal said, trying to help lighten Kalin's mood.

'When does your sword fencing start?' Asked Kalin.

'It starts shortly I think, then there is a break for the running, and then, if I am lucky to make it through, the finals will be on later today. I would love to make it that far. Father would be so proud of me!'

'You have improved greatly; you will definitely make it to the final. I don't think there is anyone that can match you here, Chal.'

The two friends moved off towards the sword area and Chal began to stretch and warm up. Kalin wanted to tell Chal about his meeting with Caitria but decided not to, as it might divert their focus from the games at hand. They moved through the crowds and over to the combat area. There were five large circles marked out on the ground and the racks of swords were lined up ready to go. The blades were blunt and there was red grease coated along the rounded edges so the fighters could see if there was a successful strike made on an opponent. A trumpet sounded out to call all fighters to the rings and names were called out by an official.

The Official then called out: 'Welcome everyone from near and far. We have a full day of entertainment for you all. Firstly, we will start with the boy's sword fighting and then we will have the foot racing. Later tonight, we will have the men's sword fighting. I hope you all enjoy it. Now, let the games begin.'

The crowd cheered and the first ten young boys walked over to the racks and chose their swords. Then they stepped into their designated rings. Each ring had a referee, and a second referee outside the ring to time the bouts with a sand timer, so all were given an equal amount of time. Every time an opponent was struck, a point would be given to the attacker. Whoever had the most points at the end of the time would move on to the next stage and his defeated opponent would leave the tournament. Kalin watched in awe, his head quickly turning right and left to try and watch as much as he could of all five rings as the competition went on. Although it was controlled, only a tournament and not for real. He felt very nervous for Chal, he so longed to be taking part himself. Chal's name was called and he turned to smile at Kalin. Kalin patted him on the back and wished him good luck.

'Go show them Chal.'

Chal walked over to the racks and tested a few swords. Happy with one, he calmly made his way to ring number 4 and waited for his opponent. His opponent was around the same age as Chal, but slightly taller. The timer was set, and the ref signaled to start. The two boys circled one another and the taller boy launched forward with an attack which Chal easily repelled, skipping forward with lightning speed, and scoring with two strikes, one to the arm and one to the chest. As the bout went on, Kalin noticed Master Ultan standing within the crowd, watching with a faint smile on his face. An official sounded the end of the bout and Chal had won with 9 points to zero, progressing easily on to the next level. There looked to be around 200 competitors entering in the sword competition. Kalin noticed the skill level was extremely good but felt that Chal was better. Chal had beaten all his opponents with ease, but as the day wore on, the skill level increased. Much to Kalin's dislike, Brin had entered the tournament and was also doing really well, also winning all of his bouts. Kalin noticed that Master Ultan was paying close attention to Brin's fights. The tournament went on, and they were finally down to the last four boys. Chal had made it through impressively with no injuries, as other boys had received nasty injuries such as cuts and bruises and one boy had two fingers broken. Also, Brin had made it through, along with a rather large, muscular boy with long blonde hair called Ram, and another boy named Jael, who was the son of one of the City's captains. The finals would be held later that day and would be the highlight of all the games. A trumpet sounded after a short while to announce the start of the hill run. Kalin started to feel butterflies in his stomach, as all the boys that were running made their way to the registration tent to receive their coloured scarves. Chal caught up with Kalin as they walked to the tent.

'Well what did you think of the sword fighting?'

'I loved it, you were magnificent, and I think you have a great chance now of winning the whole tournament.'

'You would have done just as well Kalin. You are every bit as good as me.'

Kalin sighed, 'Maybe one day I will be allowed to enter. So how are you feeling now? Will you be rested enough for the running after all those fights?'

'I think so, we still have a bit of time before the race starts.'

The two boys received their different coloured scarves and made their mark beside their colour on a large sheet of paper that documented all the runners. They then made their way to the refreshment tent to get some water. Kalin kept scanning the crowds, hoping he might get a glimpse of Caitria. Chal noticed that he was a bit on edge.

'Well are you going to tell me what is on your mind Kalin?'

Kalin looked at him with sad eyes.

'I always know when something is eating at you.'

They made their way to a patch of grass a short way from the crowd and sat down to chat and drink their water. Behind a tent on the other side of the circus, Brin and 3 other boys huddled around each other, a very small boy called Mouse and two brothers called Atal and Abtar.

'So, here's what's going to happen. The savage has entered the race with Chal, so I think we will need to play a little trick on him. After all, he is owed one from me at this stage.'

'Are you sure you want to be doing that Brin? He had the look of a wild man in his eyes the last time you messed with him. He was about to take you on, even though you had a knife.' said the smallest of the boys in the group.

Brin's hand lashed out and grabbed him by the neck and squeezed tightly.

'You keep your mouth shut Mouse. I'm sick of your nagging, you are the most irritating person that I know.'

Mouse struggled and tried to free himself, but Brin was too strong for him.

'Are you saying that he would have beaten me?'

Mouse tried to shake his head to say no, as he was being choked.

'I would have bled him that day if it weren't for that big black man that interrupted me.'

Brin released his grip and the young boy fell forward onto his hands and knees, coughing and holding his throat.

'Now, no more interruptions, here's the plan.'

The bunch moved in closer and Brin pulled in Mouse so he could hear.

'I have a small part in this plan for a small boy, so listen up Mouse.'

Kalin told Chal about his last meeting with Caitria and the fact that he had not stopped thinking about her.

'There is a lot to think about Kalin. Maybe she does not want to see you anymore?'

Kalin looked like his heart sank when Chal told him that, and Chal felt bad for him.

'I mean she might be busy and has not got the time to see you just yet. After all, she did say she was busy.'

'Yes, she did. But it wasn't what she said that hurt, it was the way she said it. She seemed sad when she spoke to me. I have not seen her like that before. There is something different. I can't explain it.'

'Well, I think that we should concentrate on running this race and then the sword fighting and then we should drink a few mugs of cider and ale and then I will help you find her. She has to be around somewhere. Sure, everyone for 200 miles is here today.'

The two friends wrapped their scarves around their necks and made their way to the starting point to begin the race. There were over 300 boys entered in the race and it seemed the crowd of spectators had grown even bigger now. The distance of the race was 14 miles. The path was marked out with ropes. Some of the terrain was through forests and rough ground. The hills were also very steep in places. The path would go around two mountains and loop back again to the finish line just outside of the city walls. It was a tough run, but Chal and Kalin had done their training and were well prepared. Chal and Kalin moved through the gathering of boys to try and get as close to the front as possible. The two friends were eager to start. They had moved into a tight area of boys at the front. Kalin tried to push thoughts of Caitria from his mind.

'Well, are you ready Kalin?'

'I am, my friend.'

'Best of luck Chal.'

'You too Kalin. I think we should try and keep a fast pace together going over the hills. That way we can push each other, and, on the return, we should make our sprint to the finish.'

Kalin agreed with a nod. A horn sounded out for all runners to get ready, and the noise among the crowd diminished. Moments later, a second horn sounded out and the runners surged forward. The race was under way. Chal and Kalin pushed forward with a very fast pace and after a while they were within the leading pack of runners. The lead pack had started to break away from the main bulk of the runners and, as they hit the steep sloping hills the running line thinned out, separating the fittest of the boys from the rest. The sun was beating down and Kalin could feel his heart pumping in his chest and his blood was flowing. He felt his lungs expanding as he took in the fresh air. His legs did not seem tired and he felt exhilarated, he felt like he could run forever. All thoughts of Caitria had vanished from his mind. There were three boys ahead of him and Chal at the lead. They were not too far ahead. He sped up to try and catch them and Chal fell behind slightly. Kalin noticed he was struggling to keep up. Kalin looked back quickly.

'Are you OK Chal?'

'Yes fine, keep going I will keep up with you.'

Kalin sped up again and was now level with the lead runner, a tall lean boy. He looked over at him and smiled as he passed him and took the lead. Chal was just behind him. The hill grew even steeper as Kalin and Chal moved away from the runners behind them, creating a gap. They were about halfway into the race and Kalin was still leading with Chal a few steps behind. They had pulled away from all the other runners now and could not see them down on the path. They crested the top of a hill and Kalin felt alive. He did not seem tired at all. They started down the other side of the hill so Kalin slowed slightly to let Chal come up alongside him. Chal was looking very tired now.

'Are you sure you are ok Chal?'

'I am struggling to keep up with you now.'

'Take the lead Chal and I will fall back and match your pace for a while. The rest of the runners are very far behind, we can relax a bit now.'

Chal did not argue. Kalin slowed and Chal took the lead and the pace was slowed down and felt more comfortable for Chal now. Up ahead on the trail, Mouse hunched down in the undergrowth at the side of the path. As instructed, he had tied a rope to a large tree on the other side of the path and trailed it across to where he was hiding.

Brin had said, 'Pull the rope tight as the savage passes and make him trip. If I don't see him coming back with bloody knees, I will give you a beating you won't forget little Mouse.'

Brin had beaten him before, and it had taken weeks for him to recover from it. He did not want Brin to do the same again. Mouse peeped out of his hiding spot in the bushes, holding the rope in his small hands. He peered down along the path and could see the savage just coming over the hill with Chal, the General's son, close behind him. He thought the savage was in the lead. He could hear the sound of running, followed by the deep fast breaths of the two runners just as they got close. Mouse pulled back hard on the rope, raising it a foot above the path with full strain. He felt the savage trip and then a thudding noise hitting the path with a groan. He let go of the rope and scrambled back down through the undergrowth in an effort to escape the savage in case he turned on him. He ran as fast as he could. He stopped briefly and looked back to see if he was being pursued and, to his dismay, saw the savage boy standing over Chal, who was lying on the ground. He had tripped the wrong person! He was certainly in for a beating now. He disappeared into the bushes, contemplating whether he would return to Kitia or not. Chal sat up, holding his arm, with a trickle of blood running down his forehead.

'Are you ok Chal?' said Kalin.

'I don't think so.'

Kalin helped Chal to his feet and he staggered slightly. Kalin braced him until he steadied himself.

'Can you still run?'

'I think so, but my arm is injured badly. It hurts to move it. I don't think I will be able to wield a sword later.'

Kalin cursed. 'It was a small child that tripped you, I saw him run off through the bushes.'

Kalin went to go after the boy but Chal called him back.

'We don't have time for that right now Kalin.' Just then, the tall runner passed by them and took the lead position. 'Kalin you can't let him win. You need to go and win this race.'

'I don't want to leave you like this.'

'I'll be ok, I just need a minute to rest and I will follow you then.'

'Are you sure?'

'Yes go. Go and win this race.'

Kalin reluctantly took off after the lead runner. It took a while, but Kalin eventually caught up with him. Kalin was amazed with himself that he was not out of breath and was not feeling tired. Kalin passed by the taller boy and took the lead with ease heading on to the final straight. There were hundreds of spectators waiting to see who would come in first. He could hear the cheering as he got closer. As he passed the finish line, the cheering diminished as they saw it was a boy from the north that had won the race. Kalin did not care. He had a smile on his face as he passed the finish line. Reesa was there with Mara, calling his name. The taller boy then came in, followed by a smaller young boy and then Chal came wearily in holding his arm. Kalin was waiting for him at the finish line. His mother was in the crowd waiting to see him finish and came running up to him.

'Are you ok?'

'Yes Mother, I had a slip on the hillside, that's all.'

Reesa ran to Kalin and hugged him. Followed by Mara. Kalin noticed the same black man that had saved him from Brin's knife was in the crowd, watching the race. He gave Kalin a smile and then disappeared into the masses of people. Then the rest of the runners started to come in. Trumpets sounded and the King and his family and associates came in and took their seats on a high, raised dais. Most onlookers clapped as they watched on. When all of the runners had crossed the finish line, an announcer stepped forward and announced the winning names from the race. Kalin was called forward and he placed his scarf on top on the ceremonial pole, followed by second, third and fourth place. Then the trumpets sounded for the last four sword fighters to come forth. Chal made his way over still clutching his arm. The crowd had grown even bigger to see the last few bouts before the feast. The officials moved everyone back to make space. The four finalists walked over to choose their swords. King Roban was sitting with the Queen, his young son Prince Rain, and Princess Thianni, along with generals and the rest of the Royal representatives. The King leaned back and spoke to General Titus, who was seated behind the King in the stands.

'I believe your son is the favourite to win the sword fighting. He must take after his father. I have heard he is the best sword fighter in the Kingdom.'

'Don't say that too loud my King, General Arthen might hear you. He might want to challenge me'

The King laughed out loud. 'Now that would be a bout worth watching.'

The King turned and drank deeply from his cup. He noticed that Titus's son was struggling to lift the sword he had chosen. He gestured to an official to come over.

'Check on that young man there, I think he is carrying an injury.'

The official called Chal over and checked his arm. He went to move it and Chal gave out a yelp. The official came back to the King and spoke quietly. The King then stood. The crowds became silent as he spoke.

'It appears that one of our fine young sword fighters has an injury. Please come forward Son of Titus.'

Chal walked over to the stands. He gave a low bow, feeling embarrassed now as all eyes were upon him, including his fathers.

'The official has informed me that he thinks your arm is broken. Is this true?'

'I think so too, your honour.'

'How did this happen?'

Brin was standing with the other two finalists, watching the conversation take place between the King and Chal; sweat was beginning to form on his brow.

'I fell while taking part in the hill run your honour.'

'And you were still going to take part in the sword fighting, even though you had hurt yourself badly?'

'Yes, my Lord.'

There was a moment of silence. Chal stood there with his head bowed, feeling ashamed. Then the King's voice boomed out.

'What a brave young man you are, don't you think so?' he addressed the crowd, and a huge cheer went up. The King signalled for quietness.

'As you are not able to take part, I will allow you to choose another boy to take your place. Is there someone you would like to ask to take on this challenge?'

Chal looked up with a smile on his face. 'I wish for my friend Kalin Ruane to fight in my place.'

A whoosh of talking took place amongst the onlookers and Brin wiped his brow. The official leaned into the King uneasily.

'I believe that will not be possible my Lord as he is a…'

The official paused, 'a foreigner, my Lord.'

'And?' The King retorted.

'And foreigners are not permitted to handle any weapons in our Kingdom, my Lord.'

The King leaned towards the official. 'I do believe I am the King and I make the rules around here. In any case, it's my Birthday. I feel like doing something new. Let the foreign boy fight for his friend Chal.'

The official went bright red. 'Yes, my Lord, as you wish.'

The official walked forward to the centre and called out.

'Could Kalin Ruane come forth?'

The King looked at Queen Lesta and she gave the King a dirty look. 'I do believe you are becoming soft in your old age.' The King's laugh boomed out. Princess Thianni had a silk scarf draped across her face and looked like she was trying to hide in her seat. As Kalin walked forward there was a mumbling amongst the onlookers. He stopped in front of the Official.

'You have been chosen to enter into the tournament to represent Chal Cassian as he is no longer able to compete. Do you accept this?'

Kalin nodded enthusiastically. 'Yes, I do.'

'Go then and choose your sword.'

As Kalin walked off to the sword racks, he could see Chal beaming with pride, and the look of disappointment in Brin's face. The first bout was between Brin and Jael. Jael came out fast and aggressive, but Brin was able to defend and then counter. Both fighters were skilled with the sword and well matched. In the end, Brin emerged the winner, scoring 16 strikes to Jael's 14, and progressed to the final bout of the tournament. Then Kalin and Ram were called. Kalin could feel the nerves building in the pit of his stomach. Ram was impressive looking; he had huge broad shoulders and not an ounce of fat on his body. He stood a full head taller than Kalin, Kalin wondered if his size would slow him down? He had to be good though, as he had made it this far. Kalin would have the element of surprise as no one had seen him fight yet, and no one would know he had months of practise with Chal and was using Master Ultan's techniques. The sun had started to drop in the sky and Kalin could feel a cool breeze on his skin as the two boys faced each other and the Official gave the word to fight. Ram instantly leapt forward, surprising Kalin with his speed. Kalin parried the attack and continued circling. Ram attacked again, this time it was more focused and Kalin struggled to defend it. Ram's sword glanced off Kalin's side on a return cut, leaving a small red mark on his tunic, and he was awarded a strike. The crowd cheered at the level of skill that was being performed. Kalin launched his own attack, scoring two strikes. The Queen noticed that Thianni was on the edge of her seat watching the bout. The time seemed to stand still for Kalin, as he focused on the moment. Ram was a very skilled swordsman, and Kalin could not help but like him. Kalin forced the pace of the fight and was able to score several more strikes but Ram gained a few more of his own. The Timer shouted time and the bout was over. The scores were added up and Kalin was awarded the win with 8 strikes to 5 and moved to the final against Brin. The crowd cheered and a break was announced before the final by the Official.

'We will resume in one hour so the finalists can rest before the final.'

The crowd dispersed and the stalls were busy serving fine food and drink. Brin made his way over to his friends, Atal and Abtar, where they congratulated him on his win over Jael.

'Where is that little Mouse? I am going to kill him. He could not do one little thing. Trip the Savage up.'

The other boys remained quiet in case they got brought in on the antics.

'Well, we'll have to catch this Savage out and I have an idea. You two.' He pointed to the fighting ring. 'When the official is not looking, I want you to clear the racks from all the swords bar two. Leave the sword I was using. You'll know it because it has a red handle and if you look at the back of the racks there is an old mock display sword that weighs the same weight as a small horse, leave that in the rack too. Only leave those two, OK?'

The two boys rushed off to complete their instructions. The official looking after the swords re-greased the swords that were used in the two bouts. Satisfied he walked off to get a drink leaving the swords unattended. The Queen stood and bowed to the King.

'I think I will have a walk and try some of the foods.'

She left the stand and an empty seat between the King and the Princess. She was followed by two royal guards. The King shuffled over to the Queen's seat beside Thianni.

'Well what do you think of the sword fighting my dear?'

'I like it a lot. The fighters are very impressive, especially the last bout.'

'I understand that the Queen has had a talk with you about your new friend.'

Thianni looked at the King, shocked. 'Did she tell you?'

'No, she does not know that I know.'

'Well how did you find out?'

'I have my spies too Thianni. I have known you sneak out of the palace now for a while, and to be honest, I don't blame you.'

'Are you angry with me?'

'No, not at all, how could I ever be angry at you? Everyone needs their freedom and time away from their responsibilities. Sure, how else are you to make new friends?'

'That is true, thank you for not being angry with me.'

'Why would that make me angry. I am pleased that you want to explore and meet new people. You should go and mingle, make new friends.'

'And, what if some of these friends are foreigners?'

'Some of my best friends are from foreign lands too, you know, Thianni. That should not matter one bit. I will assign a Royal guard to you full time. You will be protected when you want to go outside of the Palace.'

Thianni lifted the scarf from her face and leaned over to give the King a hug and kissed his cheek.

'Thank you, this means a lot to me.'

'I know I am the King, but first and foremost I am your uncle, and I have sworn to look after you.'

'Will the Queen be angry about this?'

'Leave that to me my dear. I know how to handle her. Now go and enjoy the celebrations. Be back here in time for the finals, it should be good.'

The King called over one of his Royal guards.

'This is Paran, he is a Captain of the guards. One of my finest and most loyal. Paran, your new position is to guard Princess Thianni in all her roles.'

Paran bowed, 'As you wish my King.'

Thianni rose from her seat, nodding to Paran, and walked from the stands out into the crowds, followed closely by her new guard. Kalin and Chal were standing by a seated area with a cup of water in hand.

'Well, didn't I tell you someday I would find a way for you to hold a sword in thc Kingdom?'

They both laughed.

'Yes, you did and thank you for that. I was scared, but I loved every minute of it.'

'Don't thank me just yet, you have a final to win for me first.'

Kalin was laughing and then stopped suddenly as he looked into the crowd. Chal looked to see what he was looking at. Thianni came waltzing up to Kalin. Chal instantly bowed.

'Your highness!'

Kalin looked confused. Thianni looked beautiful in her long dress and her hair all up high on her head.

'Kalin, I need to speak to you please.' Kalin laughed at Chal's response,

'What are you doing Chal?'

'I am paying my respects to Princess Thianni, you should do the same.'

'No, this is Caitria I was telling you about.'

'Kalin we really need to talk.'

Thianni took Kalin by the hand and led him away a few steps.

'I am sorry Kalin, I lied to you. My name is not Caitria, your friend is right. I am Princess Thianni, niece to King Roban second in line to the throne. Caitria is, was, my mother's name.'

'I don't understand.' said Kalin confused. 'How can this be? Why would you lie to me?'

'I will explain everything to you. It has been eating at me for a long time now and I don't want to lose you.'

Just then, a trumpet sounded for the last bout to begin.

'Sorry Caitria or Thianni or whatever your name is, I must go.'

'Please Kalin, talk to me after the bout. I need to tell you everything.'

Kalin turned and walked away, frustrated and angry. Kalin and Brin were called to the centre of a huge circle that had been marked out. The Official announced both their names and gestured for them to choose their swords. They walked to the rack together. Brin spoke low so no one but Kalin could hear him.

'You know that trap was meant for you and not the General's son, don't you? So, I will just have to show everyone what a savage you are by giving you the worst beating right now.'

Kalin stopped and faced Brin. Brin sniggered at him.

'You have always been weak, all Savages are. I bet you can't even lift that larger sword out from the rack.'

Kalin felt his blood starting to boil and, in his anger, walked the last few steps and lifted the large sword from the rack and instantly knew he had been tricked. The sword felt really heavy and he struggled to hold it in one hand, immediately he regretted it, but it was too late. He had chosen his sword. Brin walked over and drew his sword with the red hilt from the rack and pushed by Kalin with a smug smile on his face and walked over to the circle. Kalin followed him struggling to hold the sword. He could hear some of the onlookers laughing at his dismay. Both fighters took their starting positions. Kalin quickly scanned the crowd, looking for Chal. Chal gave him a nod and as he did, Kalin also noticed the black man was amongst the crowd. He could make out faces in the crowd. His Auntie and Uncle were there. Chal's parents and all the Royals and their court. Everybody. He could feel the pressure on him now. He tried to focus. Taking a dry gulp, he readied himself. The Official stepped forward and asked both fighters were they ready. Kalin wanted to say no and ask could he change his sword, but it was too late. He had let Brin trick him into choosing the heavy sword and would now have to deal with it, all eyes were on them now. The Official shouted start, and straight away Brin launched an attack. Kalin had to hold the sword with both hands if he were to have any chance of keeping it raised in front of him for his defence. The swords clashed and they echoed out over the crowd. Brin smiled when he noticed how slow Kalin was on the defence. He jabbed the tip of his sword at him to make fun of him. The crowd responded with laughter. Kalin could feel himself getting angry again. He lifted his sword with a shout and attacked Brin, but Brin side stepped it and launched a punch into Kalin's face as he passed by. Kalin could not block the punch, as his two hands were on the sword, and winced in pain as the blow landed flush on his face. Blood started to trickle from his nose. The official gave Brin a warning for an illegal strike. Kalin let the tip of his sword rest on the ground and wiped his nose. Brin didn't give him time to get back into position and attacked again, hitting Kalin on the shoulder scoring a point. Kalin lifted the sword again and Brin was upon him once more and striking out with his sword at Kalin's face, but Kalin moved his head in time and the sword passed by his ear, just missing him. Kalin drove his shoulder into Brin's, pushing him off balance, and gained some distance between them. Kalin was getting tired now with the weight of the weapon. Again, Brin attacked with a thrust and then a reverse strike, but Kalin managed to evade the attack. Now it was Brin's turn to get angry. With each attack Kalin moved out of the way, his arms were too tired to make his own attack. The more Brin attacked, the more Kalin moved out of his way. The crowd were in awe at Kalin's movement. A wave of peace flooded Kalin, and he started to relax. This feeling was exquisite, he could feel its energy moving through his body. He no longer felt the pressures of the crowd and focused solely on his opponent. He had no thoughts or worries, and his opponent was his sole focus. It was as if the whole world had slowed down and Kalin could move fast and with ease. Time was running out, and Brin was winning the fight with two strikes to zero. Brin could feel the crowd starting to cheer Kalin on as he moved out of the way of every attack from Brin, hardly moving his own sword to defend himself. No matter what Brin tried, he could not hit Kalin. It was like fighting a ghost and now Brin was getting tired. In a rage, he launched another attack straight for Kalin's throat. Kalin dummied a move to the left and then spun to his right. As Brin followed through with the strike, Kalin used every ounce of his strength to lift his sword high up in the air and then brought it down hard, hitting Brin on the side of his jaw as he passed by. Brin fell to the ground, unconscious. The Timer Official called time, and the final match was over. Brin had won with two strikes to one. The official walked over to Brin lying on the ground still unconscious and raised his arm as the winner and dropped it. It hit the ground with a thud. The crowd clapped and cheered at the display of combat they had just witnessed, not for Brin but for Kalin with his defensive movement. Chal came running over and Kalin dropped the heavy sword to shake Chal's uninjured hand.

'That was amazing Kalin, where did you learn how to do that?'

'From fighting you.' Kalin said with a weary smile. 'I lost the fight though.'

'You won in my eyes Kalin, and everyone else's eyes too.'

They looked around and some of the people were still clapping for Kalin.

'You never cease to amaze me; I have a huge amount of questions to ask and most of them involve you being friends with the Princess. Now let's get a drink and celebrate.'

As the two friends walked off, Kalin looked over to the Royal stand, but it was empty. They had all left, including the Princess. The night came in fast and there was music and dancing and food and drink. Everyone was happy. Kalin and Chal were sitting on a haystack after watching the men's sword bouts. Barra, The Kings Champion, had won again this year, retaining his title. Kalin and Chal each had a cup of ale in hand and were deep in thought. Chal had had his arm looked at earlier by a doctor and it was in a sling. Chal was mocking Kalin about the Princess when Chal's Mother and father came over to them, arm in arm.

'Well my son, how is your arm?'

General Titus was looking a bit tipsy.

'It's OK Father, the doctor said he thought it was broken, but not badly. Maybe cracked. He did not have to reset it and said to keep it well rested.'

'That is good to hear, and how about you Kalin? You fought very well today and did Chal proud fighting in his name. You took first place in the race and second in the sword fighting. Not a bad day's work for you. I have never seen anyone defend in a sword fight with such speed, well done!'

'It felt good, being able to hold a sword.'

'Well, you are part of history now. I cannot remember any other north man being allowed to hold a weapon in the Kingdom, let alone being able to enter into the tournament.'

'Thank you General.'

Chal's father leaned in to the two boys, 'You young men take it easy on that ale and have a good night. I am proud of your actions today; you both showed respect and acted like true men. See you in the morning.'

Chal's mother also leaned in; she kissed her son on the cheek and then ruffled Kalin's hair.

'You boys have fun now.'

They both walked off.

'So Chal, what next?'

'What do you mean?'

'What's next for you?'

'I am going to have a few more drinks and then look for a good-looking girl with big breasts to dance with.'

Kalin laughed, 'I meant, what next in your life?'

'Oh, that, what's next. I will be 16 next week, and then I will be old enough to join the Royal army.'

'You might have to wait until your arm is fully healed before you start the training.'

'Yes, that is true, but I think the first few weeks we have to work on our fitness. Then there is lots of theory, and rules to be learned before we start our combat training and are allowed to hold real weapons. My arm should be good by then. What about you Kalin? What is next for you Kalin?'

'I'm not sure, I think I will just still work for my uncle. I won't be 16 until the end of the summer, so I won't be able to choose a trade until then, but I might learn how to bake like my uncle.'

A group of four girls walked past, and all looked at the two boys as they passed. They were all giggling. One girl gave Chal a broad smile. Chal looked at Kalin with a mischievous grin.

'Never mind about those other ales I have just seen the love of my life!'

With that, he jumped up and ran after the group. Kalin laughed as Chal let out a yell. He had forgotten about his arm and had tried to push off the hay bale he had been sitting on. He looked comical as he ran off with a waddle, holding his injured arm. There was a thud next to Kalin and he turned to see Thianni sitting beside him on the bale. Thianni was wearing a different dress now, simpler than the one she had been wearing earlier in the day, but she still looked beautiful. She was smiling at him and Kalin wanted to grab her and kiss her right there and then, but he did not. He wanted her to know he was still unhappy with what she had done. He turned from her and took a drink from his cup.

'Oh, Kalin don't be mad at me. I am sorry for lying to you. I wanted to come here tonight and explain why I did what I did. Will you listen to what I have to say?'

Her smile was starting to fade.

'I will. But before you start, I just want you to know that you hurt me, and I thought you were different from everyone else.'

Kalin immediately felt bad for saying that and turned away again. He could see that there was a Royal guard watching them from off to the side. He turned back around so they were face to face.

'I am sorry too Thianni, I should not be speaking to you like this.'

She smiled and nodded.

'Let me begin at the start. I had to sneak out of the palace so I could get a break away from my duties as a princess. I loved going to the marketplace and looking at what the stalls have to offer and talking to new people. I am not allowed to leave the Palace most of the time because of who I am. My life is very boring. Then I met you. I really liked you and was afraid that you would not like me if I told you that I was a Princess.'

'Why would I have not liked you? I know what it is to feel disliked, coming from the north.'

'Thank you.' She said and held his hand. 'I know you must often experience a lot of prejudice, living here in Kitia, and it must have been really hard for you and your Auntie. At times I feel ashamed of my people, that they would look down on outsiders like you. I know you have had it hard living here, and they have been mean to you, but,' she paused for a second, 'I am a girl living here, and I am treated the same as you. All girls are looked down on and seen as second class. We have no say and are expected to go along with what the men want. We are not even allowed to enter into the Summer Games, as you were. We are also not allowed to carry any weapons. I am the niece of the King and I experience these things. I know what other girls or women have to go through in their lives living here. So, you can see I understand how things are. I am truly grateful for meeting you and I promise I will not lie to you ever again. Will you forgive me?'

Kalin felt a little ashamed now, hearing what Thianni and other women had to go through too.

'Of course, I will, Thianni. I had never looked at it from a girl's point of view before. So, I want to say sorry to you too.'

Thianni moved in close. Kalin looked into her brown eyes and realised again how beautiful she was. Just then, Thianni moved her lips to Kalin's and kissed him. It was the first time a girl had kissed him, and he felt his head spinning and did not know if it was the kiss or the ale. Her lips felt soft and warm and he pulled her in tight. All his anger, fear and doubt dissipated in that instant and nothing seemed to matter anymore but this kiss. She pulled away and looked over in the direction of her guard.

'I must go now Kalin. It is the King's birthday tomorrow and the celebrations will carry on. I have lots to prepare for this, and other work has to be done for the Queen. If I sneak out tomorrow night, can you meet me?'

'I would love to.'

'I will meet you here tomorrow night.'

She stood and Kalin looked up at her. She quickly kissed him again and ran off. Her guard followed her. Kalin was left with his mouth open, gazing into the night sky. He could not believe she had kissed him. He felt wanted and needed by a girl that was beautiful in every way. The feeling was amazing. He felt like the luckiest person alive. Chal came staggering back over, he was sweating from dancing and red in the face.

'Are you OK?

Is that drink going to your head?'

Kalin realised he was sitting there with his mouth open.

'Chal my friend I have never felt better in my whole life.'

Kalin sat upright in his own bed. He had had another one of his bad dreams. He could feel his head thumping with pain from all the ale he had drank the night before. He got up, dressed and walked to the kitchen. His auntie was there, cleaning plates in a bowl of steaming water. She heard him coming into the room.

'Good morning sleepy. How is my champion today?'

She turned around to meet him and saw that he was hungover.

'You don't look well Kalin, did you have too much to drink last night?'

Kalin mumbled something and sat at the table, pouring himself a cup of water and drinking it all down in one go and then wiping his mouth with the back of his hand.

'I feel like my mouth is a desert, and yes, I think I had too much to drink.'

'Well you will have to get yourself together. I was just about to wake you; you have a lot of work to do with your uncle today. This will probably be the busiest day of the year for him, baking for the King's birthday. His orders have gone through the roof and the Palace has even requested a lot of baking from him.'

Kalin filled his cup again and sank it again.

'I guess I may get going so.'

Reesa placed a plate of food in front of him. 'Not before you get something to eat, an empty sack won't stand.'

'I honestly don't think I can eat right now.'

'Trust me, after a night of drinking some food will do you the world of good. Before I go out, I just want to say that I am very proud of the young man you have turned into. You performed exceptionally well yesterday in the games. Everyone is talking about it.'

Kalin noticed that his auntie was in a particularly good mood. This agitated him as he was feeling delicate and was not able for her good humour. His auntie had been right on both statements, the food did help, and it was the busiest day of the year for the bakery. He felt like the day would never end. Every time he got back from delivering food, Mara had another order that needed to be delivered. Kalin got home later than usual and went straight to his bed. He was asleep before his head hit his pillow, but as usual his bad dreams woke him. He felt much better now and prepared to head out to meet Chal for the final evening of the celebrations, The King's Birthday.

The King's birthday celebrations went well. There was a parade that ran from the front main gate, through the marketplace and right up into the Palace courtyard where all the entertainment was. Singers and dancers performed. Acrobats and jugglers were also part of the celebrations. The King and all his family and associates were there. Most of the Generals and Captains were given time off from their duties, as were most of the Royal army. Only a few hundred Royal Guards were in uniform to keep the peace with the odd aggressive drunk that got out of hand, and these were very few. There were thousands of people present, and there was a great feeling of enjoyment amongst everyone. The King stood and made a speech.

'Thank you everyone for coming today to help me celebrate my 60th Birthday. Not only is it my birthday, but it is also the 10th anniversary of my reign as King. We have suffered in the past and lost family and loved ones, but these last 10 years have been really good to us all. We have had peace for a long time in our land now, and long may it last. I know I am 60 but I intend to keep this Kingdom of ours safe and healthy for a while longer. So, I want to say enjoy these celebrations. Don't let aging get you down. It's too hard to get back up.'

The crowd laughed.

'Let us drink to The Kingdom.'

He held up his cup and drank, and everyone there did the same. The crowd cheered and the festivities continued on. Kalin made his way to the courtyard to where the main festivities were being held. As he walked up the main road, he saw Brin standing with a few of his friends. Brin had a large bruise along his jaw line where Kalin had caught him with the heavy sword. There was also a small skinny boy with a thin face and mousey hair that was sporting two black eyes. Brin looked over and saw Kalin walking up the main road and gave him a bad look as he moved past. Kalin gave him a smirk back and kept walking. He could hear him giving out and saw his friends trying to hold him back as he tried to go after Kalin. Kalin knew it was all show though and ignored him, heading off to find Chal and enjoy the last night of celebrations. Chal was chatting to a girl and, by the looks of it, he was telling her about his injured arm. She looked very concerned about Chal's misfortune. Kalin decided not to interrupt them and wondered off amongst the crowds to look for some food to eat. He had never felt lonely or sad about spending time alone. He had been alone almost all the time when he was younger, until he had met Chal, but being by himself had never been a problem. I will catch up with him later, he thought, and headed over to a meat stall. He bought a meat pie and sat down to eat it, thinking about the last few days events. Who would have thought he could have ended up in the finals of the sword event? A Savage been allowed to hold a real sword, it was unheard of! Who would have thought he would win the race? Who would have thought he would have met a princess and fallen in love with her? The last few years, his life had been a normal boring day to day life, now it was full of excitement and wonder. How can my life get more adventurous than this? He thought.

17

There she was, Princess Thianni. She looked beautiful. He watched her from afar. Kalin did not know how to deal with his feelings towards Thianni. Was it the fact that she liked him too? Or was it that he thought she was the most beautiful girl he had ever seen? Or the fact that he knew that she was a princess? This last thought he dismissed almost immediately as he knew he felt this way about her before he knew she was a princess. It was her way. She had a wonderful way about her. She was kind and always curious. Her smile rarely left her face and she seemed content within herself. She was kind and righteous and, in her presence, she would inspire you. She was beautiful inside and out, but it was her delightful way that he liked best. Kalin knew that he had fallen for her. She was sitting down on a log bench talking to the other girls from the palace. She looked over at him in mid conversation and, as she noticed Kalin standing looking over at her, her smile beamed at him. A tingling feeling shot down his back at the sight of her. She stood and walked away from the girls and towards Kalin. She took his hand and for a second, he thought she was about to kiss him, but then she stopped and looked around at her giggling friends.

'Let's find some place where we can be alone.'

Kalin looked over and could see Thianni's guard Paran was watching them.

'Where would you like to go Thianni?'

'Wherever you want to bring me? Once it's just the two of us and it's quiet, I don't mind where we go.'

'I could take you out to Chal's parents farm and show you their villa? It is beautiful out there and they would all be here at the celebrations.'

'That would be perfect Kalin.'

'How can we get away from your guard? He hasn't stopped looking in our direction.'

'We will have to make a run for it.' Thianni said mockingly.

They both laughed at the thought of the idea and then stopped, as they knew it would be the only way to get away. They would have to run. The two walked casually away from the area and stopped to look at a stall, followed closely by Thianni's guard. A big cheer went up from the crowd as the King entered the celebrations. With that distraction, Kalin grabbed Thianni's hand and they ran through the crowd, dashing in between stalls and out onto a side street where there were less people. They then rushed down a small alleyway. Kalin knew the alleyways well from his delivering for Mara. They made their way towards the main gate. There were guards there, and people coming in and out of the gate from the tents outside the wall. As they got close, they slowed down to a walk and passed out through the gate unnoticed. Kalin steered them in the direction of the Villa on a path that turned right heading south. He noticed in the heat of the run that he was holding Thianni's hand very tightly now and he let go. She grabbed hold of his hand again and hugged in tight onto his arm with her other hand.

'You're not letting go of me that easy.'

Kalin felt like he had not a care in the world. It was dusk now and the moon had just crested the hills. There was less light outside the city and the stars shone magnificently in the clear, early night sky. They talked and laughed as they walked, comfortable in each other's presence. Kalin kept looking back, expecting to see Thianni's guard running after them, but there was no sign of him. They arrived at the villa in what seemed like no time at all, it was very dark now. The place was silent except for the farm animals settling in for the night in the surrounding fields. Kalin opened the large gates and turned back to Thianni to tell her to be quiet in case there were any farm hands around. Thianni pulled him in to her and kissed him. The kiss felt warm and wanting. They parted breathlessly.

'What was that for?'

'I've wanted to do that all day.' She paused and looked up at him. 'And every day!'

'Well in that case, please don't let me stop you.'

They heard talking in the distance and Kalin could just barely make out the silhouette of two men walking across the field, checking on the sheep. Kalin shut the gate and took Thianni's hand and they ran in through the open door to the hay barn. They listened for a while, trying not to giggle as the two men walked past the villa and faded into the night. It was dark in the barn, but Kalin could see Thianni's face, which was now lit up by a shard of moonlight that was coming in through the open doorway to the barn. She removed the pin holding up her hair and it fell free on to her shoulders. Her blonde hair almost glowed in the light. Kalin moved in close and kissed her zealously. They kissed for a while and then moved further into the barn towards the soft hay. Thianni lifted Kalin's tunic off over his head and ran her hands down his chest. She then pulled away and stood back, undoing her dress and letting it fall to the ground. Kalin could feel his arousal as he looked at her body. He could not take his eyes from her breasts. She smiled and moved towards him and kissed him again. Thianni moved her hands down to Kalin's trousers and untied the cord and they also fell to the ground. They were both naked now and they slowly lay back onto the hay. Thianni moved on top of him and he let out a sigh as she took hold of his swelling and guided it inside her. She started to move very slowly at first and it took Kalin a while to match her rhythm. Her body felt amazing, smooth and soft as she moved on top of him. Kalin felt like he was one with her. They gradually sped up, their breathing got heavier and Kalin could feel a wondrous burning sensation build up deep within his loins. As she climaxed, she clung to him tightly. He then gave one last thrust and exploded within her with a feeling he never could have imagined. They lay there holding one another in completeness. Kalin did not want this moment to ever end. They did not speak for some time, comfortable with each other's silence, they just gazed into one another's eyes. Finally, Thianni laughed.

'What should we do now?'

'I'm not sure what would you like to do?'

'There is a secluded beach just West of the city. Sometimes I go there and swim, and on occasions there are dolphins there. Swimming with them is amazing. It is one of the best feelings in the world. Apart from being with you here with you tonight. Shall we go?'

'Yes, I would very much like that, but there's just one problem.'

Thianna turned and rolled over and laid her head onto Kalin's chest. 'And what is that Kalin?'

'I can't swim.'

'Well in that case I will teach you.'

'Now that sounds like a plan to me.'

Kalin then pulled her in close and kissed her. Thianni pulled away breathless, and hugged Kalin.

'I wish we could stay like this forever.'

'Me too, but we really must leave this barn before we get caught.'

'I don't care who catches us.'

It went silent again. Then Thianni giggled.

'I am starving, let's get back to the celebrations and get some food and then I shall give you your first lesson in swimming and hopefully the Dolphins will be there.'

They both dressed quickly and slipped out of the barn and through the Gates towards the city, still holding onto one another. It was getting late now, and as they got close to the main gates of the city, they could see that the festivities were still going on. They walked in through the gates and Paran surprised them as he jumped out and grabbed Kalin by the neck.

'Where have you been with the Princess?' He shouted.

Kalin instinctively lashed out and caught Paran on the side of the head with a punch. This staggered Paran and he let go as he fell back.

'You'll pay for that foreigner.'

Paran attacked again, this time he launched his own punches. He missed with the first one as Kalin ducked, but the second blow hit Kalin on the forehead and knocked him on to his backside. Kalin went red as he saw Thianni looking at him with her mouth open. Kalin jumped back to his feet quickly and fired off blow after blow in rage. Thianni shouted for him to stop, but he kept hitting Paran.

'Stop this Kalin, stop!' but in his rage he did not hear her.

Paran fell to one knee with his hands held up high.

'I surrender I surrender!' Kalin did not stop. Paran fell backwards with the blows and then Kalin was on top of him, striking downward. Thianni ran over and pulled Kalin off him. Kalin turned and went to hit Thianni. He stopped himself just before he struck out at her. Thianni stood there in shock at what Kalin was about to do.

'I am sorry Thianni. I would never hit you.'

He could see the sadness on her face.

'I don't know what has come over you Kalin, but I do not like it. Paran was just worried about me, that is all.'

People had gathered around now to see what was happening. Thianni felt embarrassed.

'Get yourself home and I will talk to you tomorrow.'

Thianni helped Paran back to his feet and walked away, leaving Kalin there with the onlookers. Kalin felt his heart sink. He quickly walked away with his head down. He thought about what had just happened and felt ashamed. The night had been going so well. He was feeling on top of the world until Thianni's guard had grabbed him. I have ruined things, he thought. He got home and went to bed straight away. Bad dreams kept waking Kalin throughout the night and the thought of losing Thianni was breaking his heart.

18

As Karra drew closer to the Capital, he could see the huge walls that protected the city and the masses of people camping outside and around the shadow of the city's walls. Some had started to leave the celebrations, as they were at an end. He was weary now, and was looking forward to seeing his sister Reesa, and eating some of Mara's honey cakes. For the last few weeks now, bad nightmares had started back again. They were starting to be a drain on him, and he felt himself becoming short tempered with any little thing. The further he travelled from the gateway, the worse the dreams became. His mind kept drifting and he found himself thinking about bad things in his head. Killing and fighting and battle. He started to recall conflicts that he thought he had long forgotten. He tried to think about happier times. He hadn't seen Kalin since he was a very small boy and wondered what he looked like now. He made his way on towards the main gate. There were camps and tents on both sides of the road. It was early in the day and there were people still drunk from the night before. Karra rode on and dismounted just before the gate. There were guards there but they were busy chatting amongst themselves. A couple of them were drinking ale from large cups. Karra was able to walk through with his two horses without being stopped. He led his horses to a public stable and a man came out to him.

'We have no more room to stable horses today, we are full. If you come back in a day or two, we might have room.'

Karra reached into a pocket on the saddle and produced a leather pouch. He opened this and took out a gold coin.

'Will this be enough for two horses for two nights?'

The man's eyes gleamed at seeing a gold coin.

'I will make sure they are well looked after sir.'

Karra tossed the coin to the man, who caught it and instantly examined it. Karra took a couple of bags from the mounts, handed the reins over to the man and headed in towards the heart of the city. He was very tired now and was looking forward to a good night's sleep in a soft bed. His memory of where his sister lived was very vague and the city had changed a lot since he last visited. He had to ask a couple of city folk for directions. Most looked at him warily, seeing his long black hair and that he was from the north, they would just keep walking and ignore the question, but one kind lady took the time to give him directions. It was getting late when he finally reached his sister's house. He knocked on the door and waited patiently for someone to answer. He heard footsteps and then the door opened and Reesa answered the door. It took her a few seconds to realise she was looking at her older brother. She threw her arms around him and gave Karra a hug.

'Oh my, it is truly good to see you.'

'And you too my little sister. How are you keeping?'

'I am well, but you look like you have been dragged through a bush backwards. Please come in.'

Reesa took one of his bags and brought Karra through into the kitchen. His huge frame crowded the hallway.

'Please take a seat.' She gestured to a chair by the table. 'You have called at a good time. I am just about to start to make some food for Mara and Kalin. They are out at the moment. They should be home soon. It has been a long time since you were last in Kitia.'

'I think it has been 12 years or maybe even more.'

Reesa poured two cups of water and sat at the table with her brother.

'How long can you stay?'

'I have to leave to go back in two days.'

Reesa looked at him. 'I suppose you will be looking for a bed for the night?'

'Aye, I will.'

'So, what has brought you all the way down to the south? Besides Mara's baking'

Karra took a drink from the cup. 'I have come for the boy.'

There was silence; Reesa looked at him coldly. 'You are not taking him Karra.'

'Reesa, he must go. He cannot stay here. You knew this from the start, it will tear him apart.'

'He is not going anywhere Karra; he has a life here and he is content.'

'I know how this must look with me showing up out of the blue like this and I apologise for that, but we do not have any other options.'

'Karra, he has friends here, well one friend, but he is a good friend to him, and he has a job and soon a trade if he wants it and he has just started seeing a girl. Things are starting to come good for us here. He won the race in the tournament and came second with the sword fighting.'

'I am sorry Reesa but we have no other choice. It has been a hard decision, but the time is right for him now. He must come north and touch the stone.'

Reesa slammed her cup down on the table, making the water splash out. She shook her head.

'This cannot be happening. It is too soon. He is still just a boy.'

'He will be 16 soon Reesa. He is nearly a man. If I don't take Kalin north now, things will get really bad for him. You know what happens if he does not touch the gate. Have the nightmares started yet?'

Reesa nodded and looked away.

'If I do not take him, he will slowly go mad with the Calling from the Gate. I have seen it happen before to our uncle. His nightmares will get worse and he will start to get violent. The people down here will not understand, and he will be in danger. This has to be controlled and the only way to do this is to take him to the Gate.'

Karra could see that Reesa was struggling to deal with the reality of things and went to hold his sister's hand as he spoke, but she pulled away from him.

'I will look after him, little sister, and he will be trained to do his job.'

Reesa shook her head. 'I have sworn to take care of him Karra.'

'I know, and you have done a great job but, we knew this day would come.'

'Yes, but not this soon.'

They both turned as they heard the door open and Mara came walking down the hallway into the kitchen. He paused as he caught sight of

Karra. Karra stood and Mara ran over and wrapped him in a big bear hug.

'It is good to see you Karra, to what do we owe the honour of this visit?'

'He wants to take the boy away.' Reesa said in a low tone.

'Oh, that is an important matter.' He looked down at the cups of water. 'I think we might need something slightly stronger than water tonight.'

The three sat and drank wine while Karra explained the reason for his visit. Reesa had never fully explained their family's background and Mara had never asked questions about the boy staying with them. Karra felt it only right to tell Mara everything at this stage.

'Around a hundred years ago, our Great Great Grandfather, Karractus, involved himself with a dark magic. Through his dealings with this magic, he accidentally opened a gateway to another world. This world was a dark and evil place. It caused a bad energy which in turn affected our land. This unbalance then awakened The Shord, the Old Man of the Land. The Spirit of the land. The Shord tried to return the balance to the land but could not, and he punished Karractus for this negligence, setting a curse in place on our family because of Karractus's wrong doings. All the males in our family are now bound to this curse. Our job is that we have to guard the gate between these two worlds, for this magic could not be undone. If we don't guard the gate, unlimited evils can come into our world and unleash chaos. The curse is a simple one. When each male in the family becomes a man, they will be drawn to the gate, and it is their duty to guard the gate from all evil that tries to come through to our world. If we do not take up this task, it will affect us greatly. We become angry and violent, we start to lose our minds and we are tortured by the Calling of the Gate until we journey to it.'

Mara sat there trying to take it all in.

'That is immensely interesting and tragic. Reesa had tried to tell me about this story and some of the history to it years back but not in such detail. I had always thought that was just an old folk legend. I had no idea it was this serious.'

'It is very serious Mara. We can't ignore this. Our family has been tormented by this for a long time now and it will continue to torment us.'

Mara looked at Reesa and held her hand.

'I understand that this must happen, and I think you agree that this needs to happen too, but we have forgotten about one thing. Kalin. He might not want to go. We haven't asked him yet. What if he says no?'

Karra shook his head. 'He must go. There is no other option.'

They all talked into the night, waiting for Kalin to arrive home. It was very late when he did. He could hear laughter coming from the kitchen. Kalin came in all happy and beaming with a smile. The kitchen went quiet as he walked in.

'We were all just about to head to our beds, but we were waiting for you to get home. Kalin I want you to meet your Uncle Karra. He has travelled all the way from the north to see you.'

Karra stood and loomed over Kalin. He held out his hand to his nephew. His frame looked strong and sturdy. Kalin was in awe of the sheer size of the man. He was powerfully built with a thick black beard and his long black hair, which was tied back behind his head, had streaks of grey running through it. His forehead was wide with deep set pale blue eyes and his presence gave off a sense of danger. Kalin could feel energy between them and could not make out what this was, but it felt powerful. Reesa also stood and took a plate of food from the counter, laying it on the table for Kalin.

Kalin took his uncle's massive hand and shook it.

'Pleased to meet you sir.'

He could feel the power in this man as he held his hand. They both sat at the table.

A deep voice sounded out.

'You probably don't remember me; you would have only been about three when we saw each other last.'

'I do not recall,' said Kalin, trying to figure out what was going on.

'Ah, you were a small boy then, but look at you now! You are almost a man.'

Karra slapped Kalin on the shoulder making Kalin and his chair move to the side with a screech. Karra then turned around to Mara and Reesa.

'Would it be possible to talk to the boy alone?'

Reesa looked slightly panicked and placed a plate on the table with food on it with a bang in front of Kalin. She did not take her eyes of off Karra. Mara stood and took her hand, leading her from the room and closing the door behind them.

'Now you can eat, and I can talk.'

Kalin sat back and pushed the plate of food to one side.

'I am not hungry right now. I don't like the way my auntie looked when you asked her to leave, did you say something to upset her?'

'She was upset by what I told her and why I have come here. Do you know why I am here?'

'No!' Kalin said, concerned now.

'I have come here for you, Kalin. You do not know the importance of my visit yet, but I will explain everything to you.'

Kalin sat there and listened to what his uncle had to say. Karra told him everything from his Great Great Grandfather 100 years ago and all the way through up to the present. He explained about every one of his family before him that guarded the gate, and the importance of Kalin's part in taking up this role too. They were there for some time. Kalin felt numb now. He had no idea about any of this history. He did not know what to say to his uncle.

'You won't remember your father, for you were only a baby when he was killed guarding the gate, but do you remember your mother?'

'I have very vague memories of her, but I do remember some things.'

'It was heartbreaking when she passed. She had a very bad fever and it took hold of her. She was a strong woman but when your time is up it's up. You were only around four when we decided that your auntie should be the one to raise you and I have to say, she has done a great job so far.'

'Reesa and Mara have been very good to me and I owe them for that.'

'There are no debts owed to family, boy. Everything that a family does for one another is not for personal gain. It is done out of love.'

'What will happen to me now?'

'You have two options. You can stay here and try to fight off the Calling, but you will fail. Things will gradually get worse. Your nightmares will increase, and your mood will change, and you will start to feel bad in yourself. You will have a short temper and you will start to get aggressive and you will push away the people that you love. Things will get bad for you, even if you think you can control it.'

'And what is the second option?'

'The second option is that you come with me and once you are near the gate you will start to feel fine again, things will get better for you. I will teach you how to fight and guard the Gate and you will become more powerful than you can imagine.'

Kalin thought for a while. It was too much to take in all at once. He felt overwhelmed and caught between happy and sad. The thought of going with his uncle was quite appealing to him, but the thoughts of leaving Reesa, Mara and Chal and especially Thianni would be too much.

'How long would I have to be gone for?'

'It would be indefinitely Kalin, but you can come back and visit for periods of time. The gate stays closed for most of the time. This enables us to plan around it like I have done, but to be far from the gate for too long can be harmful for us. I know this is a lot to take in. I cannot make you take this journey with me to the north, to the gate, but know this. If we do not guard the gate, hell itself will come into our world. It is getting very late and I am very tired from my travels. Let us go to bed and you can sleep on it and we can talk more about it tomorrow. But think very strongly on what I have said, for all men, women and children will be protected because of our family's curse.'

Kalin woke to the sound of screaming. He rose from his bed and tried to open his door, but it would not open. He could hear horrible sounds. They were coming from outside; he ran over to his window to look out. What he saw shocked him to his bones. There was an opening like a void hovering a few feet above the ground in the air. There was a black mass coming from this void. It poured out onto the ground beneath and was moving slowly outwards, the movement was very bizarre. The streets were full of people who all seemed to be running from the blackness. As they tried to run, they looked like they were stuck to the ground as their legs would not move and the black mass slowly engulfed them. More and more of the blackness poured out of the void, like fog creeping along. Dread took over him and he tried to break out through the window, but it would not break. He then saw his auntie

Reesa standing looking at the blackness, with Thianni standing by her side. He shouted to them. 'RUN!' but they could not hear him. The blackness was nearly upon them. He turned and ran for the door. Not stopping, he ran into it with all his might in the hope of breaking through it. The door broke open and he fell out onto a desert plain on his hands and knees. No longer was he at his home in Kitia. He was somewhere else now. The ground beneath his hands felt dry, and the air was hot. He stood up still looking around to see his aunt and Thianni but there was no one to be seen. He was alone. His throat burned as he breathed in the hot air. He stood on the hot sands and looked around. There were two enormous sized moons almost touching in the red sky. One moon was silver and the other one gold in colour. Kalin walked over to the edge of what looked like a plateau he was standing on and looked down to a valley below. He could see a column of what could only be described as monsters or beasts, all walking in a long line. Their skin was a grey green colour and they were all armed with weapons. They looked bigger than a man, maybe twice the size; even at a distance they looked huge. They were all lined up and waiting their turn to pass through a gateway. It looked like a mass migration or an invasion? There were carts and supplies and some kind of dog-like creatures with them. As they passed through the gateway, they seemed to disappear. For some reason, Kalin knew that they were all heading to his world, thousands of them, and fear touched him like cold hands. This did not feel like a dream, it felt real. He heard movement coming from behind him and as he turned, a huge creature was bearing down on him. It was also holding some kind of weapon that looked like an oversized axe. The creature raised its huge muscular arms up and brought down the weapon on Kalin. He raised his hands in defence, but the weapon crashed down on to his head. Then there was blackness.

Kalin suddenly woke and sat upright in his bed, dripping with sweat. His head thumped with a headache. He felt like he needed to get sick. He turned in his bed and retched but he did not vomit. He felt very emotional after the dream and was glad that it was over. He remembered what Karra had said to him the night before, 'Things will get worse!' He could hear talking and laughter coming from the kitchen. He recognised the sounds. It was his auntie's laughter and Mara's booming voice. He went to get up out of bed but fell back. To his dismay his legs felt very weak. He tried again to stand and managed to get his balance. He dressed very slowly and shuffled across his room and out his door and went to join them. There were several empty plates in front of Karra and he was sitting looking very content rubbing his belly.

'Good morning Kalin, I have to say your auntie and uncle know how to cook.'

Reesa got up from the table and started to prepare a plate. She looked more at ease this morning.

'You look like you have seen a ghost Kalin, are you OK?'

Kalin sat down beside Mara. 'I had another horrible dream and I am feeling a bit weak.'

'They will keep happening to you until you head north Kalin.' Said Karra and then let out a loud belch.

'This dream was very strange, although it felt very real. I think I have seen what is on the other side of those gates. They all looked like monsters and they were all preparing to come into our world. It was very frightening.'

Karra turned and looked at Kalin.

'The gates normally open for a short period of time. This only allows but a few of these creatures to pass through from their world into ours, but every few years the gates hold open for a long time. In this time there can be hundreds that pass through. It is an enormous task trying to stop them coming through. Have you thought any more on my proposal?'

'Yes, I have, I don't want to go. I know how important this is, but I have met a girl and I think I am in love with her.'

One of Reesa's eyebrows was raised. 'And who might this lucky lady be?' she asked Kalin.

'It is Princess Thianni.'

There was a loud uproar of laughter in the kitchen. It left Kalin red faced and he could feel his anger building.

'Why are you all laughing? It is true. I am in love with her and she is in love with me.'

Reesa tried to stop laughing but could not. 'And the princess loves you too?'

'Yes, but the fact that she is a princess has nothing to do with it.'

They continued to laugh. Kalin jumped up and pushed his chair back and walked out from the kitchen.

He heard Reesa calling him. 'Please come back Kalin we did not mean to laugh.'

After the laughter had stopped, Mara sat back into his chair and thought for a while. He then suddenly sat forward.

'Now that I think of it, I think the boy is telling the truth. There is a young girl that has befriended him, and she looks like the princess.'

'Don't be so silly Mara. Kalin and the princess, how absurd.' Reesa started to laugh again.

'No, it is her, I am sure of it now that I think about it. I know it sounds silly, but it is true. It is the princess.'

Karra shook his head. 'This is proving a lot harder than I had first thought.'

Kalin headed for the front door, slamming it shut on his way out, and swiftly walked down the street and out of sight. He was upset now. He had not been able to shake off the dream, and it was playing on his mind what Karra had said to him. It was all too overwhelming for him. He decided to head out to see Chal and tell him about everything that had happened. As he walked through the streets, he saw Brin's friends Atal and his younger brother Abtar sitting together talking at a food table. There was no sign of Brin and Kalin could feel his mood darkening even more. Kalin walked over to the brothers.

'Where is your friend Brin this morning?'

The two brothers looked at Kalin and shrugged their shoulders and then turned and started talking to one another again. He could feel his anger build.

'Do not ignore me.' Kalin shouted with anger.

The two brothers looked shocked and went to stand. Kalin found himself attacking the two. Atal stood and was about to talk when Kalin punched him straight in the face. As he fell, his brother lashed out at Kalin from the side, catching Kalin on his right cheek. Kalin ducked under a second punch and landed his own blow to the other boy's body, knocking the wind out of him and following up with another blow to his jaw. The boy fell down on the ground beside his brother. Kalin stood over them with his fists clenched and his eyes blazing.

'Get back up,' he spat, 'I'll kill you both here and now.'

'What's wrong with you?' Abtar cried out as he looked up at Kalin with fear.

He was rubbing his bruised jaw. His brother was still unconscious lying beside him, from the blow to the face.

'I was only going to tell you Brin is not with us. We are sorry for changing the swords at the tournament, it was Brin's idea not ours.'

Kalin was about to attack again, but realised what he was doing. He unclenched his fist and looked at the two brothers on the ground and decided to turn and walk away. He left them behind him and as he walked, he started to feel his anger rising again. His hands were shaking now. What is wrong with me, he thought. He headed out through the main gates and on towards Chal's parent's farm. The area outside the walls of Kitia was starting to look bare now as all the people that had travelled for the summer festival had gone home. There were some scattered tents left, but they were starting to pack up and leave too. The walk to Chal's villa gave Kalin time to think about everything that had happened in the last few weeks. Everything from meeting Thianni, fighting with a sword in the tournament and his uncle Karra showing up out of the blue and explaining to him that he was cursed all started to weigh on him. How would anyone have been able to predict it all? There were a few trees along the left-hand side of the path and as he passed the first one, he noticed a wooden sword laying on the path in front of him. He bent down to pick it up and heard something coming towards him from his left side.

'I'd sell your genitals if I was you, with a face like that you won't be using them much.'

Kalin turned and saw Chal there with another wooden sword in his left hand and his right arm in a sling. Kalin smiled at his friend and spun the sword in his hand, pointing it at Chal.

'If you were twice as smart, you'd still be stupid. You know I came second in the Sword Tournament?'

Chal broke his serious face and burst out laughing.

'Second!'

They both laughed and lowered their swords.

'Oh, you are funny Kalin. I was on my way to the city to see if you wanted to practice, then I saw you coming down the road towards me. I decided to surprise you. We definitely have to work on our name calling and I need to work on using my left hand too. Although you don't look like you are up for some practice.'

'You are right Chal. I am not in a great mood today.' Kalin pointed to Chal's arm.

'How is your arm now?'

'It feels a lot better now, thanks, but I am playing it up, so I don't have to do as much work on the farm.'

The two boys sat down on the grass and talked for a while. Kalin was waiting for a break in the conversation to tell Chal about his uncle and everything he had been told. He wanted Chal's advice on the whole situation. Chal was talking about how excited he was to be going to sign up for the Royal Soldiers. Kalin felt like it might take away from his happiness.

'I know you must be sick of hearing about this Kalin, but I can't stop talking about it. It's all I have wanted to do since as far back as I can remember. Sometimes you can't hide from your destiny, right?'

Chal's words hit home in Kalin's mind. They made sense to him. Right there and then, Kalin knew he had to go north. Sadness swept over him.

'You are right Chal; sometimes you can't hide from what is meant to be.'

Kalin stood and Chal followed suit.

'Are you OK Kalin? You look a bit worried; did I say something to upset you?'

'I am fine Chal; you always have the answer for me, even if you do not know it. I have to go now. There are things that need to be done. You have been a great friend to me and even though we don't get to see each other, sometimes for a while, I want you to know that the time between us will not change our friendship.'

Kalin held out his hand to his confused friend and they both shook in the warrior's handshake. Kalin turned and walked back towards the city. Chal watched as Kalin walked away and whispered at him.

'You will always be my brother.'

Kalin made his way back to the city and walked to the main gate to the Palace. There were two guards talking behind the closed iron gates. They stopped talking as they saw Kalin approach.

'What is your business here boy?'

'I wish to see the Princess.'

They sniggered at him. 'And what business do you have with the Princess?'

'It is private business.'

They sniggered again. 'Be gone with you boy. Even if the Princess has any business with you it is too late for a meeting with the Court. The Court is closed for today.'

Kalin knew they would not let him in. He walked away and tried to think of a way he could get into the Palace and see the princess. He had been in the palace many times before when he had to deliver to the kitchen there, and his plan now was to enter the Palace in the morning with a delivery and try and seek out Thianni. He made his way home. Karra was waiting at the door to the house, drinking a cup of wine. His huge size filled the whole entrance and the top half of his body was bathed in sunlight as the sun shone down. As Kalin approached him he started to speak.

'I always love watching the sun go down and it's especially nice here in the south. I think when I am old, I might retire here in this land. How are you Kalin?'

Kalin stopped to watch the sun set with his uncle.

'I am good now. I wanted to talk to you about this trip to the north.'

'Have you changed your mind?'

'Yes, I have. My friend helped me to make a change in the way I was thinking. I think I am meant to go north with you, but first I have some things to take care of. When are you leaving?'

'I want to leave as soon as I can. I was planning on leaving tomorrow morning.'

'Would it be too much to ask to delay that until midday tomorrow? I have to say goodbye to someone before we go.'

'I can work with that. We can make up the time on the way. Tomorrow midday it is.'

Karra held out his hand and Kalin shook it.

'I am very pleased you have decided to come with me Kalin. The road ahead will be a hard one for you, but it will be very rewarding. Nothing worthwhile ever comes easy.'

Kalin was up and out early the next morning. It would be his last day delivering for Mara. Mara handed him the boxes he was to deliver, and they seemed not as many as usual.

'When you come back from delivering these, I will close the stall early today and head back home so myself and Reesa can see you off. She is very upset that you are leaving us.'

'Thank you, Mara. Thank you for everything you have done for me. I will try to get back as fast as I can.'

Kalin headed off on his way. The delivery rounds were easy and went by fast. After he had finished them, he headed towards the Palace. He went to the side gate that led to the kitchens where he had brought in deliveries before. There was a guard there. He walked up to the gate as casual as he could. The guard stepped out as soon as he saw Kalin walking his way.

'What is your business here?'

'I have supplies for the kitchen.'

The guard looked confused. 'I was not made aware that we had deliveries today.'

'I think it might have been a last-minute order. Mara the baker at the stall said I was to come as fast as I could. They are waiting on stock to be brought into the kitchens.'

The guard looked him up and down and then decided to open the gate and let him in. Kalin made his way to the kitchen. There was a large table just inside the door with vegetables and some fruit on it. There were a few cooks working at the far end, but they did not bother with him. Kalin left the delivery box on the table and walked across the kitchen and out through a door onto a long corridor. The corridor was empty in both directions. He turned right and made his way down along the corridor, this would bring him deeper into the palace, he thought. There was a turning at the end and as he turned, he nearly bumped into a young girl.

'Oh, I am very sorry sir.' She said instantly.

Kalin was startled by her. 'I am sorry too.' He said in a polite manner. 'Could you tell me the whereabouts of Princess Thianni? I have a delivery for her.'

The girl stepped back slightly. 'You are her friend; I know your face. Kalin, I think. Is that your name, Kalin?'

Kalin's heart sank. He had been caught. This was the one and only chance he had to say goodbye to Thianni and explain why he had to go.

'Yes, that is my name. I really need to see her though. I will pay you in silver if you can take me to her please.'

The girl looked at him for a while. 'I will bring you, not because you want to see her, but because I know she will want to see you. Follow me please.'

The girl turned and led Kalin down a few different corridors and then up a wide staircase. They passed a servant on the top of the stairs, but he did not even look at them and carried about his business. She then brought him into a small room with brooms and clothes and other cleaning equipment.

'Wait here and I will fetch the Princess.'

'Can you not bring me to her?'

'No, her room will be guarded, it is best that I bring her to you.'

The girl left and Kalin waited patiently. A while passed and Kalin was beginning to feel angry. He tried to calm himself by breathing in deeply. All sorts of things were going through his head now. Had he been led into a trap? Should I try and make my way back to the kitchen? No, I must see the princess before I go. He concluded. He heard distant talking and it was getting closer. The door opened and the Princess walked in. She was in shock to see him. 'Kalin what are you doing in here?'

'I am sorry I needed to see you.'

The princess closed the door behind her, leaving Sabby outside in the corridor.

'Is everything OK?'

'Yes. I just wanted…'

The Princess cut him off. 'How did you get in here?'

'I had to sneak in, I'm sorry. I needed to see you as I have to go away for a while.'

'Go where Kalin? the princess asked in a sad voice.

'This is going to sound extremely strange. Even outrageous; I know it will because I still can't get my head around it. My uncle arrived a few nights ago from Gantia and has asked me to go to the North with him.'

Kalin spoke at length about everything that had happened. When he had finished, Thianni's eyes started to fill up.

'Will I ever see you again?'

'Yes of course. I will be back next summer. Karra has said I can return then. That's if you still would like to see me then?'

'Oh Kalin, you know I do. I love you.'

Kalin reached out and pulled the princess close to him and kissed her.

'I love you too,' he replied. 'and I promise I will never be with another as long as I am with you.'

'I will make the same promise to you, Kalin and yes, I will wait for you, no matter how long it takes for you to come back to me. When do you leave?'

'Midday today we leave.'

Thianni then turned and locked the door and turned back to him.

'We do not have much time then.'

The Princess then slipped her dress off. Sabby was waiting outside the room. She could hear what was going on behind the door and felt embarrassed but could not help smiling. Paran, the Princess's guard walked up the stairs and down towards The Princess's chambers. He passed Sabby standing outside the door to the broom closet. She looked nervous, so he decided to turn back.

'Are you OK Sabby?'

'Yes, all is good.'

'I thought there might be something wrong when I saw you just standing outside this room.'

A noise came from the room and they both looked at the door.

'Oh, I think I saw a rat in there, and I don't like rats'

'Do you want me to go in and deal with it for you?'

There was bang that came from the room.

'It sounds like a rather large rat.' Said Paran.

'Ah, no I have just left down some poison and I am just waiting for it to take the bait.'

'Ok then, let me know if you are in need of any assistance. Before I go, have you seen the Princess?' Sabby blushed for a second. 'I don't believe I have.' Paran swore. 'If hiding was a talent, that girl would be a champion. Satisfied Paran walked away about his duties. Kalin and Thianni heard the conversation that took place and decided that they would have to go. They giggled as they quickly dressed.

'Before I go, I want to give you this.'

Kalin took out the silver chain with the dove attached and handed it to Thianni.

'Oh my, how did you know I liked this?'

'I saw you at the stall admiring it, so I bought it and I wanted you to have it.'

'I love it Kalin, thank you.'

She kissed him again.' I do not want you to go, for this will be the last time I will see you in a whole year.'

'I will be back, I promise, Thianni.'

'I will leave first, and I will ask Sabby to show you the way out. I will be thinking about you every minute of every day. Please be careful and make your way back to me.'

'I will.'

Thianni kissed and hugged Kalin for the last time and left the room. Sabby was still waiting outside the door. The princess came out and fixed her hair and dress as Sabby looked on with a red face.

'When I have gone make sure you show my friend out the same way he came in.'

'Yes, my Lady.' Thianni strode off towards her chambers with tears in her eyes.

19

The winds were good, and the Sea wolf was moving north steadily along the West coast of Latonia. Before long they could see the opening of the bay to the Capital City, Kitia. The crew were tired and weary, but they gave out a cheer at the sight of the two huge gatehouses that protected the entrance to the city's harbour. As they got closer, they could see a royal Warship coming in their direction from the mouth of the harbour. Captain Vimeo gave the order for the ship to come to a halt as the Latonian war ship pulled up alongside the huge Sea Wolf. The Captain of the war ship leaned out over his ship and called up to the high deck of the Sea Wolf.

'May I speak to the Captain of this ship?'

Vimeo leaned over the side and looked down at the Latonian Captain. 'That would be me. I am Captain Vimeo from Athel in Natalia.'

'I am Captain Jerra, well met. You are a long way from home, my friend. What is your business here at Kitia with this very large ship?'

'We are from Natalia and we are on the run from Imperial Dragon Ships. It has taken us a long time to evade capture and reach this port. My crew have been through a great deal and we are looking for sanctuary in your city. I also must speak to the King about this matter. Our belief is that there has been an all-out invasion in Natalia.'

The Latonian captain laughed out loud. 'That is a fine story to tell, how much of this is true? As I have heard no news about this.'

Vimeo looked annoyed. 'I can assure you that all of it is true. Now if you don't mind, I wish to be on my way to the city, time is precious here.'

'All in good time, first we will need to search your ship. Do I have your permission to come aboard your enormous vessel?'

Captain Vimeo nodded and then lowered a rope ladder down to the smaller war ship. Four Latonian guards climbed up the ladder, followed by Captain Jerra and then four more guards. Both captains met with a handshake on the deck of the Sea Wolf.

'Welcome aboard Captain Jarra.'

'Thank you. My, this is an amazing vessel. Where did you acquire it?'

'I designed and built it myself.'

'Is she fast out on the open water? Is she cumbersome in turning?'

Vimeo looked distressed at all the questions. 'With all due respect Captain Jerra, I would love to discuss the ins and outs of my ship with you, but as I said, I have something more pressing to deal with right now. I would like to set anchor in Kitia and then talk to either the King or someone I can pass on this information on to. Many lives are at risk right now.'

Captain Jerra paused and looked at Vimeo intensely. 'Very well then, follow my ship in and I will escort you into the city. I will run a search of your ship when you have docked.'

With that, Captain Jerra climbed back down the rope ladder with his men and both ships were moving again towards the harbour of Kitia. The Sea Wolf passed by the two guard towers and on into the open mouth of the harbour, following Jerra's Warship. The harbour itself was huge and filled mostly with merchant vessels and Warships. It looked to be a very busy place. Captain Jerra shouted back to Vimeo and pointed from the back of his ship to a section indicating a place for Vimeo to dock his ship. It took some time for the ship to move into its resting place. The Sea Wolf's anchor was dropped, and ropes were thrown to the dock and the Sea Wolf was firmly secured in place. As Vimeo stepped onto the dock, he was greeted by Captain Jerra and eight guards.

'I will take you up to the palace and arrange a meeting. Do my men have your permission to go on board and search this fine ship of yours?'

Vimeo looked back at Barus and gave him a nod and then turned back to Captain Jerra. 'Yes, you do have my permission, and thank you for the offer of arranging the meeting.'

'While your men wait, I will have some food brought onboard and fresh water too.'

Vimeo thanked him. The two captains walked along the dock together towards the city. Jerra was full of questions about The Sea Wolf. This time, Vimeo did not mind answering them. It was a long walk to the

King's Palace and the city was alive with people working and getting on with their daily lives. Vimeo had been in Kitia some years ago but could not remember it being this busy. The city had had a smaller population back then, while it seemed to be overflowing with residents now. They approached the main gates and two guards went to stop them from entering but they noticed it was Captain Jerra and they moved aside. Jerra brought Vimeo through a large courtyard, on through some arches and eventually through a side door into a building. They walked up a long corridor and into a large, well-furnished room. Captain Jerra poured a cup of cool water and handed it to Vimeo. He then pointed to a cushioned seat at the small table.

'Please wait here and I will see if I can get you in to see the King. I will be as fast as I can.'

Vimeo thanked Captain Jerra and sat down to wait. Vimeo was waiting a long while. No one had come into the room he was in, and he was starting to grow impatient when the door opened and Jerra came in, followed by a very tall man dressed in a long black gown and two other smaller men also dressed in black gowns. Vimeo stood to greet them.

'Sorry about the wait, this is Lord Sabat, trusted advisor to the King. The King is very busy at the moment and can't be here, but whatever you want to report, Lord Sabat will listen and make sure this will be reported back to King Roban.'

Sabat walked past Jerra and held out his hand to Vimeo. As Vimeo stood and shook his long bony hand, he felt a wave of nausea sweep through him. His first impression of Sabat was to run. Vimeo had learned a long time ago to trust his instincts with people, and he did not like this man at all. He could feel an evil presence from him. Sabat gestured for him to sit again and the three men sat at a low table. The two smaller men closed the door and stood on each side of it, waiting.

'So, Captain, Jerra tells me you suspect that there is an invasion happening in Athel?'

Feeling even more discomforted in Sabat's close company, Vimeo answered reluctantly.

'Yes, I believe so.'

Vimeo told him the story of how they had been out testing their new ship and saw the endless amount of Dragon ships coming out of the mist to attack them, and how they had to flee for their lives. That the

Dragon ships were heading for the city that he called home. He explained that they had witnessed the city of Scada being attacked by sea and how the Dragon ship had pursued them all the way to Kitia before they had managed to shake it off. Sabat listened intently and then sat back in his chair to contemplate what he had just heard.

'This is horrifying news if it is true.'

Vimeo was shocked, his face red with anger. 'What do you mean, if it is true? Of course, it is true. We have seen it with our own eyes.'

Jerra leaned over the table and spoke in a harsh tone. 'Please be calm and remember you are speaking to a noble priest who is a member of the Kings trusted council. I will not tolerate an outburst like this in his presence.'

Sabat held up his hand to dismiss Jerra. 'This ordeal must have been a horrible experience for the Captain and his crew Jerra. I am sure we can allow the Captain some understanding, considering what he and all of his men have been through. Now I just need to ask you some questions, so I have the right answers for when I tell the King what has happened here.'

The three men spoke for a while more and then Sabat stood.

'Well that is all I need to know. I will present your statement to the King at once and see what actions he would like to take.'

Vimeo seemed glad the conversation was over. 'Please treat this with the utmost concern. A lot of lives are at stake here.'

'I will captain, you can trust me.' He gave Vimeo a forced smile and then turned to Jerra. 'Can you make sure the captain is looked after and fed and put up for the night?'

Jerra nodded.

Vimeo also stood. 'I appreciate your welcome, but I would much prefer to stay with my men ship if you do not mind?'

'Of course, I know where to find you,' said Sabat as he turned and left the room with his two followers close behind him.

'I will walk you back to your ship Captain.'

'Thank you Captain Jarra and thank you for arranging this for me.'

After Sabat was clear of the room he turned to one of his followers. 'Make sure that this ship is watched and everyone on it. And make sure the conversation we had in there stays in there. None of what we talked about can get back to the King."

Kalin arrive home, he was met by his auntie and uncle and Karra. There was also a tall dark man with them. Kalin recognised him with shock. He remembered the man; he was the one he had been seeing everywhere, the dark man that had been watching him. He was the man that had saved him that day from Brin's knife.

'I want you to meet Leib.' Karra pointed to the dark man. 'Leib is an old friend of mine, we go back a long way. We have spilt the same blood in the same mud many a time.' He patted Leib on the back. Leib held out his hand to Kalin. Kalin reluctantly shook it. Leib spoke with a very deep voice.

'I am sorry if I have frightened you in the past. Your uncle had me keep a distant eye on you while you were living in Kitia. I know how hard it is trying to make a life when you do not fit in.'

Karra interrupted. 'I am afraid we will have to be starting to get ready to leave soon.'

Reesa sighed. 'Kalin you must go in and start packing all your belongings.'

Karra turned to Kalin. 'Only take what you really need, as the load for the horses will be very heavy. While you are doing that, Leib and I will fetch the horses from the stables and start loading them.'

Kalin went inside with his auntie and uncle and started to pack. It did not take him too long to get ready. Mara handed him a small leather pouch.

'This is your week's wages and all of the coins that you have saved, and I put a little extra in there for you in case you might need it on the way. I will miss you Kalin. It was a pleasure working with you and having you in our home. Remember, you will always have a home here.'

He gave Kalin a hug.

'Thank you, Mara.'

'It will be a hard job for me to finding a replacement delivery boy.'

Kalin looked at Reesa. She was starting to well up. Tears had started to form and were pooling in the corners of her eyes. She tried to speak but could not. She just grabbed Kalin and hugged him. They walked him out to the front door were Karra and Leib were now waiting with 5 horses.

Karra walked over to Kalin, leading one of the horses by the reins. He handed the reins to Kalin.

'This is your horse now. Make sure you look after it as it cost a lot, more than I had in mind.'

Kalin stood there with his mouth open. 'Thank you. I have never owned a horse before. Come to think of it, I have never ridden a horse before.'

Karra and Leib looked at one another. 'This should be a fun trip.' Karra put in. They loaded up the horses with provisions.

'Oh, I almost forgot.' Mara went back into the house and brought out three bags of food he had prepared for their journey. He handed them out to the group of three. 'I have made this food myself and I have packed it so the first of the food to go off is at the top. You have a week's worth there providing Karra does not eat it all on the first day.'

Karra laughed and thanked Mara and gave Reesa a hug and then mounted his horse, followed by Leib.

Reesa then spoke. 'Make sure you look after my boy.'

Karra nodded to her. 'He is in good hands sister.'

They watched and laughed as Kalin tried to get into his saddle. After a few attempts, he secured himself on his horse. Karra dug in his heels and the two other riders followed. They were underway. Kalin turned in his saddle and tried to wave back to his auntie and uncle and nearly fell off his horse. Slowly they moved on through the city. The main gates were open and the three passed through and out onto the long path to the north. Kalin's feelings were mixed. He was feeling sad and excited at the same time.

'Well boy, how are you feeling?'

'I feel good.' He lied to his uncle.

'This is the start of a glorious adventure. From this point on, your life will never be the same again.'

Kalin then paused. 'Oh no!'

'What is it Kalin?'

'I forgot to say goodbye to Chal.'

'We can't go back now; we are late leaving as it is. Sure, you will see him in a years' time.'

The three rode on along the north path. Just before they crested the hill, Kalin took one last look at the city of Kitia and then turned and rode on into the unknown.

20

Karra, Kalin and Leib's long journey north was well underway. Their mounts were holding up well, as were the two extra horses carrying their supplies. It was the height of summer now and the early morning sun was hot on the travellers. They intended to travel straight through the central plains of Latonia. There were no big cities on this route; there were only villages and farms, but the roads were good. It would take them a few weeks before they arrived at the city of Branti. This would give Karra and Leib plenty of time to start Kalin's training and to begin preparing him for what lay ahead. They did not cover as much ground as they thought they would on the first day, and Kalin's backside and legs were very sore as he was not used to riding horses, but he found he loved riding and was happy to own his own mount. Every so often, he would lean down and pet the horse's head and talk to him in a low soft voice.

'You will have to give him a name now Kalin,' Karra announced.

Kalin had not thought to name him, and for the next hour his thoughts were on naming his horse. They pulled off the road to stop for the night inside the tree line and set up camp. Karra set to work on getting their evening meal ready, while Leib saw to the horses, leading them to a nearby stream and letting them drink. Karra called out to Kalin as he was rubbing his backside, trying to get the blood flowing again in his ass cheeks.

'Go into the wood and gather as much firewood as you can. Make sure we have enough for the night.'

Kalin headed into the woods, it was quiet there and seemed peaceful. Even though he had been born in Gantia, this was the furthest he could remember being away from the city of Kitia, where the noise was ever-present. Even if he took a walk into the woods on the outskirts of Kitia, he could always hear the sounds of the city. He had always liked the woods, but these woods were different. There was only nature here. The hustle and bustle of the city were noticeably absent. He started to pick up old fallen wood from the ground. There was plenty of it here. Out of the corner of his eye he noticed movement. He turned to see a white owl landing on a branch nearby. The owl seemed curious as to what he was doing and watched him.

'Well hello there, owl.' Kalin called out.

They both observed each other for a while, and then he heard Karra calling. 'Have you got some wood yet? I want to light the fire.'

Kalin hurried back to the camp with some wood for Karra and returned to the trees for more. When he got back again, the owl had gone. Several times he returned to the camp with wood and there was now a heap. More than enough to keep the fire going for the night.

Leib returned with the horses, tying them to a nearby tree for the night. 'How's that butt of yours Kalin? Is it still sore?'

'Yes Leib, it hurts alright, I have never had a sore ass like this before.'

'It will get better. They say the first one hundred thousand miles are the worst.'

Kalin looked at Leib and saw that he was joking and laughed.

Leib gave Kalin a wink. 'In a couple of days, it will be fine. You just need to persevere.'

Kalin liked the man. He was funny and warm and caring. At first, he looked scary. He was very tall, taller than Karra but not as big and as wide. Leib was built for speed, lean and muscular. He had dark brown eyes, almost black, and his black skin was not common around Kitia but as Kalin got to know him he realised that his looks did not define him. Leib had said he was from far south, from a land where the sun always shined. It made Kalin consider how hard it had been for him to fit in with the people of Kitia, and how much harder it must have been for Leib to fit in too. As Karra prepared the meal, Kalin was surprised that there was any food for Leib and himself as Karra was eating most of it as he cooked. After they were finished, Kalin took the pots and plates down to the stream and washed them. When he came back, he saw Karra taking a short sword from his pack. He walked over to Kalin and handed him the sword. 'There you go boy. It's only a short sword but it might get you out of some trouble.'

'I am not allowed to carry a sword in the lands of Latonia.'

'You are a Gantian, all Gantians are warriors and what would a warrior be without a weapon.'

Kalin contemplated his uncle's words and decided to take the sword. 'Thank you, Karra.'

Karra grunted and moved away to the fire and began settling in for the night. It was dark and the night sky was filled with countless stars. More than Kalin had ever seen before. Karra and Leib were lying by the fire in full conversation, drinking some wine. Kalin was rubbing his sore bottom. Leib threw Kalin a small jar of what looked like a clear coloured wax.

'Spread a small amount of that ointment on the sore parts of your backside and it will help.'

Kalin scooped out some and rubbed it on his behind. It felt cold and straight away he could feel it was starting to work. The ache started to go away. He thanked Leib and gave him back the jar. Kalin spread out his blanket by the fire and settled down for the night. He felt very content now, he had a full belly and he was warm by the fire and in good company. He tried to recall all that had happened in the last few weeks. He wondered what Chal would be doing right now and then his thoughts wandered to Thianni. He was missing home, but he was also enjoying the trip, and wondered what tomorrow would bring. Kalin listened as the two men talked about old times, sharing stories and recalling adventures they'd had together, and he slowly drifted to sleep. The next morning, he opened his eyes slightly and warm light flooded through the slits of his eyelids. He had had a good night's sleep without any bad dreams. He sat up. The fire was nearly out, just a few still-smoldering branches. He looked around and saw Leib tethering the horses. Karra was down by the stream. He was fully naked and washing in the cold water. Karra walked back to the camp. Kalin noticed with shock all the scars Karra had on his upper body. Karra took a small towel from a bag and started to dry himself. He had very little scars on his back the majority were on the front. Karra looked over and Kalin looked away, trying not to stare at his uncle.

'Good morning Kalin, did you sleep well?'

Kalin felt uncomfortable now, as a naked man was talking to him. 'Yes, I slept fine,' he replied,

trying to look like he was focusing on something in the distance.

'We will have to get back on the road as soon as we can, so we will have to settle for a cold breakfast this morning.'

Leib untied the horses and let them graze nearby. He came back to camp. Karra dressed and Kalin got up and warmed his hands by the dying fire. The three had some bread and cold meat to eat and were back on their horses and heading north again within the hour. After a few hours of riding they stopped to rest and eat. Kalin remembered he had some biscuits left over that his auntie Reesa had given to him for the journey. He shared them with Leib and Karra. Karra almost swallowed his share. He always seemed hungry. They all sat just off the road, enjoying the morning sun. Karra wiped his mouth of crumbs and turned to Kalin, who was slowly nibbling on his biscuit while calling his horse, trying to get him to come over.

'Have you named that horse yet?'

'No, not yet. I can't think of a name that suits him.'

'He won't come to you, he's a horse not a dog.'

Kalin called him once more and the horse came walking over. 'See? He does come,' Kalin laughed.

As the horse reached Kalin, he grabbed the biscuit out of Kalin's hand and ate it. Karra and Leib laughed out loud, looking at Kalin's shocked face.

'Biscuit!' Kalin shouted out. 'I'm going to call him Biscuit.'

On the third day of traveling Kalin's backside was feeling better so Karra and Leib started his training in the mornings and then again in the evenings. As they travelled closer and closer to the north, the training intensified. Karra and Leib could see Kalin was taking to the training well, and both were pleasantly surprised at how fast he picked everything up. Leib turned to Kalin.

'Tomorrow I will teach you how to track.'

'We are all creatures of habit Kalin. You, me, all people and so are all animals too. Take these deer footprints here,' Leib pointed to small indentations in the soft ground alongside the trail they were on. 'See how steady they are? Maintaining the perfect distance from each other. This is telling me that the deer is comfortable walking along here. The deer has done this a lot and is at ease along this trail, he trusts this trail and this comfort we can use. Now, if the footprints had been staggered or uneven it would tell us that the deer was not at ease and when he walked along here, he would be alert, and look here.' He pointed up further on the trail. 'We can see his footprints here; he stopped to eat some shrubs. He feels comfortable enough here to stop and eat.'

Kalin looked puzzled! 'So, what has this to do with me training?'

'It has everything to do with it. You see if I were hunting today, I would know that this spot would be a good spot to kill this deer, he would be off guard here. It is the same with fighting, warfare, business, with everything! You must find out your opponents' weakness in order to defeat them. Deception is the key to winning, and once we know our enemy's habits, we can exploit them.'

Kalin now understood the lesson and nodded. Kalin found the journey to the north a great adventure. His backside no longer hurt, but the rest of his body was frequently sore from all the training Karra and Leib were putting him through. His riding skills had improved greatly, and he was enjoying his time in the saddle. The countryside was beautiful and there was wildlife everywhere. Sometimes they would ride all day and not come across a single village or farm. Karra and Leib hunted as they travelled, and they would buy supplies in the villages if there were places to purchase them, but they ate well and there was always food. He met many different types of people along the way. All were Latonian. Most were friendly, but there were some that avoided them as they did not look Latonian. Travelling across the central plains seemed to take forever, and the days were long and hot and clammy. There were less people here and the hunting was considerably harder. He missed his auntie and uncle a lot and he constantly thought about Thianni. As he experienced all these new things, he realised how important his friendship with Chal had been, as he now had no one to share it all with. He wondered how Chal was getting on with his training and how he was fitting in to the Royal Army. Although he knew Chal would make a great soldier, and would rise through the ranks fast, Kalin would miss out on all the stories that he had to tell. As they emerged from the Central Plains, the ground started to rise, and they were walking uphill for some time. They were at a higher elevation now and the air seemed a lot cooler. He loved the nights around the campfire. He got to listen to Karra and Leib talk and debate about all sorts of things. They talked about everything from money to politics to religion and the stars, and from women to fighting, but mostly they talked about women and fighting. Karra had started teaching him the language of Gantia. Kalin knew some words from his auntie but he picked it up well and was now having short conversations with Karra.

As they approached the city of Branti, Kalin felt less content. It was a huge place with lots of people. Not as big as Kitia, but almost. The first thing Kalin had noticed was that the city had no defensive walls. People were free to walk in and out of the city in any direction. There were some Latonian soldiers, but not many. They led their mounts down the main road and on to the trading Square and Karra stopped to talk to a stall owner who was selling furs. He had long black hair like his uncle and spoke in Gantian. Kalin could make out almost all of the conversation. They talked about news from Gantia and how the snow was all melted and the summer was in full bloom. Karra turned back to Kalin and Leib.

'We will rest here for a couple of days and then push on to the North Gate. I know a good inn where we can eat and sleep and maybe find a woman for this young man,' he said, pointing to Kalin.

'I don't want a woman. I have one back in Kitia waiting for me.' Kalin said in a concerned voice.

'Well you will soon get lonely without her.'

'I have made a vow to be true to Thianni, and I will keep that vow.'

'We'll see boy, we'll see!'

Karra moved through the streets, arriving at a large premise with lots of stables, where he paid for their horses to be accommodated for two nights. Kalin was reluctant to hand over his horse, Biscuit, as he had grown very attached to him. They were all staying in the same room, in three separate beds. Karra must have eaten his own bodyweight in food that night in the inn. After their meal they started drinking, but Kalin could not keep up and had to go to bed early. The next day, Kalin was woken early by Karra's snoring. He decided to go out and have a walk around the city of Branti. There were very few people on the streets; this gave the city a nicer feel to it. He took a run around the outskirts and back to the city. As part of Kalin's training, Leib had him running every second day before breakfast to maintain his fitness level. Kalin was used to his run now and enjoyed stretching his legs and expanding his lungs. He looped around the city and back in and then walked the main street to the market area. Most of the stall owners were starting to set up their stalls for a day of trading. This reminded him of Kitia and his time with Thianni. He sat down on a bench and gathered his thoughts. Had he made the right decision in coming north? A wave of sadness crept through him, he longed to be holding her right now.

Since he had left Kitia, he had not had one bad dream and he felt more at peace with himself than he had in a long time. What Karra had told him was true. The closer he got to the Gate, the better he would feel. He had noticed another change too, his fitness and strength had increased, and he seemed not to tire so easily anymore. His running speed had increased, and when he was practicing the sword with Leib, he could defend the attacks with ease. It seemed as though he could see what was going to happen before it happened. He knew Leib had noticed this too, and he had noticed Lieb was now beginning to visibly sweat during their bouts. Karra always watched and commented on the bouts, but he never joined in. When Kalin had asked Leib why he would not join in the training with them, he had said, 'I have been training with various types of weapons for a long time now and have perfected some of them. I am a natural fighter and I feel I can stand toe to toe and match most men, but your uncle, he is different. He is not a fighter; he is a killer. When he draws his weapons, whatever stands in front of him, dies.'

It was early morning, and Karra and Leib had headed off just before dawn to hunt for some fresh meat. Kalin was left at the camp to wash clothes and pots in the shallow river that ran nearby. They were making good progress on their travels and had decided the night before that they would stay in this spot for two nights. This would give them time to do some hunting and try and build their food supplies and give the horses some rest. Kalin had washed the pots first, then he took some clothes and washed them, laying them out flat on some nearby rocks to dry. Kalin made his way back to the camp to put more logs on the fire. Having completed his tasks, he sat back, noticing five riders in the distance approaching in his direction. He watched them as they came closer. Most of the people on his travels had been nice but he could feel something inside him that was warning him about these five. He strapped his sword to his side, slid a knife down his boot and sat back down again, waiting for the strangers to come. The strangers rode right into the camp and Kalin rose to meet them. The lead man dismounted and walked over to Kalin. 'Hey boy, those horses over there, how much for the black one?'

'They are not for sale.'

'One boy traveling alone by his self doesn't need five horses, so how much?'

'Like I said, they are not for sale. And I am not by myself.'

'Where are your companions then? I don't see anyone else here but you.'

'They are close by and they will be back soon.'

'How many are there?'

Kalin felt himself getting angry with the abrupt questions. 'That is none of your business. Now I suggest you and your friends be on your way.'

The man laughed. 'No one tells me what to do or where to go, let alone a young boy.'

The man walked closer to Kalin and leaned in close to Kalin's face. Kalin did not move. He could smell his stale breath as he spoke.

'Are you going to make us go about our own business? You and all your so-called friends?'

The other strangers on the horses laughed this time. It went quiet, and Kalin stood very still. Out of the corner of his eye he could see the three mounted horsemen drawing their long knives. The fourth man was just out of his sight, but he knew he was also waiting to attack.

Kalin looked at the leader straight in the eye. 'As a matter of fact, I think five might not be enough.' This statement shocked the leader, and he stepped back. The young boy stood there without any fear.

The intruder laughed again and turned to his men. 'An arrogant little pup. Do you think I should teach him a lesson in manners?'

Then he spun around fast, drawing his sword and lashing out at the boy's face. The sword sliced through the air, missing its target completely. The boy was nowhere to be seen. The leader then felt a sharp burning pain erupt in his stomach. He looked down and could see that the boy had ducked, dropping to one knee and driving his own sword deep into his Attacker's midsection. Panic and pain swept through him at the realisation of what was happening. The boy then twisted his sword and pulled it out fast, causing a spray of blood that arched through the air and met the oncoming men. The leader fell to the ground in agony. Three other attackers had dismounted and tried to rush the boy, slashing at him with their long knives. The boy ducked and spun, evading all their efforts to cut him. Then the boy attacked back with his sword. The fighting was fast, and the men were bewildered as to how this boy was getting the better of them. They were on the defence now. As he attacked, the front man did not move back in time and the boy's sword sliced deep into his upper thigh. He went down with a cry. The boy kept attacking. The next man tried to block a straight thrust, but the attack was too fast, and the tip of the boy's sword pushed deep into his shoulder. He also fell to the ground. The third man threw his knife to the ground, turned tail and ran for his horse. Kalin held himself back from running after him. His mind felt uneasy now, sensing there was still danger. He only counted four men and remembered that there were five of them that rode into the camp. Kalin scanned around him, looking for the fifth intruder. Just as he caught sight of the fifth man, an arrow was released from the man's bow. Kalin was a fraction too late as he turned, and the arrow pierced his left shoulder, the force of the impact turning him even further. A stinging pain shot through him. Kalin ran forward to attack the bowman. The bowman, in his panic, tried to notch another arrow, but Kalin was on him before he could fire off another shot. Kalin slashed his sword across the bow, breaking it, and the arrow fired off to the left, thudding into the ground some ways off. The bowman dropped his broken weapon, turned and ran off into the distance in terror. Kalin looked back at the three remaining men that were still on the ground. Two of them would live, but the leader would probably die from the wound in his stomach, he figured.

'Get back on your horses and get out of here.'

The two men lifted their leader and helped him up and onto his horse; he cried out in pain as they did so. Kalin watched them as they made their way off. He looked down at the arrow jutting out of his shoulder.

'Damn!' He said out loud.

He sat down and rested by the fire. A short while later, Karra and Leib came running in to the camp to find Kalin drinking some water with an arrow sticking out of his left shoulder. Karra came straight to Kalin.

'What happened here? Are you OK?'

Karra hunkered down beside Kalin and examined the arrow, while Leib scanned the area to see if there were any signs of what had happened.

'I was attacked by some men. They wanted the horses, I think.'

'How many were there?'

'Five. But they have gone now.'

Karra smiled and ruffled Kalin's hair as he stood. 'You have done well boy.'

'Thank you, but I was not that lucky.' Kalin pointed to the arrow.

Leib came over to join them. 'There is a lot of blood on the ground in several places, you did very well to fight off five of them, Kalin. All that training must be paying off.'

Karra turned to Leib. 'That arrow will have to come out.'

The two men looked down at Kalin.

'Will it hurt?' Asked Kalin.

Karra smiled. 'A little bit. But seeing as you can take on five fully grown men, I don't think you will have a problem with us taking out a little splinter like that.' He pointed to the arrow again.

Kalin looked nervous. Leib helped Kalin take off his tunic.

'The arrow looks to be in deep. You are a lucky boy, a little more centered and it might have hit your heart.'

Karra walked over to his pack and took out a bottle. He brought it over and handed it to Kalin.

'This is Bandar Fire. A drink I keep for special occasions like this.'

Karra took the cup of water from Kalin and spilled it out on to the ground and then poured in a golden liquid from the bottle and handed it back to Kalin.

'Here start sipping on this, try not to take big mouthfuls, just sip it.'

Kalin took a drink and felt his breath being taken away. He felt his throat burning as he swallowed and started to cough.

'I said sip it boy.'

Leib examined the wound further. 'It doesn't look like it hit any bone, so you should be ok. I am just worried that some of the fabric from your tunic might have got pushed into the wound as the arrow entered. If this is the case, it might get infected after we stitch it. When I take the arrow out, I will have to have a look inside and clean the inner wound.'

Leib took hold of the arrow and Kalin let out a yelp. 'Go easy there, it is starting to hurt a lot.'

'You have a few options here. We can leave the arrow in for a week or so and let the wound fester. It will then fill with pus, and then the arrow should slide right out. Or I can try and pull it out now. If the barbs are large on the arrow it might tear some flesh with it.'

Kalin wiped his now sweating brow with his hand. 'I don't like either of those options, but I don't want to be walking around for a week with an arrow sticking out of me.'

'I'll take it out now.' Leib went to his travel bag and brought back a small jar. He opened it and scooped out the creamy content.

'What is that?' asked Kalin, looking very nervous.

'It is pork fat. I use it for cooking.'

'It smells bad. What do you need that for?'

'I am going to spread it down into the wound along the arrow. It will help slide the arrow clear. Just look away and I will have it out in no time.'

Karra watched on as Leib performed the procedure. Kalin looked away and braced himself. Leib smeared the fat on the wound and pushed some down along the shaft of the arrow, deep into the wound. Kalin tried not to shout out. Leib then grasped the shaft and began to pull it free. Kalin clenched his fists and shut his eyes as the pain intensified. The barbs were holding inside, and Leib found it difficult to pull free.

'I am going to have to make two small cuts around the entry wound, to allow the barbs to come out, or the hooks will pull out a lot of flesh with them.'

Leib took a small knife and sliced two deep cuts outward from the wound. He then pulled on the arrow. At first it seemed like it did not want to move, then he pulled harder and the arrow came out as Kalin let out a long sigh.

'There you go. It's out now.'

Blood streamed down Kalin's chest. Leib then pushed his two fingers into the open wound and felt inside. Kalin let out a shout this time.

'It seems to be clear of any fabric. I will just clean it now and then stitch it up.'

After Leib had finished Kalin looked down at the wound in his shoulder. The stitches felt tight and the skin around it looked inflamed.

He took a fresh tunic from his bag and struggled to get it on, only using his one arm.

'I'm not sure I will be able to do any training tomorrow.'

'We will give you a few days rest and you can get back into it then, but you should be able to keep running.'

'I think I might need a bit more time for this to heal.'

The next morning, when Kalin woke, it was already bright, and he could hear Karra snoring. He rolled gently onto his side, so he would not stretch the stitches, and sat up. He lifted up his tunic to check on his wound and he could hardly believe his eyes. The wound was almost completely healed. It looked like it was a few weeks old and the stitches looked like they were pushed to the surface of his skin. He picked them clear with his fingers. There was a thin white line where the cut had been the night before. He stood and moved his arm and shoulder. It felt fine, it was back to normal. Kalin was astonished, he woke Karra to tell him about his wound had healed overnight. He shook Karra as he was sleeping. Karra jumped up with a startle and drew his long knife.

'What's the matter? Are those bastards back again?'

'No, nothing like that. I wanted to show you my wound.'

Kalin pulled down his top and showed Karra. Karra lifted his own top and showed Kalin that he was covered with many white lines that looked just like Kalin's.

'That's nothing new. We heal fast because of the curse. Now let me get back to sleep and don't be waking me with silly things.'

Karra lay back down in his bed by the dead fire. Kalin felt his healing wound was meaningless now and went to sit down. There was a sudden sound of rumbling in the air. Kalin thought it sounded like thunder in the distance, but the sky was clear from any clouds. The noise seemed to be getting louder. Karra and Leib jumped up out of their beds as the noise got louder. They grabbed for their swords as a large number of royal riders galloped close by along the road, heading north. They were travelling very fast, and in a matter of moments they were gone.

Leib sheathed his sword. 'There must have been over a hundred riders.'

Karra sheathed his sword too. 'Yes. I wonder why they are travelling at such speed. At first, I thought it was those outlaws coming back to seek revenge. Let us travel with caution. I have a bad feeling about things now.’

21

A sharp knock sounded on the door of the King's chambers, waking him and the Queen instantly. He arose from his bed with a jump and put on a light pair of shoes. The Queen was about to get up too, but the King gestured to her to stay in bed. 'I will take care of this, it's probably nothing. You stay in bed.' He opened the door and was greeted by one of his servants with a candle. The servant bowed at the sight of the King and apologised for waking him so late and led him to the main hall. When the King arrived, he was met by his two generals, General Titus and Arthen, The Primary Chief General and a dishevelled looking captain whose name he could not remember.

They bowed and General Arthen spoke. 'We are sorry for disturbing you at such a late hour your Highness, but we have some very grave news.' The King listened intently. 'Captain Brota has just arrived from the South Wall. He has ridden non-stop to get here to bring us news.' The General paused.

'Well, what is it?' The King said impatiently.

'The South Wall has been attacked and taken by the Empire of Eamhair. Every soldier there has been killed and the Empire is free to move into our lands.'

The King slowly took a seat on his throne. 'This cannot be. We have had peace with the Empire for a long-time now.' The King took some time to think on the news. 'How dare they enter our lands. So, the peace times have come to an end. We must make preparation now for war. I will not allow the Empire to take any part of our Kingdom. We must send troops down to meet them and drive them back to where they came from. They will feel the force of the Kingdom for such treachery. Set the flags and cloaks to red with a black lion's head, and make sure every man is equipped with the new armour you designed.'

At sunrise, all the generals were called to the war room and plans were set in place. Trumpets sounded out, and the white flags of the Kingdom were lowered and replaced with red flags publicising that the Kingdom was at war. All the troops within the city of Kitia were called to the palace courtyard and told about the news. They were ordered to change their white cloaks to the red war cloaks and put on their new armour. All the gates were closed, and the harbour was closed to all foreign ships. Extra guards and night watchmen were set in place and there was a curfew set within the city. Scouts were sent out daily to watch the areas surrounding Kitia. Royal Messengers were sent out to every corner of the Kingdom, informing them of the news and ordering all troops to return to the capital to make preparations. On the third day, the main gate to the city was opened and a force of 10,000 Royal Soldiers, in full battle armour and long red cloaks, marched south led by General Arthen and nine other Generals. General Titus was ordered to stay in the city and wait for the rest of the troops to come in. He would then march south too, in support of General Arthen. The talk throughout the Kingdom now was all about war, and a sense of fear began to grip the people. New recruits were hired, and the forges were busy night and day making additional weapons and armour. Giram, the King's Financial Custodian, arranged for the food stores within the city to be filled and supplies to be sent south to feed the army. All preparations were put in place and everyone was ready for a possible war.

The Royal army had been on the march for a week now, but the scouts that were sent ahead had reported no sign of any enemy forces yet. They knew that would change when they reached the south wall. More and more people were heading in the opposite direction toward the capital, in hopes of protection from the King. Everyone looked frightened with the prospects of a potential war. It would be a few more weeks before they arrived to confront the enemy. The closer they got, the less people they saw. Farms and villages had been deserted in fear of a coming war. It was always the innocent that suffered in times like this. The marching army consumed any livestock or crops that were abandoned on the way.

General Zukata had moved his Imperial army a few miles into the Kingdom of Latonia, along the road to Tureen. He set up a high wooden defensive wall in anticipation of an attack. Three smaller walls were then erected, creating a huge rectangular fortress. Hundreds of trees had been cut down to make this fortification. Branches were stripped off the tree trunks and placed into deep trenches and then the trenches were filled in, leaving the tree trunk standing high into the air. This formed the walls of their defence. Then there was a structured platform erected behind the fence, so the Dragon soldiers could defend the wall from a height. These platforms also helped to stabilise the walls. The wall stretched out for over a mile, with two deep trenches in front to prevent a full-on charge. He would then use the South Wall as a fallback in case they were overrun. Here he would hold the line. Although it would take a huge force to overrun a 15000 strong Dragon army. His orders were to hold the south wall for a year, and then the Emperor would arrive with another force and they would then move towards the Capital City Kitia and take the Kingdom once and for all. War was a waiting game it seemed. Once the supplies were continuously coming in to feed the army, they would be fine.

It was a few weeks more before two scouts came thundering in through the gate. They had laid first sight on the incoming Royal army. There were only a few miles now between the two nations. General Zukata questioned them about the army's advance. The size of the force was larger than he had anticipated, around 10,000 but nonetheless he would hold them off. He called for a meeting with the other Generals to discuss their war tactics. If they attacked straight away this would benefit the Dragon army. They would cut down hundreds with their archers as they tried to reach the wooden wall. This would thin out their attack. The killing ground in front of the wall was scattered with sharp stakes pointing upwards that would further inflict injuries and hamper the attackers. If the enemy managed to take the wooden fort, the Dragon soldiers would fall back to the South Wall. If they tried to pursue then they would run into his Dragon horsemen 2,000 strong. These horsemen would cut down more as they launched into them.

All the Generals and some captains were packed into the war tent. General Zukata took the floor. 'We are going to sit and wait for the Royal army to come to us. They might decide to attack us, or they might decide to wait. I see no point in us launching a charge towards them. We will hold this ground for as long as we can.'

One of the other Generals stepped forward and bowed. 'What if they do not attack? What if they are waiting for their force to grow or try and move into a position behind us? What then? Should we not attack them now while their army is smaller in numbers?'

'That is a good point, and one I have thought about in depth. We are informed that General Arthen could be reinforced with another army from their capital. It will take time for them to reach here. According to their war rules, The General will have to hold talks with me before he can act on anything. At that point, I will try to force him into making a decision and he will be forced to attack us. This will then give us the upper hand. They will have great losses. We have scouts out in every direction feeding back information on an hourly basis. If the Royal force tries to outflank us and attack from the rear or the sides, they will be attacked on the move with our Dragon horsemen.' The plan was set, and they all took their places waiting for the attack to come. It would be a waiting game now, And Zukata knew patience would be the key.

General Arthen halted his men a mile in from General Zukata's army and started to make his own fortifications and defence line. They also erected a wooden wall for their defence line. He would wait until General Titus joined him before he would attempt any attacks on the Empire. General Arthen sent two riders with a message to the enemy's line to request talks with their chief command. This would take place at noon the next day. The request also said to come alone. This was standard protocol in the dealings of war. The next morning, General Arthen had a small tent erected a half mile from their line, in the centre of the two armies, with a table and two chairs placed under the tent. Two cups and a jug of his finest wine were laid out on the table. Just before noon General Arthen mounted his horse and rode out to the tent alone. He arrived and, having tied his horse to the post of the tent, he took off his helmet, placed it on the table and sat down to wait. A short while later he could see that there was a rider approaching his position from the enemy's line. Content that the rider was alone, he composed himself as the rider got closer. The rider took his time, seeming to be in no rush. He arrived, dismounted, tied his horse and then walked towards the table. He was a small man, but Arthen felt that he was in the presence of a warrior. Arthen watched his every movement. He was in perfect balance on his approach and emanated confidence.

'My name is General Arthen. I am the prime General for King Roban's Royal army, thank you for coming to meet me.'

The small man bowed slowly and then removed his black helmet, 'I am General Zukata, leader of the Dragon Army and loyal servant to the Empire of Eamhair.' He spoke the Latonian language very well but had a strong accent.

Arthen pointed to the other chair. 'Please take a seat.'

They both sat, and Arthen poured two cups of wine and handed a cup to Zukata. 'No thank you, I do not drink alcohol.'

Arthen placed the cup to one side on the table. 'I have asked you to meet me, to see if there is any way I can assist you in leaving our lands.'

Zukata sat very still in his chair. 'That will not happen. I am under orders to hold the passage to the south by my Emperor and no one, not you or the whole Royal army, will move me from this position.'

Arthen took a sip of wine to try calming himself. He spoke again, this time his voice was more forceful. 'You have broken the treaty by invading Natalia, Cinam and Naos, and now you have attacked our southern wall and have come into our land. This Nation's Treaty has been upheld for nearly 14 years. The Kingdom will not stand for this.' Arthen thundered his fist onto the table nearly spilling both cups of wine.

'Your uncontrolled actions do not scare me General Arthen, and it is not my nation that has broken this Treaty it is yours. You sent armed troops into Natalia, breaking the first rule of the Treaty.'

Arthen shook his head. 'Those troops were sent to help the Natalian Chancellor to deal with an internal struggle. They were going through difficult times and the Kingdom lent a hand.'

'Do not try to justify your engagements by saying you were just. The Treaty is clear, and you broke it. Now you will pay the price for your doings.'

The General Arthen jumped up, sending his chair flying backwards. He grabbed the hilt of his sword and was about to draw it and cut down this disrespectful little man but stopped himself. 'You have threatened me, and my Kingdom and I will not stand for it. I will be forced to uphold the law here if you continue to speak in this way and do not leave the Kingdom.' Arthen was surprised that the little man did not even flinch; he just sat there unnerved by Arthen's anger and sudden movement.

'I have heard a great deal about you, General Arthen. I have heard you are a great warrior and a great leader of men. It saddens me that you refuse to accept my views on this subject. The fact that you are quick to anger tells me that you feel strongly about it, but that does not excuse the fact that you are in the wrong here. Tell me, do you not long for war? Do you not long for the powerful feeling that victory brings?

As soldiers, we all hope for peace, for it is the soldiers who have to carry the horrors of battle with them until their grave. But the General, he must keep his nerve, his dignity, his respect and his longing for the thrill of battle, for he is seen as a higher being than just a mere, normal soldier. For you and I are the same. Have you not longed for this war to happen? Have you not missed those days of splendour and glory?'

Arthen took his hand from his sword, picked up his chair, and sat back down in deep thought about what the little man had said. 'I have found myself longing for battle, I admit this. I do miss the days of riding into a fight with my men surrounding me and looking to me for courage and glory and for the thrill of war, but those days are behind me now. I have bigger obligations than satisfying my own ego, we must look for better times, not for us, but for our people.'

'Answered like a true General, but you cannot hide from what your heart desires. Even in strong words.'

'I have no time to philosophize about war and life with you, General Zukata, and you are running out of time. My army is waiting on my command to attack. You must pull your army back from the Kingdom. I am not going to give you much time to retreat, take this as a blessing.'

'I am not moving anywhere, General Arthen, and I have all the time I need. Your troops will be like water crashing against a mountain.'

'Time is like a handful of sand, the tighter you squeeze it, the faster it runs through your fingers. You will feel the force of the Kingdom in one day, that is my vow to you General Zutaka. You have one day to retreat your army from our lands.'

'Well then, this meeting is over. You have given me an ultimatum and I must prepare for those actions. Thank you for asking me to meet you. I hope that we can talk again under better times. Keep yourself alive until then.'

General Arthen stood. 'Well met little General, until we meet again.'

Zukata also stood and bowed, put his helmet back on, smoothly mounted his horse and rode off just as slowly as he had approached. Arthen sat back down and, draining both cups of wine, gathered his thoughts. What have I done, I have to attack now in one day. He felt angry with himself; this was not the outcome that he had hoped for, but this was always the case in war.

General Zukata arrived back to his army. His co-generals were waiting for him as he rode through the large, makeshift wooden gate. He dismounted his horse and a soldier took the reins from him and led his horse to the stables. Zukata walked to the war tent with the other Generals and they gathered inside around a table. Zukata then addressed them. 'The talk went as I expected. They have given us an ultimatum. If we do not leave their lands by tomorrow, they will attack. This is what we expected and wanted to happen. Their force is smaller than ours and we have a stronger position. They will come, and they will die. He was stubborn and easy to anger in our talks. Arrogance is the reason he will lose; this will be his downfall. We have forced him to make a move and now we will take advantage of this. The true measure of a General is not the superior position he moves his army to, but the inferior position he makes his enemy move to. Prepare the men for tomorrow, for it will be a bloody day.'

The sun had just risen above the horizon and bathed all his troops in its golden glow. The Royal Army were ready to advance on the intruders from across the sea. General Arthen was dressed in full battle armour with his red war cloak, as were all his troops. The new armour fitted well and did not restrict his movement as much as the old armour. He walked his horse to the front line where his men awaited his orders. Slowly, he mounted his large, grey, war horse and faced a 10,000 strong Royal army. His voice boomed out over the troops. 'I hope you all had a good sleep last night for you will need all the energy you can muster today. I myself had a restless night. Several times I woke and looked out to see if the night torches had been put out on the enemies' wall and hoped that they had left our lands, but this did not happen. So here we are now to make this occur. I had given them one day to leave our lands and they have ignored this.'

He fell silent for a few seconds. Then his voice became even louder. 'We will not tolerate this. We will not allow other nations to take advantage of us. We will not allow anyone to break our rules. These are our lands and we will fight to protect them. So, let us march upon them and let them feel the might of the Royal Latonian Army.'

The General turned his horse and drew his sword and pointed it in the direction of the Dragon army.

'Forward!' He shouted.

Trumpets sounded, followed by a steady drumbeat, and the 10,000-strong force began its advance. General Zukata watched the slow-moving army coming towards his defence line, who were crouched behind the wooden wall. The wall stretched for about a mile and was about 10 feet high. The two sides angled back to deflect an oncoming force. It was then joined onto a smaller wall which encircled the Dragon army within, creating a small fortress. In case of an attack from behind, the smaller wall would then be used to defend their rear.

General Zukata shouted out his orders. 'Archers! Be at the ready.' A line of archers the full length of the wall notched their bows and stood ready behind the wall of defenders, who were in turn armed with long spears to thrust down at the attackers. Zukata looked back down at the 2,000 mounted Dragon force, led by two Generals, that were ready to charge out from the back gate and attack the Royal force from the sides when they were packed in against the front of the wall. The Royal army stopped their march just out of bow shot and were ordered to raise their shields. They then launched forward at a faster pace and advanced their attack. General Zukata gave the order for the bowmen to fire. Hundreds and hundreds of arrows were shot into the air. They looked like they were traveling in slow motion the higher they sailed. As they reached the peak of their arc, they changed trajectory and tore into the oncoming army. Most bounced off or stuck into their shields, but scores more made their way through and inflicted horrific injuries and fatalities on the Royal army. But still they advanced.

A retaliatory wave of flaming arrows flew into the air from the back of the Royal Army in hopes of setting the wooden wall alight. A great deal of these fell short, but some hit home, killing the Dragon soldiers. Some reached the wall, but these small fires were put out as soon as they landed. The closer the Royal Force got; the more fatalities were inflicted on them by the Dragon Archers. Hundreds were killed before they reached the base of the wall. Ladders were brought forward and propped up against the wall and Royal troops scrambled up them to try and breach the wooden defence. Spears lashed out, stabbing and piercing them as they climbed the ladders. The noisy clash of weapons on armour rang out and the conflict was almost deafening as men screamed and shouted in the heat of the battle while thousands of the attacking force were packing in against the wall. General Zukata turned again and gave the order for the 2,000 mounted Dragon soldiers to start their attack from both sides of the wall. The back gates opened, and they thundered out. Splitting into two forces, they galloped around to confront the Royal army. An arrow flashed by Arthen's face as he peered around his shield, getting closer to the wall surrounded by his men. Then another one thudded in his shield, making him pull back in behind the protection of his shield.

The Royal army was taking heavy losses. He knew this would be the case but if they could take the wall, he would gain the advantage in this attack. This was a big task, but it was their only option at this stage; he could not just sit there and watch his enemy invade their lands. Seeing his men being killed, Arthen could not help wondering if had he made a huge mistake in attacking this early and not waiting for the backup force led by General Titus to arrive. He was in the thick of the attack with his men, they all pushed forward trying to climb the ladders. They all held up their shields high above them in an attempt to stop arrows raining down on them as they all bunched at the base of the wall. Arthen could see a section of the wooden wall swaying back and forth under the pressure of the men pushing forward. To his dismay, he could see in the distance a wedge of attacking Dragon horsemen crashing into the sides of his men. He turned just in time to see that a second attack was happening at the other end of his mass of soldiers. Some of his men were starting to panic now as the attackers became the attacked. Some men had thrown thick, hooked ropes over the tops of the wooden walls and tried to climb up to get at the defenders, with little success. The General then noticed a thick rope hanging from the wall at the section that had been starting to move. He pushed his horse through the mass of men and grabbed the rope, quickly tying it to his saddle. Long spears stabbed at him from the top of the wall as he tried to retreat. An arrow bounced from his helmet and was deflected into the neck of one of his men, who fell underneath the crush of bodies. The rope pulled tight now and the horse struggled to move forward. An arrow hit the horse in its rear, and it jumped forward. The rope snapped tight again, pulling a large tree trunk away from that section of the wall. This enabled some men to slip through the loosened wood and onto the other side. The Royal army pushed through the gap and then another two tree trunks were pulled outwards, making the gap even bigger. The Royal army rushed in.

At first, the Dragon soldiers were able to defend the breach, but the Royal soldiers continued to push through, forcing them back into the wooden fortress. The fighting was fierce. The Royal soldiers were heavily armoured, making it extremely difficult for the Dragon soldiers to fell them. The Royal soldiers on the flanks who had been taking a lot of damage, had now turned and were defending against the Dragon Horsemen. This surprise attack had turned the battle in favour of the Imperial Dragon army. The mounted horsemen had now moved and were attacking behind them. Arthen could see that they were losing the battle. They were taking too many losses. He could feel his heart starting to sink. Some of his men had started to run in fear and were swiftly picked off and cut down by the horsemen. 'Keep pushing, men,' he shouted. 'Take the wall.'

Just then, he heard a distant trumpet sound out from behind them. He could just make it out over the noise and the chaos. He turned and looked back over the sea of his pushing army. Royal horsemen, thousands of them, came into view and were galloping towards them with General Titus Cassian leading the charge. A feeling of relief encircled him, and he turned back around to face the enemy with renewed vigour. The Dragon soldiers began to panic on the wall as they saw their cavalry demolished by the thousands of mounted Royal soldiers.

Arthen looked up to the wall. He watched as a huge man scaled the ladder and swung his war hammer, hitting two Dragon men at the top of the wall. He knew this Royal Soldier as one of his captains by his huge size. Captain Loman was his name, and he was a force to be reckoned with in battle. Swords, spears and arrows bounced off his armour as he swung out in all directions, killing the defenders with his hammer. We then watched as he gained a position on the wall and held it. Many defenders attacked him, but he held firm, allowing more Royal Soldiers to gain access to the ladder and claim a section on the ramparts. More and more men flooded over the wall now. One of the Dragon Generals, Tantul, was killed as he rushed in to attack Loman, but Loman brought the hammer down on the Dragon General's helmet and crushed it with one blow, stopping him instantly in his tracks. The defenders around him started to give, allowing a number of Latonians to gain footing on the wall, and hundreds pushed through the gap that General Arthen had made. The Dragon soldiers found it hard to make a clean kill as the armour of the Latonian soldiers was almost impenetrable. The tide was starting to turn.

The Dragon soldiers were gradually beginning to fall back, and they were being killed by the hundreds. General Zukata tried to rally his troops but it was too late. Fear had infested and panic had set in. It was time to fall back. He signalled for the trumpet to sound a retreat to the

South Wall as planned. The gate at the smaller back wall was opened and the Dragon soldiers fled as fast as they could to find safety. As they ran, General Titus led his mounted army around to the back of the wooden fort and gave chase to the retreating men, cutting them down in their hundreds. Hundreds more were cut off and the mounted horsemen tore into them, killing hundreds more. There was a wooded area between the wooden defence and the southern wall they were fleeing to. This would give them the cover they needed to flee the attacking horsemen. Thousands were now running for their lives, trying to make it to the tree line. General Zukata made it to the trees and organised a line of archers to send arrows into the Royal horse men, hoping to slow their attack on his fleeing men. This seemed to work and the last of his men made it through. They pushed on until they reached the safety of the South Wall. The gates were opened, and they ran inside. They were soon followed by the thundering sound of the horsemen, but they stayed out of reach from the archers on the wall and then retreated back to their main force.

General Zukata immediately called for a meeting to take stock. Three of his Generals had been killed. Those who remained stood in a circle.

'That was a disaster. What happened to our wall defence?'

Another General bowed, stepped forward and spoke. 'I was watching from the archers' line and saw General Tantul attacked by a huge Latonian soldier with a war hammer. The large soldier managed to kill a few Dragon soldiers as he climbed, enabling him to gain a position onto the ramparts. General Tantul saw this and went to deal with this attacker. Tantul hacked and slashed at him but the armour he was wearing was too strong. He fought well but he was taken down and some of his men then fell back. This led to the enemy taking the wall.'

General Zukata looked disappointed. 'I want these men that gave ground brought to me so they can be punished. There is no room in the Dragon Army for weak men. What else led to our defeat?' He looked around and no one stepped forward. 'No body?' He shouted. 'I will tell you then what I saw. Aside from the large warrior climbing the wall and taking the ramparts, I also saw that there was a breach in the wall. Their General Arthen managed to pull a length of wood from the wall with a rope. This tells me that the construction was not strong enough and that parts of the wall were built in haste. This is not good enough. We must be more professional in everything we do from here on in. Is that understood?'

He looked around at the other Generals. 'Yes sir!' They all said.

'Now bring me the men that fell back on the wall and bring me the men that constructed that part of the wall that was breached. Then bring me some of our enemies' armour, so I can see what all this fuss is about.'

22

Jerra walked fast along the docks with four of his harbour guards. He felt a bit nervous as he approached the biggest ship in the harbour, The Sea Wolf. A shirtless, bald man greeted them as they reached the gangway to the ship. Jerra stepped forward. 'Can I speak to your captain?'

'I will inform him you are here.'

Jerra went to walk on to the gangway bridge and the bald man stopped him. 'No one is allowed on to the Sea Wolf without the Captain's permission.'

Jerra stepped back and waited with his men. The bald man arrived back promptly. 'He will see you, but your men will have to stay here and wait for you.' Jerra nodded and the bald man led him on to the ship and down along the deck to the Captain's quarters. Jerra was astonished at the size of the ship's deck. The bald man opened the door and motioned for the Latonian Captain to enter. Jerra went inside and found Vimeo sitting at his desk, looking over some papers. He jumped up and shook Jerra's hand. His welcome lifted some pressure from Jerra. 'It is good to see you Jerra. I have a great deal of questions to ask.'

Jerra raised his hand. 'And it is good to see you too. I must apologise to you first. You came here with information about an attack by the Empire and asked to see the King. I had organised for you to talk to one of his advisors, Lord Sabat. I should have taken the matter more seriously and brought this directly to the King. We have just received word that The Empire has taken Naos, Natalia and Cinam. The last report that came in said that they have taken the South Wall. The city of Kitia is currently under lockdown, and we are preparing to send troops down to counter this move by the Empire. Please keep this information to yourself for now.'

'It was only a matter of time before the news reached here. My men have been kept on this ship for over a week now. Between that and not knowing what has happened to their families and home, I think it is taking its toll on them.'

'I will arrange some shore leave for your crew, supervised, of course. Also, I will arrange for some fresh clothes and food and water to be brought on board. I am afraid that you will not be able to leave the harbour as the harbour gate is now closed. A scouting ship arrived last night claiming they had seen 3 Dragon ships off the South West coast heading in this direction. These might very well be the ships you spoke of and that chased you here. The scout ship barely managed to keep ahead of them and bring us the news.'

'That sounds like them. The waters will also be under threat now.'

'There has been an order to man the fleet and guard the coastlines to prevent any troop landings. I have a question for you.'

'By all means ask.' Vimeo said as he sat back down in his seat. And pointed at the opposite chair for Jerra to sit.

'What would it take for you to transform this ship into a Warship?'

'I had considered this when we started building her. I think it would make a superb Warship. But I no longer have my workshop and tools.'

'I will supply you with whatever you need, and we can talk about payment for you and your men for serving the King.'

'I think my men will be pleased to hear that. It will give them something to take their minds from Natalia. It will also give them a chance for revenge on what the Empire have done to them.'

'There will be plenty of people thinking the same thing. When can you start?'

'I will write up a list of all the things I will need and give it to you then. There were a few ideas floating around in my head that might be of some help, if my calculations are correct.'

'I am looking forward to seeing what you can do. I will leave you to your work and call back tomorrow with the supplies I have promised for your crew.'

Over the next few weeks, plenty of work took place on the Sea Wolf. Everything was overseen by Captain Vimeo. Some of his ideas seemed quite absurd at first, but then when completed, everyone stood back in amazement. The men were happy to be working on a new project and this kept them focused. Captain Jerra visited the Sea Wolf daily to see the progress of the transformation. He was the only one granted permission onto the Sea Wolf.

In secret, Vimeo and his men had designed and fixed a huge bow to the deck of the Sea Wolf. It was capable of firing out huge arrows, the height of a man, with broad iron arrowheads that could penetrate through thick wood. He tested these with small boats in the harbour to great effect, sinking all their targets. They were designed to rupture the lower end of an enemy ship's hull, just under the surface of the water, and cause it to sink with speed. He had tested different types of weapons, but the over-sized bow worked best. He had this attached to the front of the Sea Wolf and tested it daily. Its range covered the whole distance of the harbour with great accuracy. Vimeo had only shown Jerra drawings of the weapon. He wanted to wait until the weapon was fully developed before, he presented it to Jerra. Upon seeing the design, Jerra was very impressed with the drawings and the type of technology and had asked Vimeo for further ideas that they could use. Vimeo turned him down, saying that his other ideas would have to be saved for another day. The Royal fleet also stocked up with supplies and weapons, as scouting ships constantly scanned the waters for Dragon ships. Some ships had been sighted far out to sea but were too distant to determine whether they were Dragon ships or not and left alone. Everything was prepared for all-out war. Vimeo and Barus and his men were also ready now, and Vimeo was anxious to show the Latonian Captain his new design.

23

Arthen made his way through the mass of dead men. The ground was soaked in blood. He recognised some of the dead and his heart weighed heavy as he moved along. Royal soldiers were walking among the carnage, looking for wounded and dispatching any enemy that still lived. Riders came around and dismounted. It was General Titus Cassian. He marched over to him and saluted. 'My Primary General, how are you?'

Arthen put his hand on Titus's shoulder plate. 'I am fine thanks to you and your men. It was truly a great spectacle seeing all the Royal horsemen charging down to save us.'

'We did not think you were going to attack this soon.'

'We had no choice, but I am happy with the outcome. They will know now that we will not stop until we are free of them from our lands.'

'We would have been here faster if we had known. As we came across your camp and defence wall, we could hear the sound of battle in the distance and realised that you must have attacked. We then broke into a gallop and came across the battle.'

'Well I am truly grateful you got here in time. You saved a lot of lives, getting to us when you did. We would have had a tough fight trying to take that wall with their horsemen attacking us from both sides. You turned the tide with your charge.'

'Have we lost many men?'

'I'm not sure yet but going by the amount lying dead on the ground I would say yes. I will have a final count later today. We have many injured too. Before you left, were there any plans to send reinforcements?'

'Plans were being debated, but there are still soldiers coming in from across the Kingdom to Kitia. Once there are enough soldiers to make a century, I am sure the King will send reinforcements down to us. What are your plans now Arthen?'

'The plan now is to wait. I think we will take this wooded defence and see what their next move is. I don't think they will have the morale for a further attack now that we have sent them running.'

'We rode down and killed hundreds of them as they fled. They are now at the South Wall.'

'Well let's hope they stay there. If they come on to our lands again, they will feel our force again.' General Titus looked down and noticed that Arthen was dripping blood from the tips of his fingers. 'Is your hand OK General?'

Arthen looked down at his hand and saw the blood. 'Yes. I took a blow to the upper arm, between my chest plate and my shoulder guard. I think it is only a small wound.'

'You will have to get that seen to. Do you think you could hold a cup of wine?'

'I think I could hold several cups of wine and I think I owe a few large cups of wine to you, and our men. Everyone fought well today.' The two Generals walked off towards their campsite to start making preparations.

General Zukata stood on the ramparts, looking down at all his troops lined up below. There were eight men kneeling down, facing out towards the troops with their hands tied behind their backs and their mouths gagged. Two of these men knelt separately from the other six. Zukata walked along behind the tied men before stopping to address his troops. 'Today was a bad day for the Empire. We have failed to hold our position, we have failed to defeat our enemy, and we have taken huge losses. We have lost nearly 4,000 Dragon Soldiers today.' He walked slowly again and stopped. 'There were a number of areas that could be improved upon, and these improvements will be made straight away. I am a man of patience. I can tolerate a lot of things, but I cannot tolerate weakness. Today we have seen weakness! Weakness in our army! These men here before you are weak men, for they did not do their job today and let all of us down. As a result, we lost this battle. The Dragon Army cannot afford to have weakness, so we say goodbye to our weakness.'

Zukata looked back and nodded to one of his men. Captain Askil stepped forward and walked to the first kneeling man. A long knife glinted in his hand. He grabbed the man's hair, roughly pulling his head back. The bound man tried to struggle, but Askil drew his sharp blade across the man's neck, slicing into his exposed throat. Blood sprayed out in a wide arc as Askil pushed him down to the ground. The man slumped to one side and his whole body shook as blood flowed out onto the stone wall. The other bound men struggled now and tried to cry out. Askil moved purposefully along the line of kneeling men, killing them one at a time in the same way. One man tried to roll himself off the high wall and down to the onlooking troops, but Askil caught him before he could manage it, dragging him back and opening his throat also.

The first six were dead or dying when he moved on to the final two. He grabbed the closest man to him and, pulling his head back by his hair, was just about to slice into his throat when General Zukata held out his hand. 'Stop!' The General commanded. The last two men watched, visibly shaking, on their knees, with total fear in their eyes, but they did not struggle or try to run from their fate. Askil let go of him and stood back, cleaning his knife on his sleeve.

Zukata walked over to them. 'These two men failed to make sure that a part of the wooden wall was not securely fixed in place and as a result, our enemy were able to gain access through this point in our wall, but I do not think this mistake should cost them their lives. During battle they did not run, they fought hard, they are not weak men. I need strong men. I need strong men in my army if we are to succeed in carrying out the orders that our Emperor has given us. However, they must be punished. 20 lashes for each man.'

General Zukata walked from the wall in disgust. Not from the fact that they had lost to the enemy or the fact that his men had run, but from the fact that he had to kill the six men in order to prove a point to the rest of his army. As he entered the tent, he told his guards that he did not want to be disturbed. He undid his armour and cleaned his swords. Feeling tired now, he slept. The General left his tent at dawn and made his way to the open ground in the courtyard. He had taken his two swords with him. He started to stretch his muscles and warm up, as he did every morning. He then performed the Dance of the two Dragons with his two swords. He spun and slashed into the air like a dance. Other soldiers then came out to exercise. They joined in the exercise, all in perfect sync with one another. Soon there were thousands of soldiers, all out of their tents joining in with the fighting dance. When Zukata was finished, he returned to his tent and washed and then had a light breakfast. He called one of his guards in to arrange for a meeting to be held with the other Generals in the war tent to discuss their next course of action.

The men sat around a table with maps laid out. 'I want you all here to talk about our next plan of action. Seeing as General Arthen and his armies have taken our stronghold and changed our plans. I have a suggestion to make; due to our loss to him I would like to divert his attention. We have suffered a large number of casualties and our reinforcements will take some time to get here. Now, we can hold this position at this wall for a long time. The Latonians have done a good job in building it. If we were to send a small force to attack the city of Tureen, North of here, Arthen would be forced to divide his army in order to protect the city. This would weaken his position and would open up areas for us to attack him. What are your thoughts on this?'

General Sana stood, bowed and sat back down. 'If we decide on attacking Tureen, how will we stop the Latonians from seeing a large force leaving here at the wall and travelling north?'

'That is a good question General Sana. I have thought about this last night. I think if we can constantly despatch small forces at night, they could travel along the coastal mountains northeast of here and then change to a westerly course and head inland. Then we should be able to come around and attack the city without being detected.'

'I will lead this attack if you require, General Zukata?' Spoke Sana.

General Zukata nodded. 'Make it so. We will start tomorrow night.'

General Sana bowed. Each night over the next few weeks, 100 Dragon soldiers sneaked out from the protection of the wall and moved stealthily towards the mountain range. They congregated at an isolated cold camp at the base of a mountain far from the wall. Each day another 100 soldiers would arrive after traveling from the wall. When their forces reached 2500, they moved inland, straight for Tureen. They dispatched any farms and villages they came across, making sure no one survived to give away their position. There were only a few hundred Royal soldiers guarding the small wall around the city of Tureen. These were killed in the first attack. The number of inhabitants of the city was greatly reduced as most had fled to the capital, Kitia, seeking refuge. Some travelled north to be as far away as possible from the invading Empire. Once they had taken Tureen, they allowed a score of Latonians to escape so they would bring back word of the attack to Arthen. Their plan was set in motion. As long as they had control of the city of Tureen, they could launch attacks westward on the supply chain that fed the main bulk of the Latonian army.

24

Chal's mother kissed him for good luck as some of the farmers and workers waited at the door to see him off. It was a bright sunny morning and Chal made his way to Kitia with his belongings over his shoulder in a travel bag. As he walked along the path, he turned to wave goodbye. They all waved back at him. He wanted to run but he decided that he might need his energy for later that day. His arm was healing well, and he had full movement of it now. He was keeping up with the exercises the doctor had shown him how to strengthen his arm with a series of exercises. The feeling was a bit surreal. He thought it would have felt different than this, leaving home and joining the Royal Army. The recruits were not supposed to start their training for another week but when the news was brought to King Roban about the invasion in the south, everything changed. The city of Kitia's flags changed from white to red, indicating that they were at war. All the city gates were closed, and the harbour was locked. People from all over Latonia were coming into Kitia seeking safety. The city was almost full and soon they would have to start turning people away. A huge army was sent south to deal with the invaders, led by Arthen, and then Chal's father left with another Royal Army to support him.

These were frightening times.

The Royal army had commenced recruiting almost immediately and Chal had gotten his letter early. He checked it was still in place in his top pocket as he walked. He arrived at the city; it was unusual to see the main gate closed. A guard shouted down and Chal waved his recruiting letter at him and the gate opened a few feet to let him in. He then made his way to the barracks. The city was full of people, there were nearly as many here as there had been during the summer celebration. A long line of young men and boys led from the barracks out to the parade square. Chal quickly joined the queue. It was not long before he made it to the desk and handed in his letter. The man read the letter, looked at it and then looked back at Chal.

'Chal Cassian… Ah! General Titus Cassian's son. We are pleased to have you here, young man. I watched your sword fight in the summer games. You were very unlucky to have been injured. How is your arm now?'

'It is nearly back to full strength.'

'Good, we will need strong young men like you in weeks to come. Please follow this corridor here down to the hall and you will all be met by Captain Barra.'

Chal signed a sheet of paper and thanked the man, then moved along the corridor. He could hear a lot of talking as he approached the hall, and the noise was very loud. There must be around 500 young men all gathered in the hall. He recognised some of them and he could see Brin had signed up as a recruit too. He was chatting and laughing with some other boys.

There was a loud shout. 'LISTEN UP EVERYONE!' The room fell quiet. Captain Barra was standing at the top of the hall and all eyes were on him. 'Thank you all for committing yourselves to the Royal Army and to the service of the King. Your lives will change from here on in. You will obey orders from your superiors, and you will train and learn and become part of the strongest army in the known world. Some of you will find it hard and some of you will excel. We have a big task at hand. As you all know, we are at war, and the training you will receive will be harder than anything you have done so far in your lives. Time is precious here as we need reinforcements sent south to help in the war. During your training over the next few weeks you will be assessed and then you will all be broken down and matched with a suitable category. Some of you will become Royal guards; some of you will become Royal Chargers and own your own horse.' Captain Barra walked in amongst the new recruits as he spoke. 'Some might become a captain like me but most of you will make up the bulk of the Royal Army, every job is important here. So be ready and do not be afraid to be at your best as it will pay off here.'

The captain left the hall and the new recruits were broken down into different sections. Each section was assigned a leader. Over the next few weeks, they were put through training that involved fitness and skills with sword and knife. Chal loved every minute of it and excelled in all aspects of army life. He particularly liked the study of war and its history and the tactical side of warfare. After three weeks of training, they were put through some tests and all accumulated in the hall.

Captain Barra read out all the names and they were separated into groups.

'Well done to all. We only lost a few recruits to injuries and poor fitness. You all have been assigned your new roles. Some of you will march out in two days and head south to reinforce General Arthen to fight against these invaders from the Empire. Each group will be assigned a captain. Your training has not finished, it has just begun.'

Chal had made it into the Royal Mounted Chargers. He was delighted with their decision. Captain Barra made his way through the young soldiers congratulating them. He made his way to Chal. 'Well done young man, your father will be very proud of you. You have completed the training with flying colours.'

'Thank you, captain. I have loved every minute of it.'

Captain Barra looked around and then looked at Chal. 'Don't be loving it too much as your unit is being sent to protect the supply chain that feeds your father's and General Arthen's armies in the south. It will be a tough job for you and the other new recruits.'

Some weeks had passed. Chal and 120 mounted troops were around 100 miles from Tureen. Everything had gone as expected. They had guarded the supply wagons as they made their slow way down south to the main bulk of the army. There was no sign of the enemy on their travels. Their Captain's name was Amin, he was newly appointed to his position and was not too popular with his men. He had made some bad calls along the way already. Chal had disagreed with him on several occasions. He was trying his best to like the man, but he just could not. Chal had been promoted to the Captain's Second before they left Kitia but had found it difficult to follow some of the Captain's orders. He was beginning to question the man's mental capacity. The closer they got to their goal of delivering the supplies, the more dangerous it was, and in the heat of things it would be catastrophic if they made silly mistakes.

They had pulled off the road for the night and made camp. They were still some way from General Arthen and General Titus. Chal was looking forward to seeing his father and telling him all about what had happened since they had last seen each other. They had heard reports that the two Generals were situated in a wooden fort that the enemy had built. This was located between the city of Tureen and the south wall protecting the lands from the empire. The Empire still had possession of the south wall. Plans and tactics ran through his mind every night as he lay down to sleep. He would try and think of ways that would defeat the enemy at the wall. All these thoughts played through Chal's mind as he drifted off to sleep. The next day, the convoy set out again on its journey. It was a pleasant morning with a light bit of rain. Captain Amin sent out some scouts at first light, but they had not reported back as yet. Chal had a feeling that something might be wrong. He rode to the head of the line to inquire about the scouts with the Captain.

'Captain, have we word back yet from our scouts?'

'No, not yet but they should be back soon. We will soon be with the Generals and have the supplies delivered,' he replied.

Chal could feel his frustration building and interrupted Amin as he was speaking. 'I have a funny feeling that something has happened to them. My recommendation would be that we should stop and hold our position until they get back?'

The Captain shook his head, unhappy with being interrupted by his subordinate. 'They will be back shortly. Don't be worrying. We will keep going. Now get back in line and do your job.'

Chal could see all eyes were on him, so he moved back along the line and took his position. This was nonsense, he thought, but he had to follow his orders. They marched on.

After another hour, Chal could not help himself and approached Amin again. 'Have they come back yet?'

'Don't bother me about this Chal I have enough to deal with, without you complaining, again.'

Chal pulled his horse in front of his Captain's, causing him to stop. The whole line behind them came to a halt. 'With all due respect Captain, the correct procedure in our Royal Training Book is to stop and assess. If we keep marching forward without knowing if the road is safe ahead then we could be walking into a trap. The scouts have not come back to tell us that the road ahead is clear and safe. These supplies are vital for our army. We can't afford to not deliver them.' Chal noticed his voice was raised and looked around. All eyes at the head of the convoy were on Chal's actions.

Captain Amin had been challenged by his second a few times now and he had to react. His face was starting to turn red. He was angry. He also raised his voice. 'My orders for this mission are clear. To get these supplies to our troops and I will do so under any circumstances. Your orders are clear too. You are my second in command here and you will also follow orders, or I will have you stripped of this position and have you flogged. Do you understand?' Chal nodded in retort. 'Now get to the very back of the line and keep it moving.' The procession moved on.

After a short while, they moved into a small valley with a wooded area on both sides. A chilling yell came out from the trees and arrows started flying, cutting into the line of Latonian men. Cries let out as royal guards fell with arrows embedded into them, and horses went down. Captain Amin was in shock. He jumped from his horse, using his horse as a shield and he could hear screams and arrows whizzing past him. He did not know what to do. He was frozen with fear. One of his men shouted to him from the cover of a wagon behind him.

'What do we do Captain?'

The captain just looked at him and then down along the line. He could not answer the question. He felt helpless. None of his training had prepared him for this. As Amin was about to run, he heard a shout ring out. He looked out from his hiding place. Chal was galloping up along the line shouting out orders. 'SHIELD WALL ON BOTH SIDES.' The guards instantly formed a defensive line on both sides of the line of wagons. An arrow deflected from his shoulder armour, but he was unharmed by it as he made his way up the line. He sped to the front where the attack was concentrated and jumped from his horse to join his captain.

'I am sorry Chal, I should have listened to you,' the Captain whined.

'We don't have time to discuss that right now.' Chal took his bow from his saddle. He shouted back down along the line. 'NOTCH ARROWS AND FIRE BACK!' The guards started to fire back at their attackers in the woods and Chal joined them. This slowed the number of arrows being fired at them. The attack stopped for a few moments. Then a shout could be heard, and a rush of attackers came from the woods, charging from both sides. Hundreds of attackers ran for the line, all dressed in black armour. Chal dropped his bow and drew his sword. 'SPEARS AT READY.' Both lines stood ready and long spears came out from the shield walls. The Royal guards had taken losses. The attackers slammed into both lines of shields and for a moment, Chal thought that the line would give, but it held. As the attackers pushed on the shields, spears came thrusting out from behind the defensive shields, killing scores of the men in black.

A second wave of attackers came from the woods and joined their black armoured comrades. The shield line on one side broke under the attack. Chal gave the order for swords to be drawn and the battle was joined, but the attackers were gaining the upper hand. Chal launched himself into the thick of the fighting. His training with Master Ultan kept him alive. Some of the guards joined him. He hacked and sliced, downing man after man in black. The tide started to turn and soon they were pushing the attackers back. Once a few turned and ran, the rest followed. They sprinted back to the protection of the woods. Some guards followed, despatching them as they fled, but Chal called them back. Chal appointed a few scouts to go see if the attackers had gone or had regrouped to prepare for a second attack. While he was waiting, he saw to the wounded and the dying. He walked back to the front of the line to find Captain Amin lying in a pool of his own blood. He knew straight away he was dead with a wound in his neck. Chal reached down and took the Captain's Sash from his armour. Chal was his Second and knew it would be his duty now to take command of the remaining Royal Guards and deliver the supplies to the Generals.

He called over his friend Alain. 'The Captain is dead.'

'You will have to take his position as you are his second' Alain said.

'I know, it is a sad way to be promoted.'

'This is always the way with war Chal.'

Chal nodded. Even though he had often disagreed with the previous Captain, he was sad that he was dead.

'The guards will be better for this, Chal. When we were attacked, I saw Amin cower and hide, he looked terrified.'

'Let us not speak ill of him Alain, he tried his best as our Captain and did what he thought was right.'

'Yes, but if he had listened to you earlier, we would not have fallen into that trap and the dead would still be alive.'

'Well, let us hope we do not have any more surprises.' Chal took off his Second Sash and handed it to Alain. 'Will you be my Second?'

'Yes of course.' Alain took the sash from his new Captain and put it on. Chal made sure there was food and drink handed out. 34 Royal Guards had been killed in the attack and 18 injured. They buried the dead at the side of the road. After some time, the scouts came riding back to the line. Chal walked to greet them.

'They have fled.' The rider looked down at the captain's sash that Chal was wearing. 'They have fled Captain. We also found the other scouts dead just beyond the woods.'

'Good work, thank you! We should get the line moving again. I want you two men to scout ahead and report back every hour. I don't want us to be walking into an ambush again.' The scouts sped off along the road ahead. The line of supplies was underway once more, but this time under new command.

General Arthen and General Titus were sitting in the war room looking over maps. A guard knocked on the door and a scout entered and saluted. 'We have spotted a large convoy coming towards us from the West sir.'

'Ah, that will be our much-needed supplies. Thank you.'

The scout saluted again, spun on his heel and left. Arthen turned to General Titus. 'Your son is with the supply guards, is he not?'

'Yes, he is. It will be good to see him.'

They all met the convoy as it came through the gate. A cheer went up from the men as the food supplies arrived. They knew they would be eating well for the foreseeable future. Chal jumped from his horse and walked to the two Generals and saluted. They could see he was wearing the Captain's sash and that some of the men were injured.

General Arthen spoke first. 'I see you have been through some action. Is Captain Amin not with you?'

'No Sir. We were attacked along the road and we lost 34 of our men.'

'That is a shame. War is never a nice thing, it only takes. Get yourself and your men some food and some rest and then come to us in the War Room and we will hear the full report.'

'Of course,' Chal replied. Chal then removed his sash and handed it to the General.

'This was Captain Amin's Title Sash. I took on the role temporarily as procedure states, as I was his second. I am now handing it over to you as required.'

The General looked at Chal and then patted him on the shoulder. 'It is yours now Chal. I need good Captains under my command. You have earned this title. I will send word to Kitia of your promotion. You have done excellent work Chal, delivering these supplies that will keep our men alive for a long time. I am looking forward to hearing your report.' He turned and walked back towards his quarters.

Chal's father then stepped forward and hugged his son. 'Thank the Gods you are alive. You are not long in the service of the King and already you have been promoted. I am very proud of you, my son. Come! We have lots to talk about. I will show you to your sleeping quarters and show you to the food court.'

Chal reached into his tunic under his armour and pulled out a letter. 'From mother.'

His father took it and kissed the paper. 'Thank you Chal. I have been longing to hear how she is. I miss her alot.' The father and son walked off and the long line of men started to dismount as other guards ran forward to help them unload all the supplies and look after the wounded.

Later that evening, Chal and his second, Alain, were sitting in the War Room with General Arthen and General Titus, sipping on wine after a large meal.

General Arthen ordered more wine and a jug was left on their table. 'So, you had a rather tough journey down here then.'

'Yes sir, but our men handled everything as well as could be expected.' Chal reported on everything from their departure to the delivery at the wooden fort and explained how they were attacked and how they defended the supplies.

After listening to this, Arthen turned to Chal's second, Alain. 'Is there anything you want to add?'

He cleared his throat. 'Yes Sir, I think Chal might have left out some areas.' Alain described the previous captain's orders, outlining how he had ignored Chal's concerns and advice, and how Chal had taken charge when they were attacked, turning the tide.

Both Generals nodded as they listened. 'Well Chal, it seems you were quite the hero. I think you must be following in your father's footsteps.' They all laughed, and Alain was relieved that the attention was taken off him. Arthen brought them up to speed with what was happening on the front line, how their battle had gone and how they came to be garrisoned in the wooden fort. The four talked late into the night and the Generals told old battle and war stories about each other to the two younger men. Two days later, Chal and his 85 remaining men set out on their long journey back to Kitia to obtain more supplies and to continue their mission of bringing them back down to Arthen's army. It was hard work, but someone had to keep the army fed.

25

It was midday and the temperatures were much cooler. Kalin, Karra and Leib were almost at the North Wall. It had been a long trek and all three companions were feeling tired. They could see the mountain range in the distance that separated the North lands from the Southlands. As they continued on towards the North wall, it began to rain. At first it was just a light, misty rain, but then it began to get heavier and soon it was pouring down, the riders found they were soaked. The three made their way to the edge of a small wooded area for shelter. After an hour, the rain let up and they continued their way. In the distance, Kalin could see the mountains more clearly now. Then he noticed the north wall. It stretched out between two large mountains. The wall itself was almost the height of the mountains themselves. He could see the second wall on the north side too. It was immense and he realised then why the north had never invaded the south. It would be almost impossible to breach these walls. When they arrived at the south side of the walled fortress the gate was closed.

'That's unusual,' said Karra 'this south side gate is always open.'

A guard shouted down in a grumpy voice, 'What are your names and what is your business here?'

'I am Karra Ruaine from the north lands, and I am with my nephew and my friend. We are seeking passage to the north.'

'No one is allowed to travel north, and no one is allowed to enter through these walls unless they are part of the Royal Army or have written permission from a superior.'

Karra looked angry and was about to give the guard a piece of his mind when the huge gate made a loud noise. It opened slightly and Captain Groth walked out with six armed guards.

'I was looking out over the wall and saw you making your way towards us. As you came closer, I realised it was you Karra. How was your trip?'

'It was long,' Karra replied, grouchily. 'Why is the gate locked?'

'Haven't you heard yet?'

'No!' Karra grunted, shrugging his massive shoulders.

Groth walked forward and greeted Karra with a warrior's handshake. Karra introduced the Captain to his dark friend and his nephew. 'What is it that I have not heard?'

'We are at war Karra, with the Empire. We heard word a few days ago. They have invaded Natalia and taken the south wall. Come through and I will tell you all about it.' Kalin felt his heart sink at hearing the words, 'we are at war.' All he could think about was Thianni back at Kitia. It sent a chill down his spine. They all went through the gate and it closed behind them with an ominous bang. It was busy inside, there were troops training and preparations were under way. There were a lot of homes and buildings between the two walls. Kalin could see the far wall to the north and it looked even bigger than the wall they had just come through. It spread out between two mountain ranges, decisively separating the north from the south.

Karra turned to his two travelling companions, 'I think we will cross on through to the north today. I don't fancy spending a night here. We will load up on supplies and keep going.' Leib nodded in agreement.

They all followed the captain who led them all to a tavern and stopped just outside the door. 'Will you and your friends be looking to stay the night Karra?'

'No, we must be getting back as soon as we can. I have already been away from the north for far too long.'

'Well, come inside and have a drink with me and I will tell you all about what has happened.'

The four of them sat down for a drink. Captain Groth rested his drink on his large round belly and recounted everything he had heard so far. Karra did not seem to be affected by the news and seemed more interested in his drink than what the captain had to say. 'There could be some troubling times ahead for the Kingdom. But I don't think it will touch us here in the north wall. We are too far from any of the conflict in the south.'

Kalin looked concerned. 'What about Kitia? Will that be attacked?'

The captain sat back in his chair and crossed his arms. 'I think our armies will demolish any threat well before they get anywhere close to the capital. We will have to send troops back to Kitia for support though. That will leave us undermanned here. I am surprised you have not heard anything on the road up here.'

'We have met very few people in the last few days. It was quiet enough apart from some raiders that attacked the boy here.'

The captain turned to Kalin. 'Did you get to see some action young man?'

Kalin nodded as he drank. 'You could say that.'

The captain turned back to Karra. 'The raiding will get worse if there is to be a full out war. I have seen it happen in the past. People get scared and when panic sets in they can be capable of anything. It is the normal folk that suffer the most from wars.'

Karra finished his cup and placed it on the table. 'It won't concern us. We have our own agenda and with that we must be on our way.' The Captain walked them to the gate on the North wall and signalled for the gatemen to open up and let them pass. He gave Karra back the weapons that had been confiscated from him when they had entered the first gate. He then bid his goodbyes to the three. The huge gate opened, and they started to walk through. Kalin stopped, still halfway through. Karra and Leib walked a few steps forward and stopped, looking back at Kalin.

Karra walked back to him 'What is wrong Kalin?'

'I'm not sure if I am doing the right thing here?'

'Why wouldn't you be?'

'With all this talk of war with the Empire, I feel like I am deserting my Auntie and Uncle and Chal, and especially Thianni.'

'Kalin we have a lot of work to do. I cannot just turn around and take you back to Kitia. People's lives depend on me guarding the gate, and soon they will rely on you too.'

Leib joined them and looked to Kalin. 'Kalin. Kitia is probably the safest city in the world. Its walls have never been breached.'

Kalin sighed.' I know I am being silly, but I can't help feeling this way.'

Karra put his hand on the boy's shoulders. 'The Gods made rainy days so gardeners could get the housework done. I am not going to lie to you, there is a storm coming and there will be times of hardship ahead. I have seen what war can do, but you can't put your life on hold. There is a destiny you must follow. I will make sure we have the latest news available to us on the mountain. I promise you this, if you need to go back and need me to go with you I will, but first I must guard the gate for the next few openings.'

Leib also put his hand on Kalin's shoulder. 'And I promise you, if you have to go back and save the princess, I will ride alongside you.' Kalin accepted their promises and the three walked forward into the lands of Gantia, with the slamming sound of the gates closing shut behind them.

Kalin felt more alive than he had ever done. He felt at peace with himself, he felt at home. The trees looked like they could touch the sky, and the sweet smell of pine surrounded him. The mountains could be seen for miles as they faded out into the distance. As they travelled further and further into Gantia, his concerns about the war started to become less and less. The land was covered mostly with trees and there were very few meadows and fields compared to Latonia. There was wildlife everywhere and the hunting was good. The further north they travelled, the colder it became. Karra and Kalin did not seem to be affected by the cold, but Leib disliked it immensely. After travelling for just over a week, they reached Karra's cabin, high on the side of a mountain. The sun was starting to set in the distance. Straight away Kalin loved it. The views were astonishing in every direction. They entered the hut and there was wood set in the fireplace ready to be lit.

Karra showed Kalin around while Leib saw to the horses. 'Tomorrow I will take you to the gate. It is located at the top of this mountain and we will start working on making you your own cabin.'

'This place is amazing Karra; I am so glad I decided to come here.'

'Let's see if you still feel the same way when the gate opens.' He ruffled the boy's hair and Kalin gave a smile. 'I'll get the fire on and start to cook some food for supper.'

A short while later, Leib entered the hut and Karra dished out some stew he had heated up. They ate in silence. After the food was finished, the three sat back in their chairs in complete contentment. The next morning, Kalin rose early. Karra and Leib were still asleep so he decided to go and have a look around outside. The sun was just up and there were birds singing in the early morning brightness. Kalin walked down the hill some ways and washed his neck and face in the stream. He looked back up towards the cabin and could just make out that there were some old ruins at the top of a mountain that was attached to the hill. He made his way back to investigate. Kalin followed the path that wound around the mountain. It was a steep walk to reach the top. When he arrived, the first thing he noticed was that all the defence walls around the enclosure were facing the wrong way. They were facing inwards as if they were guarding something that was trying to get out, not in. It looked to be an old stone fort. The grey stone walls looked to be very old and some sections were cracked and crumbling. The entrance had no gate. As he walked through the opening, he nearly gasped as he saw two large black pillars protruding from the ground at the centre of the ruins. He walked over to them. They looked so out of place here. He had never seen black look so black before. There was a stone table directly behind the pillars. It looked to be some kind of ceremonial altar. This was also a deep black like the two large pillars.

His eyes were drawn to the pillars again. They looked so unusual. His mind swirled to try and make sense of this stone fort with its unusual design. Kalin moved in to examine the pillars more closely. Up close, he could see that the black pillars were not smooth. They were covered with indentations in the shape of strange symbols, as if someone or something had carved them into the blackness of the pillars. He felt drawn to them. He reached out to feel the carvings and as his hand touched the pillar, he felt a wave of energy rush through his body. This energy increased and there was a noise like crackling. Within the carvings, the two pillars started to light up with a soft, golden light. Kalin's hand felt like it was stuck in place, he could not remove his hand from the pillar. The light and noise increased and, with a flash, Kalin was thrown back some ten feet in a burst of golden light. He landed on his back, looking up at the blue sky. All was quiet again now. Slowly he rose and checked himself for any injuries. Happy that there were none, he looked over at the pillars to see that they were just as he had first found them. He heard a shriek and looked around. A white owl flew into the centre of the ruins and perched itself on the stone altar, watching him intently with its large, brown eyes. In that moment Kalin could feel an energy emanating from within his chest that flowed out to every extremity of his body. Never before had he felt this powerful. He felt sharp. He felt alive.

Kalin looked over at the owl again and this time he could hear the thrumming of the bird's heart. His sense of hearing was heightened. He could hear every sound around him as if the volume of the land had increased all at once. He looked out over the mountain and was amazed that he could make out all the fine details of the top of the neighbouring mountain, he had never been able to see that far before. His eyesight was also heightened. This was incredible!

Kalin walked back to the cabin. Everything felt new to him now. As Kalin approached the cabin he could hear Karra and Leib's deep, steady breathing through the wooden walls and knew they were still fast asleep. Kalin decided to start preparing breakfast for the three of them. The smell of the oats cooking must have stirred the two older men out of their slumber and as they emerged, Kalin had bowls placed on the table containing hot oats, honey and a sprinkle of wild nuts.

Lieb came out first. 'Good morning Kalin. Did you not sleep? I heard you going out early this morning.'

'I did sleep well. I haven't had a nightmare in weeks now.'

'Ah that is good. Like Karra said, being this close to the gate must be good for you indeed.'

Karra came out next, ruffling Kalin' s hair and sitting down between the two.

'I visited the gate this morning, and something happened.'

Karra looked at Kalin with interest. 'Did you touch one of the pillars?'

'Yes.'

'Did it feel like getting hit by lightning?'

'Yes, that's exactly what it felt like. It threw me back some distance.'

Karra smiled. 'Good, what you experienced is called The Briskin. It is like being energised for the first time. I remember when it happened to me too. I take it you are feeling…' he paused for a second 'feeling a little… different?'

'Yes, it feels amazing. I can hear things I could not hear before and I can see really, really far away now. I feel like I need to run now and keep running.' Kalin quickly ate the rest of his breakfast and was away for a run, leaving Karra and Leib at the table.

'You will have to change his training now Leib.'

'This is all very interesting to me. I have never known such things. I know you had told me the stories before about the gate and its powers but seeing it first-hand is even more compelling.'

'I am glad you are here with us, my friend.'

'I would not dream of being anywhere other than here.'

'I will need your help even more now, especially with Kalin's training. He will be faster than ever before and even stronger now that he has touched the gate. Our job is to guide him in the right direction and put this new gift to good use.'

The next day, Kalin awoke with the same energy. He dressed and went to prepare breakfast. He sensed that Karra was not in the cabin and went to go find him. He checked his room and he was not there. As he thought of his uncle, his mind told him he was up at the gate. He decided to listen to his own thoughts and made his way up to the gate. On arrival he could see his uncle was gathering a large amount of wood in a pile.

Kalin walked over to him. 'Can I help uncle?'

'Yes, please. I slept in for too long and I am now pressed for time.'

'What are you doing?'

Karra reached into his pocket and pulled out a small, crescent shaped chain with a black amulet attached. At the centre of the amulet he could see that there was a very small light glowing. 'This here is my only indication of when the gate will open next. It starts to glow before the gate is opened. I have been trying to record all the times, so I have a history of all the opening dates. I have been doing this for 6 years now. Most of them accrue on the same date each year, but there is the odd one that just happens. This is why I was in a hurry to get back to the gate when we were in Latonia. I was afraid that I would miss being here when it opens.'

'What would have happened if you did miss it?'

'If I am not here to guard the gate and defend our world, hell will enter our world and people will die.'

Kalin looked frightened. 'So why are you piling all this wood?'

'The pile is for a fire. It's kind of a tradition for me. I can prepare myself for the coming fight. It also aids me, especially when the gate opens at night, and all is dark. It is a constant glare in the enemy's eyes and if I keep my back to the fire, the enemy can't manoeuvre behind me, so I always have them in my vision.'

'I will guard your back uncle.'

'Not this time Kalin. Maybe in a short time you can. I want you to stay back and watch. I don't want you to get involved just yet. Watch and learn. That is your job for today. Now help me build this fire.'

The two worked tirelessly gathering the wood and after a while, Leib joined them preparing for what was to come through the gate. Karra constantly checked his amulet. Every time he looked at it, it appeared to be getting brighter. Karra took one final look at the amulet. A bright white light shone from it, causing both Kalin and Leib to turn away as it was like looking straight into the sun.

Karra put the amulet back into his pocket and turned to Kalin and Leib. 'Light the fire and stay back. Do not come to my aid, no matter what happens here. Do you understand?'

They both nodded their heads. They lit the fire with torches they had prepared. As the flames grew higher, a strange eeriness fell upon the mountain top. Karra placed his forearm guards on and drew both his swords. Kalin and Leib watched as a mist grew between the pillars and then lightning flashed from one pillar to the other. The carvings in the black pillars shone with a bright, golden light. There looked to be a light trying to shine through the mist. Karra stood boldly waiting for whatever was to come through. He had heard his uncle refer to demons and creatures, but Kalin had no idea what he meant. Kalin watched on in amazement for what seemed an eternity. Then a huge shadow surged forward, erupting from within the mist and lunged at Karra, its giant muscular arms holding an axe- like weapon. Karra side-stepped, bringing down one of his swords with great speed and cutting through the grey skin of the creature that was pushing through the gate. The creature attacked again, slashing at Karra's head. Karra ducked under the attack and then leaped high into the air, bringing down his two swords deep into the side of the creature's neck. It reared up and let out a blood curdling screech. Kalin had never seen anything like this creature or beast before. It stood upright and had two arms and two legs just like a human, but it was no human. He could not take his eyes from it. It stood around eight feet in height and was powerfully built, making Karra look like a small child next to it. Its skin was a grey colour and its huge broad head looked like it was sunken into its huge upper body.

As the fight was unfolding, Kalin could see more shadows coming through the gate. He drew his sword and attempted to rush in to help his uncle, but Leib caught him by the arm and pulled him back. 'Remember what your uncle said, we must stay here.'

'But look at the gate! There are more coming through. How will he be able to fight all of them?'

Leib counted the shadows that were nearly through the gate. There were seven other creatures on their way. 'We must trust in him. If he needs us, he will call.'

Kalin and Leib watched from their hidden vantage point. The first creature was killed, leaving Karra just enough time to reset for the next oncoming creatures. Seven beasts pushed out through the mist and attacked Karra simultaneously. He could not stop them all at once in their advance and they pushed him back from the gateway. One beast broke away from the group and moved straight towards Kalin and Leib. Karra was aware of this but could not stop him as he was trying to control the rest of the creatures. Leib moved in front of Kalin in a stance to protect the boy. The beast swung his weapon in a wide arc at Leib. Leib countered the attack with his broad curved sword. The two weapons clashed, knocking Leib' s sword clear from his hands. The creature then swung in the opposite direction and hit Leib in the face with its huge hand. Leib was knocked backwards, stunned by the impact. The creature walked forward toward his next opponent. Kalin drew his sword and leaped into action. The creature swung and chopped at Kalin but Kalin was too fast for it. Every time the creature missed with its attack, Kalin would slice and hack at its legs. Finally, it fell to one knee. Kalin, seeing an opportunity, spun and thrust his sword just under the creature's chin and deep into its chest. Dark blood spilled out of the creature. Leib was watching both Karra and Kalin now. The speed at which Karra and Kalin were moving was mind blowing. Karra had dispatched three of the creatures by the time Kalin had killed his first. Kalin moved back to Leib to see if he was OK. 'Are you hurt?'

'I think I will be fine.'

'Good, I will help my uncle then.' With that, Kalin ran over to Karra and the two took on the remaining creatures together. At first, Kalin tried to stay out of his uncle's way as he hacked and sliced at the huge intruders. Then Kalin found the rhythm of the fight. As Karra attacked, Kalin would draw back and defend. Then Kalin would move forward and attack from a different angle. The creatures could not adapt to this and soon they were all slain. The mist swiftly disappeared from between the pillars and the gate was now closed once more. The huge bodies of the creatures were scattered on the ground around the pillars and there was a very dark, red blood splashed around the battle area. Karra and Kalin had splashes of the blood on them too, but neither one was injured from the fight. Leib made his way towards them. 'Are you two OK?'

'Yes!' replied Karra. He started to clean his swords on the brown leather clothing of the fallen.

Karra turned to Kalin. 'What about you boy, are you OK?'

'Yes, I think so.'

Karra nodded his approval. 'You have done well today Kalin. You handled the fight like a true guardian. I am proud of you boy.'

26

Cahira had spent a few days traveling through the mountains, hunting and camping out in the open air. She loved it up here; it was away from Four Vales and away from all the drama of life there. She especially needed a break away from Akala. His advances on her were becoming more forceful and she was finding it extremely annoying. It wasn't that she did not find him attractive; he was a very handsome man and a good hunter. It was the thought of being tied down to one man for the rest of her life. Everyone was expecting her to choose a husband now that she was 18, but she just could not commit herself to such a perpetual agreement, and besides, she loved to tease him.

She made her way up the side of a wooded hill. She could hear the sound of the waterfalls in the distance. She loved it here; everything around her was in harmony, and besides, the hunting was good. She had already shot four rabbits with her bow on the way up the hill. She followed the sound of the water. On hot days like today she often would strip down and take a swim in the lake at the bottom of the waterfall. She reached the sandy shore of the lake and had started to strip, when she noticed someone on the other side of the small lake. It looked to be a man or an older boy running along the deer trail. He was moving fast and heading uphill. She did not recognise him but at this distance it wasn't easy to make out facial features. He had not noticed her yet as he ran, so she moved back into the foliage behind her. She moved up hill on her side of the river to watch what this stranger was doing. She lost sight of him momentarily and then she spotted him again. He had stopped by the river's edge above the waterfall and was kneeling, taking a drink of the freshwater. She moved to a closer position to try and make out if she knew who he was. Ducking down behind a bush by the shore, she was close now and could make out his face. She wondered who he was and what he was doing in this part of the countryside. Was he just passing through? He looked Gantian and she could see that he was a young man, and very handsome at that. He had no beard, but he was well built and had a long hunting knife attached to his belt and moved well. He then stood and skipped out onto a large stone that was protruding from the surface of the water and untied his trousers and took out his member and started leisurely urinating into the water. Cahira could feel her anger building as she had been just about to bathe in the water at the bottom of the waterfall. If she had not noticed him running past she would be now bathing in his waste.

Cahira jumped from her place in the undergrowth and let out an angry yell. 'WHAT DO YOU THINK YOU ARE DOING?'

The boy was startled. He slipped from the stone where he had been standing and fell backwards into the deeper part of the water. The young man came up splashing and thrashing around in the water in panic. 'I can't swim!' he yelled.

The current took hold of him, quickly pulling him towards the fall. Cahira went to reach out and help him but she was too late, the water pulled him over the waterfall and down to the lower lake with a splash. She took flight and ran to the bottom of the falls to see if he was OK. He surged upwards from beneath the water, his wildly thrashing limbs driving him towards the shore almost accidentally. Cahira stepped out onto a stone within arm's reach of him.

'Please help me I can't swim,' he cried as his head went under water again muffling his words. She reached out and grabbed him by the hair, lifting his head clear from the water.

'Put your legs down.'

'What do you mean?'

'Put your legs down,' she repeated, louder this time. This time the young man listened and obeyed her. He stood up and the water was shallow, only waist deep. He looked very embarrassed now. Cahira turned around and jumped back to the sandy shoreline and then turned to confront the stranger. He was walking to the shore also, his trousers falling down as he walked, exposing his member. Cahira pointed at his trousers and tried to look away. The young man, in panic, reached down, pulled his trousers up and tied them. He looked even more embarrassed now.

'Why were you urinating in the river?' she finally said.

'I thought it to be as good as any other place to do it.'

'Well, you shouldn't.'

'Why not?' he replied, wiping his face clear from water, and making sure his trousers were still in place.

Cahira thought for a bit. 'Because…!' she also felt embarrassed now. 'Because I was going to swim in it, that's why.'

'Oh! In that case I will do it down river next time.'

She wanted to laugh but held back. She could see now that he was young, around the same age as her, maybe slightly younger. His height had given her the impression that he was older when she had seen him first. He removed his tunic and wrung it out. She glanced at his muscular upper body and turned away so he would not catch her looking at him. He was a very handsome young man, and she could feel herself starting to blush.

'What has you out running these mountains anyway?'

'I run most mornings. It is part of my training.'

'Training for what?'

'I am staying with my uncle. His name is Karra. Do you know him?'

Cahira raised her eyebrow. 'Karra is your uncle?'

'Yes, do you know him?' he asked again.

'Yes, everybody knows who Karra is, he is a legend around here.'

'Really? I always figured him to just be a grumpy old man.' This time she laughed out loud. 'Would you like to come around and see him and have some food with us? It's the least I can do after you saved me from drowning.'

'I have yet to see anyone drown in a few feet of water. Thank you, but no. I must be going. I have a lot of hunting to do today.'

'Well I will owe you then.'

'You owe me nothing, for it was me that startled you in the first place and made you fall into the water.' With that she reached into her bag and pulled out two of her rabbits. 'Please give these to Karra.'

'Why would you give them to him?'

'Because, he is the one that keeps us all safe from the demons beyond the Gate.'

Kalin took the rabbits. 'Thank you for them.' Cahira nodded, took up her bag and her bow and went to walk off. Kalin watched her. She was very beautiful. She was tall and lean, and her braided black hair fell down one shoulder and on to her small breasts. 'Hey! What is your name?'

'It's Cahira. What's yours?'

'Kalin. My name is Kalin.' She heard him call from behind her as she walked away.

'I will remember that,' she said quietly as she disappeared into the undergrowth of the forest.

27

Autumn was nearly gone, and the first signs of winter could be seen on the tops of the mountains. White tips were starting to show on the distant peaks. Kalin had finished making his cabin and was ready to move into it. He was looking forward to having his own privacy away from the two older men. He was still training and running daily. Leib had changed his training, making it harder and more intense, but Kalin felt it was easy. Karra had kept to his word; he had travelled into the nearest village every week to get updates on how the war was developing in the South. Kalin was satisfied that there were no advancements into the land of Latonia and there was no fighting happening on the west coast near Kitia. As Karra said, it would take half a year to move an army from one coast to the other. Kalin decided to go for a walk down by the river and let his thoughts wander. Most of the time when he was alone, all he thought about was Thianni and the short time they had spent together. But today, his friend Chal was on his mind. He could not help but think about him.

He reached the trail that ran along the river. Up ahead he noticed a large buck drinking from a small inlet. Kalin cursed himself for forgetting his bow. As he got closer, the buck noticed him and stared at him for a few seconds before turning and running into a more densely wooded part of the forest. Suddenly, Kalin had a feeling that he was being watched. He stopped walking and looked around. He could not see or hear anyone, but the feeling was strong. He decided to keep walking. After a few steps, he turned around and could see a man walking towards him on the trail. His hand moved towards his knife, but he decided not to draw it from its sheath. Kalin waited for the stranger to come to him. As the stranger got closer, Kalin could see he was a small man, but extremely stocky. He looked to be around the same age as his uncle. The stranger was smiling now. He started to talk just before he reached Kalin.

'Well hello there. You must be Kalin. Your uncle has told me a great deal about you. Although you seem a lot bigger than I had imagined.' He put out his hand and Kalin shook it. 'My name is Tucus. It means Tree Stump. I am a good friend of Karra'

'I am pleased to meet you Tucus.'

'I knew your father when he was with us. He too was a big man, and I miss his company. We are heading up to Karra's cabin.'

'We?' Asked Kalin puzzled.

'Yes, my son is with me.'

Kalin looked back down along the trail and saw another man emerge from the woods with a buck draped across his shoulders. Kalin was pretty sure it was the buck that he had spotted earlier, drinking by the river. The man appeared to be a good deal taller than his father.

'Oh, and we have brought dinner with us too.' Tucus said with a laugh, rubbing his round belly. The second man made his way to them. Laying the buck on the ground, he held out a bloodstained hand. 'This is my son Blan.'

'Pleased to meet you, Blan. I am heading back to the cabin too. So maybe we can all walk together, and I can help carry dinner.'

When they arrived back at the cabin, Karra met them at the door and was genuinely pleased to see them. Only on rare occasions did Kalin see Karra smiling.

'Well boy, I see you have met some of my friends.'

'We were tracking him when we found deer tracks crossing his path. Blan decided to go after the buck and I wanted to meet your nephew.'

The mood felt friendly and a homely feeling swept over Kalin. That evening, the five men roasted the deer that Blan had killed earlier. They cooked it outside, over an open fire. After they had eaten, they all sat around the fire exchanging stories. Kalin took to Blan straight away. Even though Blan was a little older than Kalin, it was nice to have someone to talk to closer to his own age. Tucus had a huge personality, and his stories were all made funnier by his facial expressions. Kalin could see why Karra liked him. Talking to Blan made Kalin think of his friend Chal, back at Kitia. He wondered how he was keeping and longed to talk to him and tell him all about his adventures and all the new people he had encountered here in the north land.

28

The Conri waited with his men on the outskirts of Four Vales. There had been trouble with a large neighbouring village called Fenrich. There was a dispute last autumn over cattle that had wandered onto the fields of Fenrich and the farmer had claimed them as their own. This had caused a lot of enmity between the two villages which had, over time, escalated to violence. Two men from Four Vales had tried to retrieve the cattle and both had been killed. A war party had left the village that morning seeking retribution and The Conri and several warriors stood guard, awaiting their return. The Conri was feeling anxious as he had tried to advise against an attack, but the two men that had been killed had large families in Four Vales who wanted revenge. How could he deny them their rights? There was no sign of any of the warriors returning.

The Conri turned to the man standing next to him. 'I have to meet someone. If any of our men return, make sure I am informed about it immediately.'

He walked towards Old Sallin's house. The Seer was sitting on a chair outside his home, enjoying the sunshine. He had a large straw hat on to shade his eyes from the sun. 'Good day to you, Chieftain. I must be blessed. Two visits from you in such a short time. I am beginning to think you must like me.'

'Of course, I like you, but I haven't time for jokes today.'

'There is a difference between liking someone and needing them.'

The Conri was starting to get annoyed. 'I have come to seek your help.'

Sallin sat back into his chair with a smile. 'I am all ears.' Sallin closed his eyes, as the Conri spoke.

'I am worried about the conflict between our village and Fenrich. I think this misunderstanding could cause an all-out war between us. Can you predict if there is a hospitable outcome?'

'I already know the outcome of this. Have you thought any more about what I had told you the last time we met?'

'No not really. I wanted to know about this dispute. If you know something, then tell me.'

'The trouble with our villages will increase until we are visited by a certain young man. Then, all will be at peace again between us.'

'Do I know this young man?'

'No, not yet, but you will.'

'Well! Does he have a name?'

'He is the nephew of Karra The Guardian. His name is Kalin Ruane.'

After his conversation with the Seer, The Chieftain walked back to the edge of the village to his men on guard. He arrived to find that some of the warriors had returned. It appeared that only half of the men had returned, and those that had returned looked bloody and battered.

'Where are the rest of the men that went with you?' he asked the nearest warrior.

'We were ambushed before we got to the farm that is holding our cattle. They set upon us with spears and killed all but us few.'

The Conri shouted orders. 'Get these men seen to and ring out the bell for a village meeting. We must put an end to this matter once and for all.'

All of the important figures and most of the adults were packed into the village hall. The Conri stood at the head of those assembled and spoke. 'Men and women of Four Vales, we have some work to do. I am sure most of you have heard about our troubles with the people of Fenrich, and the fighting that has taken place. With the threat of an all-out war between us, I think it is time to make plans. First, we must increase our watch towers and then start making defensive walls and preparing our warriors for battle.'

A hush fell over the crowd. 'I know this news is not pleasant, but this is what we must do in order to protect ourselves.'

A shout came from the crowd 'Why could we not just give them the cattle, and all this would be sorted?'

'To let them keep the cattle would be a form of submission in their eyes and we cannot show ourselves as weak. This has proven costly in the past.'

'So, you would rather let good men die at the expense of us not looking weak?' came a woman's voice.

'I know how this must look, but we have come up against Fenrich before and have prevailed. Now they have killed more of our people and it is time to make a stand.'

Another man in the crowd spoke out. 'Have you consulted Sallin on what to do?'

'Yes, and he advises us to fight.'

A cacophony of voices erupted within the hall. The Chieftain raised his hands for quiet. 'So, let us start at first light tomorrow. I am sure that there are some young men in Four Vales that would like to be given the opportunity to prove themselves. If we plan things right, we will all be protected.'

The next morning, all the men and a great deal of the women gathered in the centre of the village. The Conri empowered Rovan, the village's champion, to have the strongest warriors divide the villagers into groups and to go through plans for building walls at each of the four entrances into the valley. Other villagers took up weapons and started to train and carry out fake battle situations. All was starting to come together as he looked around. As he scanned, he looked to the south and could see in the distance three horsemen riding into the village. He squinted at them and, recognising the middle rider, he smiled. It was Karra. A sense of relief came over him. He knew Karra would help the situation no matter what. Karra and his two companions rode through the village, right up to The Conri, and dismounted. All eyes were on the three men. The Conri could see that one of the riders had very dark skin. He was very tall and lean, and his movement was well balanced. The other rider was a young man. He looked Gantian. He also moved well. He bore some small resemblance to Karra.

Karra strode over to The Conri and shook his hand.

'Well met, my old friend,' the Conri said and pulled Karra into a hug.

'I see you are all busy in Four Vales today.'

'Yes, we have some preparation to make.'

'Let me guess. You are getting ready for war?'

'That is true Karra.'

'I see some things will never change here. I want you to meet my friend, Leib, and my nephew, Kalin.'

The Conri turned and shook both their hands and pulled them into a hug. He welcomed them to Four Vales. Leib looked amused, as most people he had met for the first time in Latonia were very stand offish because of his dark skin. They seemed much friendlier here in the North.

The Conri then turned back to Karra. 'So, what have you three coming down here from the mountains?'

'We wanted to start building up our supplies for the winter, and I wanted Kalin and Leib to visit my home village. Kalin was born here.'

The Conri looked at Kalin. 'And you must be Shun Ruane's son. He was a great man, and you have turned into a fine young man. Your auntie Reesa has done a good job raising you. I remember when you were born. Your mother and father looked the happiest I had ever seen them. That must make you around 16 years of age?'

'I turned 16 not so long ago. I like hearing about my mother and father.'

'They were good people Kalin, and you look a lot like your father. I owed him a few debts. So tonight, the village will celebrate your return, Kalin, and I might even allow you to help with our preparations here in Four Vales.'

He winked at Kalin and then turned to Leib. 'And you, big fellow. Do you like drinking alcohol?'

Leib smiled and nodded and spoke slowly in the Gantian tongue 'What man doesn't?'

'Good! Because tonight you can be my drinking partner.'

They all laughed. Most of the onlookers then turned and went back to work. As the crowd cleared, Kalin noticed Cahira, the girl that had pulled him out of the river, standing there looking and smiling at him. She then turned and walked away. A little while later, Kalin and Leib were helping with putting up a wooden wall that would enclose the village. The men there all looked strong and worked tirelessly. The women also helped with the labour. They all chatted to Kalin and Leib as they worked, as if they had known them for years. The differences between the Gantian people and Latonian people were quite diverse.

The Gantian people seemed more friendly and open and really welcoming, far from the savages that the Latonian people thought them to be. They even took to Leib quickly without any obvious prejudice.

A large warrior walked up to Kalin and held out his hand. Kalin shook it immediately. 'My name is Rovan.'

'I am Kalin.'

'I am looking for help chopping some wood and your uncle said you might be my man?'

'I would be glad to help, Rovan.'

The two walked some ways away and they both got stuck into work, chopping the wood that would be needed for stakes to hold the wooden walls in place. They chatted and talked as they worked. Kalin felt very at home here. That night, the Conri called all the villagers to the centre of the town and handed out drinks and there was food cooked for everyone. Some of the older men started to play instruments and sing, and people started to dance.

Kalin was sitting talking with Rovan and some of the young men of the village when Cahira walked up to him. 'I see you are keeping good company.' She then gave Akala an angry look.

He was among the group and was talking to Kalin at the time. 'It's always a pleasure to see you, Cahira. My heart beats a little faster when in your presence.'

The other men laughed and Rovan clapped him on the back, nearly upending him. They all laughed out loud again. Cahira could feel her face starting to heat up and knew she must be starting to go red.

'Thank you for the rabbits, they were delicious.' Kalin spoke to try and change the mood.

'You are welcome. Could I talk to you alone?'

'Of course.' Kalin and Cahira walked away leaving the other young men behind them. A cheer went out from them to jeer Kalin as they both walked away. Both smiled as they walked in silence.

Cahira finally spoke. 'I hope you are not still trying to swim in that river.' She gave out a giggle.

'It is one thing I need to learn how to do.'

'I can teach you if you want?'

'Yes, I think I would like that.'

'How long are you spending here in Four Vales?'

'I think Karra said we would be stopping for about a week. The Conri has put us up in his house while we stay. I must share the room with Karra and Leib. They snore very loudly,' Kalin said, laughing.

'I have room at my home if you need a bed?' Cahira said as she looked into Kalin's eyes.

Kalin froze. He looked to see if Cahira was joking, but the look on her face said she was very serious.

'You are a very beautiful woman, Cahira, but I am promised to another.'

'That is a shame, Kalin. Who is this lucky woman?'

'Her name is Thianni.'

'That is a very nice name. Where does Thianni live?'

'She lives in Kitia, in Latonia.'

'In Latonia? That is miles away. How can one be so committed when their lover is so far away?'

'Because I love her, and I have promised I would only love her, and she promised that she would wait for me.'

'Now that is a shame' said Cahira. 'Well we can still be friends, right?'

'Yes, I would like that.'

'OK then, I will meet you here in the centre of the village at first light tomorrow and I will take you to a lake that is nearby, and I will teach you how to swim. It might take more than a week for you to learn.'

'I am a fast learner' he said proudly.

'I have no doubt that you are.'

Kalin thanked her and they separated. As he walked back to the young village men, he could hear them cheering and whistling. Rovan lifted him up in the air with a bear hug. 'You stay away from those nasty women, you hear?' He let him down and slapped him on the back with a booming laugh. Then handed him an ale. Akala watched Cahira as she walked back in the direction of her house at the edge of the village and then turned his attention back to the group of young men. He watched Kalin as he laughed and joked with the others. He was a handsome man. Young, but handsome. He could see why Cahira liked him. Akala could feel the envy building up within him. He watched Kalin as he drank. There was something strange about the young newcomer. Then it hit him. His eyes, it was his eyes.

As Cahira got closer, she could see the towering wooden wall in the distance. It seemed out of place. The wall that was being erected was close to her home and she did not like this at all. She felt angry now and thought hard to see why. It was not the wall; it was the fact that Kalin had turned her down. She was not used to men turning her down, for she could have her pick of any man in the village or any neighbouring villages. The first day she had seen him by the river she had fallen for him, and since then she could not stop thinking about him. She reached her house and went inside and lay on her bed, thinking about Kalin. Her plan tonight had been to find him and kiss him and bring him home to her house and make him hers, but she knew by his tone straight away he would not consent to her will. Now she was alone and in the mood for love making. She thought hard on a way she could seduce him. Then there was a knock at the door. She instantly thought Kalin had changed his mind and followed her home.

She leapt from her bed and ran to the door, pulling it open. 'Have you changed your mi…!' It was Akala. Cahira sighed with disappointment.

Akala put his hand on the door so she could not shut it on him. 'Before you close the door on me, I just want to say…!'

Before he could finish his speech, Cahira grabbed him. 'You'll do for tonight.' She pulled him inside, shut the door and kissed him hard.

Kalin was waiting when Cahira walked up and without a good morning or a hello, she said, 'Follow me.' She walked out past the newly built wall and headed towards a distant hill with a thick forest on top. Kalin followed close on her heels. They walked for some time, speaking very little on their way up to the high lake. Kalin was starting to get concerned so he stopped walking to get her attention.

Cahira noticed he was not behind her. She turned and walked back to him. 'What is wrong Kalin?'

'I feel I owe you an apology?'

'An apology for what?'

'The way I reacted to your offer last night.'

'Oh, don't worry about that. I was just feeling a bit lonely last night and was hoping you could have helped.' She said lying.

'Well I just want you to know that I appreciate your offer, and if it were not for Thianni I would have accepted.'

The fact that he had mentioned Thianni's name again annoyed Cahira. 'If we stand here talking, we'll never get there so let's keep going and get to the lake.'

The two walked on, this time they chatted as they walked. They spent most of the morning in the lake. Cahira enjoyed the time with Kalin. He made her laugh often. He was a fast learner and by the end of the lesson he could swim a few feet. He was thrilled to be able to do this. All the time they were chatting about each other and their past. Cahira was fascinated with Kalin's past and how he was drawn to the gate and had to become a Guardian alongside his uncle. Kalin would talk a lot about Thianni, but Cahira would change the subject. Afterwards, they walked back to Four Vales where they helped with the reinforcing of the defence walls and joined in with the other villagers' training. The villagers were captivated with Kalin's sword skills and his speed. He would join in with the other young men as they trained with wooden swords. Rovan had taken an instant liking to the younger man and was amazed that he could not score a blow on him with his sword.

Kalin and Cahira continued to swim at the lake for the next five days, by which time Kalin could swim the full length of the lake with ease and Cahira struggled to keep up with him. She was astonished at his progress. On the last day, word came in that there had been no more conflict with the village of Fenrich with farmers fighting over land and herd ownership. They had just helped finish the last section of the wall when Karra and the Conri approached Kalin. Karra was looking concerned as he spoke to Kalin. 'We have just heard that The Empire has moved into Latonia and taken the city of Tureen.'

Kalin felt a chill go down his spine. 'What does that mean? Will they move toward Kitia?'

'I can't see them pushing up into Latonia this late in the year. Winter will soon be upon us and I don't think the armies of the Empire would fare well, even in the mild Latonian Winter. They are suited to much warmer climates.'

Even though Karra's words made sense, Kalin was still alarmed. 'We will have to be heading back to the cabins soon as there will be an opening of the gate happening shortly and I might need your help Kalin.'

As the three men started to get ready for the trek back, Cahira sought out Kalin. 'So, you are leaving us already.'

'I am. We must head back to the mountain now. Thank you for taking the time to teach me how to swim. I really enjoyed our time together. You are more than welcome to visit us up at the cabins.'

'You are very welcome Kalin, and I just might take you up on that offer. I will be doing some hunting up around there to stock up on meat for the winter.'

'Well then, I will look forward to seeing you soon.'

Cahira was suddenly overwhelmed by a feeling of deep sadness. She leaned in close to Kalin and was about to kiss him when the Conri pulled Karra aside. 'I may look for your help in the days to come Karra.'

'I do not get involved in Village disputes, Chieftain. My job is to guard all our people here in Gantia from external forces. Not to fight and go to war against them.'

The whole village came out to see the three men off. The Conri felt saddened as they left. Not that he would miss the drinking and company of the men, but the village would be less safe without Karra around. Cahira stood watching them leave. She knew there and then that she was in love with Kalin. She hated the feeling and loved it at the same time. She felt a hand on her back and turned around. It was Akala. 'Now that your friend has gone, we should spend some time together.'

She pushed his hand away. 'Don't touch me.'

'But I thought we would be close now after that night?'

'I gave you one night with me because I was lonely and that's all you'll get.' She walked away to her house.

Akala looked very confused. 'Women, who can understand them?' He said out loud.

Cahira could not get Kalin out of her mind. Even if she kept herself busy, her mind would keep going back to thinking about Kalin. She decided to go and visit Old Sallin and ask his advice. She had not been to him in a while. Before she was able to knock on his door, a voice came from within his old house. 'Come in child.' Cahira went inside the dimly lit room. Sallin was sitting at a small table by the fire and he was pouring out two cups of hot water he had prepared for them. 'Please sit and join me.' He pointed to the chair opposite him. She sat and he dipped his hand into a pouch and sprinkled out some herbs into the hot water of the two cups, passing one to Cahira. 'How are you keeping young lady? We haven't chatted in a long while, but I have been watching you with interest.'

'I am well Sallin. How about you? Are you keeping well?' She knew what he meant by watching her as everyone in the village knew, Old Sallin sees all. This bothered her slightly.

'I was pleased to hear you had saved the young girl in the woods. She was lucky and now her life will change forever.'

'It pleased me to be able to find her.'

'And I think the gold coin you received from the Conri also pleases you. You will need it in the future.' Cahira looked puzzled now. 'What seems to be bothering you Cahira?' 'I have come here today to seek advice.'

'My mind is troubling me.'

'Young love is always hard. The young have not yet learned to cope with these feelings.'

'I can't seem to stop thinking about the newcomer, Karra's nephew Kalin.'

'If it eases you, I have been thinking about him a lot lately too. He is a good young man. He will have a lot of decisions to make soon. Tell me Cahira, are you in love with him?'

'Yes, I think I am.'

Sallin went quiet and his eyes closed. At first, Cahira thought he had fallen asleep. Cahira took a sip from her herbal water. After a few moments he opened his eyes again. 'You also have a very important role to play Cahira.'

'What do you mean?'

'You must keep close to Kalin, he will need you when pain will course through his body.'

'I don't understand Sallin. Will Kalin be injured?'

'He has a power within him that normal people will never know. This power will keep him alive and yes, he will be injured. You must help him when this happens. An Evil is coming for him. After this happens you must seek me out and I will help you through this difficult time. Do you understand?'

'I think so. You have frightened me Sallin. I am beginning to regret coming to you now.'

'These things would happen if you had not come too. It is better to know than to not know.'

'I came here because I could not stop thinking about him and I have no one to talk to about my feelings. Now I suspect I will never stop thinking about him.'

'Like everything else, this will come to pass., but when this trouble does come, you must bring the light to him.'

Cahira shook her head. 'Now I know for sure I am regretting coming here. I am not understanding this conversation at all.'

The next morning, some Four Vales scouts came riding into the village at speed and announced that there was a large force of warriors heading in the direction of Four Vales. A bell rang out as men and women scrambled to get their weapons and head to their appointed areas at the four newly constructed walls that protected Four Vales. The force arrived at the north wall of the village and the Chieftain of Fenrich, Kamas, walked up to the wall and called out to the Chieftain of Four Vales. 'Come out Conri, come and talk to me before this bloody battle begins.'

The Conri looked down from high up on the wooden wall. He was much older and smaller than the Fenrich Chieftain. 'You have no business here at Four Vales.'

'Your men had no business at my village last week, but that did not stop them. They killed three of our people. So, we are here today to settle our differences.'

The Conri looked out at the Fenrich warriors. All armed with swords and spears and large round shields. They had at least 200 men. They far outnumbered the fighting force that Four Vales had. 'Well, what do you propose we should do? If you attack you will receive huge losses trying to get through our walls and then, if you do, you will face a fresh force of Four Vale warriors that are ready to kill.'

The Fenrich Chieftain looked up at the new walls and the Conri could see he had not been anticipating such a defence awaiting him. 'Maybe we could settle this between each other? Just you and me.'

The Conri knew he would not stand a chance against Kamas. He was a proven warrior and Chieftain in his prime. All was quiet and eyes were on the Conri of Four Vales. 'Do you think me a fool? Do you think I would risk coming out and facing you with an army at your back? I am too old and wise to fall for your trickery.'

'Well well, you won't fight me then. I thought as much.' Kamas turned to his warriors. 'See this my men, behold a village chieftain that is a coward.' They all cheered and laughed. 'I will give you another option. Seeing as I am in a good mood today, I will let you choose a champion to fight for you, and I will choose my champion. If my Champion wins, you take down these hideous walls. If your champion wins, we will turn and walk back to our village with no hard feelings.' Kamas turned to his warriors once more and called for his son. 'TORNOS! Come forward.' He shouted. A large warrior walked from the gathered army and stood alongside Kamas. 'This is Tornos, my son. He is one of our best. Pick your champion and send him down to his death so we can go home.'

The Conri of Four Vales nodded. 'I have heard of your son and know he is a great warrior.' Akala watched the Conri turn from the wall and looked along the line of warriors that stood with him. He was searching for Rovan the village champion. None put themselves forward to take on the deadly task. Akala looked at Cahira. She was also on the wall with her bow. She looked like she was about to step forward. A wave of panic came over Akala at the thought of it. Quickly Akala stepped out and offered to fight for the honour of Four Vales before Cahira could. 'As Four Vales Champion, it is my place to fight. I will fight for Four Vales.' He said with pride. The Conri felt relieved.

Then Rovan stepped out. 'It is my place to take on this task.' He nodded towards the Conri. Then several other warriors offered to fight also. The Conri contemplated on who would be best to send down to fight. He was talking amongst his men when a commotion went up.

Everyone turned to look back towards their village and saw Kalin riding alone towards the wall. He dismounted and walked up to the rampart to the Conri.

'I would be honoured to fight as your champion of Four Vales.'

The Conri put his hand on Kalin's shoulder. 'Are you sure you are ready to take on this task? Tornos is a mighty warrior.'

'I am your man Conri, and I haven't trained yet today, so I need the workout.'

All the village cheered as Kalin walked through the gate below and out onto the battleground to face the Fenrich Champion. Akala looked over at Cahira and he could see the excitement in her eyes and the disappointment in Rovan's.

Kamas laughed out loud as he saw Kalin walking towards them. 'I give you the chance to send out your best warrior and you send out a boy.'

Kalin smiled as he walked to meet the father and son awaiting him. He stopped a few feet back. 'Very well then, if you want a slaughter then you will get one!' Kamas shouted. The two fighters eyed each other. Kalin could see that his opponent looked strong and skilled. His eyes would not divert from him. He looked to be in his early twenties and had already acquired a lot of battle scars.

Kamas stepped in close to the boy. 'What is your name boy?'

'It is Kalin.'

'I am not sure I know you, but I am pleased to meet you. You are very brave to take on this task for your village. Do you have a family name so I can honour them later for your bravery at our victory feast?'

'Yes, I do. I am Kalin from the Ruane Clan, son of Shun Ruane and nephew to Karra Ruane, The Guardian of the gate.'

Kamas gulped in shock; the smile now gone from his face. 'Your father was Shun Ruane? And your uncle is Karra, Guardian of the Gate?'

'That is correct.'

'Well who would have thought!' Kamas turned to his son. 'Be careful my son and remember everything I have taught you.'

'Why do you look so shaken father. I will make him suffer for his people.'

Kamas leaned in close and embraced his son. 'Listen to me Tornos, try and kill him fast, you hear? And know that I am proud of you.' Kamas walked back to join the rest of his army in silence. Both Tornos and Kalin stood still staring at each other. Each waiting for the other to make the first move.

Kalin then spoke. 'Well will we begin then?'

Without a word Tornos drew his long sword and swung it at Kalin's face. Kalin back stepped and drew his own sword. Kalin was surprised at how fast Tornos was, but after training with Leib he was ready for anything this champion could throw at him. Tornos attacked again with ferocity and speed but Kalin easily parried all the strikes. Kalin was happy to remain on the defence throughout the bout. Cheers went up on both sides. Kamas looked on with fear in his eyes, knowing his son was no match for Kalin and consequently, that this might be the last time he saw his son alive. Even with Tornos's great strength, it was obvious that he was getting tired as the fight wore on. Each time he thought he had landed a slicing attack, Kalin would suddenly move out of range and his sword would just slice through the air. He could not hit him. All his life he had prided himself on his not inconsiderable skills with the sword, but none of his techniques seemed to work against this young man. It was like fighting a ghost. As Tornos got more tired, the cheers from the Fenrich warriors got less and less. They could see he was losing badly. He looked exhausted now. With one last effort, Tornos lunged at the boy. Kalin moved into the attack and deflected the sword with his, hitting Tornos with a left punch and knocking the man to his back and his sword from his hand. Tornos lay on the ground with the point of Kalin's sword just tipping Tornos's neck.

Kamas shouted out in horror. 'NO!' A cheer went up from all the villagers on the wall. Both sides waited for the killing blow to be struck. Kalin looked over at Kamas and then withdrew his sword and sheathed it. He turned towards Tornos and held out his hand. 'You fought well my friend.' He pulled Tornos to his feet. 'I am not willing to take the life of one of my Gantian Brothers under any circumstances and certainly not one with such great skills as yourself.' He then turned towards Kamas and his army. 'Now let this be an end to this dispute between our neighbouring villages.' Kalin picked up Tornos's sword and handed it back to him hilt first and walked back towards Four Vales, leaving Tornos speechless.

Kalin heard his name being called out. He turned back around and saw Kamas shouting to him. 'I take it back Kalin. Your Conri didn't just send out a boy, he sent out a great warrior. Hear my words now. Thank you for sparing my son. I am in debt to you now. This debt will be paid to you. When you are ready call upon me, and I will grant you a favour when you need it.' With that he turned and all the warriors for the Fenrich village left and headed back to their village, including the tired and bewildered Tornos. Kalin walked in through the gates of the wooden structure and was meet by the entire village all cheering his name.

The Conri came down from the wall and shook Kalin's hand. 'Thank you Kalin. You have saved plenty of lives today and have restored peace between our villages for now. Can I ask you a question?'

'Yes of course?'

'Why did you decide to come back?'

Kalin laughed. 'I had forgotten my sword and Karra sent me back as punishment for leaving it behind.'

Conri could see the boy still in him. 'Well, we are all grateful for your forgetfulness.'

Akala watched after Cahira as she made her way to Kalin and congratulated him on his win with a kiss on his cheek. He could see by the way she looked at him and the way she was around him that she was very much into him. He could feel his heart sinking as he walked away from the crowded area.

29

Alain rode at the front of the line of Captain Chal's men. The scouts had come back saying that they had met up with scouts from the City of Kitia and all was well there. They were nearly home. It was nearing the end of Autumn and all the men were weary from their trek back home. They knew it would not be long before they would have to set out again to bring a new shipment of supplies back to General Arthen. Autumn was nearing its end, and winter would soon follow. The next trip back down would be even harder than the first. Alain thought about his parents and his younger sister. It would be good to see them. He heard hooves coming up fast along the line. He looked back and saw his Captain riding up to him.

Chal pulled his horse alongside. 'We are nearly home Alain.'

'Yes Captain.'

'Have you any plans?'

'I do indeed. After I collect my pay, I am going to visit my family. I hope they have not forgotten me. What about you Captain, have you any plans?'

'I too will visit my home and see my mother. She will be wanting news of my father also. After that I think I will visit a few taverns and get drunk and maybe find a woman.'

'That sounds like a good plan. You might see me in there also,' said Alain with a smile on his face.

The line of men crested a hill and the city of Kitia was in full view. A horn sounded within the distant city, indicating that there was a force approaching. The city looked very impressive from the distance with all the colours of autumn set around it in full bloom. Closer now, Chal could see that the walls were well manned. They moved towards the East Gate which opened to admit them, and they passed through into the packed city of people. They were met by the watch captain and his guards. The horses and wagons were taken from them to be fed and replenished. All the men made their way to the barracks where they were fed and paid for their duties. Chal gave his report and they were all given leave for four days, after which Chal and all his men would report back to the barracks to prepare for their journey back down south to General Arthen in five days' time. It was only a short visit home, but they needed to get food to the army. Chal took a fresh mount from the stables and, after some debate with the gate guards, he left the city to visit his mother out on the villa by their farm. The gate to the villa was shut when he got there. He banged on it loudly and one of the farmers opened it.

'Welcome home Master Chal.'

'It is good to be home.'

He stabled his horse and went inside. His mother was in the kitchen preparing food and placing it into a bowl. She dropped the bowl and ran across the kitchen to her son and hugged him for a long time. 'Oh, Chal it is truly great to see you. How is your father? Did you get to see him? Is the war raging down at the South Wall?'

'He is good Mother, and no, there has not been much fighting. Just skirmishes.'

'I am glad to hear that Chal. You look tired and you have grown too.' She pulled back from him still holding his hand and looked him up and down. 'You are just in time for food. We have been on rations since all this war started. The city insists on taking more than half of our harvest to feed the troops. We have been ordered to keep the gates locked. I have moved in most of the farmers to the villa as it might not be safe for them in the fields.'

'If the war comes up this far, mother, make sure you bring in all the men and arm them. The villa might get overlooked as all the attention will be focused on the city. If the city falls, make sure you ride South to the mountains. You will be safe there. Father and I will find you then.'

'Do you think they will come this far?'

'I think they are capable of anything Mother.'

'Look at you all grown up and talking like a man.' She hugged Chal once more. 'How is your father doing? Is he keeping well?'

'He is doing just fine mother. Don't you worry about him. You know how strong he is.'

'Yes, I do but I can't help but worry about him down there. Hopefully this war will be over soon, and we can all get things back to the way they should be. Now you sit yourself down there and tell me all about your trip while I finish off preparing the food.'

Chal told his mother all about what had happened but left out the attack on them and losing men. That would only worry her, and she had enough to deal with, running the farm while he and his father were away.

'Oh, I almost forgot.' Chal pulled out a letter from his tunic for her. 'Father asked me to give you this.' She thanked him and placed the letter on the side of the table.

'I will read that later. There is no rush. Once you have told me he is well my mind is at ease now.'

Chal spent the three enjoyable days with his mother. He helped around the farm as best he could in the short time available to him and tried to spend as much time with his mother as possible. They talked and reminisced about when Chal was a child. On the fourth day he said his goodbyes to her, and she gave him a letter for his Father to bring back down with him. Chal made his way back to the city. Along the road he noticed the tree where Kalin and himself used to meet. He walked over to it. He reached into the hollow in the trunk of the tree and took out the two wooden swords that they used to play with. He recalled with a smile the times he had spent with his friend, running and chasing each other in mock battles and playing around the woods and meadows without a care in the world. He wondered what his friend might be doing all the way up there in Gantia. He looked down at the swords in his hands and the carved names in the wood.

'Those were glory days. I miss them' he said out loud. Wondering if he would ever see his friend again, he placed the wooden swords back in the crevice of the tree and continued on his way to the barracks in the city. Most of his men were already in their quarters. Alain was there too playing a dice game with some of the men. They all stood to attention, saluting Chal as he walked in.

'Good to see you Captain. How was your visit?'

'It was good, but not long enough.'

'Yes, me too.'

'So are you all set for another trip with supplies.'

'I am dreading the thoughts of another one,' said Alain.

Chal clapped him on the back. 'Hopefully this one will be uneventful.'

The next day, Chal and his 100 men set off on the long road to the Generals at the front line. They had a few new men join his unit to replace the numbers that they had lost. Chal had addressed these new men that morning and welcomed them under his command. He noticed that two of the new soldiers were Brin's friends, the two brothers Atal and Abtar. He was pleased to see some familiar faces. The 100 soldiers and the supply wagons moved from the city of Kitia along the stone road heading East and started their long journey to General Arthen and his army. There were still people making their way to the city of Kitia looking for protection from the invasion in the East. Most of them looked hungry and weary. Chal helped them out and gave them what rations he could spare. The further they travelled, the more the land began to look desolate and with that, the mood among the men changed. Most of them were starting to look fearful. The weather had changed and with that came the rain. Chal would not arrive at his destination until winter was in full swing and would probably not see his mother again until next spring or even summer. This would be a hard journey for them all. Chal would have to use all his skills to keep his troops focused on the task at hand. The days of playing in the woods with his friend were but a distant memory.

30

Leta was enjoying her time in Athel. Summer was over and the colours of Autumn were vibrant. Everything was working out for her as the new ruler of Natalia. The city was secure and was starting to look as it once had, thanks to all the work being done. The farms were now bringing in a healthy amount of food so the city could sustain itself. She had seduced the Captain, Velez, and they shared a bed frequently now. He was a handsome man and she enjoyed his company. He could be a little more adventurous in bed, but she could live with that. The only reason she had made this advance on her captain was to get back at Skarin. She could not wait to see the look on his face next summer when he would arrive with her father.

The Emperor's Mystic, Oranius, was also busy in Athel. He had spent his time setting up a new temple for The Dark Sect. He walked at a fast pace down the long corridor from the living quarters to the temple with some of his followers. He stopped and turned back to his men. 'We must act fast now. We are running out of time. Make sure to bring me 3 slaves tonight. Bring them to the Temple. We have some work to do before we can rest today, but first I must contact my brother.' He left the men and made his way into the temple and started to set up for the task ahead. Oranius Looked into the flames of a small fire that was held on a bronze tray. Red flames flickered to blue, and the face of his brother could be seen within.

'Hello, my brother, how are the plans coming along?'

'We are making headway, but we need to be swift now.'

'Have you a name for me?'

'Yes, I contacted the Dark Lord yesterday and he gave me the name. He is a young man from Gantia. He must be killed as soon as possible as he will be the downfall of our plan. This task is supreme. His name is, Kalin Ruane.'

Oranius could see Sabat close his eyes and concentrate. Oranius felt a connection and then Sabat projected an image of the boy, Kalin, to Oranius's mind. 'Do you see the face of he who must be killed?'

'Yes, my brother. I will make sure this happens.'

Later that night, Oranius was waiting in the temple beside the altar. He was dressed in black robes. Six followers walked in with three slaves. The slaves were gagged and bound, with their hands tied behind their backs. They were marched forward to Oranius and pushed down onto their knees in front of him. Oranius looked into their eyes one at a time.

'You have been chosen for a great cause, for there is no greater cause than to serve the Dark Lord.'

He turned to the altar behind him and took a golden goblet. He held it up high above his head and spoke words that were unknown to the followers and slaves within the Temple Room. He then turned to the first slave and pulled the gag down from his mouth and held the goblet up to his lips. 'Drink deeply for your Lord.'

The slave turned his head and refused to drink. Two followers came forward and held his head back, forcing open his mouth. Oranius poured the liquid in in and the gag was pulled back into place to stop the slave from spitting out the liquid. He then moved on to the second slave, this time a woman, and his followers held her and poured it into her mouth too and then onto the third slave, another woman. All three fell forward onto the floor and started to shake violently from consuming what the Priest had given them. Oranius then turned around, putting on black gloves and opening a black box on the altar. He picked up a steel tongs, using it to take a small red seed from the box. He nodded to the followers and they once more pulled down the gag and held open the mouth of the first slave. They all seemed to be unconscious now, but still their bodies were shaking. He dropped the seed into the slave's mouth and then did the same with the next two.

'Move back everyone and do not make any movements or sounds.'

All the followers moved to the outer perimeter of the room, along the walls. Oranius held his hand high in the air, all the while chanting in the same strange language. The room unexpectedly felt very cold and there seemed to be a rush of frozen air swirling around the centre of it. The two fireplaces and the torches that lined the walls all changed colour to a pale blue. The flames started to flicker faster, and a strange, high pitched, screeching noise started to come from all the fires. The swirling intensified and rose to the height of the ceiling. Oranius waved his hands and directed the frozen air. It split into three separate swirls as they gathered momentum. Oranius 's hand pointed down to the slaves and the swirls then shot down towards the three slaves and disappeared into their bodies. The first slave's body jumped violently. He rose up and then slumped back down on the floor. Then the second and third slaves did the same.

The room was quiet now, as the bodies of the slaves had stopped moving. Then, one at a time they started to jerk again. Their heads tilted backwards, and movement could be seen under their tunics and then under their skin. This movement pulsed upward and around their necks. The skin bulged outwards and started to swell as it pulsated. Their jaws opened and a black substance poured out of their bodies through their mouths. There was blood spilling out all over the floor. Oranius stood back and three tall slim figures were born through the bodies of the three slaves, pushing their way out into the world. They seemed to grow in size and then stood tall, towering over Oranius. They were at least eight feet tall. It was unthinkable that something the size of these demons could have come from the broken and torn bodies of the slaves lying dead on the ground. The black beasts hissed loudly with long, forked tongues that darted out over their long sharp teeth. Their mouths opened wide enough to engulf a human head. They looked around the room at the followers. One follower stepped back in a frightened motion and a beast leapt forward to attack. Oranius shouted. 'Stop.' The slim black beast came to a halt, snapping its huge jaw shut only inches from the follower's face. The Shadow Hunter looked back at its master, its long fingers with their razor-sharp talons remained outstretched.

'I said, do not move. These are Shadow Hunters, Night Beasts. They will tear you apart in seconds, and do not touch any of its saliva as it is highly poisonous.' Oranius moved slowly to the two large doors that opened out to the night air. He pushed these open and stepped aside. He pointed at the beasts and forced the projection of the boy's face into their minds. 'Shadow Hunters, I order you to kill. I order you to kill the young man that goes by the name Kalin Ruane. Now go and do as I bid.' The three beasts jumped forward at tremendous speed out the door and into the black night.

The Shadow Hunters could only travel at night, as the sunlight would burn their skin. After four nights of running they had nearly reached the South Wall. Their long limbs and prodigious strength made them capable of covering a huge amount of ground without tiring. It would not be long before they were well into the land of Latonia. They sheltered for the day in a cave along the edge of the mountain range that connected to the wall. As the sun went down below the horizon, they emerged into the night's darkness. A Dragon soldier stood guard on the wall looking out to the north with his hands on the cold stone. There was no movement out on the planes of the Latonian lands. He moved away and looked down along the ramparts. There was another guard some ways away. He was starting his shift too. He waved to him and he waved back and walked back to the other side of the wall. It got lonely at night on the wall, just watching for the enemy, and it was getting colder each night. He looked up to the sky. It was a starless night with dark clouds filling the night sky. Each guard had a burning stove to cook on and to keep them warm throughout their shift. The Dragon Guard opened the iron door on his burner and loaded it with some logs that were piled up against the wall, to keep the fire lighting. He warmed his hands from its heat. He looked out to the south and wondered when he would see the Emperor marching along the road towards them with the rest of the Imperial Dragon Army, making their way north and taking Kitia. Those will be days of glory, he thought.

Clouds drifted away from the half moon, bathing the wall with a silver light. Just then, he saw a movement. It looked like there was a shadow moving towards the wall. Then another, and another. At first, he thought it was just his imagination and the shadows of the clouds passing by the moon making silhouettes on the ground, but the shadows were moving in the wrong direction. He looked closer. The shadows had reached the base of the wall. He leaned out to get a better view. They were coming up the wall with inhuman speed. He knew then that these were not men. The guard jumped back as the first Shadow Hunter leapt from the wall onto the ramparts. He looked up at the tall black figure in terror. He tried to shout out, but sheer terror had stolen his voice. The Shadow Hunter moved on him fast. The guard didn't have time to even draw his sword. A black hand shot out and talons ripped through the skin of the guard's neck. He fell to his knees as two other Shadow Hunters rushed past him, down along the wall and into the lands of Latonia. The Attacking Shadow Hunter moved in on his dying victim and twisted his head. Huge jaws snapped down onto the man's face, ripping skin and tendons and muscle. The guard fell in a pool of blood, still holding his neck and with no face. The last Shadow Hunter then took off after his fellow Hunters, disappearing into the darkness of the night. The other guard that had waved back noticed the guard was lying down on the ramparts. Was he sleeping while he was on guard? he thought. He walked over to wake him so he would not be in trouble. To sleep while on guard would mean punishment by death. He looked around to see if any others had noticed him sleeping, but there was no one close by. Just a few guards down along the wall who were too far away to see. The guard shook the sleeping man, but he did not respond. He turned him over to talk to him and jumped back, falling onto his backside when he saw the man had no face. He then noticed the pool of blood. The guard stood back up, grabbed the brass horn from his belt and blew out a long signal to alert the rest of the guards.

31

Kalin was warming his hands by the fire in his cabin. The winter was in full swing, the snow was coming down hard now and it was getting dark. The snow had come unexpectedly and was getting heavier and heavier. Karra and Leib had been out setting traps and had not come back for supper. Kalin had made a mixed meat broth ready for them. He figured they had gotten caught in the snow and stopped off for the night at their hunting hut a few miles from their cabins on the hill. Kalin dished out the broth into a bowl and was about to start eating when there was a sharp bang on his door. He unsheathed his hunting knife and opened it.

Cahira was standing outside, looking wet and cold. 'I'm very sorry to disturb you, Kalin. I am at a bit of a loss. I knocked on Karra's door but there was nobody home there and I saw that there was a light in your cabin. I got stuck out in the snow and have no shelter nearby.'

'Please come in.' Kalin brought her in and pulled out a chair by the fire. 'Please sit and get yourself warm.'

Cahira was shivering uncontrollably now and the skin on her face was bright red. 'I'm sorry Kalin, I misjudged the weather and was out hunting for rabbits when the storm came upon me all of a sudden.'

'You are lucky, I have just made some broth. You are welcome to have some with me. It will help warm you up.'

'I would love some, thank you.' Cahira said with a trembling voice. Kalin filled a bowl and brought it over to her. She took it from him with blue coloured hands.

'Don't take this the wrong way, but you will have to get out of those wet clothes if you want any chance of warming up.'

'You are right.' Cahira stood and, looking at Kalin, slowly began to strip out of her cold, wet clothes.

Kalin also stood and looked away, embarrassed. 'I will just get you some of my clothes that you can wear while yours dry by the fire.' He left the room and went into his bedroom, pulling the door behind him.

He took out an old, small pair of leggings and a wool tunic. He was about to go back into Cahira but stopped at the half open door. He did not want to walk in on her when she was naked, so he peered around the half open door. She was naked. Her body glowed in the firelight and Kalin could see how beautiful she was. She turned suddenly and caught him looking at her. He ducked back in behind the door.

'I'm sorry,' he called out.

'It's OK Kalin, I don't mind you looking at me.'

Kalin held out his hand holding the clothes for her to take from the other side of the door. For a second, he was left holding the clothes in mid-air, then he could feel her hand slide down over his hand unhurriedly and she took the clothes. 'How come you are hiding behind that door? Are you afraid of me?'

Kalin did not answer, instead he tried to force an image of Thianni's face into his mind. He waited behind the door for a bit more and then came out. Cahira was now covered up with just the tunic on. It was big on her and came down to just above her knees. She picked up the bowl and sat on the chair by the fire. 'The leggings are too big for me, but this tunic will be fine for now until my clothes dry.'

Kalin walked over and took his bowl and sat beside her. 'Good, at least you are getting warm now.' He could see that the shaking had stopped, and the colour was starting to come back to her skin. 'You were lucky you came here, that weather can kill a person fast if you get caught out in it, and you are not prepared.'

'I was lucky and thank you for your hospitality. I think it will be a cold winter, this one.'

They sat in silence for a while, eating their broth and listening to the crackling of the fire. Cahira finished hers first and placed the empty bowl on the table. 'How come Karra and his friend are not home in this weather?'

'They went out earlier to set traps and never came back. My guess is that the bad weather has forced them to stay at the hunting hut. They have done that in the past when they have lost track of time.'

'So, you are telling me I have you all to myself?' Cahira said with a smile.

'Well, they could come back at any time.' Kalin said uneasily. He finished his broth and placed it on the table also. 'You may stay the night here tonight and see how the snow is in the morning. There is no way you would make it safely back to Four Vales in this weather.'

'Thank you Kalin. I will owe you now.' They talked for a while. Cahira had lots of questions about the gate and the creatures that tried to get into their world and Kalin was glad to answer. Eventually, Kalin stood up from the fire and stretched. He could see Cahira was looking sleepy now.

'It's getting late. I think we should turn in for the night. You can have my bed. I will sleep out here by the fire.'

'I don't mind if you want to share the bed with me Kalin.' She looked at him to see his reaction to the statement. He looked embarrassed. She gave a giggle, 'I promise I will keep to my side of the bed.'

'I had better stay out here in case Karra and Leib come back and are in trouble and need me. There is a candle by my bedside if you need light.'

'You are very honourable, but if you change your mind feel free to join me. Good night Kalin.'

'Good night Cahira.' With that, she walked into the bedroom leaving the door half open behind her. Kalin took some blankets from a small cupboard and made a bed on the floor in front of the fire and tried to get some sleep. It took him a while to fall asleep.

Kalin woke with a startle. He was not sure if the noise was just in his head or was real. He sat up and looked around. The fire was almost out and was just giving a slight glow. The door to his bedroom where Cahira was sleeping was still half open. A bad feeling swept over him. He heard another noise and this time he knew it was coming from outside. It sounded like hissing and then shuffling through snow. It went quiet again. Kalin rose from his bed and was reaching out for his sword beside the table, when a huge crashing noise sounded out and the door burst open to reveal an enormous black creature. It was standing in the doorway looking in at Kalin. Its hands with long talons curled around the frame of the door as it moved its black slender body inside. It had a long snout with sharp teeth and a long tongue that darted out into the air. It tried to stand tall as it entered the room, but its head hit the ceiling and it had to stoop. Kalin slowly moved towards the doorway to the bedroom where Cahira slept. His sword was outstretched as he backed into the door, closing it shut. He could hear Cahira inside the room. It sounded like she was coming out.

'What was that noise?' she called out.

'Stay in the room,' he shouted back to her, slowly pressing back against the door. The black creature lurched forward, its jaws snapping and biting at Kalin. Splashes of its saliva sprayed into the air with each movement. Kalin lashed out with his sword and the creature jumped backward to avoid the strike. It moved very fast and moved forward again towards Kalin. He could see two more creatures making their way inside the cabin. The first one attacked again. Kalin moved quickly to the side and drove his sword upwards under the creature's neck. As the sword pierced its black skin, it let out an ear-piercing screech and moved back.

Cahira called out. 'What is happening? Are you OK Kalin?'

'Stay in the room, do not come out here,' he called back to her. The three beasts were in the room now. The one Kalin had struck with his sword was shaking its head in pain. Any other creature would have died from that injury. This confused Kalin. They spread out around the room and Kalin stood ready for another attack. This time they attacked from both sides and from the front. Kalin found it hard to defend all three angles in the darkened room. These creatures were fast, even for Kalin. Teeth snapped and talons struck out at Kalin. Kalin fought back with his sword, slicing and hacking at them. Then one creature charged Kalin, knocking him from the doorway, and he crashed down on the table. The three Shadow Hunters jumped upon him. Kalin stabbed one in the chest as it bore down on him. It screeched out loud. Then one came in from the side and bit into his arm. The pain was unlike anything Kalin had felt before. He instantly felt weak. He kicked out at the third, sending it flying backwards. Talons lashed out and ripped the clothes from his upper body, leaving long bloody scratches across Kalin's chest. Then they all jumped back, hissing.

Cahira had opened the door to the bedroom and entered with a candle in her hand. The room lit up and the light from the candle appeared to be causing pain to the strange, unearthly creatures, who hissed at Cahira. They started to move in toward her, shrieking with pain. One leapt forward to attack Cahira. Kalin then jumped back to his feet and launched his own attack. With two hands, he brought his sword down on to the attacking creature and, with one swift swipe, he beheaded it.

Its head spun off and hit the floor and its body dropped and started to shake violently in front of Cahira. She was frozen to the spot with fear. The other two turned to attack Kalin but they were too late. Kalin launched into them, cutting and hacking. They lashed out at Kalin, biting and scratching, but this time he did not stop his attack on them. One creature lost a leg and fell to the ground. Kalin stabbed at it with speed until it stopped moving. The last one jumped onto Kalin's back, biting down on his shoulder. He twisted around, knocking it clear, and as it attacked again Kalin met it with his sword and cut through the creature's neck, taking its head from its body. It also dropped to the ground and shook. Kalin could see a black cloud leaving the dead bodies of the creatures and then the cabin fell quiet once more. Kalin slumped to the ground and Cahira ran to him, holding his bloodied, unconscious body to hers.

The next morning it had stopped snowing. Karra and Leib made their way back home. As they crested the hill and the two cabins came into sight, Karra could see that there was something wrong. As they got closer, they could see the door on Kalin's cabin had been broken inwards. They started running towards the cabin. As they entered, they could see the bodies of the dead, black creatures on the floor. They opened the door to the bedroom. Kalin lay on the blood-soaked bed with wounds all over him and Cahira was asleep beside him on the floor. She opened terrified eyes as they came in.

'Thank the Gods you are here. Kalin wont wake. He has been badly injured. I have cleaned his wounds, but they keep bleeding.'

'Don't worry Cahira, we will help now,' said Karra as he looked more closely at his nephew's wounds. He then turned to Cahira. 'His wounds don't seem to be healing and look infected. When did this happen?'

'Last night. I was sleeping in the bed and Kalin was outside sleeping by the fire. I woke when I heard a loud noise. They just broke through the door.'

Leib investigated the dead black bodies and the trashed room. 'There was a great fight. Kalin did well to kill all three. Do you think these came through the gate?'

Karra shook his head. 'I don't think so. I have never seen anything like these. They look like demons. I have heard stories about creatures of dark magic called Shadow Hunters that fit the description of those dead bodies.' He looked back at Kalin. 'They say that the Shadow

Hunters have a venomous bite and that no one can survive it. This might explain the fact that Kalin's wounds are not healing.'

Cahira slumped back. 'It was my fault that this happened to him. One of the creatures was about to attack me and Kalin jumped at it and stopped it. Then the other two attacked Kalin. It was horrible. The worst thing was, I just froze. I didn't know how to help him fight them. He told me to stay in this room, but I came out to him with the candle to see what was happening and to see if he was ok.'

Karra put his huge hand on her shoulder. 'There was nothing you could have done, if anything you probably saved him by bringing out the candle. What I have heard is that they can't tolerate any kind of light. It can kill them. That is why they only travel at night.'

She then knew what old Sallin meant. She recalled his words. '*but when this trouble does come, you must bring the light to him.*'

'This was foretold to me by old Sallin.' She looked at Karra.

'Tell me what he said?'

'He told me after this happens, I must seek him out and he will help Kalin through this. Will I go and fetch Sallin?'

'I don't think Sallin would make it all the way up here. We will have to bring Kalin to Sallin.'

The trek back down to Four Vales was long and hard. Karra had tied Kalin to one of the horses. They could not travel fast with the horses as the snow was too deep. Kalin was a dead weight and they had to stop often to rest and fix his position on the horse. As they got closer to Four Vales, some men came out from the walled village and helped bring Kalin to Sallin's house. He was waiting for them at the door. They brought him inside and laid him on a bed that was ready for him by the fire.

'Now I must ask you all to leave.' Karra and Leib and the other men left the room. 'And you too Cahira.' She was reluctant to go. 'You have done a good job here. I will look after him now.'

She started to walk out and stopped by the door. 'Will he live?'

'He will live, but I must act fast in order for that to happen.'

'I will come back tomorrow and see how he is.' She left, closing the door behind her. Sallin could see the love for the young man in Cahira's eyes.

32

Sallin stripped all clothes from Kalin and cleaned his body with a wet rag. His skin looked a pale blue in colour and he had lost a considerable amount of blood. His wounds were deep, and the venomous poison had started attacking his flesh, working its way in deeper into his body. Kalin's breathing was ragged and shallow. A normal man would not have survived these wounds. He could feel the energy emanating from Kalin's body, fighting hard against the infection. He knew that there was a raging battle taking place within this young man's body. His job now was to assist in this battle and hopefully turn the tide. He wiped sweat from his own brow. He had lit a few fires to keep the temperature high in the room and it was extremely warm now inside the house. He carefully prepared a green paste and packed it into all the wounds. Holding his hands over the largest wound in Kalin's chest, he closed his eyes and concentrated on the poison. His hands began to shake, and he could feel the poison being extracted from the young man. He used his powers to pull it to the surface of the skin and dark liquid started to seep from the wound, pouring down along Kalin's body and onto the bed. He repeated this with every wound on Kalin's body before slumping back into his chair to rest.

He awoke sometime later with a startle. The room felt cold now. The fire had died right down and was just a mere glow in the darkened room. He turned to his left and a figure came forward from the shadowy corner. 'I see you have been hard at work?'

Sallin drew back with fright at seeing the Shord, the Spirit of the land. 'What business has The Shord in my home?'

'I have come to see the boy.'

'The boy is not up for visitors today.'

'Ah, I am a very special visitor. I can help heal him if you wish it?'

'I will not be tricked into making wishes, by you or the Shann. The last time I asked you for something it nearly cost me my life. Now tell me Shord, what have you really come here for?'

The Shord ignored the question, gliding across the floor and peering down at the still naked figure of Kalin. 'He is a handsome young man. I felt his energy even before I entered this room. It woke me from my sleep. I have been watching him for a while now but now that energy is fading. It is fading fast.'

'He will not die while I am looking after him' retorted Sallin.

'You speak of hope old man, but deep down inside you know you are not strong enough to hold his soul to this world. Many forces are drawn to him and many forces want him. He is special.'

'That may be true, but I will fight for his soul to remain in this world.'

'I have no doubt that you will fight, but you do not have to. All you have to do is ask for my help and it will be so.'

Sallin looked at the old spirit of the land in front of him and felt a feeling of dismay.

Kalin was aware that he was lying down. He forced himself to sit up. He could see that both of his legs were tied together by a rope that disappeared into the darkness. He looked around in the darkness but could see nothing. He reached down to the rope that bound his legs together, but suddenly it tightened, and he felt it start to drag him along the ground. He struggled to get himself free but could not loosen it. He kicked out with his legs, trying to shake off the rope, but still he could not loosen it. The rope sped up, pulling him along the ground. He could feel the back of his legs starting to get scratched, so he turned and lay on his front, trying to grab at the ground to stop himself being pulled. A small root was sticking up from the ground and he managed to grab hold of it. He looked back down along the rope. He could not see what it was attached to, or what was pulling him. The rope just disappeared into the darkness. It tugged harder now and he lost his grip on the root. He slid even faster along the ground. He sat up again to look. He could just make out that the rope was being pulled over the edge. As he got closer, he could see that it was the edge of a cliff. Panic started to rise within him now. His body hurt. As he was dragged along the ground at speed, it cut and scraped at his flesh. He was about to get pulled over the edge and he clawed at the ground, trying to get something secure to hold. As his body was about to be pulled over, he managed to get a hold on the edge. He hung there, with what felt like a great weight at the end of the rope pulling him downward. He could feel blood running down his body from the cuts that he had sustained being dragged along the sharp stones on the ground. His fingers began to slip, and he started to lose his grip. The strain was too much. He let go and was pulled downwards, engulfed in darkness. Then all was black.

Kalin woke with a gasp. He thought he could hear voices talking. Not to him, but about him. Then they faded and the pain came, ripping through his body. His hands were now tied and outstretched in both directions. The ropes were pulled so tight that he was lifted from the ground several inches. The pain was excruciating. Blood was coming out of the numerous wounds on his body. Pressure started to build as both ropes were pulled even more tightly. He felt like his arms were going to be torn from his body. He looked down along the rope to his left and could see that it disappeared into a blackness. The blackness beckoned to him. He felt terrified. Freezing coldness emanated from its darkness, and he wanted to get far away from it. His instincts told him to run. He looked to his right and could see the rope disappear into a bright light. This light felt warm and pleasing. This was the direction he wanted to go. The Blackness pulled even harder and he cried out with the pain of its pulling. His body shifted closer to the coldness and he could feel it drawing him into its chaos. He felt hopeless. He could not move either way. Everything was out of his control. The blackness pulled at him again and the rope pulled even tighter. The pain was excruciating. Blood was streaming down his body from deep cuts. Kalin felt his strength fading until finally, everything went black.

On the table, Kalin's body started to spasm violently. His wounds began to reopen, and blood started to flow from the young man's body again. Sallin moved towards him and tried to steady him.

'You are losing him, old man' said the Shord with a crooked grin. Sallin concentrated, drawing on his energy, and held his hands over his chest and focused on Kalin. His spasms slowed ceased, and his body started to relax on the table. The blood ceased to flow. Sallin fell back exhausted, his legs nearly giving way. A weakness took hold of him and it was all too much for him.

'You were lucky, old man. His heart nearly gave out.'

Sallin sat back into his chair. His breath was ragged, and he struggled to stay conscious. 'Do you require my help?' enquired the Shord. Sallin was too weak to speak and just waved his hand in the Shord's direction as if to push him away. 'Ah, the weakness of the living flesh is a sight to behold.' The Shord rose high into the air, looming over Sallin, and his voice boomed out in a deafening screech. 'ASK ME TO HELP YOU.'

Kalin came around again and the pain instantly shot through his body. He wanted to go back to sleep so he could not feel it anymore, but he was awake now. His hand was nearly touching the blackness and he let out a shout. Then he was pulled quickly to his right and closer to the light. As he got closer to the light his wounds started to seal and the blood stopped flowing. Just as his hand was about to touch the light, he was pulled back again towards the darkness. His wounds opened and started to bleed again, and he let out a scream of pain. His hand was pulled into the blackness and he felt his soul being taken from his body and then there was nothing…

Sallin was now too weak to help Kalin. He tried to conjure up the strength, but he could not. He was drained of his powers and it would take time and rest before he could recover. Time, he did not have. He could see that Kalin's life was slipping away, laying there in a puddle of his own blood with vile poison running through his body.

As the Shord looked on at the scene, he smiled. 'Do you want him to die?'

Sallin shook his head. Kalin's body was now still. The bleeding had stopped and so had his heart. He was dead.

'In the end no one can say you didn't try.'

Sallin tried to speak. It came out as a mumble. 'Speak it again Old man.' The Shord moved in close. Sallin raised his head and tried again. This time the words came out slowly and the Shord heard and felt the power of the Old Man's words. 'Help me. Save the boy?'

The Shord rose up again, 'Your wish will be done.' The Shord moved to the body and held Kalin's lifeless head in his stick-like hands. Then he tilted Kalin's head back, causing his jaw to drop and open slightly. The Shord spoke ancient words as his breath flowed into the dead boy's mouth. 'LIVE!'

Kalin was awake again and this time there was no pain. His body was free from the nothingness of the Blackness and he was being pulled toward the light. The closer he got the warmer he felt, and a feeling of contentment filled him with warmth. He was pulled into the light and the brightness embraced him and blissfulness flooded through his body. He felt alive.

Kalin's chest heaved as his heart sprung to life again. The blood stopped flowing as his wounds started to close once more. His skin looked healthy again and he lay there peacefully sleeping. The Shord moved to Sallin now and placed his hand on the old man's head. The effort to save Kalin had taken its toll on Sallin. He was drained, but sleep would rejuvenate his strength. 'Unknown are the true heroes of this world. Sleep now, Old Man, for you have done well this day.' The Shord then disappeared. The fire sprung to life and was full of warm flickering flames. The room seemed to get brighter and there was heat in the air again.

Cahira could not sleep. The terror of the Shadow Hunters' attack kept playing through her mind again and again. She rose from her bed and dressed. She wanted to go to Sallin and see how Kalin was. It was still night-time. The air was cold, and the moon was full. She pulled her cloak around her shoulders and, shutting the door behind her, she started to walk. As she got to the centre of the village, she noticed how quiet it was and it then suddenly got colder. She caught a movement out of the corner of her eye to her left and noticed an old man sitting by the village well.

'It is too cold for you to be out here alone tonight' she said.

'My bones like the cold' came a voice back at her.

She stopped to see who he was but did not recognise him. 'Can I help you to get to your home?'

'That is very kind of you.'

Cahira walked to him and held out her hand to help him up. He did not move. She looked into his eyes and could see he was very old. His skin looked like the bark of a tree. 'You love him, don't you?'

She was shocked by the question and drew back her hand from him. 'Love who?'

'The young Guardian, Kalin.'

'How do you know this?' she retorted.

'He is a fine young man and you have a part to play in his life.'

'I do not know what you are talking about. I think the cold out here has got to you.'

'You know what I speak, and I can help you. Do you wish my help?'

Cahira was puzzled now. 'How can you help me; you can't even help yourself to your home.'

The man laughed out loud. 'You want to sleep with him, don't you?'

Cahira blushed. 'That is none of your business, but if you must know yes, I like him and, I do want him.'

The old man reached out with his skinny hand and grasped Cahira's arm. She tried to pull away but felt herself frozen to the spot. A surge of energy shot through her body and for a second, she felt she had passed out. He then let go of her. 'Not all you see is what will be. There are greater causes in life.' Cahira felt dizzy now but shook it off. 'I like your spirit, now I will ask you one last time. Do you wish for my help?'

Cahira found herself saying again, 'Yes, I want your help.'

The old man smiled widely with his thin lips. 'Let it be done so. The boy will live, but you must give him time to rest. He has a great deal of healing to do. Come to him in one week's time and pour this into his drink and he will see how beautiful you really are.' The old man reached out and handed Cahira a small dark vial of liquid. As she took it from him, she noticed his stick-like hands. She held the vial up to the moonlight to better see its contents and when she looked back to the old man by the well, he had gone.

The next day, Karra and Leib knocked on the door to Sallin's home, but there was no answer. Karra opened the door and peeped his head around. 'Good morning!' He called out. There was still no answer. Karra opened the door fully and moved inside. He could see that Kalin was still asleep on the table and on a chair beside him was Sallin, also fast asleep. Karra and Leib walked over to Kalin. He looked a lot better now, much to the relief of both men. However, Sallin looked very old and frail, slumped as he was to one side in his chair. They both moved to wake Sallin. Karra shook him gently and he woke with a start.

'Get out of here, you demon spirit.' he shouted out. Then he realised he was looking into Karra's eyes. 'Oh, I am sorry Karra, I thought you were someone else, an unwanted guest. But you and your dark friend are welcome here.'

Karra laughed. 'You look tired Sallin. We thought we'd check in to see how the boy is doing and if you needed anything?' Sallin tried to stand and fell to one side on wobbly legs. Karra caught him in time and laid him back into the chair. 'Stay where you are. You are in no state to be moving around.'

Sallin tried to stretch to look up at Kalin on the table, to see how he was but he could not. 'Is the boy OK?'

'He looks fine. Much better than he did when we brought him in last night.'

'Good.'

Leib took a cup, filled it with water and brought the cup up to Sallin's lips so he could drink it.

'Thank you.' Sallin said under shallow breath.

'Are you going to be OK? Leib asked.

'Yes, I will be fine. I just exhausted my powers last night trying to save the boy.'

'Thank you for that' Karra said.

'We are lucky he is still alive. Any other normal man would have not survived. Only for the Shord, he would have died last night.'

'The Shord?' Karra said, surprised. 'What was the Shord doing here?'

'He saved Kalin. He has taken a great interest in your nephew.'

Leib refilled the cup and brought it back with more water. 'I have heard that name before. Who is the Shord?' Leib asked.

Sallin brushed away the next cup and Karra looked at Leib. 'The Shord is the Old Man of the land.'

Sallin wiped his mouth, 'He isn't just the Old Man of the land, he is part of the land. He is part of every living thing you see around you.'

Leib looked confused. 'Is he a God?'

'Some say he used to be a God and was banished to this world. Now he must look after all nature.'

'He sounds likable.'

'He is a devious spirit and there is always a trick with him. He will only offer you something in order to get something else. I have been tricked by him before.'

Karra butted in, 'Well if he saved Kalin, I am glad he was here.'

Sallin nodded in agreement. 'I could not have saved him, Karra. We were lucky the Shord came.'

Karra turned and looked down at Kalin. He looked very peaceful now. Even though there was a lot of dried blood on the table, Kalin's wounds were almost closed and healed now. 'So Sallin, what can my friend and I do to help here?'

'I am feeling hungry.'

'I am glad you said that, Sallin, as I am feeling quite hungry too. We will muster up a meal fit for Kings. Sit back and watch what magic I can do.' Karra started to unload food from his bag and was looking for a pot in Sallin's kitchen area.

Leib shook his head and looked at Sallin. 'I have never met anyone like him. I don't know how he can be hungry; we have just eaten breakfast.'

Later that evening, Sallin sat by the fire with Karra and Leib in silence. Sallin could not remember ever eating as much as he had today with his guests. His stomach was full, and his strength was starting to return. There was a noise and all three looked at Kalin, who stirred on the table. His eyes opened and he slowly sat up and looked over at the three men who were now staring at him. Kalin licked his lips. 'Is there any food?'

Leib looked at Karra and noticed a wide grin form across his face. 'You would know he was your nephew.'

Cahira left her house and set off for Sallin's. It was almost dark now and all her thoughts were on Kalin. As she came around the corner, Sallin's house came into view. She was just about to continue onward when she saw the door opening. Karra and the Dark man, Leib, came out assisting Old Sallin. She moved back out of sight to see what was happening. The two men were helping Sallin out of the house and along the path to the wooded area of the village. She could just make out what they were saying. Sallin was saying he wanted to go and pray at the shrine and it looked like Karra and Leib were helping him get there. Cahira waited until they were out of sight and then made her way to the house. She opened the door and went inside. Her heart leaped as she saw Kalin sitting at a table eating. He turned around as she spoke. 'Thank the Gods you are alive.' Kalin smiled as he saw her. She ran over to him and he stood, and she hugged him. 'I was so worried about you Kalin.'

'Well I feel fine.'

'You were very lucky to survive.'

'So, everyone keeps telling me' he said with humour. 'Come sit down and have some food with me and we can talk.'

'Kalin, I think I owe you an apology.'

Kalin looked at her. 'For what?'

'I should have helped you when… when those creatures attacked us. I just froze.'

Kalin let out a little laugh. 'That's no problem Cahira. It was my job to protect you. After all, they came into my house uninvited.'

Cahira felt a bit better now that Kalin was joking about it. 'Well I have to make it up to you now, seeing as you nearly died protecting me.'

Kalin pulled down his top, exposing his upper body. 'Look! The cuts are all healed now.'

Cahira looked closely. He was right. Where there once had been deep wounds, there were now just thin lines on his skin. 'Well you heal very fast Kalin. I have never seen anything like that before.' Kalin pulled back on his top and continued to eat. 'Where are the others gone?'

'Karra and Leib have taken Sallin out to pray at the shrine. Karra said he needs the cool winter air. They should be gone for a while, but they said I need to stay and rest here.'

'So, it's just the two of us for a while?' Cahira stood and walked over to a sideboard where a jug of water and some cups stood. 'Do you want a drink of water?'

'Yes please' replied Kalin. Cahira poured two cups. Turning her back to Kalin, she then produced the vial of liquid the old man had given her. She emptied the contents into one of the cups and turned and walked back to the table, placing the cup with the liquid in front of Kalin and sitting down. A sense of wrongdoing came over her. She knew what she was doing was not right, but the voice of the Old Man with the stick hands came into her head. 'You are doing the right thing.'

She felt like this was all a dream. Kalin thanked her and then took the cup and drank it all down. She suddenly wanted to stop him, but the voice sounded again in her head. Cahira sipped her water, watching Kalin. After a few minutes, Kalin rose from the table and swayed a little. 'I am feeling very tired. Will you join me by the fire?' He then moved a chair closer to the fire. Cahira noticed that his speech was starting to slur. He was acting strangely, like he was drunk. She watched him as he slumped into the chair and closed his eyes.

'Kalin, are you OK?' she called out. She thought he had fallen asleep, but then his eyes opened wide.

He looked over at her. 'Thianni, is that you?' Cahira did not know what to make of the statement. Kalin jumped from the chair and ran over to Cahira. 'Oh, I have missed you so much.' He pulled Cahira into his embrace and kissed her. Cahira did not resist the kiss. Instead, she held him tight and kissed him back. Kalin pulled away from the kiss, still holding her, and looked her up and down. 'Let me see you. I can't believe you are here with me now.' He kissed her again.

Kalin started to take her clothes off and she helped him remove his. Moving to the chair by the fire, Cahira pushed him back on to the chair, climbing on to his lap without breaking the kiss. Cahira reached down and guided him into her. They moved together until he climaxed and then Cahira moved from him and quickly dressed. Kalin was asleep now. She gathered his clothes and folded them, placing them on the floor beside him. Then she took a blanket and covered him, kissed his forehead and left the house, heading home.

Sallin sat on the snow-covered ground by an old standing stone, repeating the same ancient words over and over. Karra and Leib were standing a short way away, talking quietly. After some time, Sallin stood and hobbled over to Karra and Leib. 'Time to go back now. I feel much better.' The three made their way back to Sallin's home where they found Kalin, still asleep on the chair.

Sallin stopped just inside the door, closing his eyes for a second and then reopening them. 'Kalin had a visitor.'

Karra went over to him and tried to wake him but couldn't. 'I can't wake him.'

Sallin moved to Kalin and placed his hand on the young man's forehead. 'He is OK. He is in a deep sleep.' He then picked up the second cup that had been left on the table and smelled it. 'Strange! He was not alone. Someone else was here with him. He has been drugged. He will be ok though. We will let him sleep.'

Karra went to fix his blanket and noticed he was not wearing any clothes. 'Why is he naked?'

Sallin turned to him. 'It was a woman that visited him, and for some reason I think the Shord is behind it.'

Kalin woke after a few hours and called out Thianni's name. 'Where is Thianni?' he asked Karra.

'She is not here Kalin. She is back in Kitia.'

'No, she was here with me.'

'It must have been a dream, Kalin.'

Kalin felt silly now as it had felt so real. He longed for her even more now. Sallin came to his side. 'I think you might have been tricked.'

'As soon as the winter has ended, I will travel back to Kitia.'

Karra nodded. 'The pass will not be clear until the middle of spring, but when it is clear I will travel with you for as long as I can, Kalin.'

Content now, Kalin pulled the blanket around himself and went to sleep. Over the next few weeks, Kalin built back up his strength and when the weather improved, he moved back to his cabin near the gate with Karra and Leib. He continued to train with Leib and ran when the days were not too cold. He found himself waiting to hear from the south about how the war was progressing. Kalin was back to full health nearing the end of the winter.

33

The winter came in hard with very low temperatures and freezing snow blizzards in Gantia. The tribes had not seen such a hard winter in years. They could only travel from village to village between the bad spells. The lands of Latonia were badly hit too. Food was scarce and as a consequence the advance by the Dragon armies from Eamhair had ceased. They felt this drop in temperature more than most as they were not used to such cold weather, their homelands being much milder and hotter. Because of this, back in Kitia the King had found some security that came with such a harsh winter. He knew that this would slow any attacks on his land and give him time to plan and prepare, if they were to bring the war to the capital. It also gave time for his new young troops to train and sharpen their skills, for they might have to rely on them in the months and years to come. It would also allow them time to make, and fit their troops with, the new armour they needed. Through these times he would have to rely heavily on his advisors. He also kept his personal guards close to him, especially Captain Barra, The King's Champion. The Mystic Lord Sabat also stayed close to the King, but out of them all Giram, the King's Financial Custodian, was the busiest. He was under a great deal of pressure trying to control the food stocks and rationing them out daily. Keeping the overpopulated city's bellies full was a hard job. There was less food coming in from the farmers, especially those in the south of the land, as they were either burnt out or ransacked by the Empire. To the delight of Giram, prices increased on the sale of goods within Kitia, and the King's finances started to gain momentum. The farms that had survived in the South and South East were being used by the Empire to feed their troops, either at the south wall or at the sacked city of Tureen which was now occupied by Dragon soldiers. In the Royal Palace, Princess Thianni was miserable. She was not allowed to leave the palace under any circumstances, even with her guard. This saddened her greatly. All the time she wondered how Kalin was and what he was up to in the North. The amount of people seeking refuge in Kitia had slowed down, but there was an uneasy feeling in the city. Everyone was waiting for word that the Empire was marching against Kitia.

A few hundred miles West of Tureen, Chal and his 100 troops were making their way back to the wooden fort to Arthen and his father, Titus Cassian, with food and other provisions to see them through the rest of the winter. They were desperately waiting for new supplies as their stocks had run very low. The men were down to small rations and this always brought morale down. Chal made sure his men were well looked after. After being attacked the first time they had brought supplies down, Chal made sure that all the land up ahead of them was very well scouted. He was determined to make his role as captain a success.

Back in the Empire of Eamhair, preparations were underway to advance the invasion of Latonia. Weapons were being forged. Ships were being built and new armies were being assembled. Skarin had joined his battle-hardened forces to the Emperor's, and he personally took charge of all the training and tactics. By the end of their mild winter, their army had grown. The Emperor was happy with the preparations and plans that had been put in place. They were now ready to set sail and start the second part of their plan; to march on Kitia, take the city and merge Latonia with the Empire. In only a few weeks it would be Spring, and the Empire would then set sail for Athel and bring the Dragon's fire to the King.

The Kingdom was laid in ruins. The countryside was destroyed. Many farms had been ravaged for livestock and food. The people that had managed to flee and survive the Imperial invasion were now starving and living in fear. Any remaining wild animals were killed and used to feed the Dragon army. Thus, was the price of war.

34

The 20 dragon ships of the Emperor's fleet sailed into the harbour of Athel, followed by the entire fleet of the Empire of Eamhair. The ships filled the sea as far as the eye could see. The Emperor's ship docked smoothly, and trumpets sounded out as the Emperor walked from the ship and onto the dock with General Jargo and Skarin and all the other Imperial Generals. Chariots were waiting for them and they all moved up through the city and on to the palace. As the Dragon troops started to arrive and unload supplies and equipment, Leta and Oranius were waiting for them at the top of the steps back at the palace. Her Captain was always close by her side. The streets were lined with soldiers and the residents that had survived, now slaves to the Empire. They could hear the cheers in the distance as the Emperor made his way closer to the palace. The chariots turned the last corner to the main road up to the palace as the noise of the cheering intensified. The chariots stopped at the bottom of the steps and more trumpets sounded out. The Emperor stepped out and everyone bowed. He was dressed in a golden fabric with gold plate jewellery attached to his long gown. The sun was shining down, making the gown glint in its rays and illustrating the origin of the name the Emperor's people had bestowed upon him. The Human God.

Skarin stepped out beside him, and then Jargo and the rest of his generals and personal guards. They all made their way up the steps closely behind the Emperor. Leta waited for her father. Her eyes were on Skarin as they came up the steps. The emperor reached the top steps and embraced his daughter. 'I have missed you my daughter.'

'And I have missed you, father.'

'I am looking forward to hearing all about your stay here.' He then turned to the crowd that had moved closer to the base of the steps and raised his arms high into the air. The crowd roared.

Skarin leaned in to Leta and whispered into her ear. 'I have also missed you.' She smiled Widely at the words as she waved to the crowd. Skarin kissed her slowly on the cheek. As he did so, he noticed her captain looking at him with jealous eyes and Leta took a quick glance over at him. He pulled away. 'I see that you have been busy over here.'

Leta knew he would know straight away that another man had her attention. He had an eye for it. It was one of the things that attracted her about the man. His attention to detail. 'A woman has her needs.' She said, still smiling and waving. 'And so, does a man.' They both looked forward out over the steps now and waved.

'I want to see you tonight,' whispered Skarin.

'If you are nice to me, that can be arranged.'

'I am always nice to magnificent women.'

'I will look forward to it,' retorted Leta. The Emperor turned and walked into the palace with the entire party behind him. Later that evening, he held court with all of his Generals and Leta and Skarin to inform every one of the details of the second wave of the invasion. The Emperor addressed the room. 'We have a bigger army now than our Empire has ever seen. In one week, we will march to the Wall that divides Latonia and Natalia and join our forces with General Zukata, and together we will march to the gates of Kitia and take the city. The King will be overthrown, and I will sit on the Royal Throne and command the biggest Empire that this world has ever seen. This is my legacy and you all will be part of it with me. We also have a fleet of ships ready to travel along the south of Natalia, past Cinam and on to the south of Latonia. This fleet will then take the city of Bandar and wait there until we reach the Gate of Kitia. Then the fleet will attack the city of Kitia from the sea. Simultaneously attacking them on both sides, sea and land, will give the empire more opportunities to enter the capital. The walls of Kitia have never been breached, but they have never stood in front of the mighty Empire before. We will bring these walls down.' A cheer went up in the room. 'We will also attack and take the city of Talmine, to the north. Within the year, we hope to make these three cities part of the Empire. From there we will take the rest of the lands that currently belong to the Kingdom, and from there, who knows what the Empire will do next.' There were more cheers. 'But for now, please drink and eat and enjoy this night.'

Everyone in the hall looked happy. Leta glanced over at Skarin and could see he was staring at her. She knew she had him right where she wanted him. Throughout the night, Skarin kept his eyes on the Emperor's daughter, waiting for the moment he could steal her away from the crowd. Finally, his moment came. She had walked over to the banqueting table to look at the food and Skarin approached her. 'Are you enjoying the evening?'

'Yes, it is very pleasant.'

' I shall be retiring very soon. Would you care to join me?'

'I would very much like to, but I have my duties here tonight.'

It was clear Skarin did not like her response. She could see that she was teasing him, and she knew she could only keep it up for so long as he would start to get angry. 'Come to my room after the party has finished.' She turned and went back to the party leaving Skarin alone and feeling angry at the table.

Leta rolled out of bed and walked from the room, leaving her cousin Skarin in bed, still breathing heavily. He watched her body's movements across the room as she took a silk robe and put it on. It fitted the form of her body perfectly. She was truly the daughter of The Human God. He kept watching her as she walked. She was genuinely a beautiful woman. Aside from her childish ways, she had a lot going for her. Leta made her way to the dining area to look for some water. The guards outside her room bowed as she walked by. She filled a jug and brought it back to her room. She then poured two cups and brought one to Skarin. 'A drink for The Taker of Nations.'

'Don't call me that.'

'Why not? Everyone calls you that.'

'Not to my face they don't.'

Leta saw in his face that he did not like to hear these words. There had been plenty of rumours about the man. Especially in battle. They said that he was ruthless and would do anything to win the fight, anything. This she was ok with, after all, war was war, but she then had heard other rumours about him that troubled her. They said that after he had killed his enemies, he had a man working for him that would drain his dead enemies' blood. This man had developed a technique to extract the iron content from the blood and Skarin was now using this iron to make a blood sword. She longed to ask him was this true, but by his reaction at being referred to as The Taker of Nations she refrained from doing so. She would just have to wait longer to see if this was true. She moved onto the bed and pulled herself up next to his warm body, running her finger down his muscular chest.

'Are you excited about the march to Kitia?' she asked him.

'It has been a dream of mine to someday travel to this great city. When I was a boy, I heard stories about this city and all its great heroes. It will be an honour to take this city for your father.'

'He will reward you greatly for your contribution, Skarin.'

'It is not the gold I am doing it for, but the glory.'

'Well, it will be glory you shall receive.' 'It is a pity you cannot come along with us, but I suppose war is not for women.'

Lita sat up on the bed, angry now. 'You think I am weak?'

'All women are weak.' Skarin said, unconcerned with Leta's reaction to his comment.

'You have not had a good education on the opposite sex Skarin.'

'I know well enough how the human body works, both male and female.'

Leta shook her head. 'Physically yes, some men are stronger, but that is just flesh and blood and bone. The mind is the strongest element of the body, and this is where we excel.'

Skarin looked at her inquisitively. 'You think women are stronger in the mind?'

'I know they are. We have control over men, and we know how to use this control to our advantage. Men are the weaker sex. Let me demonstrate this to you.' She paused for a second and then she lay back on the bed. 'Leave me to my rest.' Skarin waited for a joke to play out, but there was none. 'Leave me now, Skarin, as I need my rest. I have my captain calling first thing in the morning to… go over some things.'

Skarin could feel his annoyance building up in him. 'Well I see now.' He climbed from the bed and got dressed. 'I bid you good night.' Then he turned and left the room. Leta felt sad now that he had gone, but she would not tolerate any man degrading her.

She thought about what it would be like to go with her father and travel to Kitia. At first, she was angry that he had said she had to stay, but thinking about it now, this would prove to be a better position to make her own plans and do her own ruling. She covered herself with a silk blanket and fell asleep. The next day, preparations were made for the army to march to the wall. Within three days, the Emperor set off with Skarin, travelling north with the biggest army that anyone had ever seen. Along with him was the Emperor's spiritual advisor, Oranius. Leta was glad to see him gone from the city. She watched the last of the long line of Dragon Soldiers leave the city from her balcony, high up on the palace tower. Skarin had not spoken to her before he left, and she wondered whether their relationship was over. She smiled at the thought of him. She still had Captain Velez to keep her company through the lonely nights ahead. You will learn the hard way Skarin, she thought, as the army disappeared from her city. You will be mine again soon.

35

An eerie horn echoed out across the wooden fortress, sounding out the return of the scouts. General Titus put on the remainder of his armour, sheathed his longsword into place by his side and then left his tent. The soldiers outside were still busy preparing for what was to come. The General made his way to the War Tent. The evening sun was starting to go down in the sky, bathing everything in its red rays. He felt a soothing light breeze on his face as he walked. The air outside was fresh, but not as cold as previous evenings. He entered the War Tent to find General Arthen inside talking to the scout that had just come in. He saluted his Prime Chief General Arthen and took his place by his side. Arthen nodded in return. The scout looked tired and out of breath. 'They have arrived sir, with an army of such size that I could not see an end to them.'

Arthen looked at Titus and then back to the scout. Both Generals could see the fear in the scout's eyes. 'How far away are they now?'

'Only four miles South East of here, sir.'

'I need an honest calculation; how many do you think there are coming our way.'

'It is very hard to estimate sir, but at my best guess, I would say over fifty thousand men sir.'

The General sighed at the man's answer. 'Well, there is not much we can do now. They are within striking distance of us. Leave a full report with your Captain and I will read over it later. Good work soldier, you are free to go and rest. You are dismissed.'

The scout saluted and turned and left. Arthen sat at the War Table and Titus joined him. 'It does not look good. We know the Emperor has joined General Zukata and their army is now vast.'

'All the more for the slaughter' said Titus with a grin.

Arthen shook his head. 'I know our men are better armoured, but that will only hold them for so long. I do not know if we can hold such a large force. Our main objective now might be not to hold them at bay, but to kill as many as we can, thus reducing the size of the force advancing on Kitia.'

The next morning, the Generals were standing on the wooden wall looking out to the South East along the plains. A lone horseman could be seen travelling in the direction of the fortress. General Arthen left the wall and mounted his warhorse. The gates opened and he headed out to meet the lone rider. Titus shouted down to him as he moved away. 'Be cautious, my friend. They are not to be trusted.'

Titus watched as Arthen moved close to the enemy. Both riders stopped some distance from one another. 'Well met, Great General.' Zukata said with a broken accent.

'Well met, little man.'

'I hope the winter has been kind to you and your men, for I feel you will need the strength. My Emperor has come to take what he wants to make as his own.'

'We are well prepared for whatever your Emperor has to offer.'

'The reason I am here is to make one last offer.'

'Speak what you have to say, little man.'

'My emperor wishes to make you a deal. He wants you and all your men to lay down your weapons and move out of the path of the Dragon army.'

Arthen laughed out loud. 'Your Emperor is a bold man. Tell him I do not accept this offer for, it would be beneath me and all who serve my King. We do not bow or yield to threats.'

'I had assumed you would answer me with that kind of statement. I know in my heart you will not move for anyone, and I respect you for that. But know this, because of your arrogance, many of your men will die today.'

'My men have sworn an oath that they would serve the King and the lands of Latonia. They would lay down their lives for him and our lands. So yes, my men will die today but so will yours.'

'Well, there isn't much more to say to you Great General, except I hope I do not meet you on the battlefield. I would hate to kill such a great man.'

Arthen felt like drawing his sword and cutting this small invader down from his horse, but then he saw the little General smiling. Arthen smiled with him.

'I feel thankful for having met you. Stay alive, Great General Arthen. I would like to meet you in a more peaceful time.' With that, the Dragon General turned his horse and rode off into the distance. Arthen watched until he went out of sight. Then he turned and rode back to the fort.

Titus was waiting for Arthen just inside the fort's gate. 'How did he take that news?'

Arthen dismounted. 'As we expected.'

'How long do you think before they arrive to do battle?'

'I'd say they are moving on us as we speak.'

'Well we should use our time wisely then.'

Trumpets sounded out and all the Royal soldiers sprang to action. Every man had the new armour that Chal and his wagons of supplies had brought down from Kitia. Everyone was in their places, waiting for the Emperor and his Dragon soldiers.

Emperor Casimir stood in his golden chariot as the advancing line moved forward. He could feel the excitement in his stomach as he thought about defeating the army of Latonia that stood in his way. The wooden fort was close now, and he could see past it and make out the shapes of hundreds of tents that spread out behind the fort housing the Royal army. All their men would be behind the protection of its walls now. Looking closer, he could make out the men on the walls and see the Royal red flags flying, each bearing the head of a lion. A trumpet sounded out and the advancing Dragon army came to a halt. Imperial General Jargo shouted out an order from his mount and a low rumbling noise could be heard. Ten lines started to appear among the massed men as ten enormous catapults were pulled forward and set in position in front of the Dragon army. Men went to work, winching at the mechanisms, lowering the long arms back into place with levers and priming the cups with a large round clay boulder in each one. They then waited in the ready position for their orders. The Emperor whipped down on his reins and the four horses jumped forward, moving the chariot with a jump. He moved up along the front line just behind the catapults. Then he stopped his chariot and gazed back over his army.

'What a magnificent sight it is to look upon you all. My time to rule over all has just begun. Today is the next step at taking what belongs to me. Each one of you will be part of it. For there is no army in this world powerful enough to stop us. Now let us watch as they feel the heat from our Dragon Fire.' The Emperor moved back onto the hilltop with General Jargo to watch the battle begin. General Zukata raised his sword high into the air and men rushed in to cover the boulders with a brown oil, then a second wave of men lit the oil with long torches. The clay boulders were now all on fire. Zukata then slashed his sword down and ten arms shot forward, propelling fireballs into the air towards the fort with streaks of smoke behind them. A cheer went up from the Dragon Army.

On the walls and within the wooden fort the Royal army waited. They watched as the Dragon army advanced and then stopped some distance for the fort. They saw the huge war machines pulled into place, the likes of which they had never seen before. Then, to the shock of everyone, ten fireballs were launched towards the fort. Men panicked as the fireballs crashed down just short of the fort. As they hit the ground, they exploded with massive plumes of flames, engulfing their surroundings. This fire lit up a huge area of the battleground in front of the fort. Through the smoke they could see that the catapults were being adjusted and reloaded for another attack.

General Titus moved along the wall and shouted out a command. 'Make sure to take cover.'

General Arthen moved in close to him. 'I don't think these wooden walls will give our men much protection from those weapons.'

'You are right. Maybe we should change our strategy from defence to offence. I would much rather take my chances with a cold, sharp blade than face a huge ball of flames.'

Shouts went out and ten more fireballs were launched at the fort. This time they hit their targets. The fireballs exploded as they hit the walls and landed inside the fort. Men screamed in agony as their bodies were consumed with fire. Some men tried to protect themselves with their shields, but the fire was everywhere. Men broke formation on the walls and ran down to the courtyard below. Horses broke loose and were running around, frantically trying to escape the terror. Then more fireballs hit, and more men died a horrible death. Arthen shouted out 'Leave the fort and gather outside the West wall.'

The Royal army poured out the gate of the fort and organised themselves into their units. After several more volleys of fireballs the fort was now abandoned and ablaze. They could hear drums beating in the distance as the Dragon army moved towards them. Arthen and Titus rushed to restore order in the ranks. The army spread out their line, their spearmen at the front with shields at the ready. The bulk of the army gathered behind these lines and the archers formed behind them. Over 4000 Royal horsemen ran to mounts that were waiting in the large tented area behind the now fiery fort. The Imperial Dragon army moved ever closer. The drums were beating more loudly now as the men marched in sync with the rhythm. Some men of the Royal army grew restless as they waited. General Titus stood among the men at the front line. 'Steady yourselves now.' He bellowed. 'They will break on our spears.'

General Arthen took command from the rear. 'Notch arrows.' He shouted out over the archers. 'At the ready.' There was a pause. 'Take aim.' Then another pause as the Dragon men came into striking distance. 'FIRE!' he shouted. Two thousand arrows were sent into the front lines of the oncoming Dragon army. Many fell with the first wave of arrows.

Again, Arthen shouted out. This time faster than the first. 'Take aim, FIRE!' More arrows hit into the marching army, but they still drew closer. Arthen could see that the men were starting to look scared. The numbers that the arrows had downed were merely a drop in the ocean, but then again, every drop count, he thought. Three more times he yelled out FIRE. The drums suddenly stopped and there was an eerie silence from both sides. A trumpet blasted out and the Dragon men charged forward. Titus was at the ready with the front line of spearmen. The Dragon army smashed into the front line. Many died on the tip of the Latonian spears. Still they came. The fighting was frantic as both sides hacked and stabbed at one another. At first the line seemed to be holding well, but then they began to tire as fresh attacks came forward from the Dragon men. The front line began to break. General Arthen had anticipated this from the back of his army and gave orders for the bulk of his men to push forward in support. The fighting was intensified now. Both sides were taking huge losses. The

Dragon men found it hard to penetrate through the armour of the Royal soldiers, but still they came in their thousands.

The Emperor watched from afar. He was known for his superior war tactics. The battle was proceeding exactly the way he wanted it to. Timing was everything. After the Royal army was forced to leave the fort, his plan was simple. He would attack straight away, not giving them time to regroup, by sending Zukata in a full out attack straight to the front line with the bulk of his troops. While they were engaged in battle there, he would send Skarin to attack from the side with his mounted army, finally crushing the main Royal Army. General Jargo stood ready to reinforce General Zukata if needed. The battle raged on. The time was right now, as he saw the rest of the army moving in to help the front line. He turned and nodded to Skarin.

Skarin smiled and bowed to his Emperor from his horse. 'Let the blood flow.' he said, as he put on his black helmet with two protruding curved horns that splayed out from the sides of the helmet. This gave him a demonic look. He then turned his horse and moved to the back of the Emperor's guards. He gave his men orders to follow, and they moved back out of sight. They then cut across and looped around in a wide arc to come in at the battle from the side. As Skarin and his men moved closer, they started to speed up from a trot to a canter and then they were in a full gallop. Spears came down, pointing forward ready for the attacking charge. Arthen watched the battle intensely, giving orders to reinforce and strengthen the weak areas of the line. The line was holding well. His men had no give in them, and this pleased him. The new armour was a remarkable design and was working well. He heard a shout go up from the archers behind him.

'They come from the north east.'

He turned to see what the commotion was about and saw with horror the horsemen coming straight for their unprotected flank. He shouted out orders for the archers to form a line facing the oncoming force. He then gave orders to the mounted Royal horsemen to form a counterattack. He had no available soldiers to form a protective line in front of the archers. As soon as the attacking horsemen were in range, the archers let loose a volley of arrows that cut into the enemy, cutting down horses and men alike. The 4000 Royal horsemen surged forward, but they were too far back. The archers fired a second volley of arrows into the oncoming charge just before they were engulfed by the attacking horsemen. There was nothing Arthen could do to save his archers now. They were either cut down or trampled to death where they stood. Some at the back tried to run but were killed as they fled. The force then split in two. One half charged to meet the incoming Royal horsemen and the other charged towards the unprotected rear of the Latonian army. Arthen felt hopeless now. Whatever chance they had of trying to hold the Dragon army had now disappeared. They were surrounded.

He drew his sword and turned to face the enemy horsemen. The front line of fighting raged on, unaware that they were being attacked now on both sides. Arthen shouted orders for his men to turn and face the new attack. The horsemen reached Arthen and chaos erupted. The horsemen pounded into the troops, killing scores with their charge. They pushed the line and compacted the army. The tide had turned, and the Dragon army were winning the day while the Royal Army were fighting for their lives. The ground beneath them was drenched with human blood. Dead bodies covered the ground, yet the fighting continued. Men rallied around their Generals. Arthen killed with efficiency but there was no end to the Dragon army, they just kept coming. Arthen's men looked exhausted, but they still fought on. Hacking and slicing with swords and spears as screams and shouts went out and men lost their lives.

Arthen was pulled backwards and turned to face General Titus. The two men nodded to each other, they both knew that this could be the last few moments of their lives, this was their last stand. They both turned and milled into the Dragon horsemen. Arthen sidestepped an oncoming spear thrust and, grabbing the spear with his left hand, drove his sword up into the neck of the attacker with his right hand. He then pulled the dead man from his saddle and mounted the horse. He looked down at Titus and watched in admiration how efficiently he killed his enemies. Another horseman jumped at him with a slashing spear. Arthen moved to the side and the spear missed his face by inches. He kicked his heels into the Dragon horse and the horse jumped forward, clashing into the attackers' horse and nearly knocking the man from his saddle. As the man tried to right himself, Arthen brought his sword down onto his shoulder. The sword pierced the black leather armour and embedded itself in his shoulder. The man fell from his horse, dead, with the sword still lodged in him. Arthen looked around for another weapon to use. He looked back out over the wall of attackers and could see the Royal horsemen charging towards them to reinforce the fighting. They must have defeated the Dragon Horsemen and were now coming to their aid. Just then, he felt a thud in his right side just above his hip. He turned and saw to his surprise that a spear had slipped under his armour and stabbed him in his side. Pain shot through his body. The black armoured soldier who had attacked him, pulled the spear free and thrust it at Arthen's face. Arthen had no weapon to defend himself. Suddenly, a sword intercepted and deflected the spear from hitting home. Arthen looked to see Titus jumping at the spearman, slashing his sword across his chest and then, with a back thrust, stabbing him through his neck. Blood splashed out and the man was killed. The Royal horsemen slammed into the back of the line of Dragon horsemen. A cheer went up from Arthen's men that saw it. Titus took a discarded sword from the ground and threw it to Arthen, who caught it by the hilt just in time to parry a thrusting spear and kill the attacking man. Titus looked around; he could see the Dragon General in the thick of the battle slaying men. He stood out with his black horned helmet and the fact that he looked like he was enjoying the killing. A great fear swept over him as he watched. He wanted to try and fight his way through and challenge the horned warrior. A sword flashed past his face almost hitting him, bringing him back to the fighting around him. He looked to see where Arthen was. He was standing over a Dragon Soldier and plunging his sword home through the man's armour. There were Royal soldiers lying dead everywhere. They were losing the battle, fast.

Titus shouted over to Arthen. 'We must try and make a retreat.'

Arthen nodded in agreement as he wiped blood from his face. 'Push back through the horsemen. This is the only way.' Arthen mounted the horse once more and the two Generals turned their horses in to the massing enemy and fought like wounded dogs. Hacking and stabbing. More of the Royal army managed to mount Dragon horses whose riders had been killed and joined in the push back with the Generals. Soon there was a wedge formed and it drove through the centre of the Dragon horsemen. Titus looked over at General Arthen, he looked tired and he could see his leg was drenched in blood. They were nearly clear of the attackers. Titus kicked a rider from his horse and managed to get alongside Arthen and help him clear the last of the attackers. Arthen looked like he was about to fall from his horse, so Titus held him in place. Titus killed the last rider with a backward sword swipe, and they were free from the bunch. Several other Royal riders broke free too. They galloped away. There was a lone Dragon soldier with an arrow sticking out of his shoulder, moving amongst the dead men and horses that they had been downed by arrows. The Dragon soldier picked up a discarded spear and, as Titus and Arthen got close, he threw the spear at them. Titus had seen the man from the corner of his eye and could see he was aiming for Arthen with the spear. Titus turned his horse in to Arthen and then jumped from his horse into the path of the oncoming spear to protect The Prime General. The spear took Titus high in his chest, and he fell from his horse and landed on his back.

Arthen shouted out. 'NO!'

Royal riders charged the man, killing him where he stood. Arthen dismounted and went to the aid of Titus. Titus was lying still on his back with the spear sticking out. It had entered just to the side of his armour and was embedded just below his neck. Arthen pulled Titus' Helmet clear from his head. Titus tried to speak as blood seeped from his mouth. He raised his hand and clasped Arthen's as he struggled to speak again. One word came out. 'Chal.' He then closed his eyes and died. Arthen was distraught, he tried to lift him but did not have the strength.

A soldier shouted, 'We must go General, they will be coming for us as soon as the fighting stops.'

Arthen looked up at the soldier. 'We can't leave him here.'

'We have no choice Sir.'

Arthen could feel his eyes starting to well up. He did not want to leave his friend. 'This man is a great General and my friend' he shouted back.

'General, we must leave now' called out another soldier as he watched for pursuers. 'There is nothing we can do for him now.'

Arthen pulled his glove off. Taking some coins from an inner pocket with shaking hands, he placed two of them upon Titus's closed eyes. He leaned in close to the dead General. 'For your passage Titus. Thank you for saving me, my friend. Travel well and I will see you in the afterlife.' He then rose and reluctantly mounted his horse and looked down at his dead friend one last time. 'I will have vengeance for this.' The small group of riders moved away towards a wooded area and disappeared into its safety.

The Emperor looked out over the battle and was satisfied with what he saw. His men had done well, they had done their job. They had all but destroyed the wooden fort with their catapults and it was still ablaze.

When the army had fled the fires, their attack on the fleeing men had been fast. Zukata had concentrated his attack on the main bulk of their forces. He had hit them head on, giving them little time to organise. Skarin's attack had been timed to perfection, coming around them and surprising them, this made the battle and the victory even sweeter. General Jargo and his army had not even engaged in the battle, as it was over so quickly. The Emperor gave the order to kill any wounded or survivors. Reports came in that General Arthen had escaped. This also pleased the Emperor, as Arthen would have to report now to his King and explain how he had lost. This defeat of their great General would send fear into the hearts of the people of Latonia.

The sun was setting as Skarin rode back to the hilltop. He was covered in blood. He bowed to his Emperor.

'You have done well my nephew.'

'Thank you, my Emperor. Word from my men is that the General has escaped. Will I send a force to track him and kill him?'

'No. Let him run. He will report back to his King and they will all then fear what is about to come.'

'I have a request.'

'Speak it.'

'Let my men deal with the dead carcasses. They have spent the battle sitting in their saddles and have more energy than General Zukata's foot soldiers.'

'As you wish, let it be so. Make sure you are at my table tonight to celebrate our victory.'

'Yes, my Emperor.' Skarin bowed again and then moved off down the hill to his waiting troops.

He called his Captain over. 'Deal with the dead.'

'Yes Sir.'

'And make sure Bakal gets 100 bodies sent to him. With this campaign he will have my swords finished.'

'Yes sir.' The Captain saluted and went about his business. The thought of his blood swords nearly completed gave Skarin some satisfaction.

That night, all the Generals and the Emperor sat at the feast table in the large war tent. The Emperor stood from his seat beside General Jargo and raised his cup of wine. 'To all my men. I want to thank you for your help in this victory today. It is a landmark in our history. From here we will march toward the capital and take it. We should be home in one year from now, still rejoicing on our achievements. Now drink with me.'

They all raised their cups and drank.

The Emperor turned to Zukata. 'I want you to lead an attack on Talmine. I need the city sacked and I need the port for ships to land. There might be a small force protecting the city and I can't take any chances that they might attack us from behind as we bear down on Kitia. Do you understand this?' Even though he did not show it, Zukata felt he had just been slighted. He had taken Natalia and held the wall all winter, and now he would be denied the sweet taste of victory when they marched and took the capital, Kitia. He wanted to protest and explain why this post should be taken by another general, but nobody questioned Casimir, the Emperor of Eamhair.

Zukata held it in and just bowed. 'As you wish my Emperor.'

'Take six thousand men and take this city. You may kill any inhabitant you come across and make sure that there will be no counterattack from any army coming from the north. I have been told that there is one main bridge that crosses the river Rura. This bridge connects the north plain to the southern plains. It is the only bridge for miles that is big enough to support a large army crossing the river, guard this well. I will see you soon and you will be rewarded for your action. Go now. Do as I bid and make the preparations.' Zukata bowed again, then turned and left the room to organise his departure.

Arthen and eight Royal Soldiers wearily rode in through the East Gate of the City of Kitia after nearly three weeks of nonstop riding to reach home. It had been a long ride, even though they had tried to get back as fast as they could with the Empire's Dragon Soldiers close on their heels. Soldiers rushed in to help the arrivals and take their worn-out horses to be stabled. Arthen dismounted slowly and stumbled into the arms of a Royal Soldier, who stopped him from falling. Over the last week, the wound above his hip had become infected and he had been overcome by a fever, but they could not stop until they reached the safety of Kitia.

Arthen righted himself and patted the man that had caught him on his shoulder. 'Thank you!' He turned and looked up at the high gatehouse. 'Close those gates. The Empire are on their way. They will be here in a matter of days.' He spluttered out a cough and tried to fix himself. 'Now take me to see the King, we have little time and a lot to planning to do.' Arthen stumbled again. The Captain of the watch arrived over and helped the other soldier to support Arthen.

'We have got you now General.'

Arthen could feel his emotions rising. To his satisfaction, the huge gates closed, and a chariot was drawn up to take Arthen to the palace. Before it took him away, he turned back to the eight soldiers. 'Thank you for helping me get here. I owe you men my life.' He then turned to the Captain. 'Make sure these men are well looked after. Now, take me to my King.' With that, the chariot pulled away and hurried towards the palace. Over the next few days, more and more Royal Soldiers came back, having escaped the battle. Most of them were wounded and tired and hungry, but all shared the same look of defeat.

36

Kalin made his way to the village of Fenrich to meet with The Conri, Kamas, and his son, Tornos. The ride took a few days, but he had good company in Rovan. They both got along so well, it made the time pass quickly. As he rode into the village, everyone stared at him. Rovan rode by Kalin's side as they made their way to the village's main hall. They were met by nine Fenrich warriors, who blocked the path.

One stepped forward. 'What do you want here?'

Kalin look down at him from his horse. 'We have come to see your Conri.'

'Well, I don't think he wants to see you?' The nine men stood firm blocking the path.

'Move aside I don't want any trouble here today.'

'That's because you two know you would not stand a chance against nine Fenrich warriors.'

Rovan laughed. 'Why don't you go away and come back with more men. It hardly seems fair that there is only nine of you.' The Fenrich warrior looked angry and was about to jump forward when a shout yelled out.

'KALIN! How are you.'

They all looked around and saw Tornos marching towards them with a wide smile. 'Stand down men' he said as he passed the nine Fenrich warriors. 'It is good to see you Kalin.'

Kalin jumped down from his horse and held out his hand to shake Tornos'. 'It is good to see you too my friend.'

'What has you two so far from Four Vales?'

'We have come to see your father to ask of him a favour.'

'He is out on the farm helping with the cattle. He will be pleased to see you.' Tornos led them into the main hall and asked them to wait while he fetched his father. He was not long gone when Kamas, the Conri of the Fenrich, walked through the door to greet them. He also had a smile on his face.

'Well met, my friends. It is good to see you. I hope things are good in Four Vales. What brings you both to my village?'

They all sat down at a table. Kalin felt small amongst the three warriors. They were all big men. 'I have come here to ask a favour of you Kamas.'

'Kamas sat back into his chair.'

'As I said to you, you spared my son and I am truly grateful for that. When I said, ask of me what favour you want, I meant it. What is it you ask of me?'

Kalin composed himself. 'You are all aware of the war in the south, and how the Empire has invaded the lands of Latonia and taken Natalia and the islands of Naos and Cinam.'

'Yes, we have heard of their troubles. They are a long way from us, but it has affected our trade with the south at the wall.'

'I have…' Kalin stopped to think for a second. '…I have family in Kitia and I am afraid for their safety. I want to head south and help the Kingdom fight against the Empire. I would like to call on Gantian warriors to gather an army and ride to Kitia to offer help to the Kingdom fighting the Empire.'

The Conri took in a deep breath and let it out slowly, blowing his cheeks out. 'This is a huge ask Kalin.'

Kalin agreed. 'I know, and if it is out of your power to help me, say so. I will not be offended.'

'We have been at war against the Kingdom in the past, and there is still some bad blood among us because of this. I feel it would be a very hard thing to achieve, to gather an army to help the Kingdom.' The Conri thought for a while, everyone was quiet. 'I am in your debt and what I said to you I meant it. I want to help but I am not sure that I can?'

'If I can't get help to raise an army here, I am still going south to help.'

The Conri nodded,' I understand that. Thank you.' It went quiet again. Kalin looked over at Rovan. Rovan could see the concern on the younger man's face. Then the Conri spoke again. 'Leave this question with me. I will need time to think on it, and on how I can help you with this problem.'

'Thank you Conri, I appreciate your time and help.'

'Please feel free to stay the night while I come up with my answer. You can spend the night at our guest rooms.'

Kalin thanked the Conri again and Tornos left with Kalin and Rogan, showing them to their room. It was a small hut in the centre of the village with just one room inside. They could see people chatting and going about their business from the small window in the guest hut. Kalin and Rovan decided not to venture outside and to stay in their two-bed guest room. They stayed inside until night-time, discussing war and tactics. They did not want to cause any problems that might turn the villagers against them. That night, Kalin woke. He thought he could hear his name being called from outside of the hut. He stood from his bed and looked out of the window. Rovan was snoring in his bed. He could just make out a dark figure standing by another hut across from theirs. The figure seemed to notice Kalin looking out of the window and gestured for Kalin to come to him. Kalin left the hut and closed the door quietly behind him. He looked over to where the figure had been, and just made out that the figure had walked around the hut. Kalin followed quickly. It looked like an old man. He was walking away and Kalin called out to him. 'Hey you there.'

The old man ignored the call and just kept walking. He hurried past another hut and turned out of sight. Kalin ran to catch him. As Kalin got past the hut, he should have been upon him, but the figure was now even further away, making his way into a wooded area.

Kalin ran on in pursuit. 'Hey, stop there,' he shouted again as the old man disappeared into the darkness of the woods. Kalin slowed his run now as he entered the woods. He closed his eyes for a few seconds to try and let his eyes adjust to the dimmer light. He heard his name again, as if it were a whisper on the wind. He moved his hand to his sword and noticed he had left it back at the hut by his bed. He moved on into the woods. A white owl, perched on a low branch, hooted out loud and startled him as he passed by. Kalin cursed, moving further into the trees. They were starting to get thicker now and darker. Then he came to a clearing and could see the night sky was visible above. There was a small old man sitting in the middle of the clearing, alone in the night.

Kalin walked to him. 'Could you not hear me calling you?'

The old man looked at Kalin spoke with a crackly voice. 'Please come and sit with me.'

Kalin felt suddenly afraid with his name being mentioned but sat in front of the old man anyway. 'How do you know my name?'

'I know many things.'

'You know my name, so what name am I to call you?'

'I am known by many names, but you can call me The Shord. I am the Old Man of The Land.'

Kalin could feel the hairs on the back of his neck standing on end and felt like he needed to run away from the Old Man. He tried to control his rising fear. 'Do not be afraid Kalin, I have no intention of causing harm to you, young man.'

'Why have you brought me here?'

'I want to give you something and I merely wanted to meet and talk to you. I have had my eyes on you for a while now. It pleases me to watch you grow. Your father would be proud of the man you have become.'

'You knew my father?'

'Yes, I knew Shun Ruane very well, and his father before him, and his father's father.'

'That would be, my Great Great Grandfather?'

'Yes, that is correct. His name was Karractus. He was an ambitious man indeed. I liked him very much.'

'Was he as mad as they say he was?'

'No, not at all. He was a very intelligent man. Far beyond his years. But all you humans have a bit of madness inside of you.'

'Because of his action years ago I am stuck with this curse.'

'I do not see it the way you see it Kalin. You should look upon it as a gift.'

'It is far from a gift for me. I have suffered nightmares for most of my life and felt like an outcast living in Kitia and now I must be away from the woman I love.'

'Everyone has their burdens to bear, but it is a small price to pay for what you have gained. You will see your woman again and when you return, they will look at you differently.'

Kalin listened closely to everything The Shord had to say and as the conversation continued, he could feel he was beginning to relax in this old spirit's company. 'I have a question I would like to ask.'

'Ask your question Kalin.'

'Why did my Great Great Grandfather open this gateway?'

'That is a good question, and there is only one answer. He did it for love. Like you, he was in love with a young woman and her life was in danger if he did not obey.'

'Obey who?'

'There is a dark cloud that covers this world, Kalin. This cloud is controlled by an ancient evil. This evil wants this world for its own. It has followers here, doing its malice for it, and if they succeed in their tasks then it will be able to come here and rule this world. Karractus tried to trick these followers into thinking that the gate was open and tried to get his love back. He knew the danger of opening this gate was great. He opened the gate for a short period, and they killed his woman anyway. He was then taken through the gate and lost for ever, and the gate remained open. It is not my place to interfere with you humans, but I knew I needed to help mankind. The only way I could help was to cast a spell, one of the most powerful spells that I have ever cast. A spell that would protect this world from this dark force. Karractus's son was looking for him at the gate, and he was the first man I encountered. I needed to act fast, so I cast this spell on him. He was the first that held the magic. He was the first Guardian, and now it continues through your family's bloodline right down to you, and it will continue with your sons. People are fearing this war and this Emperor that is attacking the south lands, but the real threat is from this dark evil.'

'Thank you for telling me all this. I would have never known the truth about it otherwise.'

'You are most welcome Kalin. Now let me tell you the real reason why I have brought you here. I want to give you a gift. It should help you on your quest to gather an army.'

Kalin watched as The Shord held out his hands in front of him. A small glow started to emanate from the palms of his hands. The light intensified and then stretched out in a line. As the light subsided and disappeared it left a sword behind, resting in The Shord's hands.

Kalin was in disbelief as he leaned in to see the sword closer. 'It is wonderful.' The steel sword's blade gleamed in the night. Its handle was oversized, with a white carving all the way down from the guard and the grip that ended with a design head on its pommel. The Shord motioned for Kalin to take the sword. Kalin swiftly lifted the sword and spun it from hand to hand. He could feel the energy flowing up his arm and charging his body. The sword's balance was perfect, and the blade sang as he sliced it through the night air.

Kalin could feel his excitement grow as he held the sword. 'It feels perfect to hold and lighter than it looks. I have never seen its match before.'

'Good. I am Glad you like it as it is yours to keep.'

'I could not accept such a gift.'

'I want you to have it, as it belongs to your family. It is called a Moon Sword. It is made from materials not from this world.'

'It is amazingly crafted. Thank you for this kind gift.' Kalin sliced the sword through the air once more and spun with the momentum, as he turned around to face The Shord he was gone. Kalin looked around to try and find him, but he was nowhere to be seen. Alone now, Kalin examined the sword once more and then placed it down through his leather belt and made his way back to the hut.

The next morning, Kalin told Rovan about meeting The Shord. Rovan thought Kalin was jesting until he showed him the sword. Like Kalin, Rovan was amazed at the craftsmanship of the weapon. There was a knock at the door and Tornos entered. 'Good morning. I hope you slept well. We have food prepared for you in the main hall. My father is there and would like to talk to you about your request.'

The three men walked to the hall and seated themselves at the top of a long table where The Conri, Kamas, was waiting for them. He smiled as they joined him. 'Good morning, did you sleep well?'

'Yes. Well, I did anyway. I'm not so sure about Kalin here' said Rovan as he looked over at Kalin and started to chew on a slice of cold meat.

'Good. Everyone that stays in that hut seems to get a great night's sleep. I may have to move into it myself as I had little sleep myself last night.'

Kalin smiled at The Conri. 'You had lots to think about last night.'

'That I did, and I have come to a conclusion. I will honour my word and help you. It took me quite a while to think on how I could help you gather an army, as most of the Clans have been at war with each other for a long time now. First off, I will give you 50 of my warriors. Most are young and need the experience. It will do them good to taste battle. I myself would go with you, but there is too much work here for me to finish.'

Tornos interrupted. 'With your blessings father, I would like to accompany Kalin on his mission. It would be good for the younger warriors to see this.'

Kamas looked at his son and thought for a while. 'You have my blessings under one condition. That you don't take any chances and come home alive.'

'I will certainly take that advice father.'

Kalin slapped Tornos on the back. 'Thank you, my brother. It will be my honour for you to come.'

Kalin, then turned to The Conri. 'He will come home safe; I will make sure of it.'

'I hope you will Kalin. Now you have a small force, I was thinking how to get the other Clans to join with you. Now the odds will be against us, but after seeing how well you can fight; I think we might have a chance. That's if you are willing to do this? I will send out messengers to as many nearby neighbouring Clans as I can and issue a challenge in sword combat by you to all the Clans' top warriors. You can then address them all and, once they see your skill in combat, I think you might win them over. It will be a big chance, but a chance is better than nothing at all. Do you agree to this?'

'I agree, and if there is a warrior out there that can better me, this sword will be his prize.' Kalin placed The Moon Sword on the table for the Conri to see. 'This will give our people something to fight for.'

The Conri's eyes widened as he saw the sword presented in front of him. 'By the Gods, I don't believe my eyes. This is a Moon Sword. I have only heard of tales and stories spoken of this as a boy. I had never thought it was real. This is the stuff of legends. Are you sure you want to put this up as a prize?'

'Yes, I do' said Kalin, to the surprise of The Conri.

'It is exquisite. Men will fight very hard to win this, Kalin. I know how skilled you are at combat, as I have seen you in action but, are you sure you can beat them all?'

Kalin smiled at the comment. 'If I don't, I will lose this sword and if that happens, I could lose the woman I love.'

Word quickly spread out to the villages about the challenge, and the chance to win this legendary Moon Sword. After a week, warriors were starting to come into the Village of Fenrich to take up the challenge. For the Conri, his own challenge was trying house and feed them all as they arrived. The village benefited from all the trade and it was a chance for the clans to meet and catch up on news and trade. There were people everywhere. All talk was about the Moon Sword. Warriors that had come for the challenge also brought other warriors with them to watch the fighting, there was great interest. The Conri eventually had to set up camp sites outside of the village to accommodate such a large number of people. Rovan and Tornos practiced with the sword daily with Kalin, to keep his skills sharp. They would often duel with Kalin at the same time, and still Kalin would better them. Everyone was in awe of Kalin's speed and skill with the sword and would come out daily to watch him train. The Conri had set up a makeshift arena in the centre of the village for the day of the tournament. The town could not sustain any more newcomers, so The Conri announced that the tournament would start earlier than scheduled. 23 champion warriors put their names forward for the challenge, to try and beat this young man called Kalin and win The Moon Sword. The next day the masses gathered in the centre. An announcer stood and called Kalin forward to the centre of the arena. The crowd was quiet as he walked out and stood waiting.

The Conri then stood and addressed the crowd. 'Thank you, everyone, for coming to our village, you are all most welcome. It is good to see you here in such great spirits and not facing off with each other on a battlefield. I want to make some rules clear here and now. There will be alcohol dispensed later after the fights. I don't want to see any fighting going on outside of this arena. We are all here for the challenge, and that alone. So other than the bouts that will take place now, please be mindful that this is a peaceful gathering. We have 23 challengers that were brave enough to come forward to fight Kalin. These 23 warriors are mostly your villages' Champions, the best of your best. I do not want to see any bad injuries or deaths today with any of these fine men, so we will be fighting with wooden swords.'

Voices were raised amongst the crowd and then someone shouted. The Conri put up his hands for quiet. Another shout went out from a man in the crowd. 'How will we know if a strike with a wooden sword would have been a killing strike or not?'

The Conri put his hands down. 'We will mark the swords with red paint. If the strike lands, it will leave a red mark on the fighter and our three referees will determine whether that is a killing strike or not. Kalin has told me this is how they compete in Latonia. Any strike to the head or the body will end the bout.'

The crowd started to talk again. The Conri had to talk louder so he could be heard. 'This is the only way we can be sure that there will be no serious injuries today. All 23 warriors have agreed to this.'

The talking subsided. 'The 23 names will be drawn out of the bag randomly, and if a warrior is able to land a killing strike and beat Kalin, they will win the prize and the tournament will end. Now let me show you the prize.'

The Conri reached into a chest that sat on the ground in front of him and lifted the Moon Sword high into the air. 'Behold, the legendary Moon Sword.' A cheer went up from the crowd with excitement. 'Now let the tournament begin.'

A referee approached The Conri with a small bag and held it out for him. The Conri reached into it and pulled out a piece of paper with the name of the first warrior to fight Kalin. 'The first warrior to fight is Bellarus, representing the Clan Duron from the village Ramar.'

Cheers went up and a huge man walked forward from the crowd, stripped to the waist, with long black hair and a beard to match. He walked up and faced Kalin. Kalin had never seen a man so big. He would make Karra look small, he thought. Two more referees walked over to Kalin and Bellarus and handed them each a wooden sword with red paint along the blades. They moved back to the safety of the outer circle of the arena. The Conri stood once more and shouted. 'Begin!'

The two fighters took a defensive stance and circled one another. Bellarus growled at Kalin as he stared him down. Kalin looked like a small boy next to this giant warrior from Ramar. The crowd became quiet and Bellarus roared a battle cry and lunged forward in a speedy attack. His sword swung high and came down fast at Kalin's head. Just before the sword landed, Kalin swiftly moved to one side and brought his sword across the chest of the large warrior, leaving a long red line of paint across his skin. The three referees rushed in to stop the bout as Bellarus tried to attack again.

'Killing strike' shouted one of the referees.

Bellarus threw his sword to the ground in disappointment and walked off. The crowd cheered him on. The next Warrior was announced by the Conri, and Kalin dispatched him quickly too. This continued for almost an hour with the same outcome, Kalin using his speed to land a killing strike against his opponents until there was only one warrior left.

The last warrior was called. 'Atora fighting for his Clan Tallas, from the village…' The Conri paused. 'There is no village written down.' He turned to the young man waiting his turn.

Atora was a small man, but he spoke out loud. 'That is correct, Conri. My village was wiped out four weeks ago by a neighbouring village, I am the only survivor. I still wish to fight for my Clan's name, if that is acceptable?'

'Yes of course' said the Conri, looking concerned now. 'What was the name of your village?'

'It was called Malin.'

'I know this village, I visited there some years ago. It saddens me to hear the news of this. Tonight, we will drink to all the fallen from your village.'

'Thank you Conri, that will please me.'

'You may begin, Atora from the Clan Tallas.'

Atora made his way to the centre to face Kalin. Like Kalin, he was also a young man. He was a full head shorter than Kalin. Both fighters were given their wooden swords and the Conri called for them to begin. Kalin took up his fighting position while Atora just stood there with his sword down by his side. Kalin was confused why he was not readying himself. Kalin then dropped his defence. 'Do you not wish to fight me?'

Atora smiled. 'I did want to, but now I don't think I have any fight left in me. My family have been killed and my friends and everyone I knew; they are all gone. I am the only one left. They all died with honour. They died in battle, defending their homes. I have asked myself why I am the only one left. This question I cannot find an answer to. I had come here to die. I felt it a fitting way as I have nothing left to live for. But then the Conri said we would be fighting with wooden swords. So, my plan to die in battle will not happen. I have no reason to fight you now. I can only offer you my sword.' Atora then kneeled and presented his wooden sword to Kalin. There was not a whisper among the onlookers, all eyes were on the two young men.

Kalin stepped towards the kneeling warrior and took his sword. 'Please rise, Atora.' The warrior stood and faced Kalin.

'I have no knowledge of the loss you have experienced. You say you have nothing left to fight for, but you have shown great courage in coming here to die with honour. It would be a shame to have such a warrior taken from us.'

Kalin threw the two wooden swords to the ground and walked over to the Conri. He then reached down into the chest and took The Moon Sword from within and walked back to Atora. 'Hear me now. Take this sword from me and be my right-hand man.'

'But I did not win the challenge to take this sword.'

'No, but you did not lose either. The 22 warriors before you did. Take this sword from me.'

Atora did not know what to say.

'I am asking you to join my Clan, Atora. The Ruane Clan.'

Atora could feel his eyes starting to well up as he reached out and took the sword from Kalin. He could feel power surging through him from the sword. Kalin smiled and then clasped his shoulder. 'You have a Clan now, and you have a purpose.'

Atora was in shock at what had just happened. He could not help the tears from running down his face. 'Thank you Kalin. I am honoured by what you have given me. I now have a purpose. Where you go, I go.'

The crowd all cheered to see such a moment unfold in front of them. Kalin then turned from Atora and addressed the crowd. 'Who else will follow me? Who else will be part of the Ruane Clan? Tomorrow, I head south to Kitia to help fight against The Empire. I know we have had our trouble with The Kingdom, but if we do not make a stand these lands will be next to be conquered by Emperor Casimir. I ask you again, WHO IS WITH ME?'

For a few heart beats no one came forward, then Tornos and Rovan walked in to stand beside Kalin and Atora. Moments later the giant man Bellarus pushed his way through the crowd and bellowed out. 'I will follow you Kalin.' Then the 21 remaining warriors that had fought Kalin, followed by scores and scores of other warriors, filled the whole arena. Cheers went up from everyone and they started chanting Kalin's name. 'KAL-IN!' 'KAL-IN!' Kalin caught the Conri's eye and bowed a thank you to him.

He shouted back at Kalin over the chanting. 'Never let it be said, I always keep my word.' And gave Kalin a wink.

The next morning, a large force of Gantian warriors left the village of Fenrich. The Conri, Kamas, had supplied them all with food and fresh mounts. As they travelled, more and more Gantians joined them, making their way to the North Wall of the Kingdom. It was summertime now and all the snow was gone. This made the travelling easier. As the Gantian riders entered the last forest that separated them from the Wall, Karra was there waiting to meet them. Kalin had seen him in the distance and kicked his heels into his mount. The horse took off, leaving the force behind them. He pulled his horse to a skid in front of Karra. He was dismounted and holding onto the reins of his horse. Kalin jumped down and grasped his uncle's large arm and hand in the Warriors handshake. 'Well met Uncle.'

'Well met boy.'

'Thank you for coming.'

'I can only journey with you a small way as there will be an opening of the gate soon, and I don't want to let the unwanted dogs through.' Karra leaned to one side to see the army of Gantian Warriors coming towards them. 'I see you have made some new friends.'

'Yes. Kamas, the Conri helped me do this. I owe him greatly.'

'That is good to see. You have gathered quite an army there and the most impressive part is that there is a mix of Clans as far as I can make out from here.'

'They are all strong warriors. I have seen them all training over the last few days. We are just over three thousand strong.'

'Gathering an army is one thing Kalin but leading them is another. Make wise decisions boy. Their lives will be at your command, and on your conscience if they die.'

'I will try my best Uncle.'

'This is a war you will be riding into and many will die. Just be strong when it comes to pass.'

'Thank you for this advice. I know things will be tough. We will have to cover more than 30 miles a day if we want to get to Kitia in less than 2 months. Our men will be tired when we get there and then they will have to fight.'

'They are Gantian, they will fare out OK. Sure, they will rest when it is all over. I see you have many extra horses.'

'Yes, courtesy of Kamas.'

'The extra horses will enable us to cover a lot of ground fast, as we can change to fresh mounts as we travel.'

The Gantian warriors all stopped when they reached Kalin. Kalin turned to address them. 'This is my uncle Karra Ruane.'

Big Bellarus jumped down from his horse and walked to Karra. 'This man needs no introduction. We all know he is The Guardian of the Gate. I have been waiting a long time to meet you. You are a living legend in Gantia.' Bellarus picked Karra up and gave him a bear hug.

Karra smiled as the giant let him down. 'I like these men you have gathered. You have chosen well Kalin.'

'They are a strong bunch alright.'

Karra slapped Bellarus on the back, 'we shall drink together tonight, and I will tell you of some tales from the gate.'

'I would be honoured to hear them Karra.'

Karra then turned to Kalin. 'Now the tricky part is getting them to open up this damned gate so we can pass through.'

Bellarus laughed out loud. 'I will knock it from its hinges for you Karra.'

Later that day the Warriors arrived at the edge of the forest. Karra told them to stay in the woods out of sight, so he could go and negotiate for them to pass through to the South lands of the Kingdom. He made his way down and, just before he got to the gates, a Latonian Guard shouted down to him. 'Move away from the wall and go about your business.'

'I am here to talk with Captain Groth.'

'What about?' The Latonian guard shouted back down.

'It is a private matter. He is an old friend of mine and will be pleased to see me.' The wall went quiet and the gates then opened a crack, just enough for a man to pass.

Captain Groth walked out to meet Karra. 'Well Karra, another visit. I may get the tavern to stock up on drinks tonight.'

'I will not be drinking with you today, my friend. I am here to pass through to the South.'

'It is a shame that a man can't find the time to have a drink and catch up with an old friend.'

'I wish I could, Groth, but I have friends that need to pass through too.'

'I don't see anyone with you Karra.'

'They will be here shortly Captain.'

'How many friends are we talking?'

'Just over three thousand.'

'THREE THOUSAND!' he blurted out.

'Yes, that is correct.'

'I cannot allow that to happen. We are at war Karra.'

'These men are Gantian Warriors led by my nephew Kalin; they are coming to the King's aid.'

Groth scratched his head. 'You are asking for a lot here Karra. If things go bad here it is a rope around my neck.'

'If things go bad with the war, we will have no necks at all. You will be rewarded for helping us to help your King.'

Karra had a feeling he was going to refuse him and the warriors' entry. 'Remember the favour you owe me Groth.'

He nodded. 'Yes, I do.'

'If you allow us to pass through, we will be even again.'

'Will you be carrying weapons?'

'How else can we fight off these invaders?'

Groth scratched his head again and thought for a while. 'I will grant you and your warriors' passage through under two conditions. One, that you do not harm a single Latonian person on your journey, and two, that you have to spend a night drinking with me on your return?'

'That seems like a fair deal to me, old friend.'

'The things I do for friendship, Karra. Bring your men through. I will open the gate on both sides, make sure they keep moving until you reach the outer walls on the Latonian side. It is getting late you, can camp on the southern side. I don't want any confrontation with my guards past the wall. We are all on edge with this war.'

'Thank you, Groth.' Karra turned his mount and rode back to the force and led them down to the gate. The Gantian Warriors passed through silently. There were two long lines of Latonian Guards that stretched from gateway to gateway, channelling the Gantian men to the Latonian side. There were angry looks from the Guards, but there was no confrontation. Once all the Warriors were through the gate on the far side, Karra said his goodbyes to his friend, Captain Groth, and Kalin led his force South, deep into the Kingdom on the road to Kitia. They camped late that night and were all riding hard again at first light the next morning, covering as much ground as they could.

37

Thianni walked with her chambermaids along the corridor to the main hall. The doors were opened for her by the Royal Guards and she went inside to a packed hall. The King was sitting on his throne with the Queen at her place beside him. On the other side of him was General Arthen and the High Priest Ulauth. She was shocked to see Arthen looking so haggard. She almost didn't recognise him. The General was skeletally thin, and he appeared to be in a lot of pain. It had been a long time since she had seen him last.

She made her way up the hall and mounted the steps to the King. Her maids parted and moved off to the sides of the hall, waiting on her. Thianni bowed to her Auntie and Uncle. They both smiled at her. She went over to the Prime General and gave him a hug. 'Welcome home General.' She then took her seat next to little Rain. The doors to the hall opened and Sabat made his way up and, bowing, took his seat next to Ulauth.

'That seems to be everyone now' said the King 'I will begin. Ladies and gentlemen. Thank you all for gathering here at such short notice. I have some grave news today. General Arthen has returned home, just hours ago. He has borne this bad news all the way from South of Tureen. Unfortunately, our worst fears have come true. General Arthen and his men were unsuccessful in holding back the armies of the Empire and now they are making their way to our gates.'

Worried murmuring rippled through the assembly. 'Please, do not let this news unsettle you. Our walls have never been breached. We still have a large army within the city and our food stores are stocked high. We must remain strong if we are to weather this storm.' He paused for a moment to let his words sink in. 'I would like to take this opportunity to remember all the soldiers that have fallen, especially our beloved General Titus, who gave his life for us. They have given their lives to protect all of us. This is the ultimate sacrifice anyone can make. To lay down their lives for others. I know many of you here have family or friends that went to war and now they have not come home. Our Priest Ulauth will now say a prayer to remember our fallen. Ulauth bowed to the King and Queen. Taking the floor, he recited the Battle prayer for the fallen. It was very moving and a large number of those assembled were in tears. He bowed again and returned to his seat.

The King then stood. 'Now we have little time, we must prepare for this storm. I will need everyone on board to help protect this city of Kitia. Men and women. Let us make one last stand and push back these evil men that come here to take our home. Go now. Let the word spread through the city, as tomorrow we will begin preparations for this coming war.' He turned and left the hall.

The Queen, and the remainder who had been seated, followed. Thianni went with them. She could feel her heart beating hard in her chest with the news she had just heard. She could see Ulauth trying to help General Athen along and she moved in to help.

'Thank you, Princess.' He said, in a weak voice. Thianni had never seen the General so weak before. He had always been a big, strong, protective man in her eyes. Now he was a shadow of his former self.

Once inside his rooms, the King turned to Thianni. 'We have plenty to be planning here. Would you be so kind as to take Prince Rain to his bedroom please? It is getting late and he looks tired.'

'Yes, my King.' She bowed and then took her young cousin by his hand and left the room. Sabby and Tiffin were outside waiting, looking frightened. 'Follow me.' Thianni said as she moved on down the now empty hall to the Prince's chambers. Before she entered with Rain, she turned to her Ladies in waiting, Tiffin and Sabby. 'I will stay with Rain tonight; he is probably distraught from all this bad news. The poor boy doesn't know what's happening.' She ruffled his hair. 'Go on in Rain, I will be there in a moment.' Once the Prince was inside, she closed the door and turned again to Tiffin and Sabby. 'We will also need to start planning.'

'In what way, my Lady?' said Sabby.

'When the army gets here, they will surround the city. There will be no one getting in or out and there will be no food coming in. I know the King said we have plenty of food, but that won't last forever. I have read about historical sieges and they are always very bad times. If they breach the outer walls, they will slaughter the entire city's inhabitants. Then the walls of this Palace will be next to be breached. If that happens, we will have to either try to escape this city, stay here and fight for our lives, or take our own lives. If the siege lasts a long time, we will start running out of food and it will be hell within these walls.

We must start making a stock of food of our own and arm ourselves. Make a plan on how to escape the city if we can? Now, start gathering what we need but keep out of sight. Sabby, we will use your cleaning room to store our things.' The two ran off to carry out their orders and Thianni entered Rain's room and locked the door.

38

Renik had been working in the kitchens of the palace for a month now. It had taken him a while to get used to these early morning starts. He had to start work, preparing food, before the sun came up. His skills had improved quickly, and within his short time in the palace kitchens, he had already been promoted after the last chef had been sacked for constantly coming in to work drunk. It was not Renik's fault that he had been the one that was supplying him with the alcohol. He had paid for a letter of recommendation in order to secure a position in the Royal kitchens. The price of this letter had been high, but worth it, as it had given him a good starting point within the palace. One of the first disciplines he had been taught all those years ago on the island of Tibar, was patience. He must take his time above all else. This was the biggest job he had taken on in more than twenty years as an assassin. This was the job he had been waiting for, the pinnacle of his career. A price so big he could retire on it. He could live the life of a normal man and not ever have to worry about money again. He stirred the huge pot of soup and then dipped a small spoon in and tasted it. It tasted good; he was pleased with it. He heard whistling behind him, and it was getting closer.

The Head Chef of the Royal kitchen passed by and slapped him on the back. 'You're doing a great job, Limira.'

Renik thanked him immediately. 'Thank you, this is one of my best recipes. It has a secret ingredient.'

'Once you don't poison us all, it will be fine.'

Renik laughed out loud and continued stirring the soup. The Head Chef walked away, whistling once more. Renik was used to his new name now, Limira, and was able to respond naturally to it when it was called out. Staying in character for weeks on end was an ability that had always come easily to Renik. He looked at it as a chance to become someone different for a while. He had made food for the King twice now and had been very tempted to use poison both times. The chances were, he would have been caught and tortured and then killed. The real skill to his art was not the taking of a person's life. It was taking a life and then being able to get away without being caught. That was the real art.

He was getting close though. Now that he was established within the palace, his next step was to start studying the King's movements and routines, followed by his guards. Then, and only then, could he plan for the kill and the escape. The escape would be difficult as the city gates were all locked now, due to the war raging in the South. As he mused about his current job, he became aware of screaming and shouting coming from outside the kitchen area. A woman ran past Renik crying. Before he could ask her, what was happening, she was gone. Then a maid went to run past him. He grabbed her by the arm. 'What is going on?'

'They are here' she shouted. 'Thousands and thousands of them. Outside the city walls.' She shrugged off his grip and moved away at speed.

Renik's mind reeled as the realisation hit him. His job would still stand though, he was to take the life of he who sits on the throne. All the gates were shut and there was an army just outside the walls. The word impossible came into his mind. How would he manage to accomplish this? He covered the pot with a large lid and made his way to the kitchen terrace. The palace was situated within Kitia, on high ground, and from the high up terrace he would be able to see out over the far away walls of the city. There were people already out on the terrace looking out over the walls. The sky was starting to lighten as the sun was threatening to rise. His head turned as he looked out over the wall line; his eyes followed the distant line of the army that was closing in on the city. Thousands and thousands of men. The biggest army he had ever seen was massing outside Kitia. A feeling of impending doom swept over him as he could see no way that any of the city's inhabitants would be able to survive this force. He wondered if this was what his victims felt at the very moment when he took their lives.

Loud horns boomed out from within the city, alerting everyone to the pending battle. Renik moved back into the palace and made his way to the kitchen. He took the lid from the large pot of soup and continued to stir it. He had a lot to think about, and a new plan would need to be put in place in order for him to achieve his goal.

39

The Royal guard stood at the top of the look-out tower looking Eastwards, out over the flat lands. It was early morning and the stars moved slowly along the night sky. These last few nights had been extremely warm. He was tired tonight as he had little sleep. He looked straight up at the stars. They looked magnificent. He liked being up here alone on watch duty. No one to bother him. He looked back down to the horizon and noticed a faint glow on the skyline. The sun is starting to come up already, he thought. A feeling of dread came over him as he looked closer. He could see it was not the sunrise, it was the glow of thousands of torches in the distance, and they were coming straight for the city. He rushed down from his post, running down the stairs and into the quarters belonging to the Hornblower, who was fast asleep.

'Wake up, wake up, they are coming.'

The horn bellowed out over the city. Within minutes, the high walls of the city were congested with soldiers dressed in full armour and red cloaks. Bows, arrows and spears were brought up to the walls and the towers. The gates were locked and reinforced with extra beams of wood. Everyone waited and watched from the walls as the army of the Empire marched towards the city. It was like the sun was rising in the distance. Before long, the plain in front of the castle was filled with black armoured men, all carrying torches. They set up their camps a mile from the city and their tents filled the landscape as far as the eye could see. It took all morning for them to make ready. Trees were cut down to make room and used as firewood. The path to the city of Kitia disappeared into the centre of the huge encampment.

A lone rider made his way from the camp and up to the East Gate of the city. All eyes were on him as he approached. Several bowmen notched their bows and were ready to take him from his horse at the given order. He looked up at the high walls and spoke haltingly. 'Good day to you all. I speak to the King Roban?'

General Arthen limped forward. 'The King is busy having lunch. He will not be here. I am The Prime General. Anything you want to say to the King can be said to me.'

'If the King is unconcerned about the largest army that has ever been assembled outside of his gates well, he must be a mad man.'

Talking went up along the walls and then shouting. Arthen held his hand up to hush them. 'If the King's name is used wrongly again, I assure you it will be the last words you ever say. Now what do you want.'

The man laughed. 'Very well so. I am here to offer you your lives, courtesy of Emperor Casimir, ruler of Eamhair. If you open your gates to him by the day's end, everyone behind these walls will be allowed to live under his ruling.'

General Arthen let out a booming laugh. 'If you want these gates to be opened, you will have to come and try opening them yourselves. Now be gone, or it will start to rain down arrows on your lonesome ass.'

'So be it, General. We will break through these gates like wet paper and you will feel the full power of The Dragon Army.' He turned his horse and walked back to the Imperial camp.

The General looked around at the men standing around him. 'We can relax now men as he will give us today to change our minds. Tomorrow will be different; it will be a long day. Make sure everyone gets plenty of rest, you will need it.' By dawn the next day, everyone within the city was uneasy. Everyone feared what was about to happen.

Tipin was sitting on the deck of the Sea Wolf with Old Talip. The sun was high in the sky, beaming down on their sweating bodies. They had been working all morning, making ready the changes to the ship that Captain Vimeo had ordered. It had taken them a few weeks to get this far and they had been told that Captain Jerra was visiting the ship today to examine the changes that Captain Vimeo had made. Talip tore off a chunk of bread and then sliced a large wedge of cheese from the block. Placing the cheese on the bread, he handed it to Tipin. Tipin gratefully accepted it and started to chew on the hard crust. They both sat in silence, watching out over the harbour at the ships performing battle manoeuvres. No boats or ships could enter the harbour now, only the scout ships came and went through the gate at the mouth of the harbour.

Barus called out to Captain Vimeo at the other end of the ship, shouting 'He's on his way.'

The Captain made his way to Barus and waited for Jerra to board the ship. Jerra marched up the ramp and shook hands with Vimeo. 'Well met Captain. I have been waiting patiently to see these new adjustments to your ship.'

'We have been working night and day to get things right. Come and I will show you what we have been working on.' Vimeo took him to the front of the ship and pulled back a canvas cover.

Jerra's eyes gleamed as he saw what hid underneath the cloth. 'That looks dangerous, what is it?'

'It is a weapon, let me show you.' Vimeo gestured to Barus. Barus took up an iron rod and inserted it into the machine. He then started to wind large levers. This wound a rope around tight on a large spool. Then Barus opened a long crate and took out what looked like a large arrow, longer than a tall man.

Vimeo turned to Jerra. 'When I was a boy, I saw a man make one of these. It was smaller than this one here, but I was astonished at how effectively it worked. He called it a Scorpion's Sting. It took me some thinking over the last few days to recreate it. Once I had the design right, I wanted to make it bigger. This is what we have made.'

Jerra looked like his eyes were about to jump from their sockets. 'Can I see it working?'

'Yes of course. We have been practising for most of the day yesterday with it, and I'm pleased with how well it works. We had to make a few minor adjustments with it, so it is firing on target. I am happy with its aim now.'

Vimeo called out a name. 'Pittana!' The young boy raced along the ship, down the ramp and along the dock. He reached a platform that was floating on the water a good distance away from the Sea Wolf. He then pushed this floating platform away from the dock and it floated out into the bay. The boy then ran back to the ship. Jerra could see that there was a wooden target sticking out of the top of the float. Vimeo ordered Barus to arm the weapon. Barus slid the large arrow into place and then moved to the back of the weapon. He then aimed it at the target. When he was happy with the position, he pulled back a lever and the weapon jumped with a cracking sound, propelling the iron arrow from its run and shooting it with great speed. The iron arrow thumped deep into the target with a violent stop.

Jerra was astonished. 'That moved very fast, and the accuracy is amazing. You are a genius Vimeo.'

Vimeo smiled at Jerra's reaction. 'We can also attach a rope to the arrow, so when it hits its target, let us say a ship's hull for example, we can reel them in to our ship if need be.'

Jerra listened intently. 'I really like it Vimeo. It is truly a great weapon. One that the King will be glad to see, I am sure. How much damage does it do when it hits its target?'

'I am glad you asked that.' Vimeo turned to Barus. 'Load the heavier arrow, Barus.'

Barus reached down into the chest once more and took out another, larger, iron arrow. This one was different. The arrowhead was much larger than the last and the design had a twisted spiral that splayed out from the tip of the arrow. Barus placed the arrow in its casing and wound the weapon. He then took aim again. The lever was pulled back. This time the arrow made a whistling noise as it travelled at speed through the air. It hit home beside the first arrow with a much louder sound, and the wood on the target looked like it had exploded on impact, sending pieces of wood into the air that splashed out and around the floating platform. Jerra almost fell back at the sight of the damage. Vimeo was enjoying the other Captain's reaction. He always liked appreciation of his work.

'This design of arrow is made to cause as much damage as possible to a ship's hull, so it will sink it fast. A well-aimed arrow should land just below the sea level. This should puncture the strongest of hulls and sink a ship fast.'

'I would like to see how accurate it is on open water against a moving target.'

'We still have tests to do with it, but I am confident it will perform well out on the sea.'

'Well, all this has excited me immensely. I think we will have to have a drink to celebrate your invention.'

'Yes, I would like that, but it will have to be later today as we still have some work to do. We need to forge more arrows and secure the weapon to the deck.'

'I shall leave you to your work and see you later for that drink. I will go now and report to the King on your great work here. Well done to all.' Jerra went to turn.

'Just one more thing Captain, before you go. I do have a request. I will be looking for extra men to row and help on deck. The Sea Wolf is undermanned. They have to be strong men and willing to work, as the timing on board this ship is critical.'

Captain Jerra nodded. 'You shall have the men. I will pick them myself and if it comes to this ship sailing out to war against the Empire, I would very much like to be onboard The Sea Wolf too, with your consent that is?'

'We would be pleased to have you on board, but know this, on my ship I am the Captain.'

Jerra Smiled, 'Yes of course, Captain Vimeo. I will only be onboard to assist.'

Even before he reached the tent, he could smell the stink of death. The pungent smell of dead bodies emanated from the black tent. Skarin lifted the cover to the entrance and entered. It was dark inside and he could just make out that Bakal was busy working. Bakal turned as he noticed Skarin walking in but said nothing. Skarin looked around. There were human body parts everywhere. Arms, legs, and torsos, and in one corner of the tent was a large basket filled with severed heads. There were several pots on fires. They appeared to be filled with bubbling blood. It was a scene of horror, but Skarin was unaffected by the sight as he had seen Bakal work many times before.

'If I were to picture what hell would look like, it would be like your tent Bakal. Have you no pride in your living quarters?'

'My work comes first before anything. You know this Skarin.' Bakal responded with a croaky voice.

'That I do, and I am reminded of it every time I enter this tent. How are things progressing?' Bakal continued to place chopped up parts of human bodies into a pressing device. He turned a lever and a plate came down and pressed the flesh, draining it of its blood. The blood was then collected in containers below the work bench.

'They are going well, but I will need more bodies to complete the process. I have drained all these bodies and I am just getting the last of the blood.'

'There will be more bodies then you could imagine Bakal, just as soon as we breach those city walls.'

'You do know that those walls have never been breached before Skarin, don't you?' Skarin chuckled.

'Those walls have never faced a force like the one the Emperor has brought, and they have never tasted the war machine that we bring either.'

'Maybe so, but I have heard stories that those walls are over fifty feet wide, and they look as high as mountains. It will take a great deal for any force to breach them.'

Skarin moved in closer to Bakal. He could see that his clothes were saturated with blood and most of his skin stained with dried dark blood. 'I had no idea you were so interested in the construction of Kitia.'

'I am not, I only speak fact. I have little interest in this war that you and the Emperor wage. I have only interest in my work here.'

'How much iron have you extracted from the blood of the dead?'

'I have almost enough iron to complete the task of making you your two blood swords.'

Emperor Casimir left his tent, followed by General Jargo and his fifty most trusted guards. He stepped onto his golden chariot, and General Jargo and his guards mounted their war horses. The party moved towards the front line of the army where all of his Dragon army awaited his arrival. The sun had been up for an hour now, and it bathed the land in its warm summer rays. Skarin was waiting for the Emperor with the other generals and the Dragon army, all facing the city of Kitia, a half a mile from its walls. The golden chariot pulled up to the front line and the Emperor looked to Skarin. 'You may begin.'

Skarin bowed to his Emperor, then turned his horse and moved down along the line. 'First wave commences!' he shouted. Thousands of men surged forward with long ladders and large shields. They broke away from the bulk of the army and moved towards the menacing walls that surrounded the city. Skarin moved back to his Emperor to watch the start of the attack. He turned to his Emperor. 'These first attacks will cost us men, but it is vital that we test their defences. We will see if these walls have any weak areas.'

Arthen stood on the ramparts with his men as they watched the first wave of Dragon Soldiers approach the great walls of their city. They had plenty of time to make ready for this war and they had spent that time wisely. Arthen had a wooden platform constructed on the back of the wall. On this high rise he mounted his archers. They consisted of old men, women and some older children from within the city. Anyone who was strong enough to draw a bow was ordered to help. This gave room for the Royal soldiers to defend the walls right at the front. They all had trained for this attack for weeks.

As the Dragon soldiers came closer, Arthen drew his sword and held it up. 'Archers, at the ready!' The archers all notched their bows, all along the wall, and aimed them high into the air. The Dragon Soldiers were closing in now and were in striking distance. 'FIRE!' Arthen shouted, bringing down his sword. The sky was filled with deadly sharp shafts. They came down hard into the onrushing soldiers, felling hundreds. Again, and again, the arrows were sent into the oncoming black mass of the Dragon Soldiers as they drew closer to the walls, leaving many dead and wounded.

Arthen shouted once more. 'Cease fire! Royal Troops move into place.' The Royal Soldiers all moved forwards and pointed their spears outwards above the walls. Some soldiers picked up long wooden poles with T shaped ends and stood at the ready. Ladders banged all along against the top of the ramparts and the attackers began to climb the ladders to the walls. The T poles were placed against the top of the ladders at the ready.

Arthen looked along the wall line. 'Wait for them to climb the ladders men.' As the first Dragon Soldiers peered over the tops of the ladders, Arthen shouted out another order. 'NOW! PUSH!' The T poles were pushed outwards, pushing the ladders from leaning onto the walls preventing any Dragon soldiers getting close to the walls. The Ladders all fell backwards with the Dragon men desperately holding on. Most of them crashed to the ground, killing the men furthest up the ladders. Several times, the Dragon Soldiers tried to climb the ladders to gain access to the walls, but every time they were pushed back.

After what seemed a long time, a horn sounded in the distance and the attackers started to retreat. Some of the archers started to shoot into the fleeing soldiers killing more, but Arthen shouted 'Hold your fire. Save the arrows for the next attack!' A little while passed and then a fresh wave of attackers ran forward to try and take the walls. This time there were twice as many attackers as the previous attack. The archers killed hundreds more and the ladders were repelled again. Not one attacker managed to put a foot onto the ramparts of the high walls. Throughout the day the Empire attacked the walls again and again, always with the same outcome. The Dragon Soldiers took huge losses. As the night set in, the fighting stopped for the day. The gate to the city opened wide enough for men to pass out onto the blood-soaked killing ground and retrieve the undamaged arrows from the land and the dead. Baskets were lowered from the walls and men scurried back to fill up the baskets with arrows, under the cover of darkness, to be used in future attacks. The next day, enormous siege towers higher than the walls were brought forth from the Empire. They took a long time to reach striking distance. This time, the archers fired flaming arrows at the towers. Some towers started to burn and soon were engulfed with flames. The towers that got near to the wall were then stopped from getting any closer with long poles that were fixed into place stopping the towers from moving. Thousands of arrows were sent into the wooden towers and eventually they too, were in flames. A battering ram was pushed forward in place at the base of the entrance and started to bang at the gates. Boiling oil was poured down onto the battering ram, killing anyone underneath or operating the ram. This too was soon ignited with fiery arrows. Still no one was able to gain a foothold on the walls or break through the gate. The city of Kitia was now under full siege.

In the war tent, the Emperor was furious. 'Why have we not taken the walls to the city yet?' His Generals were all quiet now, including Jargo. No one dared to answer. 'I have not seen one Latonian die this last week and our own losses have been great.'

Just then, the tent flapped opened and Skarin calmly walked in and bowed to the Emperor, sitting down and pouring himself a cup of wine.

'What is your report?' the Emperor asked him.

He took another drink from his wine. 'The catapults are almost ready. We know now that we can't breach the walls with our men and their ladders.'

'And will the walls stand against our catapults?'

'That is what we will find out, your highness.'

'And if they fail also?'

'Then we will starve them out.'

The Emperor turned once more to his Generals. 'I am starting to grow impatient with all of this. There is too much failure here. I have not come all this way to lose this war. Make sure these walls are breached. The King's throne beckons to me.'

The catapults were pulled into place, well out of range of the archers on the walls. Arthen shouted for everyone to take cover on the walls. He counted 14 catapults in total. They were spread out in a long line facing the city. The long arms of the war machines were wound back, and large stones placed into the cups. Then the arms shot forward, sending the stones high into the sky. Most of the stones fell short, bar two that hit the base of the wall. Adjustments were made to the catapults and they were all reloaded again. They all fired for a second time and all hit the walls at different places, sending up pieces of rock onto the ramparts. For hours, the war machines fired at the walls, but the walls held up against the onslaught. Day and night the catapults launched rock after rock against the city wall with little effect. The walls were built well with huge slabs of stone and had very few weak spots. The stones just seemed to crumble on impact as they came crashing in. After some days, cracks began to show in parts of the walls, they were showing signs of weakening. The parapets were all mostly destroyed from the rocks pounding the tops of the walls but the walls themselves still stood. Then out of nowhere, the rain came.

The Queen sat in her chambers talking to Thianni. 'I have brought you here today to talk to you about this siege.' Thianni looked nervous. 'This could very well swing in the favour of our enemies. We have no external forces coming to help us. We are alone within this city. If the Emperor is able to breach our walls and defeat our Royal Soldiers, we will be left at the mercy of his ruling. As Royal Ladies, if this were to happen, we would not be killed. We will be raped and used and tortured in ways you could never imagine.' Thianni could feel her heart sinking listening to this possible outcome. 'We will have to make our own fate. Do you understand what I am saying?'

Thianni shook her head. 'No, your Majesty.'

There was a knock at the door, and the High Priest Ulauth walked in, bowing to both Queen Lesta and Princess Thianni. 'My Ladies. I know this is a matter of great concern and it is a delicate subject, especially for the House of Light.' Ulauth handed them each a small vial. 'This is a poisonous substance. If the time comes and you need to take it, just break the seal and drink all its contents. Just one drop of this will kill a horse. There is enough there for ten men. There will be no pain and it will act fast. You will have only moments before it renders you asleep, and it will then stop your heart from beating. This greatly troubles my soul, having to hand these over to you both, but it is your request my Queen. Let us hope that the Light shines on us in this time of need and you will not have any use for this.'

He bowed and then left the Queen's chambers with a heavy heart. The Queen then turned to Thianni. 'Do you understand now?'

'Yes, I think I do, but it will not come to that.'

The Queen nodded. 'Let us hope so my niece, let us hope so.'

40

Kalin, Karra and Leib led the Gantian army out through the gate of the North Wall and into the lands of Latonia. Most of them had never set foot in this land before. When they were all clear, they sped up their pace. They could move faster on their horses as they continued on the wide, stone road that led to the city of Branti. They would be there in a few days and then they would reach the Kingdom's plains. They only stopped twice throughout the day. The first time to give the horses a rest and the second to make camp for the night. The further south they travelled, the more the war became apparent. After a week and a half of traveling on the south road, they were on the central plains when they saw fresh tracks of a large army traveling east. They were a few miles from the river Rura when they decided to stop to make camp for the night and assess the situation. Food was running very low and all the riders were weary. The camp was spread out along the side of the road and it was starting to get dark. Karra was lighting a fire and Leib had started to prepare some food. Some warriors did not pitch tents as the weather was still warm, they just slept by their fires at night.

Kalin called two men over. 'I need you to ride out and scout the lands behind us. I am concerned about the tracks we came across. I do not want any surprise attacks from behind us as we travel.'

The two men mounted their horses and rode out. Kalin then sat down with Karra by the fire. 'You have taken to the role of leading these men quite well Kalin.'

'I'm not so sure. I am finding I need to think about everything very carefully first, before making any decision. There are lives at stake here, and I don't want them to think I am weak in my judgment. I don't want them to turn against me.'

'They would not have come with you if they thought that they were being led by a weak man. You are doing a good job.'

'Thank you, uncle. It is reassuring to hear that.'

'You need to know that there will be lives lost in this battle. You will make friends with some of these men, but not everyone will be coming back home to Gantia with us. This is just the way of war lad.'

'I keep thinking about Thianni and Reesa too. What if we do not get to them in time?'

'That is something that could happen, but you should not think about it right now.'

Kalin thought deeply on what Karra had told him. He did not get much sleep that night. The sun had just come up and the two riders had come back into camp. They came straight to Kalin. He rose from his bed by the dying fire. 'What is the news?'

'There is a huge army of Dragon Soldiers coming our way. It looks like they have found our tracks and are now in pursuit of us.'

Leib also stood while Karra was still fast asleep, snoring. Leib looked at Kalin, who looked very concerned now. 'Will I wake the men and make a defensive line?'

'No, we can't afford to waste time here and lose men in an all-out battle. We need to focus our fighting at the main battle. This is where we will make a difference. Wake everyone. We will ride to the river. If they are close, we might need to try to slow down their pursuit.'

The Gantian warriors moved fast along the stone road, trying to gain distance from the Dragon soldiers. It was midday when they reached the river Rura. The road led to a long bridge that stretched out over the river. Kalin remembered it from last year when he was travelling north. It was an immense body of freshwater, moving at a fast speed, and this bridge was the only crossing for miles.

Leib came alongside Kalin as they rode. 'We will have to rest the horses soon Kalin.'

'Yes, I know. We will rest them when we reach the other side of the river. It will take a while for all of us to cross the bridge, as it will only hold four abreast.'

The warriors tapered down to travel four abreast as they crossed over the bridge. The last men had just reached the shore when a shout went out amongst the men. 'There they are. They are coming.'

They all looked back across to the other side to see the Dragon troops moving along the road and about to reach the bridge on the other side.

Kalin struggled to think what he could do. The men were all tired and needed to rest. If they fought now, they would lose hundreds if not thousands of lives, and with their force reduced in size, they would not be as effective in the coming battle at Kitia. Just then, Kalin felt a hand on his shoulder. He turned to see Karra standing there. 'There comes a time when a man must make a decision. Today is my day.'

'What do you mean uncle?'

'Take your men and keep going. I will remain here and guard the bridge.'

'You cannot face these men alone, there are far too many.'

'Listen to me now, lad. There is no time. You must go and I will stay here. The bridge is not wide, and one man can defend it well. This will buy you some time.'

'I can't let you do this Karra. I will stay with you.'

'No Kalin, you have to go. You have to save the princess and Reesa. These men need you to lead them.' Kalin exhaled. 'You know I am right Kalin. Now go! I will see you again, don't worry. Either in this life or the next.' Karra held out his hand for the warriors' grip but Kalin pulled him in and hugged his uncle.

'Do not die here, you hear me? Do not die here.'

'I don't intend to. One thing before you go Kalin, you will owe me a favour now.'

Kalin grinned. 'I owe you a great deal, more than just one favour.'

'I only need one favour, Kalin.'

Kalin then mounted his horse and rode off south with all the warriors behind him, leaving Karra alone by the bridge. He could hear Karra calling out. 'Remember, you owe me a favour.' Kalin laughed and rode on. Karra stood alone now, waiting for the Dragon soldiers to arrive. In the distance he heard orders shouted out in a language he did not understand. Hundreds of men gathered on the other side of the river, all in black armour. He could see they were starting to start to cross. Around 20 Dragon Soldiers were making their way across towards him. He looked up into the sky. He would have the sun at his back on the bridge. He then spotted an eagle soring high above him.

'You will eat well today, my feathered friend. There will be plenty of dead flesh to feast on by the time I finish.'

He turned and walked back to his horse, removing his tunic and draping it over his saddle. He then unstrapped two arm-length axes from his mount and walked onto the bridge to meet the oncoming men. Karra spun his axes, slashing them through the air, to loosen up his arms and shoulders as he walked. As he got closer, he could see the men drawing their swords and getting ready to fight. He stopped some distance from them. He heard them shout out and then they charged.

Karra took up a defensive position. 'Come then little men, come to me and I will send you into the next world.' As they charged, Karra spun his axes through the air at a downward angle, nearly decapitating the first man as the axe hacked down on him. He fell instantly and the next two tripped over his body as they tried to get to Karra. There was little room to manoeuvre on the bridge. Karra smashed down on both men killing them instantly. More men rushed forward, only to be met with killing blows of the sharp axes from the big Gantian man. In the matter of a few heart beats, all 20 men were lying dead on the bridge. Karra stood there with blood splashes dotted all over his upper torso, waiting for more. Zukata was at the far edge of the bank, watching the scene unfold. He could not believe his eyes. How could one man kill 20 men with such ease and with such speed. He had never seen the likes of it before. He shouted orders at his troops for 30 men armed with spears to attack.

The 30 Dragon men moved forward onto the bridge. This time they took their time with their advancements. As they got close, Karra swung his axes at the spears, knocking them to the side and breaking the sharp ends off. He then charged the front four, knocking into them with his shoulder. They all fell back. One was thrown clear from the bridge with a splash. The current took him and pulled him down river. The soldier desperately tried to swim to the riverbank, but the surging river just pulled him along and out of sight. The front attackers were now disorientated by the charge and struggled to gain a defensive line. Karra hacked into them, cutting left and right with his axes, killing as he ploughed through the Dragon soldiers until there was only one man left standing. The last man then turned and ran back to the safety of his own men. Karra threw his right axe at him as he tried to escape, hitting him high in his back with a sickening thud. The man fell, dead. Karra walked forward and pulled the axe free from the body.

The bridge was slippery now with the blood of the dead. Karra was breathing heavily now and felt tired. Looking down, he could see he had several cuts on his arms and body where the soldiers had got close. One was quite deep; a lot of blood was seeping from it. Back on the bank, Zukata walked forward along the line of his men in amazement at the Gantian warrior on the bridge. Every soldier watched on at the slaughter that had unfolded.

Zukata grasped the hilt of his sword. His disbelief turned to anger. He was angry at the failure of his men. How can one man defeat 50 Dragon Soldiers? How can this be? He turned to his troops. 'Who among you can defeat this lone man?'

No one answered. Then, Captain Askil stepped out from his men. 'Let me cut this man down General.'

Fearing his Captain's life would be taken Zukata answered. 'No Askil, I need you here with your men. You are too valuable to me; I can't afford for you to get injured. I want to talk to this warrior myself.' Zukata walked past them and onto the bridge. Both men locked eyes as Zukata made his way towards the lone warrior. As he got closer, he could see that the man was wounded, he was drenched in blood. His first thought was, how is this man still standing? There were dead bodies laying all over the bridge and many more were floating down the river and out of sight.

'You look tired, big man.' Zukata said in a broken Gantian accent. 'Why don't you lay those axes down and I will let you walk away from here alive.'

The man just stood there, breathing heavily. His arms started to fall now with the weight of the axes he was holding. 'I will rest when my job is over here.'

Zukata felt a chill as the man spoke to him. He knew he was in the presence of a great warrior. 'You have fought well, but you know in your heart that you cannot win this fight. You will not win here today.'

Karra heard the eagle cry out over head and a smile formed on his face. He could feel the strength coming back into his body and his axes came back up into a fighting position. 'I don't know how I am going to win. I just know I am not going to lose!'

Zukata shook his head and looked at this warrior. He thought about drawing his own sword and cutting this man down but for the first time in his life, doubt set in on his mind. Had he the skill to kill this big man? Thoughts ran through his mind on what was the best action to take here. It would make no sense to be killed here and leave his men without a commanding General. He thought carefully about his next move. 'If you turn and walk away right now and let my men pass, there will be no retribution for the men you have killed here today. There is no dishonour in that.'

The axe man just laughed at his offer. 'If you are not here to fight me, go back and let the next man across to die.'

Zukata gave him a disappointed look. 'Well so be it. You have made your decision. If it is death you want, it is death you will receive.'

Zukata turned and walked back to his men. As he stepped from the bridge he called out. 'Send in the horsemen and take him from the bridge.' A row of horsemen galloped onto the bridge and charged the lone man. The first two to reach him went down, as Karra jumped into the air and hit both of them at the same time. The next two charged right into Karra. He could not gain footing in all the blood and slipped to one side. Karra was hurled from the bridge and into the rushing water below. A cheer went up from the Dragon soldiers as the man splashed into the river. Zukata felt a sense of shame for the man. He looked down into the river to see if the man emerged, but there was nothing. Had an undercurrent taken him down to the bottom? The line of horses had reached the other side now and still there was no sign of the man.

Just then, Zukata saw a movement from under the bridge. The man was clinging to the side, holding on to a support pillar on the bridge. In his other hand he was still holding on to one of his axes. He started to hack at the wooden pillar. Chunks of wood flew out into the river as the axe cut into the first pillar. He then moved onto the next pillar and started to cut it. Zukata shouted to the horsemen on the other side but they could not hear him. They had turned and started to make their way back over the bridge. Zukata shouted for archers to come forward. They lined up on the bank of the river and started to fire. He was a long way out and arrows hit the water around him. One arrow hit home and embedded itself in his back. The man seemed oblivious to it and kept on hacking at the pillars. The horsemen were halfway across the bridge when a loud crack sounded out and the bridge seemed to shift slightly to one side. Then the whole middle section collapsed to one side and the centre of the bridge fell into the river with a huge splash, taking most of the horses and men with it. Zukata could hear the men shouting as they were pulled downriver with the current. Zukata looked for the Gantian man, but there was no sign of him now. Had the bridge collapsed on top of him? There was no way to know. The bridge was unusable, they would not be able to pass now. The nearest crossing was a smaller bridge some miles upriver. This would impede their pursuit of the Gantian army, they might not catch them now.

41

Chal waited with his men on the edge of a forest that looked onto a plain to the north. Alain was beside him. Chal's men were all lined up behind him, all mounted. He could see the scout in the distance coming back towards them. He was travelling fast. Both Chal and Alain looked at one another in amusement. 'He looks to be moving fast.' Said Alain. Chal nodded. As the scout got close, he pulled on the horse's reins and both horse and rider came skidding to a stop right in front of Chal. He jumped from his horse and stood before his Captain. He looked panicked and his chest was heaving.

'Thousands of them, Sir.' The scout said out of breath. Talk went out amongst the line of men.

'Thousands of what, soldier?'

'Thousands of men coming this way Sir. They will be here within the hour.'

'Are they from the Empire? Where are they coming from?'

'I couldn't get too close, but I could just make out that they looked like they were from Gantia, Sir, and they are coming in our direction.'

Alain laughed. 'From Gantia! That is highly unlikely. How would they get through the North Wall? And, what would they be doing this far south?' Alain said still laughing.

Chal looked concerned now. 'Are you sure that is what you saw?'

'Yes Sir, it is.'

'OK, take up position in the line.' The scout saluted and walked his horse back to the line.

Alain turned to Chal. 'This cannot be right. He must have made a mistake, or he is going mad.'

'He is one of our best scouts and he has always been logical with his reports in the past. I have no reason to doubt the man, even if it seems absurd' said Chal.

'So, what do we do now Captain?'

'We sit and wait and confront whatever force comes our way.'

Some time had passed, and there was no sign of any force. The men were beginning to get restless and impatient. Alain was just about to say something when Chal put up his hand, indicating silence. 'Do you hear that?' a soldier said, back in the line. There was a low rumbling noise, it started to get louder. Up ahead on the plains came into sight thousands of horsemen, racing towards Chal and his small force. The rumbling got louder as they came straight towards them. Chal looked at Alain. His mouth hung open in disbelief. Some of the line looked like they were going to break and run.

Chal looked back at them and barked out an order. 'Hold the line men.'

One man shouted back. 'They will kill us all.'

'Do not move from your position until I command it' retorted Chal. The line held steady now with Chal's order. The huge force of horsemen filled the entire plain now. It was a sight to behold. As they came closer, the lead rider held up his hand and the entire force slowed to a walk. As they came in close, the leader let out a shout and they all came to a stop. The leader walked his horse up to Chal and Alain.

Chal turned to Alain. 'Do not make any sudden movements.' Alain watched Chal and saw how calm he was with the situation. Alain gulped as he could feel the fear rising within him. These were savages from the north, they were known for their aggression and hunger for battle. The leader looked very young to oversee such a large army of horsemen. He had a tall black man by his side. Alain could make out that the black man had a long scar on his face. Alain had the feeling he had seen this black man before.

The leader walked his horse right up to Chal. 'Are you the leader here?' He spoke the Latonian language very well.

'Yes, I have the command here. What are you…?'

The young savage cut Chal off in mid-sentence. 'You will move your men out of our path.'

Chal thundered back 'You are on the lands of King Roban, and we do not move for anyone.'

The young man laughed. 'You are but a handful of men. You would not stand a chance against such a formidable force.'

'We are part of the Royal army and ordered by King Roban. We have sworn an oath to protect these lands. Now turn your force around and go back from where you came, or we will enforce our laws.' Alain felt his bowels starting to move as he watched the scene unfold.

'You are a brave and ambitious man. Ambition is a good servant but a bad master. Now move aside.' A low laughing sound went out from the Gantian army.

'You are also a brave man when you have an army behind you.'

'I am surprised that your horse can hold your weight with having balls that big.' A cheer from the Gantian men went up.

Chal looked at Alain, who was white as snow. He then turned back to the Gantian leader. 'Why don't you get off of your horse and come and move me yourself.'

All went quiet now, and all eyes were on the young Gantian leader. They both stared at each other and then both dismounted and walked towards one another with their hands on the hilt of their swords. As they got close, they both stopped. Neither man took his eyes from his challenger. Alain moved his hand onto his own sword. He could feel his hands shaking as he did so. The tension in the air was so thick, Alain could have cut it with his sword. Chal looked ready as he stood defiant in front of the bigger Gantian leader. Just then, Alain could see a smile beginning to form at the edge of the Gantian man's face. Both men laughed out loud and then embraced each other in a hug. Alain nearly fell from his horse in relief. A cheer went up from both sides, but mainly from Chal's small force.

'How are you keeping my brother?' Kalin said to Chal.

'I am well, but not as well as you. My, you have grown to some size. What are they feeding you up there? Whatever it is, they must be looking after you up in the north.'

'They are. Let me see you.' Kalin pulled away and looked Chal up and down. 'I am glad to see you are unscathed from the war.'

'We have had our fair share, Kalin, but my men are good with the sword. What are you doing with such a large force of Gantian men this far south?'

'I am doing what I always do, I am here to save you.'

They both embraced again. 'I want to hear all about your adventures from Gantia.'

'Chal, we do not have time. I have three thousand mounted warriors with me, heading to Kitia to give support to the King. There is a large force of Dragon soldiers twice the size of the Gantian force I have here. They are following close behind us. My uncle Karra has insisted on staying and guarding the bridge.'

'You left your Uncle to guard the bridge? One man against a Dragon army of around six thousand men to guard a bridge?'

'I know, it hardly seems fair for the Dragon soldiers.' They both laughed.

'By the Gods Kalin, I have missed you, my brother.'

'Have you seen or heard anything about Thianni, my friend? I am constantly worrying about her.'

'I have heard when the city was informed about the Empire marching on Kitia, the whole city went on lockdown. Everyone in the Palace will be shut inside. Rest assured; she will be safe there.'

'Is there any word on your father?'

'We had come into contact with a wounded Royal Soldier trying to make his way back to Kitia. He had said that he was at the battle. He said that Arthen and his army were defeated, and some were making their way back to the capital, but not many survived.'

'The fact that you have had no word yet on the war might be a good thing. Bad news always travels fast. I hope your father is OK?'

'Let us hope so Kalin.'

'We will camp for the night and move out early in the morning. Will you be joining us Chal.'

'Yes, I think it is time we made our way back home. We no longer have an army to supply. If we travel with you and your men, we will be safer, and we are fully stocked with food. You and your men are welcome to take whatever you all need from our supplies.'

'I am glad to hear that Chal. I have lots to tell you.'

Later that night, both Gantian and Latonian men camped together. The mood was good amongst all. Chal watched Kalin interact with his fellow Gantian men. He looked comfortable and at home in their presence. This pleased him, as he knew how hard life had been for him growing up in Kitia. He noticed that Kalin spoke the language very well. His hair was longer now, like his fellow Gantians, and he could see a beard was starting to grow on his face, making him look older than he was. He watched as Kalin walked to a nearby campfire where some of Chal's men were sitting.

Kalin approached the two brothers, Atal and Abtar. Chal could hear their conversation from where he sat. 'I am pleased to see you two. I wanted to apologise for my actions last year when I attacked you both. I was wrong in doing so. For this I want to say sorry and say I am pleased to see you again.' Both brothers stood and shook Kalin's hand. Happy with the outcome, Kalin made his way back to the campfire with his men. Chal followed him and sat down beside Kalin by the fire. There were six of them, including Kalin, sitting and chatting and eating around the flickering fire. Kalin filled a large bowl of broth and handed it to Chal without saying a word. All the Gantian warriors looked big and strong and ready for war, especially one man. He was the biggest man Chal had ever seen. There was a young warrior Chal noticed. He was slightly smaller than the others. He had no facial hair. Chal was drawn to the sword that was fastened to his belt.

Kalin noticed Chal observing the young man. 'I must introduce you to these men, Chal.' Kalin firstly pointed to Leib. 'This is Leib, a good friend of my Uncle. He used to be an Arena fighter and has lived in Kitia for many years. He has taught me a great deal about sword fighting. This man here is called Rovan. He is the Champion of Four Vales. The village where I was born. Then Tornos, he is the Champion of his village called Fenrich. His father helped me gather this army. This big man here is called Bellarus, a formidable warrior and a bigger man you won't find. Legend has it he once ate a whole cow in one day.' Chal laughed at the statement. 'And then there is this young man.' He pointed to Atora. 'His name is Atora. He has agreed to be my sword bearer.' All the warriors greeted Chal with smiles and a nod. Kalin then grabbed Chal in a headlock. 'And this good looking Latonian man here is my best friend and my brother with different blood.'

Chal felt a little more at ease now. 'I could not help but notice the sword he is carrying.'

'You have always had a good eye for weaponry, Chal. That there is a famous Gantian sword called a Moon Sword. It was given to me by The Old Man of the Land.'

'The Old Man?' Chal asked, captivated.

'Yes, he is the spirit of the land. They call him The Shord.'

Atora stood and unsheathed his blade, handing it to Chal hilt first. Chal took the sword from him. It felt magnificent to hold. 'It is perfectly balanced. I have never seen its like.' Chal swung the sword a few times and then handed it back to Atora and thanked him. 'You have a fine bunch of men with you Kalin. They are a formidable bunch.'

'That they are, them and the other three thousand Gantian warriors that ride with us, all itching for battle. How about your men, Chal, have they been in any battles?'

'Yes, we were ambushed a while ago. They held up well, but our Captain then did not react well. I think his downfall was that he had no plans in place.'

'I see, is this where you stepped in and saved the day?'

Chal smiled at his friend. 'I wouldn't say I saved the day, as some of our men died in that attack, but we did win that fight. Since then, I have been made Captain and I have made sure I have plans in place for every event. What are your plans now Kalin? Have you any plans in place?'

'I just have a simple plan. I am going to ride to the city and save Thianni. Anyone standing in my way will be taken down.'

Chal smiled. 'Sometimes the simple plans are the best ones.'

'Yes, I agree. I am really pleased you are coming with me, Chal. I have so much to tell you.'

'I have too. It's been too long since we have seen each other. Maybe we'll get some sword play in on the way?'

'I hope so. We will be leaving at first light tomorrow. We should try and get some rest as the travelling will be tough.'

Both the Latonian and Gantian men finished off their food and all turned in for the night. The next morning, they were all mounted early and moving fast towards Kitia. The villages and farms they came across had all been laid to waste by the Empire. Kalin was glad of the food supplies Chal had shared with them, as the land was bled of all its livestock and wildlife by the Emperor. The Latonian people were slaughtered in their thousands. Men, women and children were killed as they tried to flee the invaders. Their bodies scattered across the land, left to rot or in burnt piles of human remains. This was the horror of war. The closer they got to Kitia, the more anxious Kalin got. Chal was also starting to fear for his family, as the level of chaos was enormous and the fact that they might not make it in time to help hung over their heads like a heavy weight as they travelled.

42

It was now Autumn, and the rain came down hard as the temperature dropped. The Dragon troops found it hard to carry out their orders as the ground had turned to mush. Everything was wet and there were a number of soldiers becoming sick. A fever had raged through the Imperial camp, leaving many soldiers unable to carry out their tasks, and now men had started to die. The food had also started to run out as the siege wore on. The attacks with their giant catapults had ceased as they had run out of rocks to fire. The Emperor was getting increasingly irritated with the lack of progress in attacking the walls. He called for a meeting to take place with his nine Generals. They all met in the War Tent. General Jargo took the floor.

'Generals, we are coming to a standstill with breaching these walls. Morale is very low among the troops, and we are now rationing food. We cannot sustain this siege for much longer.'

The Emperor then intervened. 'We have not come all this way to go home empty handed. I want this city sacked, NOW! All you so-called connoisseurs and not one of you with a plan to defeat this enemy, who continues to stand defiant before us.'

The tent went silent. Jargo then spoke. 'We can't keep sending our troops in to try and take the walls. We are losing too many in each attack. We have already lost over six thousand men with these attacks and many more that are injured and will not fight again. Now our men are starting to become sick in this bad weather. The battering ram has failed, and our catapults have had little effect on the walls. If we cannot sustain this siege and starve them out, I do not know what more we can do.'

The Emperor smiled. 'It is a shambles. You, my generals, all masters in warfare, all sit here struggling to come up with a plan and it is my Mystic Priest that has come up with the solution for me. I have been talking to Oranius for the last few days and now we have a plan in place.' With that, Oranius walked into the tent and bowed. He then looked at the Generals with a smug smile on his face.

The Emperor and Jargo sat with the rest of the generals, while Oranius presented the plan. 'I have just talked to my brother. He is on the other side of these impenetrable walls. Tomorrow, we must launch an attack on their harbour with our Dragon Ships. This will take the focus from the east wall. Then that night we must all be ready. My Brother will open the gate to the East Wall from inside, and we will have access to the city. This will be our only chance. After dark, we will have a small group ready to enter through these open gates. This group will hold the gates open until we can push our army through to the city. Once inside, make sure you kill everyone.'

A scouting ship sailed into the harbour with speed, announcing that there was a fleet of Dragon ships approaching. A horn sounded out over the harbour of Kitia, and Royal guards scrambled to their positions. Captain Jerra came running down towards The Sea Wolf with a gang of his men.

Barus was there to greet them. 'Quick get on board, we are about to set sail.' Jerra and his men piled onboard and took their positions. Most of them went below deck to man the oars. Barus then untied the ropes and pulled up the walkway board. Oars came out through the slots and they pushed the Sea Wolf sideways out into the harbour. Free from the docking port now, Vimeo shouted out orders and all the oars came out and hit down into the water. A steady drumbeat boomed out from Tipin below deck, and the Sea Wolf moved forward to the harbour gate. The gate was raised as Royal Warships moved outside to confront the oncoming Dragon ships. The Sea Wolf also moved out into open water. The Drumbeat sped up and the Sea Wolf was now leaving the other ships behind.

Vimeo moved back to the stern of the ship to Old Talip. He was at the helm. 'As soon as I say, I want you to break to the Port side. We will try to out manoeuvre these Dragon ships and get to the back of the fleet where we will have the wind with us. Any ship that tries to turn and follow us we will ram them.

Jerra moved alongside Vimeo. 'What is the plan, Captain?'

'We are going to try and get behind their fleet. Then we will hit them from behind and your other War Ships will hit them head on. Vimeo then shouted to Pittana. 'Make sure you help Barus with releasing the sails when I call for them.'

The Sea Wolf was now powering through the water with all oars manned. Vimeo felt a surge of excitement flow through him as the Sea Wolf gathered speed. Sea spray and wind passed over the deck. They were closing in fast on the attacking fleet. He looked back at the Royal Warships. They had left them behind with the Sea Wolf's speed.

'Be careful when we turn. They will try and hit us with arrows.' Vimeo shouted out to his men. As they drew even closer Vimeo waited for the right moment to turn. He could see the Dragon soldiers scrambling on their ships now getting ready for the clash. 'NOW!' He shouted. Old Talip turned the wheel as fast as he could. The ship pulled to the left with ease as it cut through the water. It was now traveling along the front line of the attacking ships. He watched them as they moved. He could see their archers lining up to fire.

'TAKE COVER!' Shouted Vimeo. Arrows thudded into the Sea Wolf. Most of the arrows fell short and no one was hit. They were nearly free from the bulk of the oncoming fleet. A Dragon ship broke away from the pack and tried to cut them off and block their path.

'Ram her, Talip' Vimeo ordered. The smaller Dragon ship cut across the path of the Sea Wolf, and at the last second Talip turned her into the Dragon ship.

'Brace yourselves!' Barus shouted. The Sea Wolf crashed into the side of the Dragon ship. A deafening crash sounded out as the bow of the Sea Wolf rose high into the air. The front of the ship had almost sailed right over the smaller Dragon ship, completely capsizing it. There were men screaming and shouting as they were catapulted into the sea. There was splintered wood everywhere from the impact. The Sea Wolf remained unscathed. The Dragon ship was pushed to the side of the Sea Wolf and was now sinking fast.

'Oars!' Barus shouted, and the Sea Wolf moved forward once more to the beat of the drum. They were free from the enemy fleet now as they moved past them. Random arrows were still hitting them as they pulled further away. The fleet were still heading toward the harbour, straight into the Royal warships. The Sea Wolf then turned again and began to give chase.

'Drop Sails!' Vimeo ordered. Barus and Pittana pulled at ropes and the sails fell into place. As the wind filled them, they stretched out to their fullness. The ship cut through the water even faster now with both wind and oars working together. Barus looked over to his captain, he could see his red scarf flapping in the wind. Vimeo looked back, they both smiled at one another at the feeling of the ship at full speed.

'Now we are sailing, Barus.'

'That we are, Captain.'

'Arm the Scorpion Barus.' Barus moved to the bow and opened the long chest and took out a long iron arrow. He armed the Scorpion. Pittana struggled to lift out a second arrow and waited for Barus. They were gaining on the fleet now. As they approached the first of the Dragon Ships, Barus took aim. He fired the first arrow and it hit home at the stern of the enemy ship, right on the water line. Wood exploded from the back of the ship. A huge hole was punched open. The Dragon ship slowed down and started to take on water, fast. The Sea Wolf passed by and on to the next ship. Pittana handed the next Iron arrow to Barus, and he quickly armed the Scorpion again and fired on the next vessel. Arrows from the sinking ships were firing on the Sea Wolf now. One passed close by Pittana, almost hitting him.

'Keep low.' He shouted to the boy. They sailed through the fleet, sinking ship after ship with their new weapon. Jerra was thrilled to see it in action. As they got to the front of the fleet, the Royal ships were attacking too. The Fleet were in disarray now. Dragon ships crashed into each other, trying to escape the onslaught of the Sea Wolf. Some tried to ram the Sea Wolf, but its hull was too strong. One Dragon ship crashed into the side of the bigger ship and tried to board the Sea Wolf, but its deck was too high. Jerra's men fired down on them with arrows, killing scores of Dragon soldiers as they manned their deck. The Sea Wolf continued to fire its weapon and sink more ships. It was unstoppable. Eventually, their flagship turned and broke from the chaos. The remaining ships followed in suit and sailed in the direction they had come from. The battle was over, and the victors all cheered as they watched the Dragon ships fleeing for their lives.

Lord Sabat lit his torch and moved quickly along the dark hallway towards the young Prince's room. His plans were well underway now, but he needed to act fast as time was running out. He had gained access to visit Prince Rain. A few weeks prior, Sabat had sprinkled some ground powder, taken from the poisonous Atrop plant, into Rain's food. It was only a small dose, but enough to make the child very sick. No one seemed to know what had made the young Prince sick, or how to cure him. The King had asked for Sabat's help in treating him, and now he had access to visit Rain once a day.

As he approached Rain's room, the Royal Guard moved across to guard the door. 'It is very late, and the Prince is sleeping now. You will have to come back tomorrow' the guard announced.

'I was unable to see Prince Rain earlier today, so the King has ordered me to see him now.'

The Guard did not move. 'Did you not hear me, soldier? I need to see the Prince.' The Guard struggled to decide on what to do. 'Move aside, soldier.' Sabat said in a stern manner.

'I have my orders, Lord Sabat. You will have to come see him in the morning.'

Sabat could feel his anger rising now. 'Very well then.' He turned to leave and then stopped and turned back towards the Guard. 'Just one more thing…' With that, Sabat raised his hand and blew a grey powder into the Guard's face. The guard instantly brought his hands to his eyes and started to cough and then choke. He fell to his knees and blood started to seep from his closed eyes. Sabat took a curved knife from his belt and struck downwards. The knife plunged deep into the Guard's neck and he fell, face first onto the ground, twitching as blood flowed out onto the stone floor. Sabat quickly entered the room and rushed over to the Prince's bed. Rain was fast asleep and looked very pale. The priest fixed his torch to the wall and then pulled back the covers and lifted the Prince up into his arms.

The boy opened his eyes. 'What is wrong?' He spoke with a weak voice.

'Don't worry, my Prince, I am just bringing you to a better place. Be still now.' Sabat left the room and moved down the dark hallway with the boy in his arms. His mind raced as he moved along in the dark. It was late, and there should not be anyone roaming around the palace, he hoped. His followers were late, they should have been there to support him. After a few more hallways, he entered the Royal Hall. At least it was well lit here. He raced across the open floor and was startled to see the Priests Ulauth and Giram moving towards him. Sabat stopped still.

Ulauth raised his hand. 'Lord Sabat, you are up late tonight. How is the Prince?'

'I have work to do, I have no time for talk.' Sabat went to move around the two men but Giram moved in his way to stop him.

'Come now, you have always time to talk to us.'

'Move out of my way, this boy is sick.'

Ulauth held out his hands. 'He does not look well at all Sabat. Give him over to me and I will bless him with the prayer of the Light.' Sabat moved backwards and was about to leave the hall the way he had come in.

'Hand over the Prince, Sabat. NOW!' Ulauth shouted at him.

Sabat could feel panic setting in. He quickly pulled out his curved knife and placed it under the boy's throat. 'Get away from me you two.'

'You don't want to do this, Sabat' said Giram, beckoning him to lower the knife.

'Move away or I will spill the Prince's blood all over the Royal Hall.'

Ulauth wiped his brow and then spoke in a low voice. 'You do that, and it will be the end of you, Sabat. Besides, we will be on you fast. You won't be able to get away. There are two of us.'

Just then they heard footsteps running. Doors to the side of the hall opened and eight of Sabat's followers entered the room, all with long knives in hand. Relieved now, Sabat smiled and looked back at Ulauth and Giram. 'Do you think the two of you can defeat me now?'

A low voice then came from behind Ulauth and Giram. 'No, but I think I might be of some help.' General Arthen limped out to stand between Ulauth and Giram with his sword in hand.

Sabat's laughter echoed across the hall. 'A coward priest, a fat tax man and you, Arthen, are half crippled. My followers will make short work of you three.'

'That maybe so, I think we might have to even up those odds.'

Captain Barra, the King's Champion, then walked into the hall and drew his sword. Sabat cursed, then shouted to his followers. 'Kill them!' The eight followers rushed in and Arthen and Barra met them head on. As the fighting started, Giram rushed Sabat and tried to grab the Prince from his grasp.

Sabat pulled back and yelled at Giram. 'Do not try that again or I will kill the Prince.'

Ulauth then grabbed for the Prince and managed to catch his arm and tried to pull him from Sabat. Sabat knew he would not be able to take the young Prince with him. He pressed his knife into the boy's neck, slicing into his skin, and blood flowed out over his hand.

Giram shouted. 'NO!'

Ulauth pulled the boy towards him and Sabat let go and ran from the hall. Ulauth, Giram, Arthen and Barra dispatched the last of the followers, leaving the hall floor scattered with dead bodies. Sabat raced from the palace. The rain was coming down heavily now and he could feel his clothes getting wet. He slowed down to a brisk walk as he approached the Palace gate. A guard, who was unaware of what had just happened, was guarding the gate that led to the streets below. He came out of his shelter and opened the gate as Sabat got closer. Sabat, having successfully left the palace, ran down along the streets to the main courtyard. He was relieved to see his followers were waiting for him. Nineteen in total.

The first follower spoke as Sabat got close. 'Is the Prince not with you?'

'No, there was a last-minute change of plan. Are all of you armed and ready to flee?'

'Yes, my Lord We are all ready.'

'Come with me, all of you. We have little time. This will get bloody.' Just then a horn sounded out. Sabat cursed out loud. 'They have signalled, this might hamper our plan as it will alert all the guards at the gate.' They walked on towards the gate. As they got close, a large number of guards came down from the wall and were running straight at them. 'Be steady, my friends.' Sabat spat out. The guards just ran past and on towards the palace to answer the signal. 'Good' said Sabat. 'This will leave less guards to kill at the gate.'

At the base of the gate there was a captain standing by the stairs. He noticed Sabat and his men approaching. 'What seems to be the problem at the Palace, Sabat? Why was the horn signalling?' he asked.

'It is a minor problem, Captain. The Palace Guards think they have an intruder. I have been sent by General Arthen to help guard at the gate while most of your guards see to the problem.'

'That would be beneficial.'

The Captain moved from the bottom of the stairs and let Sabat's followers up into the gate tower and onto the ramparts. The Captain then turned to Sabat. 'Are you coming up too?'

'Yes, lead the way please.'

The Captain turned to go up the stairs and Sabat drew his knife and grabbed the Captain by his hair. Tilting his head back, he sliced the sharp blade across his throat and pushed the dying man to the ground. Sabat moved up the stairs to watch his followers killing all the guards that were either sleeping or resting. Muffled screams sounded out but were masked by the sound of the falling rain. Sabat knew he had little time and moved fast to get the gate opened. He called out to some of his followers. 'Open the gates now.' They ran down and lifted the huge wooden plinth from the back of the doors and then others turned the wheel above the doors. The huge gate started to move, creaking open. Sabat took up two torches from the wall and waved them high into the air as a signal. He then moved back down the stairs and out through the open gates, where he could hear the rushing of men coming towards them in the darkness.

'Quickly!' He called out to his men. 'Move along the line of the walls until we are free from the gate way' he said, fearing they would get caught up in the killing. Free from the surprise attack, he looked back to see hundreds of Dragon troops moving through the open gate and into the city within. It would be a slaughter. Only a miracle could save the city now.

43

The first wave of Dragon soldiers moved into the city through the open gate and started killing the guards. Once they secured the gate, they held it open for the army behind them to start surging in. Skirmishes broke out along the walls and then battles started in the streets. More and more Latonian soldiers rushed to the fighting but were soon killed. Horns sounded out over the city to alarm everyone, but it was too late. The Dragon Army were now inside and killing everyone as they moved on through the city. The city was in chaos now, guards ran to the safety of the palace and then its doors were barred shut, leaving the rest of the city's inhabitants to fend for themselves. The Latonian people on the streets ran in terror. Most locked themselves into their homes and tried to hide from the chaos. The walls around the palace were manned with many Royal Guards. Within the palace, word had got out that the young Prince had been murdered. The King felt numb as he stood over his crying wife as she cradled her dead son. She sat uncontrollable in a puddle of his blood.

Arthen and Barra made their way over to their King. 'We must go, your highness. The enemy has breached the outer walls. We are all in danger now.' The King said nothing. Shouts and screams could be heard outside of the Palace in the distance. Giram then took the King by his arm and the King shrugged him off.

'I am not going anywhere' the King said in a low tone. 'All is lost, nothing matters anymore. My son, the Heir to this Kingdom, has been murdered. Nothing matters anymore.'

Giram sighed. 'We must take the Queen to safety too.'

'Go! Take them, I will wait for whatever awaits me here on my throne. I shall not run.'

Arthen then interrupted. 'It is unsafe here, my King. We must go now.'

'I am staying here. You go, you all go. Take the Queen to safety. That is a direct order.'

'I will stay with you.' Arthen said.

'You are my loyal General. I owe you a lot, but I need you to take the Queen and the others. They will need you. I will face this Emperor alone. This is the way it must be. These are my last orders and they will be obeyed.'

Arthen could feel his heart breaking. He drew his sword and turned it. He handed it to his King hilt first. 'This is the sword that guards the King. Take it from me, so it is with you in your time of need.' The King took the sword, and Giram and Ulauth lifted the crying Queen to her feet while Barra lifted the dead prince into his arms. The Queen's legs gave out and she almost fell. Giram and Ulauth caught her and held her up. They all moved away and left the hall. Arthen stopped and turned back to his King. 'It was an honour serving under you, my King. Make sure you bury that sword in your enemy.' The King nodded and Arthen was gone. The King made his way to his throne and settled in to wait for the Emperor to arrive, as the noises outside the palace got louder and the fighting raged on.

The group rushed along the corridors and down steep steps to the lower levels of the Palace. Some soldiers gathered with them as they went. 'Down here, we will barricade ourselves in.' Arthen shouted.

'We will be trapped' said Ulauth in a panic.

Arthen grabbed him by the shoulder. 'No, there is a river that travels under the Palace. We should be able to swim along it and can use this to escape. It comes up outside of the walls on the West side of the city.' They all moved deeper and deeper down the steep steps below the Palace.

The Queen, still crying, suddenly stopped. 'Where is Thianni?'

'We do not have time to go back now. They will be upon us.' Arthen uttered.

'No, we must. She will be all alone and frightened.'

'The King has given us orders to bring you to safety.'

'And We have given our promise to protect her.'

'I'm sure she will get out of the palace and flee the city. The palace is full of Royal Guards. They will protect her.' At the end of the stairs the was a large oak door. Arthen pushed it open and the party went inside. 'Block this door with anything you can find.' Arthen then lit the torches. He looked over at the river. It was a raging torrent. The rains of the last few weeks had caused a swell, and now the river had filled the tunnels to its maximum.

Ulauth saw the shock on Arthen's face and went to him. 'We will not be able to get out through there. How long does the tunnel run for Arthen?'

'Too long' Arthen replied with a sigh. 'Our only hope now is that the city guards will fight off the Imperial Dragon hordes.'

King Roban looked down at his hands. They were trembling now. Grief swept over him as he thought about his young son. The King tried to fight back tears and the sight of his boy lying on the floor with his throat cut kept flashing in his mind. He coughed to clear his throat. It was dry so he made his way over to the table where there was some wine. He tried to pour himself a cup, but his trembling hands would not allow it, and the red wine spilt over the table and onto the floor. The sight of the red wine triggered the sight of his son, lying in a pool of his own blood, again. His emotions flooded over him and he cried out. He pushed the cup and wine from the table, and they crashed to the floor. He tried to gather himself with deep breaths.

'I must be strong now' he said aloud. He turned to go back to his throne and found himself face to face with a young Royal soldier in full armour. The soldier was smiling at him.

'Can I help you your Highness?' he said, still smiling.

'Yes, you could pour me a cup of wine.'

The young soldier quickly picked up the cup and wiped it clean, then he poured out a full cup from another bottle with his back to the King. The soldier handed it to his King with a bow and the King thanked him and drank deeply. The soldier waited as the King drank all the cup's contents. After finishing the cup, the King wiped his mouth.

'You should take your position guarding the palace walls. Or better still, be trying to flee this doomed place. The enemy will be here very soon.'

'Yes, your Highness. I will be leaving shortly. Before I leave, can I ask you something?'

The King laughed at such a question in this time of turmoil. 'Yes, ask away soldier.'

'Do you know my name?'

The King looked at him and shook his head. 'No, I don't believe I do, but please do tell me.'

The soldier's smile started to fade. 'My name is Jann.'

The King shrugged his shoulders. 'It is a good name.'

'I wanted you to know the name of the person who kills you.'

The King looked shocked now. He could feel a sharp pain in the pit of his stomach, and it travelled up within his body. He dropped the cup he was holding, and it made an echoing throughout the Royal Hall as it crashed to the floor. He tried to take a step toward the young soldier, but his legs failed him, and he fell forward onto his hands and knees, his crown falling from his head and spinning on the palace floor. The King heaved and then vomited out blood onto the stone floor.

'You have just consumed a large dose of poison. You have only moments left before you leave this world. Have you any last words?'

The King fell forward onto his stomach and then turned onto his back. He grasped at his throat in agony and tried to speak. Jann moved in closer, to try and hear what the King was trying to say. 'Nothing matters anymore,' the King gurgled. The King then reached down and drew the sword that Arthen had given him. He tried to lash out at the soldier with the sword, but it fell from his grasp. A trembling motion erupted in his body and with one violent jerk, his body became still. His last breath left his body, the King was dead. Jann reached down and removed the King's Royal rings from his hands and pocketed them. He looked at the crown on the ground and thought about taking it too, but if he was caught with it, they would certainly know it was him who had killed the King. He shrugged off the idea and then left the hall and disappeared down the corridors.

From the shadows of the outer hall, a man stepped out. There was a whisper. 'You have beat me to my job, but I will remember your name, Jann.' He then moved back into the shadows.

The city of Kitia was in the distance now. Sabat looked back to see the fires raging within its walls were glowing in the night sky. Although his plan to kidnap the Prince had failed, he was happy to see the city fall. He moved on with his followers. 'We must be quick now. I am to meet my brother.'

'Where are we to meet him?' asked a follower.

'We will travel south along the coastline. There is a small fishing village about five miles from here. That is the meeting place.' After some time walking in the drizzling rain, the group came to the fishing village. Oranius was waiting for them with his followers. Sabat and Oranius embraced.

'I am glad you made it brother' said Oranius.

'You too. It has been many years since I last saw you.'

Oranius looked around. 'Where is the Prince?'

'It did not go to plan. I had to kill him in order to get out alive.'

'This is not good news, Sabat. We needed a sacrifice of Royal Blood in order to allow The Dark Lord to enter our world. What will we do now?'

'There is another we can use. We must start new plans now to make this happen, we must move quickly.'

'The Dark Lord will not be happy.'

'I know, and that is something I must face.'

The group of priests moved down onto the beach, where there were small boats waiting for them. The sky was starting to lighten now, as the sun threatened to rise. They rowed out to a ship and boarded it. The ship then raised its anchor, dropped its sails and sailed South.

44

Kalin and Chal galloped along with their men behind them. It was dark out now and as they crested the hill, a mass of tents came into view, glowing with campfires scattered throughout. Kalin raised his hand, signalling for all the riders to stop. The campsites looked deserted, apart from a few Dragon soldiers on guard duty around fires. In the distance, Kitia was visible. It looked like it was partly engulfed in flames.

Kalin turned to Chal. 'I hope we are not too late. By the looks of those fires in the distance, the city is under attack. Are you going to make your way out to your mother?'

'No, I will go with you to the city first and kill as many of these invaders as I can.'

'That sounds like a good plan, Chal.'

'It's the least we can do after coming this far. I am hoping they have not yet reached my home.'

'I hope so too, my friend. Firstly, I think we should destroy their camps, make sure they have nothing to come back to.'

Kalin ordered five hundred of his men to set alight and destroy the enemy's camps and then follow on into the city as support. The bulk of the Gantian force moved on fast towards the city as the 500 charged down towards the unsuspecting Dragon Soldiers guarding their tents. As they reached the East Gate, their worst fears came to reality. The Empire's forces were inside the city. They could hear screaming and shouting and fighting within. Kalin signalled for the Gantians to halt. He looked back on the force of warriors. Thunder rumbled across the hills behind them in the distance, and he could see lightning hitting the distant trees.

'Hear me now. There is a storm coming this way. It rages with all its might. It rages with us. To us it is the Gods' anger. Let us be the storm now, let the Empire feel our anger.'

Kalin drew his sword, turned his horse and sped forward with his Gantian warriors at his back. He led his horsemen through the opened gate and instantly they were met with Dragon forces.

'Kill all Dragon troops,' commanded Kalin as he hacked his sword down, killing the first Dragon Soldier. The Gantian horsemen, along with Chal and his men, moved inside, hacking and slashing from left to right from their mounts. The fighting was fierce but the Gantian forces were fresh and up against half-starved and weak Dragon Soldiers. Chal tried to keep close to Kalin. He watched his friend in awe, as he killed with great speed any Dragon Soldier that came close to him. Kalin made his way through the streets, killing as he went, with his men and Chal close behind. There were dead everywhere, men, women and children paved the streets, with blood filling the cracks of the cobblestone paths and roads. Deeper and deeper they pushed into the city, killing as they moved. Further in, most of the homes had not yet been broken into or set alight. Chal saw Kalin jump from his horse. He banged on the door of his aunt's home. It had not been touched yet.

'Auntie Reesa, it is Kalin, are you OK.'

Moments later the door opened slightly, and the scared eyes of Mara peered out. He was holding a long knife in his hand. He dropped it when he recognised it was Kalin.

'Kalin, you are a sight to see' said Mara with a shaky voice.

Reesa then came running out and hugged Kalin. 'Oh Kalin, thank the Gods you are still alive. It is truly great to see you.'

'Are you both OK?'

'Yes, we are fine, so far.' Reesa looked around at all the warriors with Kalin. 'I see you have made some new friends.'

'Yes, and fine ones at that. We have a small army of Gantian warriors hungry to cut down these invaders.'

'That is so good to hear Kalin. We have nowhere to run so we just locked ourselves inside.' The look on Kalin's face was one of relief.

'I must make my way to the Palace, but I am going to leave you with a guard. I have a large Gantian force with me. They are busy killing the Dragon Soldiers. All behind us are dead. Stay inside no matter what.'

Kalin called out for Bellarus. The big man rode up to Kalin and dismounted. 'I need you to stay here and protect my Auntie and Uncle. This is Reesa, Karra's sister.'

'I would be honoured to keep you safe Reesa, Sister of Karra.'

Reesa hugged Kalin once more. 'Keep yourself alive.'

Mara patted Kalin on the back. 'We'll have honey cakes later, my boy.'

They moved inside, followed by Bellarus. The doors were shut and locked, and Kalin and Chal set off, followed by Leib, Rovan, Tornos, Atora and the rest of the small group of men. The Gantian warriors were storming through the city on horseback. They all moved on toward the palace. The main bulk of the Gantian Warriors were spread out in groups, fighting and killing the Dragon soldiers. Fires were blazing where homes and buildings had been set alight. The storm was above the city now, and the rain poured down on the chaos below as lightning flashed across the dark, stormy night sky.

Chal shouted over to Kalin. 'I am going to make my way up to the barracks to see if there are any survivors. I will meet you back here later.'

Kalin nodded back to Chal. 'Stay alive and kill many' he shouted to his friend, and the two separated.

Most of the Dragon soldiers fought their way through the city streets and forced their way in through the palace gates. Skarin and Jargo walked in front of the Emperor as they moved inside the palace grounds. Their men were fighting well but were taking huge losses. The Royal Guards were fresh and had been fed better and well rested over the last few weeks. The Dragon Soldiers were almost exhausted. The cold, wet weather had taken its toll on them, but still they fought on.

The Emperor turned to his General. 'Jargo, have they captured the King yet.'

'I am not sure, your Highness, but it is only a matter of time.'

'Take me to the Throne Room, I wish to take his throne now.'

They moved into the Palace, killing everyone they came across. There were a large number of dead strewn on the floors within the palace, most of them Dragon Soldiers. They made their way into the main hall. The Emperor was disappointed to see the King was already dead on the floor in front of the throne, but this was the aftermath of war. He walked to the throne and turned to his men as they filled into the Royal Hall.

The Emperor's voice echoed out across the hall. 'This is a tremendous day for the Empire. We have conquered a nation that they said could not be conquered. I am now, truly, The God King I was meant to be.' He then sat proudly back on the throne, savouring his moment. Jargo picked up the Dead King's crown, walked up the steps to his Emperor and placed the crown upon his head.

The Emperor sat back and threw his arms out to his sides. 'Now go and kill the rest of them.' The hall emptied as his troops spread out through all the exits in search of their enemy. Skarin placed his black horned helmet on his head and left with his men, leaving only Jargo and a handful of Imperial Guards to protect the Emperor.

Thianni ran down the hallway, frantic. There was screaming and shouting everywhere. People were being killed and there was nothing she or anyone could do to stop it. The enemy were now in the Palace. Up ahead, she saw Sabby's head popping out of her cleaning room. 'Quick Thianni, in here!' she shouted. Thianni rushed inside and Sabby closed the door and locked it behind her. Tiffin was also inside, holding a lit candle. Sabby started to panic and cry.

'What are we going to do?' Thianni put her arms around her to comfort her. Tiffin was looking around the small room with the light of the candle. 'We don't even have weapons to protect ourselves.'

'Listen both of you. This is what we are going to do. They will move through the Palace, hopefully they will overlook this room. We will hide out here and when things settle down, we will leave this room and escape Kitia. There is a river that runs under the palace. We will wade through this. It leads out under the walls. We will then head North to Gemas. There is a stronghold there, we will seek safety.'

They could hear running outside of the room, and movement. The handle on the door was turned but they could not get in. They then heard shouting and more running, and it went quiet once more. The girls huddled together at the back of the small room, all frightened. A thunderous bang sounded on the door and all the girls jumped. Sabby was shaking uncontrollably now. A foreign accent shouted out and the banging on the door increased.

There was a large number of Latonians hiding down under the Palace in the depths of the building. Giram listened at the door. It was hard to hear anything outside of the room with the rushing water flowing from the river passing from tunnel to tunnel in the sewer. He pressed his ear against the door and listened carefully. Just then a large axe exploded through the door right beside his face. Giram fell backwards on to his backside with a thud.

'They are breaking through.' Giram jumped back up and ran to the back of the group beside Ulauth. The door was now being picked apart by the axe as it smashed its way through again and again sending splinters of wood spraying inwards. Queen Lesta was cradling her dead son Rain. Kissing him one last time on the forehead, she gently placed him on the floor and covered him with her shawl. The handful of Latonian Soldiers drew their swords and waited for the attackers to break through. Arthen moved to the front of the line of men with Barra and they drew their swords also. The door smashed open and Dragon Troops surged in and the fighting began.

Imperial General Jargo watched his Emperor as he relished the drama unfolding. All around them, the city was in battle and skirmishes were taking place. Jargo felt very uneasy, especially at how calm the Emperor was. The crown slid slightly on the Emperor's head and he adjusted it back into place, then turned to Jargo. 'It won't be long now until we have killed every last one in this city.'

'I am uncomfortable just waiting here, your highness. I think we should get to a safer place until we can take full control.'

'Nonsense General, we will be fine here. Our Dragon troops are everywhere.'

'I know, but they have been left weakened with this sickness.'

Just then, sounds of fighting could be heard from a corridor that led from the hall. Jargo looked around. There were ten Imperial Guards with them in the hall. The Emperor pointed in the direction of the fighting.

'Go and help deal with that, General.'

'I will send the Guards to deal with it and I will stay and guard you.'

'No, I will be fine here. There can't be many left alive in the palace at this stage. Go, and deal with the remaining Royal Soldiers. That is an order, General.'

Jargo turned and took off, reluctantly, with the ten guards down the corridor.

The Emperor sat back on the Throne in pure contentment at what he had achieved.

Bakal jumped from his horse and splashed his hands down into the river. Dried blood from his skin and the sleeves of his tunic was washed downstream as the running water cleaned him. He pushed his face into the cold water and drank deeply in between heavy breaths. He looked back to see if he was being followed. There was nothing. The screams of the dying Dragon Soldiers, that were under attack by the Gantian warriors, were long out of earshot. He took one more drink and then moved to his horse, which was also drinking by the river's edge. The horse was secreting foam from its mouth from the forced galloping. Bakal opened a dark brown sack and checked inside. Satisfied the Iron was there, he looked up to the black night. The rain had stopped but the dark clouds were gathering again, high in the night sky. He felt cold now, and his sleeves were wet from drinking the cold river water. He heard a distant noise and jerked his head around to try and hear it again. There was nothing. *'I must get the iron back to Parica,'* he thought. Bakal jumped back onto his horse and kicked his heels in hard and continued to travel south.

The Emperor sat alone, listening to the sweet sounds of battle. The hall was empty now. He felt a wave of weariness come over him. The Emperor looked down at the dead King and took his heavy, armoured breastplate off and let it crash to the floor. Just then, he saw a movement from the shadows of the hall. A man walked out and towards him.

'Who are you?' the Emperor's voice boomed out.

'I am the Royal Chef, your highness. I work in the kitchen.'

The Emperor was surprised he could speak the language of Eamhair. 'You speak my language very well, I like that.' The man kept moving slowly towards him. 'You are in luck today, chef. I could do with a good chef in my service. I think I will spare you.'

'That is most kind of you, your Highness, but I think I will be leaving the job as a chef and going back to my old profession.' The Emperor looked at him now interestedly. 'You see, I was sent here to do a certain job, but someone got there before me.' With slow steps, the man moved ever closer to the Emperor.

The Emperor started to get concerned. 'You are starting to irritate me now, Chef. Be gone while I am still in a good mood and you still have your life.'

'That is the thing, your Highness. I can't leave. Not just yet. I have accepted a job and I can't rest until that job has been completed.'

'And what is this job you speak of.'

'I am glad you asked that question' said the chef with a smirk. The Emperor slid forward on the throne to hear the man. 'My job is to kill the man that sits on the throne. And seeing as the King is now dead and you now sit on the Throne…' There was a pause. The chef came in close to the Emperor. 'I want you to know. When I have given my word, I always carry it out.' The Emperor's jaw dropped. The chef launched forward and, with a flash of his right hand, stabbed the Emperor through the heart with a long blade. The Emperor grabbed at the chef's hand but hadn't the strength to stop the attack. The chef twisted the knife and then let go. The Emperor pulled the knife free with a shriek. Blood pumped rhythmically out over his clothes. He fell forward onto the floor beside the King. He tried to get up, but his hand slipped in his own blood and he fell back down, powerless. As the light of the room faded, he heard a whisper in his ear. 'Even a God King can die. Now my job is done, I can rest.'

The door was starting to give and Sabby screamed as it burst open and light flooded in. A large Dragon Soldier stood silhouetted in the doorway; his black armour drenched in blood. He stared at the three inside and Thianni could see he was licking his lips with a look of lust. She thought about taking the poison, but her will to live fought against it.

'Stay away from us' she shouted at him.

He started to enter the room, but suddenly froze. The look on his face changed. A sword appeared out of his chest and he pitched forward and fell face down. Dead. Thianni could not believe her eyes. Kalin was standing there, smiling at her, where the Dragon soldiers had stood mere seconds before.

'I have great memories of the last time I was in this room' Kalin said playfully.

Thianni blinked a couple of times. Was she dreaming? She launched herself forward into his arms. Tears were flowing from her eyes now with relief and love for Kalin.

'What are you doing here?'

'You saved me that day I dropped the cake, remember? I thought it was only polite to pay it back and come and save you.'

'Oh Kalin, I am so happy to see you.' She looked up and kissed him. 'I have missed you so much.'

Just then, a scream sounded out close by, bringing Thianni abruptly back to reality.

'We must go, Kalin, there are Dragon Soldiers everywhere.'

'There are not as many as before. I brought a small army with me from Gantia and they are helping the Royal Guards to defeat the Dragon Soldiers as we speak.'

Two Dragon Soldiers rushed Kalin from the side. Kalin spun and pulled Thianni behind him to protect her. He blocked a sword attack from the lead attacker and killed him with a reverse thrust and then spun again and cut the second attacker's head clean from his body.

'You are right Thianni we should try and get you and your maids to a safer place while this battle is still being fought.' He looked back in at the two frightened maids. 'Come with me please ladies. I will make sure you are safe.'

As they left the small room, a group of Dragon soldiers came into sight at a cross section in the corridors. They started to run at Kalin and Thianni when, from the side corridors Leib, Rovan, Tornos and Atora intercepted them, killing them quickly.

Kalin turned to Thianni. 'Remind me to introduce you to my friends later.'

Leib, Rovan, Tornos and Atora joined Kalin and Thianni. They all moved on through the palace. Kalin and his men killed any enemies they came across. Once they were free from the palace, they ran towards Kalin's auntie's home. A war was raging all around them in the streets of the city. Homes and buildings were on fire and everywhere was chaos. They arrived at the home of Reesa and Mara.

Kalin banged on the door. 'Open up auntie, it's me Kalin.'

The door opened and a huge, black bearded man was standing there, taking up the entire doorway with a smile and a honey cake in his hand. Reesa pushed her way past him and came to the door. 'Thank the Gods you are safe Kalin.'

'It is nearly over Auntie. The Princess needs to shelter here until it is all over.'

'The more the merrier.' Reesa called them in.

Kalin gestured for Thianni and her maids to go inside. He turned to Thianni, 'you will be safe here until all the fighting is finished.'

Kalin then turned to Leib, 'can I ask you to stay and guard the Princess?'

'It would be my honour Kalin.'

'Thank you Leib.'

Thianni grabbed Kalin and kissed him. 'Please be careful.'

Kalin smiled at her. 'I will see you soon.' and they all went inside and Bellarus locked the door behind them.

Kalin turned to the rest of the small group, Rovan, Tornos, and Atora. 'Let us seek out and kill as many as we can. A shout went out and Chal and his second, Alain, came running over to them. Chal was covered in splashes of blood.

Kalin looked his friend up and down. 'Please tell me that's the enemy's blood?'

'Of course, Kalin, and I intend to keep it that way.'

Dragon soldiers had started to fill the road up ahead and they were making their way down to the group.

Chal looked at Kalin, 'Are you ready to get bloody?'

Kalin smiled back at Chal. 'Always my friend.'

The group advanced and met the Dragon Soldiers head on. The fighting was fierce and bloody. The large group of Dragon soldiers were no match for Kalin, and his friends and they were dispatched quickly.

Kalin let out a shout to his friends. 'Let's find more.'

Chal called to Kalin as he was walking off. 'I am going to go into the Palace to see if there are any survivors.'

'OK Chal, I will meet you back at Reesa's house. Stay safe.'

'You too, my friend.' Chal and Alain hurried off towards the Palace.

Jargo moved back to the main hall with some of his men. He could see straight away that the throne was unoccupied. He scanned the room with panic and then saw his Emperor lying on the floor next to the King. He ran to him. He knew before he got to him that he was dead. He was lying in his own blood.

Jargo knelt down beside him. 'A God has died today.' He turned to his captain. 'Sound out the retreat. The war is over.'

Deep under the palace, the fight raged on. Arthen was tiring fast now. They had killed all that stood in front of them, but all the Royal Guards were now dead on the ground. The Queen, Giram and Ulauth were standing back, away from the fighting. There were footsteps, and more Dragon Soldiers entered through the broken door. Arthen had lost count of how many he had killed and now more awaited. A shout sounded out and the Dragon Soldiers within the room pulled back. A large, dark figure entered the room. He was tall and lean with broad shoulders and clad in black armour. His helmet had huge, black, curved horns coming from both sides of his helmet. An enormous feeling of evil emanated from this man. Arthen looked over at Barra, who was smiling at the challenge that stood before them. Barra looked fresh and ready to fight on. At that moment, Arthen wished he was ten years younger. More soldiers packed into the room behind the horned warrior.

Arthen called out to Barra. 'It will be a fine send off. It was nice fighting alongside you Barra.'

'And you too, my General.' A noise sounded from up the stairway and fighting broke out. It seemed that the Dragon Soldiers were fighting on the stairway outside the room also. The horned warrior advanced and swung his sword. Arthen was lucky to block the blow. The force from it knocked him from his feet. Barra was upon the horned warrior with frenzied strikes. Arthen stood, and the horned warrior struck him once more and knocked him back down. Arthen's strength was draining fast. He could hardly get back up. Sweat stung his eyes. Barra was struggling to hold the warrior.

Arthen looked back at the doorway and for a split second he thought he could see his old friend, General Titus Cassian. He blinked the sweat from his eyes and saw that it was, in fact, his son, Captain Chal, fighting his way through the black armoured attackers, with his men with him. The sight of Chal coming to their rescue gave him strength. He pushed himself from the ground and stood.

'One last fight' he said to himself. A distant horn sounded out and the horned warrior pulled back from Barra. He shouted out to the remaining Dragon Soldiers and they started to retreat back out through the doorway. Chal moved in front of the horned warrior to block him from leaving. They both locked eyes. Chal attacked first but as he pushed off his back foot, he slipped on the blood drenched floor and lost his balance. The horned warrior took advantage of this and spun and drove his sword into Chal then pulled it free. He walked past Chal and out through the door and up the stairs. Chal fell to the ground. Barra and Arthen moved in to help Chal as he lay on the ground, bleeding.

Arthen looked back at the remaining group. 'Bring me some water please.'

Then, 'NO!' Ulauth shouted out as he rushed to the Queen. Her eyes were open in a lifeless stare and her face was snow white. She was laying by Rain's body with a small empty vial beside her hand.

Skarin fought his way out of the palace with his men. Their losses were great. There were Gantian warriors everywhere, killing any Dragon Soldiers they happened upon. There were riderless horses gathering under a shelter from the rain. Skarin made his way over and mounted one. His men took what horses they could. The horns sounded out again for the Empire's army to retreat. Hundreds of them were running to the gate they had come in through. Some were still fighting in the streets.

A Dragon soldier shouted out 'The Emperor has been killed! Retreat! Retreat!'

Skarin kicked his mount and he sped off down through the streets, pushing his way past enemy and foe. More and more Dragon soldiers were fleeing the city now. The gate was still open, and Skarin pushed his way out through all the others that were running. Once free, he made his way to the smouldering campsite. Everyone there was dead. He pushed on through the camp until he arrived at Bakal's smouldering tent. There was no sign of the man's body.

'You sly devil, you got out.' Skarin dismounted and looked around the remains of the tent. He was looking for the blood iron Bakal was collecting. There was none. Happy now that Bakal had escaped with the iron, he mounted his horse again and headed south along the stone path.

45

Summer was in full bloom, and the mood in the city of Kitia had finally changed from dread to happiness. After the Emperor was killed and his Dragon army was driven from the city of Kitia and the lands of Latonia, there was a sense of relief for everyone that had survived the war. The Kingdom of Latonia had lost many of its citizens, loved ones, family and friends, including the King and Queen and their young son. This had been a devastating blow to all. A week of mourning was announced, and sorrow flooded the land. After the mourning, it was a time for new beginnings and a time to rebuild, but first the Kingdom had to elect a new Royal Leader.

Thianni stood waiting in her long, white, gold trimmed dress. She looked out over the assembly. The Royal Hall was packed with people, all looking at her. Many thoughts ran through her head. Thoughts of doubt and fear. She looked out over the crowded hall again. Although there were many people missing now, she recognised many faces, all smiling at her. She looked to her right. Seated beside her was General Arthen in full armour. It gleamed from the lights in the Royal Hall. Giram was sitting beside him. They were smiling at her also. To her left was the Champion, Barra, and Sabby and Tiffin. She looked over to the side of the steps and could see Kalin smiling back at her. He was with his Aunt and Uncle, and the dark man Leib was by his side. He had changed since they had first met, she thought. He was not a boy anymore; he was a man now. His black hair was long, tied back at the nape of his neck, and there was a short black beard on his face that had not been there before. He was very handsome as he looked at her with pride in his eyes. Trumpets sounded out, and she jumped. Nerves erupted again in her stomach.

The High Priest Ulauth walked out in his ceremonial gown, carrying a golden crown held out in front of him. He bowed to Thianni and turned to the assembled crowd. 'Today is a very special day, a new day for our people. Today we anoint a new ruler of Latonia. She is the sole heir to the throne and the last of her bloodline of the Casca family.'

The priest then turned to face Thianni. 'Do you, Thianni Casca, swear to uphold the law of Latonia with righteousness and valour?'

'Yes, I do.' Thianni heard herself say.

'Do you, Thianni Casca, swear to rule with justice and wisdom for all its people?'

'Yes, I do.'

'Do you promise to put the Kingdom first and the rights of the people that belong to this land above all?'

'Yes, I do.'

'I, as holder of the power to the House of Light, grant you the status of ruler of all the Kingdom of Latonia. I now Anoint you with this crown our one and true ruler. You are now our Queen.'

Trumpets sounded out again. Everyone clapped and cheered. Ulauth stepped in, placed the crown on her head and stepped back, bowing. He turned to the people in the hall. 'Bow now to our Sovereign, our Queen. Queen Thianni.' Everyone stood, cheering and clapping, as the trumpets sounded out again.

Arthen sat at the table. He took a drink and placed the cup back on the table with shaky hands. His eyes showed his grief. 'I find myself thinking about him a lot over these last few days. He was a very good friend of mine. A true warrior. He was taken from this world too early, but this is the nature of war. I want to give you this.' Arthen reached down from under the table and lifted up a Royal General's sash. 'This was your father's. I want you to have it.' He slid it over the table to Chal, who was sitting on the other side.

'Thank you, General Arthen. This means a lot to me. We have lost a great deal through this war.'

'That we have. It is time to rebuild now and get strong again. Speaking of rebuilding, how is your mother?'

'She is well, considering all that has happened. I am only back from visiting her at our farm. And thankfully, the villa was not touched. She fled the villa with the farm hands before the Emperor arrived at Kitia. If she had not, she would have been slain as the farm was raided for food. She is back now and working hard on getting the farm back up and running. She has hired extra help. The city needs the food. She took the death of my father badly and is still in mourning.'

'She is a great woman. She needs time to mourn for him, as do you. I will make sure she is paid well for her produce. We have plenty to fix and rebuild.'

Chal could feel himself getting emotional and changed the subject. 'Are there any signs of the Imperial Dragon Soldiers leaving Natalia?'

'No. My scouts say they still occupy the South wall and heavily occupy Natalia. However, both Cinam and Naos have revolted and fought the diminished Dragon soldiers, gaining back their lands. They only occupy Natalia now.'

'What is our next step, General?'

'I think we must rebuild our army and then march to the South Wall and free Natalia from this scum.'

'That sounds good to me. Can I ask a favour?'

'Yes, ask away.'

'Can I be part of this fight?'

'Yes, I can't see why not. We will need good Captains with us.'

'Good, I have some revenge I need to impose.'

The General laughed. 'I think we all do.' Chal agreed with a nod. 'One more thing Chal before we close this meeting. Are you entering in the men's Sword Fighting today? I hear Ultan The Sword Master will be entering. He has not competed in years, and it would be very interesting to see him in the finals against Barra.'

'No, not with my injury. The stitches are not out long, and I have no wish to open the wound back up.'

'Pity, as I heard a rumour that some of the Gantian men will be entering in this year's tournament. I would have liked to see how their fighting styles would fair out against you and Barra and Ultan. We will have to leave Ultan and Barra to teach them all some lessons in swordplay.'

'Yes, I heard that too. With the Queen's new rules, non Latonians will be allowed to enter now. But I don't think it will matter who enters the competition as Kalin has told me he is taking part.'

General Jargo rode wearily over the crest of the hill, with General Zukata and General Sana by his side, as the South Wall came into view.

Thousands of defeated Dragon Soldiers trailed back for miles. Jargo looked back at the six black stallions pulling the large cart that held the body of the dead Emperor. A horn sounded on the wall as they approached. The gates opened and they rode through onto the lands of Natalia. Once all the Dragon force were through, General Jargo ordered the gates to be shut. The Captain of the wall approached and bowed. 'My General. How are things?'

'Not good. We have been defeated; and worse, our Emperor has been slain.'

The Captain dropped down to one knee to express his condolences. Then all the Dragon Guards from the wall followed suit. General Jargo nodded and looked around. 'Please rise.' All the Guards followed orders. 'This is not an end to this war. This is just the beginning. We will go home for now to rebuild and strengthen our armies. We will come back bigger and stronger than before. For now, General Sana will take the command here. I will leave enough Dragon Soldiers to man and guard the wall. We will not let the lands of Natalia be taken. Now, we must push on as I need to inform Leta of her father's death.'

Even though the population of Kitia and the surrounding lands had decreased hugely from the war, there were more men entered in the sword fighting competition than ever before. A large number of these were Gantian Warriors. They had stayed on to help rebuild the city before they made the long journey back to the North. Kalin stood with his men, waiting for their names to be called out and place in the tournament. They all had enjoyed watching the racing and the boys' sword fighting. The skill level was very high.

Chal made his way to Kalin. He was walking with a slight limp from the wound he had received. 'I wanted to wish you luck in the tournament, but then I was thinking, you don't need it. The other fighters will.'

Kalin laughed. 'We will see my friend. Some of these men here today are great sword fighters. It should be a good tournament.'

The Queen was announced, and she took her place in the Royal Seats with her congress. She spotted Kalin and gave him a wave. The Queen then nodded to the official. He walked out and addressed the contestants and the watching crowds. 'Ladies and gentlemen, we will start the Men's Sword Fighting shortly. These games here today mark a special celebration. Our Queen has made new rules so everyone can now enjoy the competition. We will now let foreign nations join in, and for next year women will also be able to enter in the foot racing and the sword fighting.'

Talk went up amongst the crowds. Thianni felt that the people were not happy with these new rules. She stood and addressed them. The crowd fell silent. 'To everyone here, near and far. I have changed these rules so everyone can be equal. We are entering new times and because of this we need to change the way we think and especially the way we act. Our rules before stated that no foreigners were allowed to carry any weapons while in our lands. If the Gantian Warriors had abided by this rule, they would not have been able to come to our aid and turn the tide of the war. If we had not allowed our women to handle the bows on the walls of the city, the oncoming forces might have gained a foothold on our walls and overcome our city on the first wave of their attack. From now on, I want to make it clear that we will all be equal. We all need to change to make this happen.'

A few claps went up from the Gantian Warriors and then everyone joined in. She looked to Kalin and he was nodding his approval to her. Happy now, she sat back down. The official then announced the first names to enter the circles. There were six circled areas marked out on the ground for the fighters to fight within. Each fight would only last a few minutes, with the loser being eliminated from the competition and the winner moving on to the next stage. Kalin lined up for the next bout. His opponent was a middle-aged man. Kalin looked past his opponent and could see Brin, his old foe, lining up for his fight also. He looked like he had gained in size and he was much taller than the last time Kalin had seen him. Kalin was called to his first fight. He beat his opponent with ease and moved on to the next round. He smiled to himself and thought, this time it will be different. The bouts continued throughout the day and into the night. Everyone was enjoying the competition. Kalin was untouchable in his fights as he beat every warrior in front of him with his blinding speed. He had made it to the last four competitors. The four were, Kalin, Master Ultan, the City's Champion Barra and his old foe, Brin. There was silence as the four names were put into a bowl and the official drew out the first name. He called out Brin and then reached in and took out the second name. 'Kalin!' he shouted out.

The crowd all cheered as Kalin and Brin walked into the circle.

'You may choose your swords' announced the official.

Brin quickly rushed over to the sword rack and took up his sword. Kalin watched him, as Brin turned, he was grinning. Kalin then noticed that there was only one sword left on the rack. Brin had repeated his old trick on Kalin. As Kalin walked over to the rack, all eyes were on him. He could see it was the old, heavy, practice sword he had used to combat Brin before. Kalin tried to pick the sword up. He could hear Brin laughing. Kalin pretended he could not lift it out of the rack, that it was too heavy to lift.

'I see you are still a weak savage boy' called out Brin, still laughing. Whispers went out through the crowd. Brin spat on the ground. 'You couldn't win the boys competition last time; you certainly won't win the men's.'

A smile appeared on Kalin's face and he lifted the sword clear from the rack and spun it, slicing it through the air with ease. The crowd all cheered, watching the display. Kalin stopped dead with the sword pointing at Brin. He held it outstretched with one hand. Brin's smile faded from his face.

Then Kalin spoke. 'I'll show you what a savage boy can do.'

With that, Brin leapt forward in a high attack, bringing his sword down on Kalin. Kalin was too fast and stepped to the side, out of the sword's downward path. As Brin passed by him, Kalin tapped his sword onto Brin's head, leaving a red paint mark on Brin's forehead. Brin turned and attacked again with anger. Every time he attacked, Kalin moved and countered, leaving red marks all over Brin. The contest ended with the official calling time. The official counted all the strikes. There were red marks all over Brin.

'The winner is Kalin with 16 strikes to none. He will now move on to the final and face the winner of the next contest.'

Kalin looked over at Brin. He was breathing heavily and had a look of dejection on his face. Kalin walked to him and held out his hand. 'That's one win each Brin. I think we should leave it a draw from now on. What do you say?'

Brin squinted at Kalin, and there was no response for some time. Kalin's hand was still outstretched waiting for Brin. Brin looked around at the crowd. Then he nodded. 'Yes, I think we should call it quits.' Brin Shook Kalin's hand in agreement.

Kalin then turned to the official. 'I am now withdrawing from the contest.' He turned and walked from the circle, closely followed by Brin, to the shock of the onlookers. They all then clapped and cheered the two young fighters as they walked away. The official came forward and asked for the rack to be restocked with swords. He then announced for Master Ultan and the current Champion Barra to come forward for the finals. The two men walked into the circle, never taking their eyes from one another. The crowd all went quiet again. Master Ultan had never been beaten before in any sword contest and, when he had retired from competition, Barra had taken his place as champion and had won every year since. There had always been talk about who was the better swordsman. Now the time had come to see who the true Champion was.

'Choose your swords' the Official called out. The two men walked to the rack.

Master Ultan spoke as the two men looked through the selection of swords that were now on the rack. 'That was unexpected from Kalin.'

Barra replied. 'He is an honourable man and has nothing to prove to anyone.'

Master Ultan agreed with a nod. 'If I am to better you here, I am not sure I could have beaten Kalin.'

'Nor I,' said Barra, 'I have never in my life seen someone so fast.'

'So, where does this leave us, Captain Barra? Have you to prove you are better than me to someone?'

Barra stopped looking at the swords and thought about what Ultan had said. He turned to Ultan. 'No, I don't believe I have anything to prove.'

'Then why are we about to fight?'

'You are right, Ultan, I have nothing to prove to anyone.'

'Let us call a halt to the competition, Barra, and leave as equals.'

'Then we would never know who is the better between you and I.'

'That is true' said Ultan, as he picked out his sword.

Barra chose his and they both walked back to the centre of the circle, each still watching the other. They took up their positions. The Official shouted, 'Start!' and Ultan leapt forward with a stab to Barra's chest. Barra blocked it instantly, launching his own attack and Ultan easily evaded his sword. The fight continued back and forth with neither man able to land a strike on his opponent. Ultan was a much smaller man than Barra, and much older, but his fitness was never in question. The contest ended with the official calling time. He looked at both fighters to see if they had any red paint marks from the sword landing, but there were none.

'The fight will go for one more round, to determine a winner.'

After the two fighters had a short time to rest and some water, the second and final round was announced. 'Fight!' The Official sounded out. Barra and Ultan clashed once more in the centre of the circle. The second round was the same as the first and the fighters put on an impressive display of defensive and offensive sword fighting. There was not a sound from the onlookers as they watched in amazement.

'Time!' called out the Official again, stopping both fighters in mid action. The official checked both fighters again for red marks. 'No score for either fighter. The fight is a draw.'

Barra grinned at Ultan. 'Maybe we will never know who the best is?'

Ultan relaxed his hand and dropped his sword down by his side. 'I am OK with that Barra. Are you?'

'Yes, I think I can live with that but I'm not so sure the crowd will.' The crowd were all shouting for one more round.

The Queen stood and held out her hand. The noise level dropped. 'I want to say thank you to all who took part in the tournament today. Especially to the participants in the last two contests. I am happy with the result. Now Kitia has not one Champion, but two.' The Official raised both Barra's and Ultan's hands and the crowd cheered on.

Thianni and Kalin undressed under the canopy. The sun was starting to set on the horizon, colouring everything in a deep red glow. The sound of the waves crashed onto the shore with a steady rhythm. They were the only ones on the beach, apart from the Royal Guards standing way off on the rocks. Thianni was ready first. She pushed Kalin over as he was undressing and trying to balance on one leg. She then ran down to the sea, waded into the warm water and dived into an oncoming wave, surfacing further out to sea. Kalin got back to his feet and watched her as she pulled back her wet hair from her face. She was only wearing a thin white tunic, and now that it was wet, it clung to her body. He could make out every shape and was drawn to her breasts. He felt a sense of sadness come over him. He knew he would have to travel North again very soon and leave the woman he loved behind him. His bad dreams had returned, and he knew it was because he was away from the Gate.

'Are you coming in?' Thianni shouted back to Kalin. He smiled and then ran down to her in just his under trunks. He waded out to her. As he got closer, Thianni dived under the water again and swam out further to sea. It was much deeper here, and her feet could not reach the bottom. She treaded water and spun around to look at Kalin, but he was nowhere to be seen.

She called out for him. 'Kalin!' She could not see him anywhere. She looked up and down but nothing. Just as she was about to swim back in, Kalin burst out of the water in front of her, giving her a fright. She splashed water at him. They both laughed as they treaded the water.

'I was starting to worry there. I thought you said you could not swim?'

'I couldn't before I went to Gantia. A friend of mine taught me how to swim.' Thianni looked disappointed.

'What is wrong?' asked Kalin.

'I was supposed to be the one to teach you. Who is this friend of yours? What is his name?'

'Her, name is Cahira.'

Thianni looked even more disappointed now. 'A girl?' she blurted out loud. 'Another girl taught you how to swim?'

'Yes, but she is just a friend.' Thianni splashed Kalin again and he laughed at her. Thianni started to swim back to shore and Kalin swam after her. Touching the sand now he stood, and he caught her by the arm and spun her around into him. She giggled with the action.

'You know you are the only one for me, don't you Thianni?'

She looked at him and kissed him. 'Of course, I do. I just feel sad that you have to go back to Gantia. Can you not stay for the summer?'

'I wish I could, Thianni, but I have made a promise to Karra. When I was up there, the only thing I thought about was being with you. It will be hard for us both to be apart for such a long time, but I must go back. I owe Karra this favour.'

'You know Kalin, if we were to marry, you would be King of Latonia.'

'I have thought about that but being King was never my intention. I just want to be with you. Anyway, I'm not sure you would say yes to a savage boy? Maybe I will surprise you on my next visit and ask for your hand in marriage.'

Thianni smiled. 'And maybe I might say yes to a savage boy.' A huge splash emerged beside them as a dolphin jumped out of the water and swam around them. Thianni and Kalin both laughed with fright. 'See I told you dolphins swim here.'

' I never doubted you, my Queen.' Kalin said back.

'I am glad you are here with me to see them, Kalin. I think it is a sign of better times to come for us.'

'I hope so' said Kalin. He pulled her in close and kissed her as the last of the sun dropped below the horizon.

The End

Epilogue

All was quiet in the still of the night in Four Vales. At the edge of the village, Akala pulled back the covers and sat up in Cahira's bed. Cahira was fast asleep. Akala stood and lit a candle and went to the end of the bed to check on their baby, who was asleep in his cot. They had named him Kade. He was only two months old and perfect in every way. These last few months had been the most joyful of Akala's whole life. He was with the woman he loved and now she had given birth to their baby. He looked down at the small child in almost disbelief. A wave of warmth flooded over him. His small face was perfect in every way. Kade was a good sleeper. Once he was put to sleep, he would not wake until his next feed. Akala liked to check on him during the night to make sure he was ok. Some nights he would just watch over him as he slept. Cahira would wake soon, she had to feed him every three hours and he was nearly due his night feed. Akala brought the candle closer to the cot. He noticed that one of Kade's hands was outside of his covers, so Akala reached down into the cot and went to put his tiny hand back under the cover where it would be warm. As he did so, baby Kade opened his eyes and looked up at his father. Akala smiled at him and the baby let out a low cry. 'Shush, now. Go back to sleep, little one. Give your mother a little longer in bed.' The baby looked at Akala again. His eyes opened wide, and he could see the blue grey colour with a black outlining around his iris. A shocking feeling swept through him as he could see Kalin's eyes gazing back up at him.

Just over a thousand miles away in the city of Kitia, the new Queen Thianni sat up in her bed. The night was still and there was not a sound. Ever since the invasion she had had trouble sleeping. Bad dreams haunted her, recalling the horrors of the attack on the city. She tried to put the thoughts from her head and think about Kalin, but her mind kept coming back to the attack. She still could not believe the events that had unfolded. Her Uncle and her Auntie were both dead, also her little cousin, Rain, was gone. Now she was Queen of all Latonia. The city of Kitia had been almost destroyed by the invaders. She was busy rebuilding everything. She knew she would have to be strong. She remembered the words her Auntie had spoken to her. 'You are becoming a woman now.' She thought about this and realised she had not bled in two months now. Her breasts were swollen. She touched her hand to her stomach and smiled to herself. She spoke out loud. 'I am with child.'

Leta, Empress of Eamhair, sat on the throne. She was alone, the hall was empty. She drained the last of her wine and called for more. A female servant came in from a side room with a large jug and bowed and then refilled the empty cup. The servant bowed once more and was about to leave when Leta called her back. 'Before you go, tell Captain Velez I require his presence right away.' The servant bowed again and hurried off through the same door she had come in. It was almost an hour later when Captain Velez entered the hall. By this stage, Leta was feeling very tipsy from the wine she had consumed.

Captain Velez marched up to his Empress and gave a deep bow. 'Empress, how may I be of service?' He could see she was drunk, even before she spoke with slurred words. She was swaying slightly as she sat on the throne and her eyes looked sleepy.

She smiled at him as she focused on his face. 'My Captain! Thank you for coming to me so late at night. I have been thinking a lot about what went wrong with my father's campaign. I miss him greatly you know?'

'We all miss him, my Empress. He was a great man.'

'Yes, he was. He was unlucky to not have conquered Kitia. It was not his time.' She paused for a bit. Then she took another drink from her wine. 'Back to why I have called you here. Tomorrow I want you to contact all my Generals and come to me at noon.'

'What will I inform them my Empress?'

'Tell them.' She drank again. 'Tell them it is time to plan a new campaign. Tell them it is time to plan for revenge for my father's death, and tell them it is my time, to conquer.'

'Yes, my Empress. I will make it so.'

The Captain went to bow and leave when Leta spoke again. 'I have had word from the wall in North Natalia today. General Sana sent me a full report. It was interesting. The Latonian army has started to gather north of the wall in the Kingdom. He said their numbers are low. He counted a mere 4500 troops gathering on the Latonian side. I know we have lost a great number of our Dragon Army and now Skarin has returned to his lands in the far east of Eamhair. This has reduced our force also. I think it is time we made our next move.' Velez nodded with agreement. Leta then drank the contents of her cup. 'Well if we are to meet tomorrow, I must be getting to my bed. Will you help me, my Captain?'

'Of course, my Empress.' Velez held out his hand and Leta took it to balance herself as she stood from her throne. They walked to her chambers, chatting as they went. Velez stopped outside of her door. 'Well I will bid you good night your highness.'

Leta turned in close to him. 'I haven't dismissed you yet, Captain.' The Captain looked at her. 'I know your wife and child will be waiting for you at home. Can you stay with me a little longer?'

The Captain smiled. 'Is that an order?'

Leta ran her hand down along his chest. 'I have lived by a few simple rules in my life and one of them is: If you want something, ask for it. Do you want me Captain?'

'Yes' he heard himself say.

'Well then, I order you to stay with me tonight. I have a lot to share, as my plans of conquest are vast in this world. There will be a lot of hard work ahead of us. We have much to plan, all our tomorrows depend on today. But for now, we should have a little fun.' The Empress took her captain by his hand. They both went inside and Leta closed the door behind them.

Acknowledgements

My thanks to my Wife Adele, my editor, whose patience and motivation helped me to make a dream come true. Thank you!

To my Proof-readers, Margaret Kenna, Sarah Kenna, Eoin O'Neill, Tommy O'Rourke, Paul Keogh and John Byrne. Without your feedback and encouragement, I would be lost. Thank you!

Coming Soon from Scott J Kenna

CLASH OF THE GUARDIANS

Available worldwide online and from all good bookstores

www.mtp.agency

www.facebook.com/mtp.agency

@mtp_agency

Michael Terence
Publishing

Printed in Great Britain
by Amazon

52228218R00211